THEY ALL FALL DOWN

THEY ALL FALL DOWN

A. K. Mason

ISBN: 0692519599
ISBN 13: 9780692519592

This is a work of fiction. References to major financial institutions, public figures, and events of record in the 2008-2009 financial crisis are derived from public documents. All other names, characters, events and incidents are either the products of the author's imagination or used in a fictitious manner. Any resemblance to actual persons, living or dead, or actual events is purely coincidental.

In my beginning is my end. In succession, Houses rise and fall, crumble, are extended, Are removed, destroyed, restored, or in their place Is an open field, or a factory, or a by-pass.Old stone to new building, old timber to new fires, Old fires to ashes, and ashes to the earth...In my end is my beginning

–T.S. Eliot, Four Quartets Part II: East Coker

Ring-a-round the Rosie
A pocket full of Posies
Ashes! Ashes! We all fall down

-Children's Nursery Rhyme

"How big are you?"

"Excuse me?"

"I said how big are you?"

"How big am I?"

"Pay attention. Size fucking matters here. How big are you?"

"I'm big. I'm huge. I'm as big as you fucking want me to be."

"Ok then, what do you bid?"

"Bid?"

"Yeah. Are you hard of hearing or just stupid? What's your bid? You know, what price do you pay? I'm not just gonna offer you bonds all day without knowing what your fucking bid is."

"You mean what I offer? What I offer to pay?"

"No. I'll say it one more time. I'll go as slow as I can manage without killing myself. What. Is. Your. Bid? That means what are you willing to pay to buy this fucking bond. Then, I'll counter with my offer. That's where I'm willing to sell the bond to you. If we can agree on a price, we trade. Bid. Offer. Size. That's all anybody fucking cares about. No one gives a shit about how big you want to be. Only thing that matters is how big you are right now. What's your size and what's your price. Bid. Offer. Size."

"Bid. Offer. Size?"

"That's right, Harvard. Now you're fucking catching on. Traders bet. That's just what we do. We're addicts - addicted to betting, addicted to winning, addicted to playing even. I'm not just talking about that Liar's Poker shit I know you read about before you took the job. If you've got balls, baby, you gotta bet on EVERYTHING. It's all one big game of blackjack. Betting against the house - which is always out to screw you by the way. You've got to hope the other players at the table get the fucking joke too. You gotta sit at a table with other guys who know how to play, understand the rules, the protocol, the goddamned etiquette. If they get it, you all play together. You're talking to each other without actually saying anything at all. And you're all playing against the house together. But if they don't get it - if they're amateurs or just fucking ignorant to how life works, to how the game is played, then you're screwed. They'll screw you sometimes without even knowing it. That's when you have to get up and just switch tables, Harvard. I bet they didn't teach you this up in Boston. This isn't the kind of class where you take notes, but don't fucking forget this lesson: Traders bet. Because that's just what we do."

THE BIG BANKS AREN'T DOING THIS
MARCH 15, 2009

I t had been advertised as a great charity event – one too great to miss since everybody on The Street would be there. It wasn't a *Cipriani's* soirée or a gala at The Met. It was a booze fest at a ratty bar on the Upper East Side, with an atmosphere that evoked memories of a college fraternity. It wasn't exactly screaming "epicenter for titans of industry." But then again, a night out was a night out. Out of her apartment. Out of her office. Out of reality. Wall Street Brokers invited Alex to every party. Back then, she was quick to accept.

It had been one year since Bear Stearns had been swallowed into J.P. Morgan. Washington Mutual had been subsumed too, shortly thereafter. Lehman Brothers had gone bankrupt in September just six months later, left without a date to the Fed's dance when Bank of America bought Merrill Lynch instead. Even the venerable houses of Morgan Stanley and Goldman Sachs were bellying up to the bar for government money to try and stave off the increasing public hysteria.

Business wasn't exactly booming. The Street was bored by the lack of business and disturbed by the greater public's reaction to this cataclysmic banking crisis. Everyone, it seemed, on any side of the equation was getting fucked out of sizable sums of money. Employees alternated between therapy and anger management sessions, confounded by the sudden weight that the crisis had brought to the fore: spouses, children, mortgages, healthcare, tuition expenses, job security, Social Security, superiors, inferiors, the housing markets, the financial markets, the job markets, the auto industry, the retail industry, the entertainment industry, personal debts, the national debt. All of a sudden it was all so heavy.

Some senior executives began to travel with security. Employees would whisper in sarcastic wonder whether the detail was meant to protect them outside the building or within. In an instant it seemed the orderly manner of conducting business on Wall Street was subsumed by chaos. Institutional clients pulled their investments from The Big Banks by the hundreds of millions, tucking them instead under the proverbial mattress by housing their monies in cash accounts. Retail clients dialed out to help hotlines with numb fingers and racing hearts, trying to track down their life savings when Big Banks merged, were acquired, or went under altogether.

For the most part, Wall Street was drinking its pain away. Alexandra Kramer had been a bond trader at Lehman Brothers. Her husband, Jamie, was a seven-year Investment-Banking veteran at Bear Stearns. Each had been spared as far as they could tell. Now she was working at Barclays and he was at JP Morgan. And for the past year she never skipped a Wall Street outing to which she'd been invited. It was her obligation, she argued to her husband, who frequently questioned the after-hours work jaunts. Wall Street is a people business more than a numbers business she would lecture. She could only hope to succeed if she could prove that she could cut it amongst the other traders. And if that included a few shots of tequila and an occasional seedy bar, so be it. Typically, he acquiesced, but that night he persisted in his opposition. They compromised (a feat Alex considered one of the greatest challenges and subsequent triumphs of marriage) and it was decided that Alex would bring her husband along.

Giddy with anticipation for the night, Alexandra hopped into a yellow cab and directed it up to 88th Street and Second Avenue. She felt suffocated in the middle seat of the taxi, between her husband and her best friend Daniella. Jamie peppered her with questions:

"Who is going to be there? Why are we going to this anyway? How long do we actually have to stay?"

He pressed and pressed and pressed again.

"You know they're only asking you up here because they all think you're hot, right?"

This last comment stung her like she had been slapped in the face. She inhaled deeply and exhaled slowly, silently counting to five with deliberate control. Alex turned imperceptibly towards Daniella. *See what I mean?* Her eyes asked.

"You know these events are very important to me, Jamie. Socializing is critical."

She usually had this conversation with him from her cell phone once she was already at the event and he was waiting for her at home.

"You didn't have to come with me...I mean, of course, I would always love for you to come, but not if you are going to insist we leave the very instant we get there. I thought you liked a lot of the guys from the desk, though. And it's a Thursday night!"

Alex layered on the guilt and played to his sense of machismo. She prayed he would calm down because she could barely contain the next words likely to come from her mouth: *Are we an old married couple already?!? Leave me the fuck alone and go home if you can't handle it.* Was marriage always such a difficult dance, a battle of wills?

Privately, Alex conceded that it wasn't really a huge sacrifice to bring Jamie on this particular night. It wasn't entirely spontaneous either. Tonight's party was at Tommy's bar. Tommy Good Times. Alex need only imagine how exactly Tommy earned his nickname. He was the consummate host - playfully chubby, perennially gleeful, and most important for Alex's nights out, he always appeared innocent. He was therefore supremely non-threatening to her husband. Jamie had met Tommy a handful of times and had always seemed to come away from the evening in good spirits.

Alex was the only female trader on the desk. The other traders frowned upon her bringing her husband. Women were expected to bring other women, not even more guys. And they were certainly not supposed to bring their husbands. The presence of a spouse tended to remind the married men present that they too were miserable. So for the most part, spouses were deposited like coats at a coat check: leave them where you know they'll be safe, forget all about them for a few hours while you go about your business, and then pick them up to keep you warm on your way home.

The cab pulled up to the near left corner of 88th Street, on the west side of Second Avenue. They stepped out and Daniella quickly whispered, "Is that a joke? Why is he being so ridiculous?"

"See, I wasn't fucking making this up. I really don't know what to do. He makes me want to kill myself sometimes."

Jamie jumped out the cab behind them, scowling. He either scowled or cracked jokes to mask his diffidence. Lately, that was his mood of choice. He reached for

Alex's hand but caught her right wrist instead. She tilted her head to look up at him. The blonde baby hairs on her skin prickled in tightly-controlled anger. Instead of adjusting his grasp to her hand and interlacing her fingers with his own, he held her wrist firm, shackling it with his lanky fingers. The cross-walk sign flashed its neon orange hand. *Do not cross. Do not cross. Do not cross.* In an instant, it flashed to white, and the easy gait of a nondescript passerby froze on the nine-by-nine inch screen. The three of them crossed in silence, Alex's mind bent to the left, her hand held captive to the right.

The bouncer carded her at the door.

"Really?"

"They don't pay me to just sit here and look pretty," the linebacker-sized man replied.

"Funny." Alex flashed her license and a broad, amused smile, relieved to have been carded in front of friends and not clients. Inside, a jumbo pretzel container was being used as a charitable depository. Alex dropped in one hundred dollars and scanned the room for familiar faces.

"What can I get you guys to drink?" she asked, writhing her wrist out from the marital death grip. After taking their orders, Alex hurried off towards the bar, in search of white wine and Corona. She moved towards the back of the bar, using it as an excuse to temporarily break away. She took her time as the place was filling up with happily drunken, distantly familiar faces. She could barely squeeze her way over to order.

Nearly an hour later, they were elbow-room-only in the belly of the bar, about five feet off the action, and near the mirrors just under one of the three ratty televisions. Alex occasionally checked herself out in the mirror from the corner of her eye. She tried unsuccessfully to maintain asinine conversation with a broker whose name she could not remember while she silently stepped on the foot of another, and held her breath from a third who was secretly farting every time another warm body entered their little drunken stratosphere.

He had his back to her. Alex knew immediately that it was him. As her head bobbed up and down, in mindless agreement to the conversation she was no longer engaged in, a little electric shiver ran straight down her back. Instead, she deliberated how best to solicit his attention: melodrama or nonchalance? Too impatient to decide, Alex tapped him on the shoulder and before he had even fully turned around she threw her arms around him in the friendliest hug she could muster.

"Hank! How have you been?" she gushed. "I can't believe you're here," she blabbed on, disentangling herself from the awkward embrace (*was it awkward or had she only imagined it?*). She didn't give him a chance to respond. "I mean, it makes sense that you're here, since Tommy's your cousin. I just didn't think you would be out."

Alex had deftly facilitated an invite to the last four client outings in the silent hope that Hank would make an appearance, and then drunkenly endured when he was a no-show time and time again.

"I feel like I have so much to tell you about." Was she really still blabbing on like this? Alex could feel the heat rising up her neck from under the collar of her J. Crew blazer - attire she had conceded to wearing after several husbandly death-stares from Jamie while she tried on her first and second choice outfits earlier that evening (vetoed as too short and too tight, respectively). She sipped some shitty Pinot from her wine glass and gave herself another quick once-over in the mirror.

"Miss me."

Maybe he meant it as a question, but his intonation was replete with confident presumption. But that was Hank. Work hadn't been the same without him there. He had made each day lively, crazy, intense, and competitive all at once. He was the craziest trader she had ever met. And the most complex personality. His profit and loss swings seemed erratic but Alex had spent enough time learning from him to know that he operated with deliberate control. It was part of her job to report each trader's profit or loss at the end of each day. His would swing wildly, with seemingly reckless abandon. He could lose $2.5 million one day and go up $4 million the next. He never seemed to fixate on the numbers like the other senior traders. He never seemed to care that the Big Bank executives were always watching, always counting. He seemed to keep score differently. Some people in the business said he was a complete and utter asshole. She didn't know him too well. Her superficial impression was that he was loyal and protective to a fault, but also a little rough around the edges with no patience for politics. And he wasn't shy about letting people know it. He ran a real trading desk. And Alex had hung on his every word, desperately wanting her shot at becoming a real trader.

Hank's trading book was up thirty five million dollars when he walked away. He left to go on vacation and then just never came back. After a few days of confused waiting, they finally called to see where he was. The Big Bank tried to woo him back. Hank wouldn't bite. He laughed and told them they couldn't buy him like that.

They downplayed his exit internally but pounded the phones to do damage control with clients. His absence held the desk like clouds hold water before a storm. The quiet, the silence, the anticipation were all deafening. But that was Hank. Typically, he captivated any room with his presence. But when he left, it was his absence that held them.

It had been six weeks since he'd quit. He had reportedly gone underground. No one really knew if Hank was living it up in some country south of the border or was hunkering down in his apartment, strategically planning his next career move. The details around his departure were muddled for most of them, and the stories going around had already begun to take on a legendary air.

With his chocolate brown eyes fixed on her, his grin only permitted the slightest upturn of one side of his mouth. His hand clapped down on her shoulder in Tommy's Pub and she felt the very slight squeeze of his fingers.

"Well, I missed you too, kid." The touch was friendly enough. But it still sent a slight shiver through Alex.

"Oh, Hank, this is Jamie. My husband."

She'd forgotten that Jamie was standing there. He was consciously nursing his beer. Jamie loosened his protective grip from her other shoulder and grasped Hank's thick, calloused hand.

"It's great to meet you, bud," Jamie said. "So you're the famous Hank?"

Alex almost thought Jamie might follow that with *'I would have thought you'd be taller,'* but his insecurity held him.

She laughed to break the tension. Then she introduced Hank to Daniella, gesturing in the direction of her friend's perfectly straight, long brown hair and polite, tight-lipped smiled. Daniella took Hank's hand and shook it. Pat Benatar's *Hit Me With Your Best Shot* blared from the sound system. All around them the collection of Wall Street misfits brandished a dirty mix of alcoholic concoctions, either immune to or reveling in the cheesy eighties music.

"I'll grab you another drink, babe," Alex placed her left hand on Jamie's midsection, pressing against the neatly tucked, bespoke, purple shirt that clothed his skin. "Hank, can I grab you anything?"

"All set," he said to her and grinned at her husband, while jingling the ice cubes in his still-full glass of Captain Morgan's and Coke.

◆ ◆ ◆

"Bud, I need you," Tommy came up behind Hank and grabbed him.

"Here we go," Hank replied, automatic.

Hank stripped off his houndstooth checkered black and white sport coat, and deposited it into another friend's unprepared arms. He rolled up the sleeves of his white collared dress shirt, pressed his hands together to crack his knuckles, and rolled his head from side to side, loosening any tension in his broad shoulders. Alex returned with their drinks, just as Hank was becoming more animated.

"No, not that, dude."

"What's the matter? Who do you need me to hit?"

Tommy laughed his affable laugh and slapped Hank playfully on the back.

"Thanks bud." He winked his signature *Tommy Good Times* wink at Alex. "But I just need you to say hi to a couple guys. People haven't seen you in a while and everyone's been asking about you. I just need you over in the front for a sec. Can you help me out?"

"Oh." Hank's laugh was deep and deliberate. "That's it? I thought I had to bail your Irish ass out again."

Alex shook her head in mild amusement and disbelief as she fixed her dancing blue eyes on Hank. She raised an eyebrow, as best she could, in an effort at simultaneous mockery and salute. Hank just shrugged his shoulders. She thought he had winked too but she couldn't be entirely sure.

He followed Tommy to the front of the bar, brushing Alex's shoulder, despite the available gap between them. Alex sipped her wine and refocused her mind and her conversation on her husband. Glancing around, she noticed that Daniella had slipped off. Alex could hardly blame her. She had only come as a favor to her longtime friend and was hardly as captivated by the Wall Street scene.

"So, what do you think? It's so much fun, right? I love these parties! You should see them at work. These guys are all nuts. What did you think of them?"

Jamie slid closer to her. As a banker, he was more reserved and stuck out in this type of crowd. He also socialized less and less after they were married and then, four weeks later Bear Stearns, his employer and professional temple, collapsed.

"Yeah, I'm having fun. Tommy's really nice. And that other guy I met, what's his name? Nick? He seems like a good guy. Do you work with him a lot? He said his wife might stop by in a little. I don't want to stay too late though. Big day at work for me tomorrow."

She looked down because if she would have looked at him he might have seen the doubt in her eyes.

"Sure babe," she squeezed his hand and looked down at her watch, which read only ten-fifty.

"Let's just stay for a little while. We haven't been out in so long."

A couple of the guys walked back over. "We're going to hit up another bar," Nick announced. "It's time for a change of scenery. Bro, you guys down to keep this party going?" Nick asked Jamie.

Alex nodded yes before Jamie could decline.

"Where's Daniella?" Jamie scanned the room quickly.

"I think she slipped out. Let's check if she is on her phone outside and see if she wants to join us,"

Jamie gave Alex a look that said *don't you think it's already getting late?*

Alex silently retorted with her eyes. *Don't. You. Dare. Embarrass. Me. Not here. Not now.*

"You guys good?" Nick already had his jacket on.

"Of course," Alex chirped. "Let's go."

The group picked up a couple of followers on their march towards the door. Several sweaty, sloppy hugs, handshakes, and fist-bumps later they were safely out of the dirty grasp of Tommy's Bar's.

There were seven of them assembled: Jamie, Alex and Hank plus his crew: Nick, Geoff, Jason, and Ronny.

Or as they were commonly known: Icky Nicky, Salty, CMO, and "Chinee." Nick (Icky Nicky) was a senior salesman who had grown up under Hank and loyally followed him from firm to firm. He earned his nickname from his questionable lunchtime jaunts to the massage parlor. Geoff (Salty) was a senior research analyst and one of Hank's closest college friends. Jason (the CMO) was the new kid, a first-generation Wall Street wannabe who had joined the group directly from a Big Bank analyst program. Ronny (Chinee) was also a senior research analyst. Even though he was born and raised in Manhattan, he looked distinctly Asian so Hank had every Italian waiter in Midtown calling him "Chinese" just to ruffle his feathers. The waiters themselves often had accents, so their pronunciations sounded more like "Chinee", which turned out to really sound like the unadulterated mockery Hank was hoping for.

Outside, Daniella was nowhere in sight. Alex wasn't complaining though. Now, she only had one person to look after. She also couldn't really blame her friend for leaving. The guys were usually a little rough around the edges. And they could be brutal. When they were in asshole mode, though, which Alex distinguished from their charming, woman-wooing mode, they were a tough group for girls to love. But for Alex, after more than two years as a trader, she was perfectly at home in the mostly-male, give-and-get shit environment. She actually sort of loved it. She could do without the ritualistic way so many of them would fart repeatedly and then innocently light matches to mask the stench - as if the smell of snuffed out flames and stale farts were aromatically acceptable. Even the flatulence factory was a small price to pay in exchange for being in the thick of the action.

The group split two cabs down to P.J. Clarkes on 54th Street and Third Avenue. Jamie, Hank and Alex sat in the back of the first cab, with Alex in the middle seat, her stilettos straddling the divide on its matted floor. Her armpits were uncomfortably damp against her shirt. She asked the taxi driver to please turn the radio on, which was something she rarely did anymore; she had learned on their second date that Jamie found taxi radio music positively maddening.

Jamie asked if Hank knew where he planned on working next. Hank, ignoring the question, asked how things were working out over at his new spot at JP Morgan. At home Alex had spoken constantly of Hank's seemingly abrupt departure and its impact on their trading desk. When she first came to Barclays with the group from Lehman Brothers, Hank had eyed the wedding picture on Alex's desk, asking what Jamie did for a living. It seemed both men had solid memories that could keep the awkward back-seat banter alive. Alex checked her cell phone and feigned drunken disinterest, allowing the two men to continue their banter without her.

P.J. Clarke's was housed in a two-story, freestanding building with Old World New York affectations. The popular restaurant and bar stood out on a stretch of Third Avenue that was now colored with nondescript, tall, grey office buildings that housed a row of coffee shops, drug stores, and fast-food eateries in their respective ground floor spaces. Alex, assuming it was a faux-authentic-New York tourist trap, had never been there before and was surprised and amused to find the bar absolutely packed with Wall Street guys. It was mostly a Sales and Trading-meets-hedge fund scene, though Jamie even ran in to one senior Investment Banker he vaguely knew from their glory days. The bar itself had the look of that Boston pub from the sitcom *Cheers*, and somehow she had a feeling that here, too, everybody knew at least somebody's name.

Ronny and Salty sauntered off to retrieve drinks for their group. There was a collection of people lined up directly in front of the bar and a scattered mess of patrons behind, squeezing their way forward. Six feet in past the front door, the room narrowed considerably, rendering the back of the bar virtually unreachable. So the rest of their group remained by the front, settling in comfortably near the door.

Forty-five minutes later, Alex felt drunk. The scene looked a little fuzzy. Her body felt a little too warm. They had been drinking for hours already and as usual, Alex wasn't shy about keeping up with the boys. People kept wandering over to say hello to Hank, many making a big show of introducing all the others they were with to him.

Alex vaguely recognized some of them. One of them kept calling to Hank from a few feet away. He was with a beautiful lanky blonde from the business. It was too crowded for the guy to make his way over. Alex could hear him shouting to the hot blonde so she could hear him over the boisterous crowd.

"You have to meet my new business partner," he kept saying, pointing at Hank. "You have to meet my new business partner."

He worked to woo her by association. The lanky blonde craned her neck.

"He's one of a kind; you have to meet him."

Hank nodded towards them but made no effort to meet them.

Alex noted the large number of pretty women at the bar. She was unfettered. It was part of a scene she was accustomed to by now. There was the standard bevy of women - from coed to cougar – who went hunting for wealthy Wall Street Sponsors. Alex could already identify a few of the usual offenders. Alex and her group stood in a semi-circle nearby, watching the women work and joking about the lack of a bouncer and the clear need for one.

A white-haired guy stumbled in, clearly with a few drinks in him already. He looked like an angry cop, maybe 6'3" or 6'4", with grisly hands and a big round belly punching through the buttons of his white shirt. Everyone looked up but no one intimated that they knew him. Alex approached him.

"Sir, I'm going to need to see some identification before you can come in here."

"Yeah, right," he snorted, though affably enough.

"No, seriously, I can't let you in."

"Alright, sweetheart, don't get too cute."

"Really, I'm not trying to be cute. They don't pay me to stand here and look cute," she smiled sweetly, jokingly.

"Yeah, what do they pay you to do?"

Alex batted her eyes in jest and ignored the obviously suggestive question.

He grabbed at her shoulders. "Get the fuck out of my way, pretty. Game's over."

Alex giggled, thinking they were still just joking around. It quickly became clear that she was the only one who was kidding.

He grabbed at her shoulder again and squeezed it more aggressively this time.

The shift in his temperament was jarringly abrupt.

"Honey," he slurred, "I don't have patience for this shit."

The physical contact and a handful of expletives were enough to grab the full attention of the guys. Hank looked at Jamie.

"What are you going to do about this?" Hank asked him.

Jamie half-shrugged.

The angry cop was now trying to belligerently massage Alex's shoulders.

"You're crossing the line." Her shoulders tensed. She tried to slink away but the bar was so crowded.

"This is gonna get addressed," Hank emphasized to Jamie. "Are you going to handle it, or am I?"

Jamie looked at Hank. "Handle what?"

Hank gave up with Jamie. He turned towards the groper.

"Asshole, get your fucking hands off of my wife!"

Alex felt like the wind had been knocked out of her. The groper stopped in his tracks. Jamie stared blindly. The four of them froze, perfectly still.

A measure of silence engulfed them, despite the drunken din all around. Someone somewhere hit the mute button as the four stood there, unmoving. Alex was shell-shocked. She shifted her gaze back and forth, Hank then Jamie, Jamie then Hank. Their eyes darted back and forth between one another and then over at her.

The angry, white-haired groper ultimately broke the silence, which could have been hours not seconds from Alex's drunken, awe-struck position.

"What did you say little man?" He pointed his finger in Hank's face, and moved closer as if to demonstrate his six-inch height advantage. "Watch yourself." He squeezed Alex's backside once more, still eyeing Hank menacingly.

The rest was a blur. Before anyone else knew what was happening, Hank rocketed towards the groper. He curled his right fist and smashed it into the groper's face, sending him crashing back into the wall.

"You don't talk to a lady like that."

Hank growled. He jumped on top of the groper and pounded.

Alex jumped back. One of the bartenders caught the glass he was flipping, mid-bar trick. He shouted at them with a heavy Irish accent to cut it the fuck out. Someone else yelled to get the police. Women scattered. The former colleague and the lanky blonde stood nearby, tongues wagging in disbelief. Several burly waiters closed in on the fight, blocking and tackling to get through the crowd. Nick and Ronny finally reached Hank and tore him off the groper. Hank had a rip in his dress shirt and blood trickling down his face in between his left eye and the bridge of his nose. Salty and Jason appeared next. The four of them closed in around Hank, creating a human wall. The unit moved deftly towards the door of the bar. Hank looked over at Alex. Nick said they should leave quickly. The police might come. Alex wondered if the groper really was a cop. They busted out of there like they were a group of bandits robbing a bank.

Alex's head was spinning. It was cold outside. The guys were already plowing their way down the street, heading east toward First Avenue. Jamie physically tugged at Alex's arm, pulling her southward, toward home. She resisted.

"We should at least go for one more drink," she reasoned.

Jamie paled. "Did you see what just went on?"

"Yeah," she countered. "That's why we should go have one drink with them. He just punched a guy in the face for me."

Jamie just stared at her.

An eternity passed between them.

"Fine. One drink."

They started down the street after the others, breaking into a brisk walk to catch up to the group. Jamie held her hand in his. They caught up about half way down the block.

"Holy shit," she said loudly, waiting for the others to notice she had joined them after all.

"I'm so fucking mad right now," Hank said.

"Are you ok?" she touched his arm.

"You never should have pulled me off, Ronny. I wasn't done with that asshole."

"Hank," Nick broke in, "the cops would have been all over that place. They're probably filling out a report as we speak."

Jason kept his hands buried in his pockets, shoulders hunched. Ronny and Salty walked side by side up ahead, Salty measuring about a shoulder taller. Somehow, Alex felt they'd played out this scene before. Jamie walked silently, nose tucked into his zipped up jacket, and still holding her hand.

"Are you bleeding?" she asked Hank.

"No," he replied, not noticing the blood on his face.

"Yeah, Hank, I think you are," she confirmed as he turned his head to face her.

"Shit. That fucking asshole. Are you okay? He didn't hurt you when he grabbed you, did he?"

Just then Ronny jerked left up a few stairs and into a small bar Alex had never noticed before. The rest of them followed behind. Inside, it smelled of stale cigarette smoke and was bereft of patrons. Music blared from behind the bar. Ronny pulled up at one of the empty stools and ordered everyone a round of shots. Alex hid her yawn. The sudden downshift from exhilaration to calm had punctured her inebriated daze and a wave of exhaustion followed.

She downed her tequila shot, shaking her head from side to side.

Hank got up, walked past the bar and disappeared through a door on the left. Alex followed. She pushed open the door behind him. His back was to her. It took her drunken blue eyes an extra second to adjust. They were in the men's restroom. His back turned away because he was at the urinal.

Shit.

"Uh, I just wanted to say thanks. Um, you know, for before."

Hank flipped his gaze over his right shoulder, keeping the rest of his body fixed. His face was still streaked with a little blood. He wore the widest shit-eating grin.

"Trust me, the Big Banks aren't doing this, Harvard," he said. "The Big Banks definitely aren't fucking doing this."

Then he turned back to face the wall and finish his business.

2

A lex woke at five o'clock the morning of her wedding. She was so giddy with excitement that she had only fluttered in and out of sleep. The air was crisp and still; it was a perfect and sunny February morning in New York. The Pierre was one of the city's finest hotels with prime real estate on 61st Street and Fifth Avenue. The building's interior design captured the decadent flare of early twentieth century wealth. Marble staircases introduced each ballroom, large crystal chandeliers hung in every room and entryway, Renaissance and Victorian-era murals covered many of the walls, and the rugs were rich shades of green, blue, and gold.

Alex never thought her parents could afford a Pierre wedding. She hadn't even planned to tour the venue, for fear of falling in love with what she could never have. But Jamie saw the way her eyes lit up whenever she talked about the hotel so he wrangled a meeting with the events manager. Then he wrangled some more, negotiating a deal that would cut the price tag in half. He had triumphantly recounted the meeting to her family, detailing the case he had made, arguing that their money was better than no money at all for a Sunday evening wedding in the dead of winter.

Even still, it was an enormous sum. Her dad shocked her by offering to contribute twenty-five thousand dollars. Alex didn't think that he and her stepmom could afford it; she later learned that he used part of his inheritance from her grandmother – who died one month after Alex had announced her engagement. One of the few stimulants that had stirred her bedridden grandmother from her mental delirium and physical fatigue was the burning urge to go out and buy a new pair of shoes for her oldest granddaughter's wedding.

Alex's mother was at a point in her life where she could finally save her hard-earning money after her three children were mostly off the payroll – as Alex liked to refer to parental financial support. But her mother gladly bore the brunt of the day's cost; she wrote check after check for her baby girl, spending close to three years' worth of college tuition on one evening of expectation. The family started calling her 'M.O.B.' for 'Mother Of the Bride' – but also for the authoritative role she played in the planning. M.O.B. was elated to be marrying off her daughter. The accomplishment would serve a dual mission: secure what was left of Alex's twenty-three year old virtue and absolve herself of some of the protective maternal worry that she wore like a badge of honor. (The M.O.B. once called the campus police when she could not reach her daughter on the phone at night; at the time Alex was nearly twenty, a college sophomore, and had been in her room the entire time. She simply hadn't been in the mood for talking.) Still, her mother would race between business meetings to meet Alex for dress fittings, menu samplings, and floral arrangement decisions. But M.O.B. would often sigh after writing the check and implore upon her daughter to promise that she'd only marry once. She just wanted her little girl happy and settled.

For his part, Jamie contributed a decent sum and Alex loved him even more for trying to pull the weight of his entire dysfunctional family himself. His mom gave them a small amount of money – siphoned off from the alimony Jamie's father had started delivering to her the prior year. Jamie's dad said he couldn't give them anything at all. Alex watched Jamie's heart silently break, after he had swallowed his pride enough to ask his father for help in the first place.

She hated the part of herself that felt that the money mattered. But she couldn't help it. Part of what she loved about Jamie was her belief that the two of them would make it on their own; they would mature into a powerful couple and join an elite circle of powerful, like-minded

New Yorkers. Alex had long imagined that such a society existed, where handsome couples would mingle at one another's Park Avenue homes and swap stories of professional triumph and personal accolade over martinis, served dirty and whiskey, delivered neat. So she took Jamie's efforts at overcompensation as nothing short of heroic and a telltale sign of great things to come.

Alex completely panicked eight weeks before the wedding when she discovered via New York Times article that the superb rate they had secured couldn't be attributed to their negotiating prowess alone. The hotel was also under renovation and much of the hotel would be shuttered. After several rounds of hyperventilating and controlled temper-tantrums with the hotel's events manager, Alex was informed that the renovations would only affect the guest rooms and that the palatial rooms that would house her wedding would remain untouched. Since Jamie's Kentucky family wasn't ponying up for a night at the Pierre anyway, Alex calmed down enough to continue with her dictatorial wedding planning procedures.

On that February morning she couldn't have been more thankful that the hotel was otherwise empty. Alex quietly changed out of her pajamas and into her old Harvard sweatpants and a fresh t-shirt, and put on a pair of flip-flops. Then she tiptoed out of the bridal suite, careful not to wake Daniella, her maid of honor who had dutifully stayed at the hotel with her the night before.

As she rode the old-fashioned elevator down to the first floor, Alex relished the moment of uninterrupted peace and quiet. She told herself she felt calm but her heart kept beating in rushed intervals. She silently marched in and out of each room, at times closing her eyes to try and imagine how the day would unfold, and hoping that every detail would mirror her color-coded spreadsheet. The spreadsheet doled out time and place instructions for each member of her eighteen-person wedding party and the fifty or so other assorted family members who were scheduled for pre- wedding pictures.

Finally, she peeked into the room where the wedding ceremony would be held. The florist insisted on setting the room up in solitude and she had been working tirelessly since midnight. Alex stopped short just inside the room, swooning a little. Her cheeks almost hurt she was smiling so hard. Her whole body filled with happiness. The wedding canopy was just perfect. She just stood and stared, like a very small girl might in a very large toy store, gaping at this magnificent structure. She knew her awe was silly. But she also knew she didn't care. Her tongue wagged unabashed, like any bride's might in private moments the morning of her wedding.

A billowing ivory tent-like structure stood at the front of the room. Beneath it hung a chandelier hand-made from crystals and almost four thousand white roses. The crystals twinkled, catching the morning light that was streaming through the windows. Alex imagined walking down the isle of this beautiful gold and blue room and up the five steps in front to stand underneath this awesome canopy and become a wife. She closed her eyes to picture how the antique Spanish lace of her veil would delicately fall all around her, framing her ivory-clad body.

The inner calmness she sensed building was from the certainty she felt inside herself. She felt a trance-like serenity and wondered if all brides feel it the morning of their wedding. Alex was absolutely certain, without a shadow of a doubt, that she was going to be great at being married. She was going to crush it, as she liked to say to friends. She had seen all of the mistakes her parents had made and had begun to learn from them from the time she was five years old, when they had divorced. She was practically a yogi in the field of matrimony. She could not wait for it all to begin but at the same time, she had this feeling that she wished the day itself would last forever.

◆ ◆ ◆

Back upstairs the bridal suite was slowly building into a state of complete wedding bedlam. By ten a.m. the space held three hair stylists, two makeup artists, six bridesmaids, the maid of honor, two flower girls, the M.O.B. and the G.O.B. – Alex's grandmother. They had transformed the living room of the suite into a makeshift salon, complete with stools, mirrors, and any extra lights the hotel could spare. The bridesmaids were joking around and comparing hairstyles. The caterer sent up several plates of light refreshments and finger snacks from downstairs. Alex's two aunts floated in and out to check on their daughters – bridesmaids – but also, to enjoy this girls-only moment. The bride sat perfectly still in one chair, eyeing herself in two mirrors as one stylist worked on her hair and another began in on her makeup. Her mother sat in the far corner, eying her daughter's progress in one mirror as she had her own hair arranged.

The doorbell to the suite rang. It was Alex's dad, who had come to drop off Alex's six-year-old half-sister, who was also a flower girl. Ella ran right up to her sister and grabbed her sides, hugging her as best she could while the bride sat, still statuesque and waiting for her hairdo to be completed.

"Are you really getting married today?" she asked, wide-eyed. "Can I see your dress? Is it white, like mine? Show it to me! Pleeeeaaaasssse."

Laughing, Alex confirmed that it was indeed white, just like hers.

"We'll be matching because we're sisters!"

Alex wondered if her excitement mirrored Ella's animation, her bright-eyed wonder. Another stylist, playing the part, asked Ella how she'd like her hair arranged for the big day. Moving into the stool next to her sister, Ella imitated the bride exactly, sitting as still as a statue and staring intently at herself in the mirror.

"Well, I was thinking highlights and a perm. Maybe some sparkles, if you have them," she answered with the utmost gravity.

Everyone burst into laughter. The little girl looked around in amazement and wondered why everyone was so hysterical. Alex caught a glimpse, stolen, of their dad in one of the mirrors. He had hung back after dropping his younger daughter off. He was half hiding himself in the closet where he had deposited her flower girl dress, just watching this most intimate of moments. He had this look on his face that Alex had seen a lot (or at least imagined to have seen) as she had gotten older: it was a mixture of pride, love, happiness, and awkwardness. It was both intimacy and unfamiliarity. She had first seen it when she first brought Jamie down to Maryland to meet that side of her family. She'd never been much interested in bringing any other boys home to dad before. When he saw the two of them together it was as if Alex transformed, suddenly, from the little girl he raised sometimes only from the sidelines to a woman seemingly unscathed and ready to start her own family, to build her own life. That weekend, he pulled his eldest daughter aside in the small hallway just off the living room. Like many other conversations between them, it was a conversation that started about nothing really and then shifted into a conversation about everything all at once. That was just the way they were. Father and daughter would shift back and forth between familiar and unfamiliar six or seven times in any given exchange. Suddenly, his eyes were tearing, and then he was crying. His shoulders would sink and then rise and his breaths would come out as shorter gasps. He took his circular glasses off to rub his eyes and rub away the tears that kept building. He was happy and grateful for her happiness, but couldn't, he said, grasp whether or not he deserved the happiness as his own.

He caught Alex's eye in the mirror of the bridal suite and smiled. Her dad's smile always seemed nostalgic, but she could never fully tell if the nostalgia was for something he had experienced or for something he had only imagined. Alex had grown to see him as a philosopher, a dreamer, a thinker, the smartest man she knew. No matter the topic, he always seemed to know the answer. He tipped his cap to her and smiled a little wider. Then realizing he had been caught amongst the women, he motioned that he would see her later.

◆ ◆ ◆

Hours later, Alex stood by an open window in the hall just outside of the ballroom-turned-chapel. So far everything had gone as perfectly as she imagined it possibly could. Now, she hoped that she looked like the picture of a bride. Her Vera Wang ivory dress should have been perfectly accentuated next to the billowing silk curtains. There was only one problem: she had her arms positioned in mid-air at her sides like a robot. She was sweating like a monkey. Alex even felt a dampness building behind her knees. She checked under her arms to see if the small yellowish stain of sweat was still continuing its relentless path of destruction just beneath her armpits. It was. She was sucking the air in through her nose so hard her nostrils hurt.

Laughter erupted from behind the heavy gold-painted doors, where the guests were assembled for the ceremony. The processional had started several minutes ago. She listened to the song and tried to figure out which member of the wedding party was walking down the aisle just then.

Jamie's brother. Jesus. Couldn't he just go five minutes without embarrassing her? A drink would be nice right now, Alex thought.

The wedding processional was slowly trickling out in front of her. Alex noticed her mom quietly hyperventilating a few feet ahead. Her stepdad was making small talk with her stepmother. The two little flower girls were practicing their best slow-paced processional walk. Alex's dad was nowhere in sight.

"Jesus Christ. Where's dad?" Everyone looked up. "Well, where is he?"

Extreme alarm was in her voice. Her stepmom shrugged her shoulders, giving Alex her 'Well, you know your father' look. Alex's mom stopped hyperventilating long enough to get all pissed off and give the bride her

'Well, you know your father' look. Her stepfather offered to go look for him.

Great, just what I need right now.

She begged her stepfather not to leave; she couldn't afford to have both of them missing. Her dad loved to take walks and lose himself in thought, but now, goddamnit, was really not the most opportune time to ponder the universe. Alex made a mental checklist of all of the reasons for her father's sudden and untimely disappearance: he had just gone to the bathroom and would be back any minute; he needed some fresh air since his tuxedo was a touch too tight; he was lost in thought in front of one of the murals trying to identify its famous painter; he'd had a change of heart about escorting Alex down the aisle along with his ex-wife; or he was getting cold feet about the whole thing in general...

She was halfway through asking one of the hotel's staff to go and search for her dad when he reappeared. He entered through the archway from across the room. His hands were in his tuxedoed pockets. His face was slightly flushed. He looked up at Alex, standing by the window. He hesitated for a moment and then walked over.

"I love you, dear. You are quite the vision, aren't you?"

He bent to kiss her cheek. Alex could smell the faint sweetness of whiskey on his breath.

At least one of us had managed to take the edge off, she thought.

She smiled. "Thanks, Daddy." She whispered the words, trying not to cry.

"You ready?" He held her bent arm at the elbow.

Was she ready? How would she know? She wasn't sure. She must be. Here she was, after all.

"Don't think I have much of a choice now," she half-joked.

3

After Alex and Jamie were officially husband and wife, the real party began. Alex had vowed not to drink the night of her wedding because she wanted to have a perfectly clear recollection of every blissful moment. But that was before the night had actually begun. She was so behind-the-scenes-stressed that she danced and mingled with a glass of wine fixed in one hand and a glass of champagne assembled in the other. Her cheeks burned from smiling and her head throbbed dully but she relished every ounce of every feeling. Alex desperately wanted to freeze the frame and prevent the time from passing so quickly. She and Jamie circled the room, thanking all their guests for coming, including the ones her parents had invited and she knew so vaguely that she couldn't pick them out of a line-up for all the reward money in the world. The entire Kentucky contingent only took up two tables. Her father's family and guests had another two. The balance of the three-hundred guests was a weighted average of the young couple's friends and the M.O.B.'s friends, acquaintances, and business associates. In the New Jersey town Alex had grown up in, effectively a suburb of Manhattan, weddings weren't about the bride and the groom; they were really about the family.

Towards the end of the four-course dinner the newlyweds finally had a chance to sit and catch their breath. They had been seated at a private table for two, on display for all their guests to see. The MC quieted the crowd and Alex settled back into her seat, preparing to get comfortably relaxed and mildly sedated for the obligatory speeches to come.

"Don't get too comfortable," Jamie whispered in her ear. "I've got a surprise for you."

A soft smile spread across her face as she tilted her head to one side, studying her new husband's eager, radiant face.

"Ladies and gentlemen, can I have your attention please."

The MC waited until the room was more or less silent.

"The groom has prepared a little surprise for his beautiful bride. I think she's in for a treat. I'd like to ask the bride's brother, Eli, to join me up here on stage."

Alex's younger brother walked up to the front of the room, accepted the microphone, and took a seat at the piano bench. Clearing his throat, he addressed his sister with a sense of naïve gravitas.

"Alex - Jamie came to me a few weeks ago and asked if I would perform a song for you, on his behalf. He wanted to find the perfect song - a melody that perfectly described you and that perfectly described how he feels about you. It's an honor for me to perform. This one for you, Sis. Congrats – you finally did it."

"Come." Jamie whispered softly in her ear. "I want to dance with my beautiful bride again."

He took her hand and escorted her back onto the dance floor. Eli played a few chords and then began to sing, very softly but full of emotion. Alex recognized the melody of a Billy Joel song. Jamie had played it for her on one of their early dates. They had stayed in at his apartment that evening and he had cooked them a romantic little dinner. After dessert, he had put the song on invited her to dance. Even in the privacy of his home, Alex had been embarrassed. She had always thought herself a terrible dancer and tried to avoid a two-step at all costs. But she had thought he looked so handsome that night. She had felt the butterflies in her stomach as he asked for her hand and pulled her close before she could protest. It had disarmed her. He twirled her around his living room effortlessly, nestling his nose in her hair, breathing her in as he swayed easily to the music.

"I think I'm falling in love with you."

He had whispered the words so softly in her ear that Alex wasn't sure she'd heard him right. She hadn't looked up. She was afraid of the emotion her face might have betrayed. She just smiled to herself, burying her head against his chest, letting him lead her across their private makeshift dance floor.

She's got a way about her... I don't know what it is - But I know that I can't live without her. She's got a way of pleasing... I don't know why it is - But there doesn't have to be a reason...

The sound of Eli's voice brought her back. She looked up at her husband, who had his arms wrapped firmly around her waist. The lights in the ballroom were dimmed, save a spotlight that shone down around the new couple. Hundreds of eyes were on them, but Alex didn't care. She felt like it was just the two of them again, dancing on a private, makeshift dance floor. She let herself sway to the music. Her cheeks ached slightly from smiling so hard.

"I love you, Alex." Jamie was whispering in her ear again. "This is the happiest day of my life. Let's dance forever, okay?"

She felt the butterflies again. She didn't want the day to ever end. She looked up at him.

"I love you too, baby," she breathed. "I can't believe we finally did it. We're married. I'm your wife."

She giggled. That word would take some getting used to.

"Forever."

He squeezed her tighter.

She's got a smile that heals me... I don't know why it is – But I have to laugh when she reveals me.   She's got a way about her... I don't know what it is – But I know that I can't live without her any way...

Eli drew out the last line of the song, letting the last syllables float through the otherwise silent, mesmerized room. When the last musical note finally faded from the air, he stood and ceremoniously bowed towards the bride and groom. Tipping an imaginary hat, he affectionately saluted the new couple. The room erupted in cheers.

Reluctantly, Alex eased out of Jamie's embrace. Holding hands, the couple crossed the ballroom floor to meet Eli. The three exchanged warm hugs. Alex whispered her thanks in her baby brother's ear. Then Jamie led Alex back to their table.

Next, there were the speeches.

Alex had insisted that her mother go first. In a way, it was her wedding too. Her mother had always given her so much – usually more than she could afford and then some - and Alex wanted everyone to know that this was 'her event.' Her mother was radiant throughout the evening; Alex had never seen her smile quite like that before. She looked magnificent in her bronze-colored gown – regal was the word that continuously came to mind. She had always known her mother as a relatively private person, keeping few truly close friends in their community after she divorced. Tonight, however, her mother seemed to cherish the special attention.

The M.O.B. gave the opening toast – raising her glass of untouched champagne to the bride and groom as she told Jamie that he now had her most precious gift, her baby girl.

Alex's dad followed, walking uneasily towards the front of the room to take hold of the microphone. Tiny beads of sweat covered his forehead. He pulled a handkerchief from his pocket to wipe the dampness away. He had mounds of salt and pepper white hair, a full beard, happy eyes, and a sad, tired face. He cleared his throat to quiet the room, not unlike a professor might have done.

"So every Sabbath I think about Jamie. I think about him because of a phrase that appears in an early part of the service. It reads: 'it is like a bridegroom who steps down from his marriage canopy. He is like a hero who can run the complete course.' Because Jamie is a marathoner, I can't help thinking about it, and with the impending wedding, well, I think about it a lot..."

Alex wondered where her father was going with this, though she was sure that Jamie must have been delighted to have his penchant for marathons pointed out to the rapt audience.

"So Grandma would have liked to have been here." He paused, then:

"My mother died - last August."

A lump caught in Alex's throat. She looked around the room quickly to try and gauge her guests' reactions. She couldn't tell what people were thinking.

"Alex and Jamie came down to see her a few days before she passed away.

And then they came back again a few days later for the funeral.

My mother was very much taken with Jamie, as she has been with her granddaughter for her whole life. My mother kept talking to me about two things – well several things – as her life was coming to an end.

She talked about how satisfied she was with her life and with her grandchildren. And she wanted me to make sure that she got shoes and a gown for the wedding. And she wanted me to rearrange her stock portfolio. Well, we didn't get to either."

The room laughed at that. Alex's father relaxed a little. He had rehearsed the speech three dozen times – while driving, while working, while cooking, while playing with his younger children. Alex imagined that he knew every word of the speech by heart, and only his emotion altered the cadence of its delivery.

"My mother was always telling me what a nice young man Alex has found and what a nice young couple they make - which they do...

Now, my father – who has been dead almost twenty years – would have liked to have been here too."

Oh Jesus. Alex could barely believe it. The speeches were the one aspect of the wedding she hadn't overseen with dictatorial fervor. She had provided each family member a suggested maximum time limit - and her father was pressing that limit already - but she hadn't put any restrictions on speech content. She should have stipulated that referencing multiple dead relatives was a definite buzz kill.

"And he would have been - he would have been shaking his finger under my nose telling me, 'This is a good match.' And he would have gone to Jamie and he would have said '*Eashti k'beti'*, 'which translated from Hebrew means 'my wife is like my house.' And then he would have explained it at some length."

This time, her dad chuckled at himself a little. Alex relaxed, smiling at her dad, who was smiling at the memory of his father, who had been dead twenty years. Theirs was a complicated, still unresolved relationship.

"So —My father was a philosopher." He paused again.

"By training and by inclination...I told this to somebody and he laughed and I couldn't understand why he was laughing because I was sitting there thinking, 'well, you didn't grow up as the son of a philosopher.' And he said, 'but every father is a philosopher. They all try to tell you everything about life and it's really just incomprehensible stuff that comes out of their mouths.'"

This brings another round of laughter and scattered applause from multiple tables.

"But there have been many examples of philosophers and fathers throughout the ages. One of my favorites is Polonius, who appears in Hamlet."

Alex held her breathe as her father droned on. She mentally counted the minutes thinking that he was at least seven over the time limit she had set for each speech, he had already referenced two dead grandparents, and now he was pushing the envelope with Shakespeare. Part of her desperately wanted to make him stop. But part of her didn't mind if he took all the time in the world. He was struggling with giving his little girl away, she decided. That possibility actually brought her close to tears. She snuck a quick glance at Jamie and he gave her hand a little reassuring squeeze.

Alex's father paused. He looked up from his notes and out across the room at his daughter. He smiled a fatherly smile, a nostalgic grin.

"There is a scene Alexandra and I used to practice together when she was in high school. She needed to memorize it so we practiced it together for hours. In any event, by this point in the play Hamlet has gone mad. In this scene Polonius advises the King and Queen, in a bid to help them determine the cause of their son, Hamlet's madness. And Polonius says 'I have a daughter - and while she is mine...'"

Our repetition of this scene helped me to finally figure out the meaning of a recurring dream that I had when Alexandra was a small child.

So the dream was that we were on a scaffold. And I guess Alexandra was about three or four years old. And clouds surrounded the scaffold. And we were trying to climb up and I was trying to explain certain things about the scaffold - not uncharacteristically for me. And it's completely ridiculous but she started to fall. She started to fall and I reached out to try to catch her. But I couldn't catch her. She fell into these white clouds. While she fell she just laughed and laughed. She was laughing with absolute, un-abandoned joy.

So I understood the meaning of the dream, which is - I will - at some point - let go."

Her dad exhaled, breathing heavily into the microphone.

The room was silent.

He rubbed his eyes and from across the ballroom raised his glass to Alex and to Jamie in an affectionate salutation.

"So, Mrs. Kramer – that time has come. And I believe I still do have a daughter, while she is his."

4

Once the artery had burst, any attempt to stop the bleeding was just an exercise in futility; no amount of pressure could stop the hemorrhaging. Bear Stearns finally seemed to be at death's door by Friday, March 14, 2008. The company's stock was on its way to closing down a numbing 47% on the day. Only a few days earlier the firm's newly-minted CEO, Alan Schwartz had appeared on CNBC, attempting to demonstrate optimism and instill confidence. He tried to reassure the public that there was no liquidity crisis at the bank. But it was to no avail. Perception feasted on reality until the two were indiscernible. Corporate counter-parties and investors began pulling out their money as fast as they could. No one could be sure if and for how long the Big Bad Bear would remain standing and no one wanted to be the last to find out. By Friday, there actually was a liquidity crisis of sorts, and Alan Schwartz was pressed to speak once again. This time, he hosted a conference call for all employees, investors, and a myriad of others who obtained dial-in info. Thousands around the world listened in to the "Bear Stearns Conference Call to Address Speculation in the Marketplace."

On that same Friday, Bear Stearns was the last topic Alex wanted to think about. She and Jamie finally succeeded in hailing a taxi at the street corner near their Midtown Manhattan apartment after waiting for nearly fifteen minutes as midday congestion clogged the city streets. After loading their matching black and red Swiss Army suitcases, fully equipped camera bag, and carry-on luggage into the vehicle they eased into the cab's sticky leather interior.

Alex noted happily that both she and her husband (she loved using the word) were casually dressed in Third World Country Chic attire – fitted cargo pants, low-top sneakers, and lightweight cotton button down shirts – hers floral and his white. Both of them had run late leaving work and now they were scrambling to make the flight to Bangkok for their honeymoon.

It had been almost a month since their wedding night. Alex was feeling terrific about the early progress of their marriage. They were both excited to break away from the chaos of New York and Wall Street for some far-away alone time, surely a sign that they were settling in well to matrimonial bliss.

She was thankful that the stress of getting married had passed and she could settle into a life of just being married. She wouldn't need to lie to her parents about secretly living with Jamie or feign excuses to skip the religious holidays the rest of her family observed assiduously. She was a wife now – which was a classification she had always thought would cement her position as an adult and not a child. She felt she was rushing as fast as she could to reach this point. Now that she was here, she was ready to start living. And she had it all mapped out: launch her career with the token two years in finance to build credibility; return to Harvard for business school, where she had already been accepted; perfectly time the birth of her first child to pop him out in between her first and second year of school (would any corporation really want to hire a pregnant woman out of business school?? She couldn't fathom it); secure an All-Star job and then promptly return to the work force – she was thinking in bright lights 'Corporate America' – with hubby, baby, and nanny all in tow. There, she would begin her ascent to corporate superstardom as C.E.O. of a yet-to-be-determined but highly reputable Fortune 500 Company. She had a five-year plan, a fifteen-year plan, and a twenty-five year plan all etched in her head. The details were blurry, but the main point was to perfect marriage and motherhood while dutifully charging up the proverbial corporate ladder. Her husband would remain entrenched at a Big Bank on Wall Street until he was promoted to a Managing Director – what Alex believed to be the pinnacle of

Investment Banking success. From there, he could easily transition to Corporate America, where countless companies would be banging down his door to hire him as their Chief Financial Officer.

But all that could wait. At least for the next fifteen days. She and Jamie had meticulously planned an amazing two-week expedition through Thailand. A promise of adventure had been one of Alex's marital pre-requisites: several weeks before the wedding Alex had a fleeting case of cold feet. In an angst-filled conversation she had told him that she could only marry if Jamie promised to explore the world with her. Ideally, she wanted to live abroad for at least two years, but if that ultimately didn't fit into their larger life plans, she could settle for visiting at least one or two unknown countries a year. She had a bid to see it all and expected her husband to be a willing and adventurous life-long travel companion. Jamie had assured her then that he shared her appetite for exploration and obliged her with a honeymoon that would pack a four-country punch – two weeks in Thailand with a quick day trip in and out of Cambodia and then Laos, followed by a quickie to Hong Kong – since they'd be in the neighborhood anyway. They'd earmarked a portion of the cash gifts from their wedding to spend a little extra on nicer hotel rooms – paying well above what they might on a regular vacation. She had consciously packed the most daring of all of the lingerie she'd received from her bridesmaids, prepared to step up her post-matrimonial game.

But Alex couldn't get her husband's full and undivided attention yet. This goddamned Bear Stearns conference call was in her way. Jamie had his cell phone against one ear while he was scrolling through his blackberry with his other hand. Finally locating the password, he tapped it into his phone and clicked into the call. Alex leaned in close to him and strained to listen in.

"…As we said in our release, you know, Bear Stearns has been subject to a significant amount of rumor and innuendo over the past week."

Alex thought she recognized Alan Schwartz's voice; of course she did not know him personally, but he was frequently dialed in to conference calls on banking deals that Jamie was tasked on. She typically beamed with pride and bragged to anyone who would listen that her boyfriend- turned fiancé-turned husband was a hotshot investment banker. Bypassing business school, which was the standard route after two years in banking, Jamie was instead promoted directly out of the analyst program to be an Associate in his banking group. He was considered a rising superstar, albeit an unlikely one. He was a Midwestern boy at heart with an easy, affable disposition. But he worked with precision and verve, consistently generating superior work product. Most senior bankers fought to task him on their deal teams. As a cherry on the Big Bank sundae, Jamie also taught the analyst training classes. He was the perfect ambassador into the business for many fresh-faced, impressionable, eager-to-please college graduates. He personified the model employee: a diligent, eager, efficient, non-confrontational, aspirational work-producing machine. He was a Big Bank's wet dream. Alex believed his path was pre-ordained – three years as an analyst, three years as an associate, four years as a vice president, a handful of years as a junior managing director, and then, finally, a promotion to the Holy Grail of Investment Banking Superstardom – Managing Director.

Alex nudged Jamie and mouthed her question. Jamie nodded, confirming that it was Alan Schwartz who was speaking.

"We attempted to try to provide some facts to the situation, but in the market environment we are in, the rumors intensified and given the nervousness in the market, a lot of people, it seemed, wanted to act to protect themselves from the possibility of rumors being true and could wait later to see the facts."

He was trying to call off the dogs and stop the run on the bank. The potential implosion of Bear Stearns was all anyone and everyone Alex knew talked about these days. It consumed the couple during the infancy of their marriage.

It was still a little bit surreal to Alex that this call was even taking place. Only a month before Alex's grandfather, who had officiated at their wedding, had jokingly describe their marriage as the great merger of Bear Stearns and Lehman Brothers. Their wedding guests had laughed and Jamie and Alex had exchanged nervous smiles. Only three years before, Alex had wrested a coveted summer intern position at the venerable bank. She was one of the many seemingly confident but secretly wide-eyed college juniors to earn a summer spot in an Investment Banking division. It was the first of many rites of passage, where kids bragged about pulling consecutive all-nighters working on top-secret pitch books for critical, high profile clients. In reality, most slaved away all night on small, irrelevant details of presentations that likely would never see the light of day. Alex had no goddamned idea what was going on that summer. She couldn't distinguish a Balance Sheet from a Cash Flow Statement to save her life. But she had developed a strange sort of reverence for the business, with its seemingly foreign language, powerful networks, and wildly wealthy executives. So she was more than willing to eagerly work all the late nights required.

Alex met Jamie Kramer that summer. She had arrived at 383 Madison Avenue twenty minutes before the scheduled start time for the first day of the Summer Analyst Training program. She had chosen a blue pinstriped Brooks Brothers shirt to wear with her only black suit – hoping to strike a feminine yet professional pose. She stared at all of the legitimate professionals streaming in to the glass-paneled, cavernous lobby of the building; they were all pretty much dressed identically – navy blue suits, white, blue or pink shirts, with the occasional power red tie. The shuffle of men's loafers and the occasional clatter of a woman's heels combined to sound like a mechanical whirring. That was followed by the repetitious hum of identification cards being swiped and electronically acknowledged, triggering the click of the metal turnstile.

Finally, there was the hum of the security x-ray machines. Sometimes people acknowledged passersby with a nod, but no one really seemed to speak.

Alex stood impatiently in the lobby, watching while she waited for her friend Ina. Childhood friends and sometimes partners-in-crime, the two used to spend hours sitting in the closet in Ina's house while plotting their future greatness. At age nine, Alex and Ina had settled on a plan to become high-powered corporate lawyers, intent on starting a practice together that allowed them to take Tuesdays off to be philosophers. That would placate their no-nonsense, business-oriented mothers and inspire their contemplative, academic fathers. By twenty, the two were instead convinced that Investment Banking was the most direct path to professional nirvana.

Ina finally arrived fifteen minutes late, with tiny beads of sweat building against her beautiful, fair olive-hued skin. She explained that at the last minute she had decided to walk the forty blocks to work to clear her head and enjoy the sunshine before their first day of work. Alex rolled her eyes good-naturedly and temporarily wished Ina had pursued an internship with a philosopher instead. Then, she hurried her friend through security and over to the elevator bank that led to the 36th floor.

Every head in the room turned to stare when Alex and Ina walked in to the room. There were thirty-eight other interns in their class, and Alex noted, only three other female coeds. The portly woman with curly brown hair who appeared to be in charge of the group motioned for the girls to pick up their training packets and take the two open seats left in the front row. Alex glared at Ina, who brandished a devilish little smirk at their highly conspicuous entrance.

When Jamie appeared before the training class on the second day of the program Alex and Ina were sitting in the front row like two ass-kissing dopes, not exactly the type of impression Alex hoped to assert with any man under any circumstances. Alex was hardly swooning over him in those first few days, but he certainly left her with a solid first impression. She determined that he was on the right side of handsome despite the slightly cheesy way he slicked his hair with gel. He had an infectious sense of humor, looked great in a business suit and most attractive of all, he seemed to be damn good at his job. Each time he tested the class on some detail of finance Alex cursed under her breath as Ina's hand swiftly shot up and she gave the correct answer, time and time again. Jamie increasingly focused his classroom banter in her friend's direction. *Were they flirting?* Alex couldn't help but wonder. It didn't really matter, she decided;

she was really there to master the Investment Banking Juggernaut, determined to take Wall Street by storm.

And Alex took it. Well, as much as any intern could. She intentionally chose a subdivision other than Jamie's so that she would not fall prey to any potentially self-indulgent distractions. She approached the tedious work with religious devotion and revered the building's top floor - the Management Suite - as if it were a temple. She woke early to exercise before work and then spent the next twelve to fifteen hours in a cubicle, making sense of financial statements, spreadsheets, and corporate presentations. She counted eight instances where she worked nearly through the night, encouraged by the positive feedback and the occasion friendly pat on the back from a superior. One manger assured her even before the summer was through that she was guaranteed to receive a full-time offer. Once, Alex was even staffed on a project alone with only a Senior Vice President, who had requested her specifically. Alex was so eager to please that summer that she took every sign of encouragement at face value and nothing more. She didn't associate it with the other side of Wall Street that she had also learned a little bit about: the bag of cocaine in one of the best Associate's top drawers that Ina had spotted while looking for a calculator; the assistant with the *Fran Dresser* voice and the *Baywatch* implants who was simultaneously bemoaning her bad luck on J-Date while sleeping with one of the group's very married senior bankers; the bank-sponsored black town cars that employees would use for illicit trips to strip clubs instead of taking them home to their sleeping families; the Vice President who finished his three-hour conference call with a client instead of immediately dashing off when the secretary passed him a note that his wife had just gone into labor with their third child. For Alex, all these exploits faded into the shadows against the shining light of the banks. She happily drank the Kool-Aid.

◆ ◆ ◆

But on that Friday, her gilded version of Wall Street was on shaky ground. At Alex's urging, Jamie clicked off of the conference call a few minutes before their taxi arrived at John F. Kennedy International Airport.

"Babe, there is nothing we can do about all that now. Don't look so worried."

He looked at her with his eyebrows still creased in concern. She squeezed his hand reassuringly.

"It's all going to be here when we get back. The madness, the excruciating hours, the deals, your friends, and even the assholes you can't stand. All of it will still be here in two weeks. Bear's not going anywhere, babe. But if we miss this flight, you are going to have one bitch of a new bride on your hands."

He grinned at that and kissed his new wife.

Alan Schwartz had announced on the call that the Federal Reserve Bank of New York had agreed to give Bear Stearns a $25 billion loan in order to give the bank a 28-day bridge of liquidity, Jamie explained to Alex. Surely, that would get the bank through this absurd crisis of confidence. With the camera bag slung over his shoulder and a suitcase in either hand, Jamie led the way through the terminal. He managed to convince an airline associate to check their bags through in First Class, even though they themselves were sitting in Coach Class for the thirteen hour flight to Tokyo where they would then connect on a five and a half hour flight to Thailand. *At least their luggage would travel in style,* Alex silently noted.

But once they were through security, he couldn't turn work off. Jamie kept his eyes glued to his blackberry until the flight attendants closed the cabin doors. Alex nestled up against him as he alternated between checking his work email account and checking a website that listed the minute-to-minute changes in Bear Stearns' stock price. He quickly dialed his best friend Chris, another Bear banker, one last time before they closed the cabin doors for takeoff. He finally powered everything down, assured that nothing had changed.

Nearly twenty-four hours later, they landed in Bangkok at 2 a.m. local time. Bleary-eyed, the couple made their way over to the baggage claim carousel. Alex was tasked with watching their carry-on bags so she slumped down in a nearby plastic chair while Jamie nudged himself into prime baggage-claiming position. Streams of other passengers arrived and left, collecting their belongings. Alex noticed that they were amongst the last waiting and felt her stomach sink a little.

Ugh.

She roused herself from her semi-catatonic state and joined her husband.

"Gone?" she half-asked, half-stated.

Jamie figured that there had to be some mix up; their bags had likely just been deposited to another terminal by mistake. They made their way over to what looked like a lost baggage office and proceeded to argue with several airline employees who alternated between refusing to help or refusing to acknowledge that they even spoke English. Through the hysteria, the couple managed to discern that there was no record anywhere in the system of their luggage, which meant at best it was still in New York or at worst had disappeared into the traveler's vortex somewhere between New York, Tokyo, and Bangkok.

Jamie looked like he was on the verge of a tearful, yet homicidal rage. Alex was furious at their bad luck. She could not believe that her perfectly-planned honeymoon was off to such a shitty start. She felt filthy in her travel clothing and exposed without her belongings.

With only their carryon luggage and the promise of $50 per day for clothing and other essentials - until their luggage was hopefully recovered - Alex and Jamie left the airport and headed for their hotel. Alex could hardly wait for the luxury of a Five Star Hotel, a steaming hot shower, crisp Egyptian cotton sheets, and a chilled glass of wine.

They were driven from the airport into the city where they hit gridlocked traffic. It was still the middle of the night and she couldn't believe the scene all around them. Cars were practically parked behind one another, where through-traffic should have been moving. The streets were fairly wide but in complete disarray; entire chunks of concrete were missing in certain spots and paved roads turned to dirt without warning. Their driver pointed out haphazard construction platforms above and explained that the Ministry of Interior was in the process of building an inter-city rail system. It didn't look like too much progress had been made as far as Alex could tell. Each time they stopped at streetlights beggar children would rush up to their car and with wide, sallow eyes would motion to their empty hands and bellies. Grown women and elderly men also roamed the streets, trying to pander a wild assortment of unnecessary goods. The whole scene made Alex shiver. She checked to see that the car's doors were locked, with a realization that she was very far from home.

They arrived at the hotel and explained their luggage situation to the nighttime desk clerk, who while very nice, was nearing the end of his graveyard shift and really didn't give a damn as far as Alex could tell. He promised to alert them if their bags arrived that evening and then handed them off to the porter, who escorted them up to their honeymoon suite.

Jamie and Alex collapsed on top of the bed almost instantaneously, much to Alex's delight. Being allowed to lie on a bed with street clothes on was a small luxury she had sacrificed to marriage. Apparently, a 24-hour flight, missing luggage, a foreign environment, and the seemingly-imminent implosion of Bear Stearns was just the right mix of chaos to make Jamie forget his "no outside clothes inside the bed" mantra.

Alex rolled over and pecked Jamie on the cheek.

"I'm gonna go hop in the shower. I feel gross. I need to wash this day off of me."

Jamie pulled her back onto the bed a little bit, grabbing her ass and squeezing it affectionately.

"Hmm, you feel so good, baby. Hurry in there," he said suggestively. Then, "I'm just going to call and check in with Chris and a few others at the office. I want to see what's going on there."

Alex slipped through the antique-looking double doors and into the lush bathroom, stripping off her filthy clothing. Third World Country Chic was feeling overwhelmingly Third World and decidedly un-Chic at the moment. She turned on the shower and adjusted the temperature until the room began to fill with steam. She stepped in, cringing reflexively from the initial contact with the steaming hot water. Moaning, she let the adrenaline drain a little bit from her body. Her mind wandered.

So far she felt strange more than excited. It was tough to pinpoint the exact emotion but she just had this sensation of being underwhelmed. Like, this is it? THIS is what a honeymoon is like. It felt like they were trying so damned hard. The perfect exotic location. The perfect hotel. The perfect amount of time in each region. The perfect balance of adventure and relaxation. The perfect wardrobe for each event. Had she planned too much? She was doing all the things she was supposed to do but she didn't feel even a morsel of satisfaction. She didn't feel like a sexy new bride. In fact Alex felt more like a homely wife; she was already a shade too pale, had let the natural color of her roots grow in too much, and was packing on more than the few pounds she had lost in anticipation of her wedding. She mentally reassured herself that it was just the long travel, lost luggage, and late hour that were making her feel a little dejected. But it was hard to shake that sensation of simply feeling far away.

Alex stepped out of the shower and wrapped herself in one of the hotel's robes. No luggage meant no lingerie. *So much for that,* she thought. Alex rubbed some of the hotel's lotion on her bare body, and sprayed herself with some perfume, which mercifully she had tucked into her carryon. She ran her fingers through her hair and then brushed her teeth quickly using only her finger, cursing herself for forgetting to pack a toothbrush for the umpteenth time in her life.

Alex re-entered the bedroom with the intent to seduce. She didn't want to be a pasty, unpolished bride. She wanted to be a hot sex machine, prepared to fling open her robe and jump Jamie, hungrily tearing at his clothes. She perched on the desk, intent to raise one leg seductively against a nearby chair until Jamie implored her to show him more. She stopped. Something else was holding Jamie's focus. She could have been lying naked on the desk and she wouldn't have caught his eye.

She watched him. He was sitting on the bed with his fingers clenched around his blackberry, which at the time was pressed so tightly to his ear that both ear and fingers were turning an alarming shade of red.

"What do you mean two dollars a share? Two dollars? Two dollars! There's gotta be a mistake. Maybe you heard wrong. Nobody really knows what's going on. I bet it's $20 a share and somehow a zero got dropped along the way. I mean, heck, even $20 is a total f'ing joke. It's not possible Chris. I, I just don't see how any of this is possible. What are you going to do? What are we going to do? What are they saying? Is anyone saying anything? What are guys doing? Is anyone working? I know it's Saturday over there... Really? The place is packed? Everyone's there? Packed? Shoot. Do you think I should come back? I mean, should Alex and I come back... What are guys doing? Matt, Jesse, John, Rick, Steve, Frank - what is everyone doing? ... You're packing up your desks? And loading your files and financial models onto personal drives? Shit... You seriously think they're going to bolt the doors Monday and not let everyone in? C'mon, that's just crazy talk. These guys wouldn't do that...Well, will you log onto my computer for me and grab my files too? I've got a lot of critical material on there. I've got a lot of valuable work. I mean, I've worked months on some of those models. You can't just replace that kind of work... Thanks, bud. I appreciate it. So what do you think happens now? What happens next? ... But I'd think they've got to make some sort of announcement. I'm sure Alan's spoken with Steve. Maybe I should just call Steve right now - I'm sure he'll fill me in... Oh, he's in a closed-door meeting? All senior managers have been in one all day? Jesus, I just can't even believe this. What happened to all that '30-day window' crap from the conference call yesterday? That was yesterday! God. I board a plane for my honeymoon thinking we're finally gonna pull through - that we're all gonna be okay in the end, you know? And not even 24-hours later, my luggage is lost, this city smells like shit, my wife is miserable that she doesn't have any of her clothing, and Bear Stearns is gonna fucking go under? How could this happen? JP Morgan is going to buy us for $2 a share? What a goddamned joke... It's got to be a mistake, Chris.... You really don't think I should come home... Yeah, I guess you're right. But maybe I should switch hotels at a minimum! The motel near the airport might be better suited for my budget at this point. Romancing the wife at a Thai Motel 6 - great way to start a marriage... Okay. Yeah, I know you have to take care of your own shit right now... But if you can grab my files too... Thanks Chris. Talk soon bud. Ok, thanks man... I appreciate it... Yeah, you too. Call me if you hear any other details. I'll be up. Yeah, it's like three in the morning here. But I'll be up."

Jamie let the phone drop onto the bed. He looked up at Alex. The faint lines around his eyes creased in pain, exhaustion, and confusion. She looked down briefly at the coffee table next to the desk. A note from the hotel's concierge sat atop a box of strange, exotic looking chocolates:

Congratulations on your honeymoon! Welcome to beautiful Thailand! Please do not hesitate to contact us with any questions or concerns.

She crossed the room and sat down on the bed next to him, carefully folding her bathrobe over her legs and wrapping the folds tightly around her waist.

"Baby, what happened? What's going on?"

"I don't really know yet." He sounded exhausted.

"Was that Chris on the phone? What did he say?"

"He said - he said JP Morgan is going to buy Bear Stearns for two dollars a share. He said it's all over. We're screwed."

Alex couldn't hide her confusion.

"Huh? What? What does that mean? What happened to that window thing you explained to me yesterday? From the Fed or something? What happened to the conference call? We just listened to it yesterday...I don't understand? You said everything was going to be okay?"

"I don't know. I just don't know yet. Everyone's saying something happened overnight. Something changed. I mean, no one's talking - at least none of the senior guys. But that's what everyone's saying."

"That's what Chris said? How does he know? Isn't it Saturday there?"

"Yeah. Chris told me. He's at the office. He said everyone's at the office. Like, everyone - even guys who blow off working on the weekends. He said everyone's just walking around, snooping around, you know? Guys are just trying to get information. The group heads are all in closed- door meetings in their offices. But Chris doesn't even think they really know what's going on yet. Apparently there's some hush-hush meeting going down on the executive floor."

"About what?"

"I have no idea! How the hell am I supposed to know?" He snapped.

"Jamie..."

"I'm sorry." He moved to sit closer to her on the bed. "I'm sorry, baby. I didn't mean to yell at you. Baby, I'm sorry."

He held up his hands, as if to illustrate his helplessness.

"I just don't know what to do. I mean, Chris said everyone is there loading their files onto the computers because there's a rumor going around that they are going to lock the doors on Monday. *Nobody in and nobody out*. Chris said that guys are steaming mad. Management doesn't want to have a situation with a disgruntled employee or something so they're just going to lock the doors. It's a joke. We're all going to be fucking disgruntled. I mean, they can't really sell Bear Stearns for two dollars a share. It'll wipe people out."

Alex squeezed her husband's hand reassuringly. She searched for the right words, for some sort of consolation.

"Well, at least you haven't gotten any stock yet. So we'll be okay? Only Vice President's and above get stock, right?"

Jamie tried to laugh, but it came out more like a restrained snort.

"Yeah, well that's true. But, all those guys - Ken, Steve - they've worked at Bear their entire careers. Twenty years of stock going down the drain. It just doesn't seem possible."

He shook his head.

"I thought I'd be there my whole career, too," he said quietly. Without looking at her, "do you think we should go home?"

Alex was starting to feel a little bit panicked. She took a deep breath and tried to focus on how to react.

With her free hand she reached up to stroke his face, willing him to look at her.

"Go home? Baby, it's all gonna be okay. Listen, we just got here. What are we going to go home to do?"

She smiled at him, trying to make her questions sound soothing, even a little playful. Inwardly, she was bursting at her emotional seams.

"But...but my files? How am I going to get my files?"

"Shhh. Baby, it's gonna be okay."

She could recall her mother consoling her in the same way years ago. Alex forced herself to push the images of her childish temper-tantrums to the recesses of her mind.

"We'll figure it out, baby."

"But, Alex." His voice was more urgent. "My files."

Remain calm, she coached herself. Then, "I thought I heard you say that Chris offered to take care of that for you?"

That wasn't enough to assuage his rising anxiety.

"But what if there are meetings? I'm sure there are going to be dozens of meetings. I should be there for them."

"Chris will fill you in."

She felt his body stiffen against hers.

"But, what if those meetings are about retention? How can they decide if they're going to keep me or not in the merger if I'm not even there to prove myself? Or how do I know if they're going to keep any of us? I mean,

JP Morgan guys and Bear Stearns guys aren't exactly going to get along. We couldn't be more different."

This was exhausting.

"How do you know that?"

"I just know, Alex."

He sounded affronted. But she hadn't meant anything by it. She was just trying to understand. The less confident he sounded the more she felt herself panicking.

"It's a culture thing, Alex. I've worked on deals before where JPM has been co-lead. I've had meetings and calls with these guys. They're all assholes who had their jobs handed to them on silver, pedigreed platters and think that they're the greatest f'ing commodity on Wall Street. It's like they've developed Goldman Sachs complexes over there. It could never work. But who knows if I'll even find out. What if they just fire all of us?"

"Baby, that's not gonna happen."

Alex meant it. How could they ever fire Jamie? He worked harder than anyone she knew.

"But we don't know that. How can we know?"

He looked helpless again. Alex tried to get her husband to crack a smile.

"Maybe we'll just stay in Thailand indefinitely." She snuggled up against him, laying her head in his lap. "We'll become expatriates or something romantic like that."

Jamie sighed heavily but didn't respond. He leaned back, letting his body fall back against the pillows of the still-made bed. Alex's head was still resting on his upper thigh. They lay there like that, silently staring at the ceiling, each lost in their own thoughts.

Jamie's question echoed in her head. How could they really know what would happen? She couldn't really answer him. She had no clue. She didn't know if he was going to lose his job, or if Bear could go under, or if they were going to even be able to make the mortgage payments on the apartment they had just bought nine months earlier. He had proposed to her there the very day he signed the papers for the final closing. How could they know what was going to happen now? She had no fucking idea.

Alex had heard Jamie joke on the phone about switching hotels. But was he really joking? Maybe they should switch hotels. Was it really prudent of them to be gallivanting around Southeast Asia on an opulent vacation when Jamie might not even have a job when they got home? It wasn't like she didn't make decent money too, but Jamie had been in the business five years longer and he was definitely the primary breadwinner in their new little family. What would she do if he didn't have a job? What would he do? She could tell that her husband was in complete panic mode. Bear Stearns was all he knew. The bank had popped his professional cherry when he was a summer analyst and he remained loyal ever since. And he was thriving there. *Skipped business school. One of only three analysts promoted directly to associate. Worked directly with the most senior bankers and was fast-tracked to someday hold a senior position as Managing Director.* She had proudly bragged about Jamie so many times.

He had applied for sixty summer internships his junior year of college. He just happened to land the job on Wall Street like a roulette ball falling on Black 32. He could have ended up in Corporate at a place like Staples, Inc. as easily as he had ended up on Wall Street. But he was humbled by a job on Wall Street. And he was proud. Back in the Midwest these were coveted credentials. Back home he was seen as a Hot Shot Investment Banker Living In New York City. Most of his friends had moved back home after college or had opted for jobs in a less-stressful environment. Jamie could count on one hand the few who, like himself, chose to grind it out in New York. He was an outsider looking in. That's why he loved Bear. He identified with the firm. It was the underdog in the city, just like he was.

"Hey."

She moved up in order to lay her head down on his shoulder, extended her body along the bed to meet his.

"We'll figure it out okay?"

She wrapped her arms protectively around her husband.

"We're in this together now, remember?"

Looking up, she kissed Jamie softly on the lips. Then she raised herself up onto her arms and moved in again, kissing each of his eyelids, forcing him to momentarily close his tired, scared looking eyes. Jamie finally exhaled for the first time since he'd made the phone call back to New York.

"How'd I get so lucky to land a wife like you?" He cupped her face in his hands. "Let's enjoy our honeymoon. I promise. Nothing will stop us from doing that."

He reached over to switch off the light, hungrily reaching for his bride in the dark.

5

BOND BABY
APRIL 2008

A lex's first day back from her honeymoon was also her first official day as a junk bond trader. As far as she was concerned, that was a pretty big fucking deal. Lehman Brothers required all new Fixed Income trading recruits to spend time as research analysts before transitioning over to the trading desk. So when she joined the firm in 2007, they made her rotate into research. The research was interesting but she knew she wouldn't build her career there. As far as she could tell trading was the epicenter of absolutely all of the activity in the building. Alex just wanted to be where the action was. While she was prone to being highly impatient, Alex was willing to bide her time in the annals of research and to overlook this small career layover; she rationalized the move by figuring that it would give her ample time to learn all of the finance she could, or at a minimum give her the tools to successfully mask her inability to do complex math in her head. It turned out that one year as a research analyst had armed her with a little bit of both.

The trading floors at Lehman Brothers were expansive. Fixed Income was on the fourth floor. To enter, employees had to swipe their identification cards by the elevator bank and walk through two enormous beveled-glass doors. Rows and rows of computer monitors filled the floor, which was easily the length of a football field. There were forty rows with twenty people in each. Each employee sat in a reclining office chair in front of three, sometimes four, computer monitors. Phone turrets with two receivers each were next to every computer. There was roughly twelve inches of space between each computer terminal. One's only hope at personal space was a small metal filing cabinet with three drawers. There were a handful of glass-encased offices that ran against two of the long walls, but they were mostly for show, housing perfunctory meetings and granting a handful of the most senior management a vestibule for self-flagellation. All of the real action was on the floor where nothing could be hidden behind the walls of an office. Alex thought the ceilings were unusually high by office-building standards. The lights that hung above each row were shockingly bright, casting a florescent hew across the floor. Any place that had room for color was distinguished in green, Lehman Green. There was a steady buzz across the entire floor, but the decibel level escalated when moving from the research side of the floor down to the rows that housed the salesmen and the traders. There, phones were constantly ringing with people taking orders from clients and yelling across the rows at one another, trying to execute trades. Most of the time the atmosphere was jovial but intense. When they weren't trading for the firm, the guys would boast about their personal trading conquests and compare notes on the multi-million dollar renovations they were undertaking at their summer homes out in New York's notoriously wealthy enclave, The Hamptons. There was also the typical boys-only banter that mostly included retelling crude jokes, recapping sports highlights, and reliving a dirty night out with one of the many attractive female executive assistants that worked the floors of Lehman Brothers. Alex usually described it to people as a cross between a fraternity and a locker room. But the truth was she had no goddamned idea what either one was really like from an insider's perspective. She just liked the idea that this job might afford her the opportunity to find out.

Fresh from her honeymoon Alex swiped her card as usual. She inhaled deeply and pushed open the glass doors onto the fourth floor. It wasn't even six a.m. yet. The floor was still relatively quiet. Alex's four-inch stilettos clicked softly as she walked past the research rows and towards trading. She allowed herself one last lingering glance at research. Fuck. She was nervous. Maybe research hadn't been all that bad. The senior analysts were a little quirky, to say the least. But she could hide in research. There was no hiding in trading. There was no hiding, no whispering, no crying, and no fucking up in trading. There was just trading, and betting, and yelling, and cursing, and winning. If you wanted to last as a trader, you had to prove you could win.

Just go for it. Just act like you know what the fuck you are doing until either you actually do know what you're doing or they discover you're a fraud. Don't be such a pussy. You wanted to be a big shot. You wanted to be one of the boys. Here's your chance. Just don't fuck it up.

Alex arrived at her new desk. She looked around the trading rows. Another young trader was already in his seat typing away. He'd been on the desk for eight months already. He looked up briefly and nodded hello. Alex made a mental note to arrive even earlier the next day. She took her coat off and then realized she'd have to double back down the floor to hang it up. She walked over to the coat closet and made another mental note to arrive an extra five minutes early. She returned to the trading area, sat back down at her desk and tried to get comfortable. She took her cell phone out of her purse and then slid the bag underneath her feet. Thinking twice, she dropped the phone back in to her bag. No distractions today, she told herself. She wiggled the mouse and waited for the computer monitors to light up. Nothing happened. She hit the power button on the hard-drive that sat by her knees. Still, nothing happened.

Fuck.

She had to get this goddamned computer started before everyone else showed up. She could only imagine what an asshole she would look like in front of three black computer screens. Pushing her chair back, she crawled under the desk. She fidgeted with the wires trying to find the one that belonged to the monitors.

"Is this some new innovative trading strategy I haven't heard of yet?"

At the sound of the voice behind her Alex quickly crawled out from under the desk, a wave of panic spreading over her.

"You'll be more successful at trading bonds from up here." He paused. "At least that's been my experience."

Alex smoothed her hair and adjusted her skirt. She flashed a quick smile, which she hoped looked confident and not sheepish, as she felt the heat rising inside her. She silently prayed she could control her face from turning a deep shade of crimson. Lindsey, one of the most senior traders, had apparently arrived while she was trying to get her computer monitors to turn on. She had no idea how long he'd been standing there but she was pretty sure that her ass had been sticking out from underneath the desk while she was hard at work. She cringed at the thought of being the topic of side conversations on the desk that day. She couldn't be sure though if Lindsey would even say anything to the other guys. He did not intimidate her like some of the others did. As far as Alex was concerned he was a grown man with a woman's name who thought it was a good idea to get orthodontic braces in his late thirties. He wasn't exactly oozing machismo. If they were at a bar instead of on a trading desk, he'd probably be hitting on her, and their meters of interaction would be wholly reversed. Still, his style of interaction was aggressive enough to warrant full attention whenever talking to him. Lindsey had a way of putting people on the spot by asking them a series of questions in front of a large group. He seemed to have a vast chamber of knowledge that included the most random, irrelevant facts. She had never seen him actually trade but Alex had watched him drill someone on the details of some obscure ocean mammal and then deftly switch subjects to ask the other's opinion on inflation. Alex lived in fear of being caught in Lindsey's verbal crosshairs. She considered herself lucky that she didn't have to report to him directly and she hoped their interactions would be limited.

"Hi Lindsey. I was just trying to get my computer going. Can't be of much use around here without one!"

"Well, looks like you've succeeded," he said, nodding towards the monitors, which were now humming to life. "Welcome back. How was your honeymoon?"

"It was really nice, thank you."

Alex answered quickly, opting not to divulge the part about Bear collapsing, her husband having a minor meltdown, and going shopping for cheap clothing in a Thai mall after their luggage was lost. She also left out the fact that she found Thailand strange, overcrowded, and that while the itinerary had all the makings of a grand adventure, Alex had felt strangely numb and distant. All that would certainly be too much information. Alex thought it was an awkward question to answer anyway. As far as she was concerned, people went on their honeymoons for two reasons: to see an exotic location they wouldn't otherwise spend the money traveling to and to have copious and possibly offensive amounts of newlywed sex. Both hadn't quite lived up to Alex's expectations. She did not want to engage Lindsey in a conversation about some obscure facts about Thailand and she certainly had no interest in having any conversation of any remotely sexual nature with anyone on the desk. She wanted them to see and treat her as a trader and nothing else.

"Good. Well, if Clarke doesn't give you enough work you know where to find me. I'll always find something for you to work on. There is plenty to be done around here."

"Absolutely, you got it," Alex replied, grinning. She made yet another mental note to make sure she asked for plenty of work from Clarke and the other Distressed traders.

Alex sat back down at her desk. She opened up a few web browsers and started paging through newspaper and market websites as quickly and efficiently as she could. With nothing to trade yet, she wanted to be completely up to speed on the companies everyone else was trading. Maybe she'd find a breaking news item someone had missed and she could prove that she could add value to the desk immediately. She scanned multiple sites for headlines on retailers, airlines, publishers, and subprime lenders, industries which at the time were all in focus in the world of corporate bankruptcy.

By six forty-five, most of the traders had arrived. The smell of cologne and after-shave filled the row. No one else said a word to Alex yet. There wasn't much chatter in general. It was all business in the morning. Everyone scanned news articles to check for headlines that might affect their positions. An unexpected event could catch a trader off guard and cause him to lose millions.

At seven fifteen, all of the traders and salespeople got up and made their way down the floor to one of the large conference rooms. Alex had no clue if she was invited or not but she grabbed a blank notebook and a pen and followed suit. The room was packed beyond capacity with some people sitting around a long mahogany conference table and the rest standing with their backs up against the glass walls. Alex saw an open seat and moved to take it, but thought twice after Caroline, the most senior saleswoman gave her a sideways glance that Alex pretty much assumed said *don't even fucking think about being that brazen*. Seats are for senior people. There was a very strict and structural hierarchy at Lehman. As an eager employee, Alex drank much of the Kool-Aid about the company being different (i.e. superior) to all its competitors. But she drank it knowingly. She knew that the no-nonsense corporate culture, the excessive arrogance and the illusion of perfection were no different than at any other Big Bank. Alex was brazen but she knew to respect the culture, the hierarchy, the Lehman Way. Alex chose a spot in the far corner where she could stand while perching herself up against the back wall.

Ted and Andrew, the duo who oversaw everything, kicked off the meeting. First they briefed the group on upcoming economic data that the market was anticipating for the coming week as well as their take on the overall macroeconomic outlook. Then they discussed the calendar of new issue bond deals expected to be marketed and sold to institutional investors – the firm's clients – and how those deals would affect the overall market. Despite the market turmoil from the Bear Stearns "episode", as they called it, investors continued to turn a blind eye. All indicators pointed towards a sorely anemic economy, but it seemed to them that the bond market was nevertheless willing to stomach endless supply.

Next, Lindsey discussed the desk's risk exposure. In his mind they were overexposed. He wanted the reins pulled back in. Alex noticed that the High Yield guys nodded knowingly while the Distressed traders exchanged looks that were partially indifferent, partially skeptical. When Lindsey finished each trader took a turn reviewing his working agenda, highlighting the largest trade orders. Each trader was brief, quickly and tersely listing the name of the company, size of the potential transaction, and price context of the market. After the traders were done the salespeople were given the opportunity to voice any comments, concerns, or general themes their clients had mentioned. Only a handful of salespeople spoke up; the others waved off their turn. Finally, the research analysts took the floor, detailing any relevant news items. Alex kept her head tucked, furiously trying to keep up and scribbling down everything each person said. She made a small asterisk next to the points she wasn't sure she understood and made yet another mental note to consider asking someone later that day. Before Ted wrapped up the meeting, he asked if there was anything anyone else needed to cover.

Greg, one of the most senior traders, spoke.

"Yeah, one other quick item Teddy. I wanted to make sure that everyone knows that today is Alex Kramer's first day on the trading desk. After what seems like a very long time, she is joining us from the research group. I'm sure you all know her already but if you don't, please say hello. We expect her to be a huge asset for our group."

Alex felt a rush of adrenaline as all eyes followed Greg's and turned to look at her. She gave a little wave and smiled, unsure if she was supposed to do more. She was both excited and embarrassed that Greg had so publicly called all attention to her. But she felt that he had always looked out for her so this must be for her own good. Greg had interviewed her for her summer internship as a trader two years before and he had taken her under his wing when she was an intern. While she had been in research over the past year, they had had several sit-down meetings where they discussed her career path and he helped coach her. She found herself confiding in him even though Jamie had warned her to maintain a professional distance with her colleagues. He had close friends at work, why couldn't she?

After Greg's final announcement, the meeting wrapped up and everyone shuffled back out to the trading desk. Alex returned to her seat and waited. The desk was coming to life now. Alex took a mental inventory of each trader's location. Offices might not be important but where a person sat on the trading floor at Lehman was the symbolic equivalent of measuring a trader's manhood. The biggest dicks always sat closest to the isles. As the most junior trader, Alex's seat was in the middle of one row, marking the end of the Trading section and the dividing line with Sales.

A senior salesman sat to her right. Bobby DiVeccio was a veteran salesman who had cut his teeth at Solomon Brothers before joining Lehman. He had a strong American Italian accent, kept a meticulously clean desk, sat slouched in his chair with one foot perched up on his desk, and as far as Alex could tell, spent the better part of most afternoons scratching his balls.

"Hey, how you doin? Welcome to fucking paradise. Keep your shit off my desk. Never read my computer screens. And if this phone rings and I'm not here," he motioned to his phone, "don't fucking answer it under any circumstances. You get all that, you'll make it next to me. Got it?"

Alex just stared at DiVeccio. *Was he fucking serious?* She'd never spoken to him before. She took a mental inventory of possible responses but nixed them all. A couple of the other traders and salespeople had overheard and turned to watch the show. Alex felt like the words "fresh meat" were imprinted on her forehead.

The salesman couldn't hold himself together any longer. He burst into laughter, throwing his full weight back against his chair.

"I'm just fucking with you, kid. Don't look so serious. You're liable to hurt somebody. I'm only kidding. Well, not about keeping your shit off of my desk. I meant every word of that. All I got here is twelve inches of space to myself and that's all I own for twelve hours a day. So I like to keep it fucking neat. Keep my little kingdom clean and we'll be best fucking friends. Capish?"

Alex nodded slowly. "Chrystal clear. I appreciate the warm welcome Bobby."

And just like that, the conversation ended. The salesman turned back to his computer screens and gave no further evidence or acknowledgement of Alex's presence. Twelve inches just as easily could have been twelve city blocks. The salesman started to pound his phones, dialing out to each of his accounts in his bid for business. He didn't turn left again in her direction for the rest of the day. It suddenly dawned on Alex that twelve inches of space was going to be what she made of it – either too close for comfort or light-years away.

6

S he dreamt about Lehman Brothers almost every night. Alex was consumed with her job. She was obsessed with being perfect at it. She lived in fear of making even the smallest mistake. She would have died for the praise of her superiors. She slept with her blackberry and her cell phone by her pillow.

Jamie didn't seem to mind. In those first few weeks after they returned from Thailand he worked like a dog. Since J.P. Morgan had bought Bear Stearns there was a selection process underway to see who would make the final cut in the new merged company. Alex listened patiently to Jamie's stories about the spiteful rivalry building beneath the surface at his company. On the nights when Alex was still awake when he got home, Jamie would sit on the couch in his suit pants and white undershirt, sipping Jim Beam Whiskey as he recounted his day. She would ease off his Italian loafers, taking his feet in her lap so she could massage them.

But more and more, Alex was already asleep by the time Jamie got home. She tried to stay awake but exhaustion consumed her until she couldn't keep her eyes open anymore. She was up at five each morning so that she could squeeze in a trip to the gym before work. Jamie was on the opposite schedule, often home well past midnight and sleeping in until seven or eight in the morning. Sometimes she would wake from his touch, as her husband slipped into bed, rubbing his body up against hers. But she dreamt about him more than she saw him as their schedules intensified.

The dreams started to repeat:

> *"So, do you have any questions for me?"*
> *She bit her lip to suppress a smile. But she couldn't stop the memory of the night before from dancing through her head.*
> *Alex resisted the urge to twirl a strand of hair between her fingers, like the schoolgirl that she really was.*
> *"Alex." The man sitting opposite her cleared his throat importantly. "I asked if you had any questions for me."*

Alex forced herself away from her inappropriate thoughts. She looked around the corner office and quickly remembered her place. The Lehman senior executive stared back at her, growing impatience twitching in his fingertips, as he drummed them against his mahogany desk. He leaned back in his chair and picked up her resume, eying it one more time while waiting for her to answer.

Alex tried to think of a question that would require a lengthy response.

"Can you explain to me how your job works here?"

John Coughlin was part of the executive committee at Lehman Brothers. He also ran the Harvard recruiting for the firm. He was therefore Alex's last stop on her 'sell day'. She had worked diligently to secure a summer internship at the prestigious firm. Once she had landed an offer, the tables seemed to turn and the Lehman team worked hard to sell her on accepting. As they did with all recruits, they had flown her in to New York City for the day. She had visited with several departments where all of the traders had been on their best behavior, puffing out their chests, brightening their computer monitors, and giving their well-polished sales pitches.

Facing her future employer, Alex mustered up the will to stop smirking. But she couldn't stop her mind from wandering.

What a first date, she thought.

She had ignored the mini crush she had on the cute but quirky investment banker the summer before at Bear Stearns. She hadn't seen or even spoken to him in the nine months that had passed. But she was coming down to New York anyway so she thought it wouldn't hurt to reach out.

Alex wasn't sure if Jamie was single or not. So she had sent him an innocent email, with a casual subject line, "Coffee…?"

It was a proposition of sorts.

It had taken Jamie three days to respond to her email. But she decided to meet him anyway. So Alex had come to New York a day early, deposited her overnight bag at a friend's apartment and then made a beeline for the Bear Stearns building. She had carefully chosen her outfit – jeans, stilettoes, a powder blue blouse, and a navy blazer. Professional meets sexy. Summer intern meets available college coed. Her outfit said, "I emailed you for career advice over coffee but I wouldn't be opposed to a date with a few drinks instead."

Their first meeting didn't pan out the way Alex had expected. Jamie met her by the couches on the mezzanine level, just outside of the little bodega where employees would come to buy quick snacks. He didn't offer to take her to lunch. He didn't even invite her to join him in the corporate cafeteria.

Adding apparent insult to undeniable injury, he had shaken her hand when greeting her. Alex thought that a casual peck on the cheek or even a hug could have been appropriate. They chatted benignly for less than twenty minutes before he begged off, checking his wristwatch and claiming that he had to get back upstairs to work.

Clearly, she told herself, Jamie Kramer had zero interest.

Alex had spent the rest of the afternoon window shopping and wallowing in self-pity. She had somewhat seriously dated three guys in college: a musician, an athlete, and an academic. Now, they were each seriously dating other girls. And she was alone again. She had tried being artsy, being sporty, being smart. She pretended to dance at concerts, cheered on the school football, baseball and hockey teams, and even audited classes down the street at M.I.T. Nothing seemed to stick. Her mother called no less three times a week looking for status updates on a status that never changed.

"You're not getting any younger, honey. This is the prime of your life. I was already engaged-to-be-married at your age. Women aren't like wine – they don't get better with age."

Alex was twenty-one and single with no salvation in sight. In private, melodramatic moments, she was sure she would die alone.

Her phone buzzed, signaling an email:

Dinner instead? 8pm tonight? Date probably better than coffee;)

Alex smiled. She had totally misread him. She was happy to have packed for all occasions. She looked down at her watch. It was almost six. She debated whether or not to wait a bit before responding. If she responded right away she worried she might look a little desperate. On the other hand, if she waited too long he might make other plans. Instead she opted for available but not too available. After waiting five minutes, she responded:

I have dinner plans with some friends but I would love to have a drink. How about 9pm? Where should I meet you?

◆ ◆ ◆

Just after nine Alex descended the small metal stairs into a bar she had never heard of before. Jamie had proposed a place at the corner of Houston Street and Lafayette, a popular intersection in Soho - the trendy New York neighborhood whose shops, restaurants, people, and overall ambiance always left Alex drooling.

Alex paused just inside the entrance to take in the scene around her. A quick Internet search in the cab ride down had given her some advance notice - a Russian subterranean speak-easy that specialized in Vodka martinis and caviar. Alex looked around at the beautiful people cozied up to one another at tiny, intimately arranged tables. Music from another era floated effortlessly through the air. The lights were romantically dim. Pravda. Alex had read on the website that the word was Russian for "truth."

Maybe Jamie Kramer was full of surprises after all, Alex thought.

She hadn't even noticed him standing there at first. Or maybe she just hadn't recognized him out of a business suit. The dark blue jeans and checkered shirt were better suited for his gelled hair, she realized. He was nodding approvingly, almost imperceptibly in her direction. She smiled and gave a little wave in his direction, descending the last three steps into the bar.

Jamie kissed her warmly on the cheek and offered to take her coat. Then, with his hand tucked against the small of her back he escorted her to a corner table. She took the seat in the booth and he slid in next to her instead of taking the chair opposite her.

An attractive waitress in a little black dress appeared to take their order. Asking her permission first, Jamie ordered for both of them.

"Trust me," he winked. *"This will be the best martini you've ever had. The Russians know their vodka."*

"I'm not worried. I've never met a glass that I've had to send back."

They both laughed.

Alex looked at Jamie, apprising this stranger she somehow felt she knew. He caught her looking and held her gaze. They stared at each other for an extra beat. Jamie Kramer was getting in to her head. She wanted to know more about him. Where he grew up, what his family was like, what his favorite book was, what sports he loved, who his oldest friend was, what kept him up at night, what his lips tasted like.

"So…tell me something you never tell anyone." she began.

◆ ◆ ◆

"And that," he concluded, *"Is how my role at Lehman Brothers has evolved over the last twenty years."* John Coughlin pushed his chair back from his desk and leaned back in self-congratulating satisfaction.

"Does that answer your question?"

No answer.

"Alex? Alex, does that answer your questions?"

"Alex!"

Nudged out of her dream, she realized someone was really calling her name.

"Alex! C', mon baby, you've got to get up or you'll be late for work."

She felt a hand on her naked body, tracing an imaginary line from her breasts, down her stomach.

"Five more minutes," she mumbled dreamily, squirming while trying to catch the dream.

"Since when does my wife ever have five minutes to spare in the morning?"

The hand moved lower.

She squeezed her eyes tighter but spread her legs, just a little.

"Just five more."

Jamie pulled back the covers completely, exposing their naked bodies to a rush of cooler air.

"Jamie!"

Alex tried to reach down for the covers but Jamie was already on top of her.

"I feel like I haven't seen you in days. If you've got five minutes, I'm taking them."

She tried to laugh but his mouth had already enveloped hers, kissing her with unexpected ferocity. He hungrily crawled up and down her body, kissing every inch of her while she squirmed, eyes still closed. Finally, after she thought she might die from anticipation, she successfully pulled him back up so that his face was next to hers. Then he kissed her even harder, biting down on her lower lip as he thrust himself inside her. He had her arms pinned above her head, controlling both of their movements. Dripping in sweat he leaned down. She thought he was going to lick the back of her earlobe but instead he whispered:

"Come on, baby."

She came undone, eyes still closed, giving herself to him, which in turn, caused him to do the same.

He lay panting and sweaty, on top of her for an extra minute before rolling over, back into his side of the bed.

"You should shower. You don't want to be late."

He was smirking at her.

She couldn't move yet.

"That was the best dream ever."

He laughed.

"We closed the deal last night. The big one I'd been working on. That'll show those J.P. Morgan guys. I just know they're gonna love me now."

His hands were tucked behind his head, self-indulgent apparently in more ways than one.

"So that explains it," Alex half-joked, finally pulling herself out of bed and towards the bathroom. "I've never seen you like *that* before."

"Just wait till they see what I'm made of."

Jamie was staring at the ceiling, happily. Alex wasn't even sure if he was talking to her or to himself. *So that's the secret to marriage,* she thought to herself, *a self-congratulating husband and morning sex.*

Okay, she could work with that.

7

W eeks felt like years on a trading floor. There was such a high level of intensity all the time that it aged people. If a trader let himself forget about his positions during the day, even for a minute, he was always reminded when he "marked himself to market" each evening before leaving. Marking to market was like pressing the reset button in advance for the next day. Traders had to adjust the prices of their positions to reflect that day's shift and then report their individual gains or losses to their superiors. Each trader's results were tallied, a report was generated, and then an email of cumulative profit or loss was sent out to the entire group. If a position kicked somebody in the nuts, everybody else knew about it and watched him sweat it.

Alex started getting into a groove on the desk. Her boss gave her a couple of names to trade. Her focus was in the Gaming and Casino space, which Alex determined was decidedly sexier than Mining or Chemicals and still not an industry that would be a cliché for a woman to have expertise in, like Retail.

She started to become increasingly confident in her grasp of the language used on the floor and the rules of engagement required during a trade. Early on, she had confused the terms "bid" and "offer" and nearly ruined an important trade. But now this language was second nature. She no longer stuttered when speaking about bonds in terms of fractions; "tinies" (1/16) and "stinies" (1/32) were part of her vocabulary now. She didn't hesitate when a salesman asked for her bid or her offer.

The nuances of life on the floor were revealing themselves too, but these revelations took a little longer to process. Alex was slowly weeding through the fiefdoms across the floor and discerning friend from foe. She found that most salespeople were out for young blood. There was one in particular who seemed to relish in giving her hell: Jon Jacobs. He was middle-aged and leaning into those years without grace. He was fat, bald, and ugly. He carried an extra thirty pounds on the waistline and his bottom lip hung lower than usual, revealing garish purple gums. He grew his hair out, despite increasing baldness in the middle of the top of his head, resulting in an unsightly comb-over that hardly masked his situation. His verbal assaults were consistent and painstakingly methodical. Each time Alex would approach him to discuss a trade he would make her repeat herself multiple times, like a punished school girl who had erred and was then subjected to the public humiliation of writing her indiscretion on the chalkboard five hundred times: "I am a bond trader. I am a bond trader. I am a bond trader."

Then, using exaggerated facial expressions, he would ask a question she had already answered, enunciating each syllable deliberately and painfully slowly. He would give her a pointed stare with his lower lip hanging limply, waiting for an unnecessary response. It was maddening and terribly embarrassing. Each time Jon spoke to her in this way he would raise his voice an octave, drawing the attention of other salesmen towards the conversion, as if he were giving a lecture for all to hear. At first, Alex always kept her composure but one day she snapped back.

"Jon," she seethed, interrupting him. "English is my first fucking language. No need to speak so slowly. And I'm not fucking deaf either, so no need to raise your voice to me. I'm just trying to get the trade done."

Jon eyeballed Alex in very minor disbelief. He was used to traders mouthing off to him. He appeared mildly shocked though that any verbal lashing would have come from her. Salespeople sat below traders in the hierarchy of Big Banks. But junior traders sat beneath absolutely everyone until they learned to command respect. People pretended to be nice to junior traders. But they didn't really actually give a shit. Juniors had to earn the right for people to give a shit about them, let alone trading with them. As far as Alex could tell, respect came from the way people handled themselves, from the way that they traded and from the way that they bet. Respect came from how much money a trader could make for the firm.

Jon lowered his voice and focused his attention squarely on Alex's face. "I know you speak English," he seethed. I was simply clarifying for myself, to make sure that you have clarified for yourself, exactly what you have for sale here."

Well, that made no fucking sense.

"Have I adequately clarified it for you, Jon?" She smiled benignly.

"Yes. You certainly have. I'll make the call and let you know what the client says."

Thank you. I appreciate that." She smiled sweetly.

Turning on her heel, Alex retraced her steps down the sales row and back over to her seat. She tried not to look up at the salespeople she knew were watching while trying equally hard not to look down and give the appearance of not looking at people. Alex knew that people hadn't actually stopped what they were doing. A complete halt of activity on a trading floor was a very rare event. It was usually precipitated by a very loud shouting match, which in turn, was precipitated by a disagreement over a trade. This was hardly the case here but Alex could still feel the eyes on her. She wondered how they were digesting her remarks: would it be seen as a well-timed stand against the schoolyard bully that would gain her more respect or as a hissy fit by a young trader who didn't know her place? Time would tell.

The short walk back to her desk was all the time Alex was afforded to ponder her outburst and its reception. Before she had even sat down her boss, Clarke yelled for her from down the row. She quickly joined him at his desk, hovering as he pointed to the computer screens in front of him. He was studying several stock charts of comparative companies on one screen and had what looked to Alex like several options models up on another. There wasn't a single screen with a corporate bond on it. Alex had grown accustomed to this. She was told that the business cycle was slowing, clients were doing less trading, which was generating fewer opportunities to make money trading the 'good old fashioned way.' Clarke and several others on the desk were attempting to pad the profits of their trading books with bets in stocks instead of trafficking in traditional bond and bank debt trading, which was their mandate.

"Alex, you have you Series 55, right?"

"Yup, of course."

Alex had just skimmed by with a passing grade on the regulatory exam required to execute equity trades. She had taken the test hours before leaving to catch her flight for her honeymoon.

"Good, and you know how to use our equity trading platform?"

"Yes, I'm familiar with it." Alex had seen the technology platform on other traders' desks and had once asked another junior trader to give her a quick tutorial, but she'd never actually used it before. She was in the habit of yessing everything that was asked of her on the desk though and she wasn't about to change that up with the boss himself talking to her.

"Excellent."

He pointed at one of the stocks on the left screen.

"This is the stock you were telling me about this morning, right?"

Alex leaned closer to see the name of the company displayed in the top left hand corner of the computer monitor. She recognized it and nodded her head 'yes'.

"Great. I like it. Love the idea. Go buy me five hundred thousand shares of this one. Make sure the average price is sub twenty-five dollars. If you have any questions just ask Whatshisname."

He pointed generically in the direction of another junior trader.

"Go."

He looked up at her, perplexed as to why she was still standing there.

"That's all. Go."

Alex's eyes popped. She leaned in closer over Clarke's shoulder to make sure she saw the correct stock symbol. She had no fucking idea how she was supposed to do what he was asking.

Clarke was still looking at her. She could feel his breath and realize she was standing too close.

"Make sure you get the order filled before the market closes. "C'mon Harvard, get on it."

"Sure. Yes, will do. Thanks Clarke."

Alex quickly walked the few feet back over to her desk. Her mind was already racing. She clicked on the equity trading icon on her computer monitor and three boxes popped up onto her screens. She centered them on one monitor while on another monitor she pulled up the same stock chart Clarke had just been contemplating. *Not rocket science, Harvard. This is not rocket science,* she kept telling herself. The technology was programmed so that a trader entered the stock symbol, desired price, number of shares, and buy or sell order into the system and the order was electronically distributed to multiple floor brokers across the exchange. The system allowed traders to set price limits and to decide whether to send the order to every possible equity broker, which was known as 'actively sweeping the market' or to send them only to a few. From what Alex understood, an Active Sweep was the preferred method because execution was faster with more brokers distributing or buying up the stock at once.

Alex entered all the specifics into the system. She noticed that the markets on the boards were only for thirty thousand shares when she was supposed to buy five hundred thousand but didn't think much of it. She expected that her Active Sweep would carry her order to so many dealers that she would be able to accumulate all half a million shares before the closing bell. She realized that she had no idea how long it was actually supposed to take to fill a stock order. She quickly took a mental inventory of everything the other junior had told her about the system and compared that to what she'd entered. For a moment, she thought about running over to double check everything with him but decided against it. She didn't want it to look like she needed help with a silly little equity order. That would almost certainly reverse all possible effects of her earlier triumph over Jon Jacobs.

Alex clicked on the large green rectangular button that read "BUY" and held her breath. There was a small box on the screen that tabulated the shares purchased and the purchase price as the system filled the order. In a matter of seconds, Alex watched as the share count climbed at lightning speed. On the other screen, the stock chart suddenly popped. The line that indicated the stock's price jumped so high so quickly that Alex thought it might pop off the page altogether. Something was so wrong. Her mind registered only a single word:

"Fuck. Fuck. Fuck. Fuck. Fuck. Fuck. Fuck."

She just wanted to scream *Stop!* at the top of her lungs. But it all happened too quickly. In an instant, it was all over. Her heart thumped in her chest. To her, the sound of it was nearly deafening. She looked around to see if people could hear too. No one else was paying any attention to her at all. The room was otherwise humming with its usual pace of activity. She forced herself to look back at her computer screens. She was positive she would vomit. The box with the share count was flashing on her screen.

"Order Complete" it read, pulsing in blue.

Could a computer system even be mocking her? Alex had executed the equity order for her boss is twenty-seven seconds. She looked at the average execution price in horror: $38.17. Alex could only hear two words in her mind: *You're fired.* She couldn't imagine Clarke saying anything but that to her when she relayed the news of her idiotic execution. Alex approximated the cost of her error. She had, on average, bought the desk five hundred thousand shares of stock thirteen dollars above the order price Clarke had given her. She had just cost him six and a half million dollars.

"Holy fuck," she whispered to herself. "Oh my fucking god."

Alex imagined how long it would take her to make that much money in trading profits. How in the hell had she managed to lose an equal amount in twenty-seven damned seconds?

She stood up slowly. She forced her feet to carry her over to Clarke's desk. She stood behind him. She was too afraid to speak. She waited for him to just sense her presence. Finally, he turned to look at her. He appeared slightly taken aback that Alex was back at his desk so quickly. She looked towards the empty seat next to him and without asking for permission, sank down into it.

"Back so quickly?"

"Um, yes."

She paused.

He stared at her expectantly.

She took a deep breath.

"Do you want the good news or the bad news?"

"Excuse me?"

"Well," she cleared her throat. Her stomach was in knots.

"Well, the good news is that I bought the stock."

She laughed nervously, unnaturally.

"The bad news is that the execution price is, um, slightly higher than what you had asked for."

Alex decided she may as well just come straight out with the news. There was no beating around the bush here. She was fucked.

Clarke raised one eyebrow in question.

"Higher?"

"Yes, well, I'm not exactly sure how it happened. I mean, I thought I did everything perfectly. It just happened so quickly. I didn't really have time to stop and –

The phone ringing interrupted Alex. It wasn't the shared trading line that rang on everyone's desk. It was Clarke's personal line. He held one finger up to silence her and then answered the phone. He listened for a moment.

"Yeah, it was us...No, no, she's sitting right here in front of me...Yup, in the middle of explaining herself as we speak...no shit, they called to ask you that? Fucking priceless...Yeah, okay. Sorry for the confusion... Erroneous, huh? Fucking priceless...Yeah, I'll take care of it from this end. Thanks for calling Dan...yup, make sure to tell 'em we don't know anything about anything. I don't want them drumming up some insider trading accusation bullshit. Who knows what that could trigger in this media-frenzied environment. Just a trigger-happy junior fucking trader. Plain and simple."

He hung up and turned his attention back to Alex. He looked like he might erupt and Alex braced for her inevitable termination. She had been holding her breathe throughout his phone conversation, trying to decipher what it all meant and she was sure she was a fancy shade of purple by now. Clarke must have taken one look at her face and aborted the tongue-lashing she was owed. Instead, he erupted into fits of laughter, literally howling in hysteria.

"You, my friend, are one fucking lucky broad. Jesus Christ Kramer. You're fucking lucky we all like you so much."

Alex gave him a quizzical look. She was sure she wasn't hiding her confusion.

"That was the head of the firm's Equities Department who just called. They saw the spike in the price and thought there was news out on the stock. Then, his phone started ringing off the hook with people asking what we knew and what was going on. Word on The Street was that Lehman just took down a block of stock in a trading flurry that sent the equity price skyrocketing. He stormed around his desk demanding to know who the fuck had executed an order in such a fucking hammerhead fashion. Finally, he stopped when the regulatory branch of the New York Stock Exchange called to ask who Alex Kramer was. And you know what he said?"

Alex shook her head demurely. She had never seen Clarke talk so quickly and she wasn't sure if he was really looking for an answer or not.

"You know what he fucking said? He said 'I have no fucking idea!'"

Alex cringed as Clarke fell into fits of laughter again.

"You single-handedly sent the stock up so quickly and so aggressively that the Exchange called to cancel your trades, saying they were too far out of the normal range of trading. Clearly Erroneous is how Danny said they phrased it. Clearly Erroneous, Kramer. Jesus Christ you're lucky. You nearly cost me - "

He paused and looked up at the ceiling, doing the math in his head.

"You nearly cost me 6.5 million bucks you fucking knucklehead."

Alex still wasn't sure if all of this meant she still her job or not.

"No, I'm not going to fire you," Clarke laughed, reading her mind. "I'm just going to call you Clearly Erroneous Kramer from now on until you fucking start pulling your weight on this desk again. Get outta here before I change my mind. This is a first Kramer. A fucking first."

8

"Excuse me! Ladies! Would you hold that pose? You look gorgeous! This will be a great shot for our upcoming newsletter!"

Alex obligingly wrapped her arm around her friend's waist in response to the nasally voiced request. The girls held their pose for the staff photographer. Alex smiled wryly at Daniella, who returned her amused look. The photographer was still snapping away when both girls erupted into fits of laughter.

"Do you think she really works for the charity or is she undercover for JDate?" Alex joked.

"Please, JDate's not looking all that bad lately," Daniella lamented. "I can use all the help I can get these days. I mean, could it be any harder to find a cute, successful, single Jewish guy in this city?"

"Depends - are you open to dating assholes?"

"Don't joke. I wouldn't even rule that out at this point! Not all of us are lucky enough to be married, Alex. We can't all score the nice guys like you did."

Alex paused, still mirthful. "Well, to be fair, I did pluck him from the Kentucky dating pool so I'm not sure what that says about my skills either."

She motioned to the photographer that they would take another picture.

"C'mon babe, let's take one more. Who knows, maybe your prince charming habitually reads fundraising newsletters, scouring every photo and caption because he knows you are out there somewhere, just waiting for him."

Daniella shot Alex a look that was mixed with an odd pairing of reproach and gratitude. Alex felt bad for a minute. She hadn't meant to hurt her friend but she had clearly struck a nerve. It had been nearly six months since Daniella had ended a tumultuous three-year saga-filled relationship with a nasty boyfriend. Her parents were relieved that she ended it but were also unapologetically pushy when it came to getting their daughter back in the saddle. Daniella had been set up on so many blind dates that she could barely keep their names straight, let alone allow for any deeper, relationship-worthy connection to marinate.

Alex decided she would help her friend man-hunt that night.

The girls turned their attention to the photographer and posed again, in earnest this time. They grinned straight at the camera's lens with a mixture of demure and coquettish expertise.

"Thanks girls," the photographer acknowledged, handing them a small business card. "You can view the pictures on the website printed on this card. I'll have them posted within twenty-four hours. I also do private events - you know, weddings, things like that..." she winked, her voice trailing off.

"Awesome," Alex said dryly, accepting the card with her left hand, careful to flash her diamond ring. "Good to know." Subtle was not a strong skill set for people who peddled their wares at a meat market like this one.

"Do I look okay?" Daniella asked. "This dress works, right? It's not slutty or anything?"

Alex assessed her friend's outfit approvingly. The little red dress hugged Daniella's slight, feminine frame to perfection. The neckline plunged in exactly the right place, perfectly suggestively just above her petite breasts. The material ended four inches above her knee. A scarlet manicure-pedicure combination complimented the frock. And her friend polished off her look with a stick straight blow-dry, so her hair fell evenly against her shoulders. She added a subtle touch of smoky eye shadow to accentuate her hazel eyes. She was the perfect combination of sex appeal and appropriate-future-wife-and-mother-of-your-Jewish-children appeal.

"They're going to be falling all over you tonight. Trust me. You definitely look hot."

She linked arms with her friend and steered them in the direction of the bar.

"C'mon, D. If I can't flirt, I might as well drink."

Daniella gave Alex a wary, knowing look.

Alex couldn't help but smile. Her best friend knew her so well. She could practically read her mind.

"Fine, well maybe a little flirting. I mean, I'm married. I'm not dead."

Now it was Daniella's turn to laugh. "That sounds more like the girl I know and love. As long as I've known you, you always flirt. And you always drink!"

"True," Alex admitted. "And I guess no one knows me better than you."

They had been thick as thieves since freshman year of high school. In the beginning, Alex had felt intimidated, awkward and unattractive because she was curvier than all of the pin-thin teens. She also knew she couldn't afford an expensive, in-vogue wardrobe or holiday vacations in exotic locations, like the others could. She felt like an outsider who had somehow made her way to the inside of the prestigious, preppy Upper East Side Manhattan School. Daniella, on the other hand, seemed to know everyone. She was bubbly and social, with a knack for making everyone like her. They had nonetheless gravitated towards one another in that inexplicably cosmic way that opposites attract.

For a period, they did everything together, consulting each other on everything from boy trouble to parental stress to clothing options and college decisions. They stayed close in college too, enabled by the proximity of Harvard and Boston University. There was nothing Alex did that Daniella didn't know about. The minute she had gotten engaged she knew she'd ask her friend to be her maid of honor. Now, she wanted to help her friend find the same success.

Alex watched Daniella scan the room for potentially eligible men.

"Well, we both know I'll be more help if you get a martini or two in my bloodstream. Plus, when is the last time we've been out just the two of us since I got married? It's been forever. I say we toast to a girls night out - and to finding you a man!"

Daniella's eyes lit up.

"I miss hanging out with you, too babe."

Alex led her friend into the main ballroom. The event was being held at the Metropolitan Pavilion, the Mecca of Jewish fundraising locales. The cavernous banquette hall was in a trendy section in Chelsea. The space easily held one thousand people. That night the room looked festive, with cocktail tables scattered throughout, multiple well-stocked bars staged in each corner, a band set up on stage, and a section of casino-style card tables arranged for the obligatory charity poker tournament. The invitation called for **black-tie-optional attire, but no** one ever opted out. It was the place to see and really be seen. Everyone dressed accordingly. If you were single, Jewish, under forty and breathing, you were likely to be there on the prowl that night.

This was Alex's second time. The only other time she had attended was during college, before she had known Jamie. The girls had made the trip down from Boston together, gambling that they could work their way in to the twenty-one and over event with fake I.D.'s and a few extra- wide smiles.

"Do you recognize anyone yet?" Alex asked.

"Hmmm. I see a few guys over in that corner but I can't deal with them right now." Daniella motioned towards one of the poker tables, rolling her eyes. "They're all still really friendly with Jay I think," she added, referencing her ex-boyfriend.

Alex followed her friend's gaze, eying the group: greased, slicked back hair, slim-fitting expensive suits, one too many buttons left intentionally open on collared shirts revealing gold chains. They were ostentatiously noticeable, even in this crowd. Alex cringed.

"That was a good miss, babe. You're so much better off without him."

"I know." Daniella paused. "But it's not like the guys I've been dating lately have been any better. Jay may have been as asshole but at least he wasn't a total weirdo. I mean, you wouldn't even believe some of these guys I've been out with. I don't even know how they are permitted to participate in the general dating pool. I actually agreed to go on this date with my Grandma's best friend's doctor's son. I mean, first of all, why am I letting my grandmother set me up?! At first, I thought it wasn't that bad. I mean, he was really cute and interesting. And I was sitting at dinner thinking to myself 'good work grandma!' But as soon as I think I may have scored a winner, the guy kicks into full on weirdo mode."

She paused.

"Alex, he talked in different accents all throughout dinner."

Alex would have thought she was kidding if Daniella hadn't looked so mortified. Bemused, Alex waited for her friend to elaborate. Daniella indulged her.

"He was a total talker, self-involved storyteller, name-dropper – you know, the works. He had all these stories about traveling to all of these different countries: Brazil, Mexico, Israel, Germany, Russia, Japan, and on and on. Every time he tells a story about a country he visited, he'd switch into an accent from that country. Then, he started speaking in different languages! I mean, do I look like I speak Japanese?!"

Alex couldn't contain her laughter. "What did you do? And how am I only hearing about this now?"

"Oh. Wait. It gets better. I couldn't even tell you right away. It was so embarrassing. So, of course I don't know how to respond because he is speaking in languages that I don't understand! So I just keep smiling and laughing, nodding my head in agreement, which I guess is encouraging him. So he slides his hand under the table, onto my thigh. Obviously I am totally taken aback. I mean, this is our first date. So I am starting to think he is just another sleaze ball when he starts to slide his hand down my leg."

"Down your leg?" Alex interrupted, confused.

"Oh yes. Down my leg. He reaches all the way down to my foot. Takes my shoe off. Takes it off. At the restaurant. And he starts to massage my foot! Alex, he was actually massaging my foot in public while he kept on talking like nothing was even happening."

"What?!" Alex was hysterical. Her stomach ached from laughing. "Shut the fuck up. He did not do that!"

"Oh yes. He most certainly did."

"Was he talking in an accent then too?" Alex couldn't resist asking.

"Alex! It's not funny. It is so embarrassing. I can't even believe I told you. You can't tell anyone."

Daniella looked mortally offended just thinking about the whole episode.

Alex giggled again.

"I swear. As much as it pains me, I will take it to the grave. I still can't believe it though. What a weirdo. What did you do?"

"What could I do?" Daniella shrugged. "It was too ridiculous for me to do anything. I just pretended like it wasn't even happening."

"How did you get your shoe back on?" Alex was beside her self.

"He put it back on my foot!" Daniella was indignant. "Like nothing ever happened!"

"Did you tell your grandma?" Alex couldn't resist asking. She knew Daniella's entire family as well as her own. She could picture the conversation unfolding.

"Did I?! Please. You know I did. I called her up the second I got home and told her that she could never ever, ever set me up ever again. Ever."

They had reached the bar. Alex's wiped the tears of laughter from the creases of her eyes. Their families would never learn.

"C'mon, babe. What are you drinking? You clearly need one. From now on, let's leave your grandma out of this. I'm getting involved. I promise I will screen for foot fetishes and any other irregularities."

Daniella scanned the room again, on the prowl. Alex ordered them two dirty martinis, straight up. Drinks in hand, they turned to face the crowd. Alex motioned towards two guys standing across the room.

"What about that one? On the left?"

Daniella crinkled her nose. "Too short."

Alex looked some more.

"What about him? He looks cute. A little familiar though."

"No chance. He dated my little sister, remember? He is cute though," she added.

"Wow. I totally didn't recognize him." Alex took a closer look, trying to be discrete. "You're right. Shit, how old is he?"

"Twenty-nine. Perfect age," Daniella said, chagrinned. "How my sister got to him first, I'll never know," she added with a hint of competition in her voice. She scanned the room some more. "Look over there," she motioned to Alex. "I think we went to summer camp with him back in the day. Doesn't he look familiar? He looks pretty cute now. Let's go talk to him and his friends?"

Alex squinted. She vaguely recognized the guy but couldn't be sure.

"You're the boss. Let's go."

They made a beeline towards that group of guys across the room.

"Alex!"

A tall, handsome figure stepped in front of their path. Alex looked up.

"Sam!"

He fixed his wicked blue eyes directly on her and then engulfed her in an affectionate hug. Standing back, he held Alex at arm's-length and inspected her.

"I haven't seen you in ages."

He looked her up and down again. The floor-length whimsical, magenta gown she had selected for the evening hugged her curves and showcased her breasts.

"You look spectacular." He paused. "I guess married life agrees with you."

Alex felt herself turning a deep shade of crimson. She took a sip of her martini.

"You're not looking so bad either."

She couldn't help herself. His sandy blonde hair was trussed, with a few wisps falling over his crystal clear blue eyes. He was wearing an expensive looking Italian dark navy suit with a slim-fitting tie. Alex smiled at the contrast against all of the other guys in tragic-looking tuxedos. Of course, he had opted out. Sam always had. Her first real boyfriend – the musician, the poet, the playwright, the thinker. He reminded her of the Peter Pan in her imagination. He never wanted to leave **Neverland**. She hadn't seen him in at least a year. She had to admit she was shocked to see him at this sort of event.

"Fancy meeting you here. This is probably the last place on planet earth I would expect you to be. Is everything okay?" She joked.

He laughed his knowing laugh.

"I'm doing some research."

His voice was mischievous.

"It's for a new play I'm working on."

"I'm sure you'll get more than enough material here," she said with a conspiratorial grin.

"Indeed. I expect I will."

He turned to Daniella.

"Daniella, you are looking well. Great dress."

His voice was warm. He checked her out too.

"Single these days?"

Daniella blushed. Sam was always direct.

"Hi Sam. Great to see you, too."

She gave him an impartial peck on the cheek and added with a frown, "Yes, I'm single these days. But hopefully not for long." She looked in the direction of the guy she had her eye on. Then she looked back at Alex. "I think I'll leave you two guys to catch up. I'm going to go say hello to an old friend, too."

Alex smirked.

"Good luck. I'll be over in a few minutes."

Then she turned back to face Sam. They stared at each other for a beat.

"Married, huh?"

She smiled softly, nodding.

"Crazy, isn't it?"

"Yeah. I have to admit, I was surprised when you called to tell me you were engaged last year. It seemed sort of sudden."

Sam had been dating his current girlfriend for nearly four years.

"I know. But it just felt right. I was so ready."

That's what Alex always said to people. Sam looked at her intently.

"Why didn't you invite me to the wedding?"

The question caught Alex off guard. She had planned on inviting Sam to her wedding. But their initial guest list had far-outpaced their budget for the event. She had kept Sam on the list through as many rounds of attrition as possible. Each time he made it through to the next round, Jamie had questioned her rationale. Alex had always explained that she and Sam had remained good friends. After all, she had only been eighteen when they had dated. At twenty-three, five years had felt like five lifetimes ago. Finally, Jamie admitted that it made him uncomfortable. That had made Alex wonder if she should be uncomfortable too. When she reviewed his list of friends she confirmed that he had no prior paramours in attendance. She wanted her husband to be happy. A good wife always compromised. So she acquiesced.

Sam continued, interrupting her thoughts.

"It was a bit strange that you called to tell me you'd gotten engaged and then you didn't invite me to the wedding. Why did you even call to tell me then?"

Alex was silent. She stared into space for a little.

"I'm sorry, Sam. I didn't know you'd take it like that." And then sheepishly she admitted, "You were on the list but Jamie asked me to take you off at the last minute and – I don't know. I just did."

Alex held her hands up, as if to display her helplessness in the matter.

Now it was Sam's turn to look surprised. Alex tried to explain again.

"When you are married it will make more sense."

"Is that so?" His eyes twinkled. "Well, if and when that day comes, I'll make sure to ring you for some sage advice."

"Good. You should. I am full of it."

Alex shot back, in jest, trying to prove her authority in the matter.

"Full of what?"

Alex spun around.

"Jamie!"

Her husband swept her up in an embrace, kissing her hard.

She kissed him back.

"Baby, what are you doing here? I thought you couldn't come because of your work event?"

He was wearing the tuxedo from their wedding night. She felt Sam watching them. She squirmed until Jamie set her back down on the floor.

"I couldn't stand to stay there for too long. Typical J.P. Morgan politicking. It was just a bunch of phony bullcrap. You can't have a mixer with people who don't mix. There's too much bad blood between the two groups right now. I did the best I could and then I split."

He paused, seeing Sam.

"Plus, I wanted to spend the night with you. See what this event is all about. You talked about it all week. Wanted to see for myself."

He nuzzled his nose against her neck softly, whispering in her ear.

"You look stunning. I think I also need to keep an eye on my beautiful wife."

"Jamie, you remember Sam, right? We went to see his show downtown last year?"

Alex turned, to establish their re-acquaintance.

Jamie eyed Sam, extending a cautious hand. He wrapped his other arm protectively around Alex's waist.

"Good to see you again, bud."

"Likewise."

Sam nodded, accepting the handshake.

They all stood silently for a moment.

"So – this is it, huh?"

Jamie looked around the room.

"Pretty impressive. You come every year?" He asked Sam, who nearly snorted his sarcastic response.

"No, sad to say this is my first."

Alex laughed.

"Baby, this isn't exactly Sam's scene. I was surprised to see him here, actually." Alex intentionally added. "We just bumped into each other a few minutes ago."

"I see."

Jamie feigned nonchalance, running his free hand through his hair. He looked down at her full glass.

"I'm gonna go grab a beer from the bar. Looks like you're okay for now?"

He turned to Sam.

"Can I grab you anything, bud?"

Why don't I come with you?" Sam offered. "I think your wife needs to go check on her friend."

Sam tilted his head over in the direction of Daniella, who was now surrounded by no less than five eligible bachelors.   Alex bristled at the remark. As much as she loved being married, she hadn't adjusted to being known purely as someone else's. *Your wife*. It sounded so unnatural when Sam said it.

"Yes," Alex said brightly. "Why don't you guys go together and I'll go see if Daniella needs to be rescued. Though she looks okay to me from here," Alex smirked.

"Like moths to a flame," Sam muttered under his breath.

"What did you say?"

He laughed affably.

"You never did miss a beat, did you Alex?"

Then he answered, "Just an idea for a storyline. Don't mind me."

And then to Jamie: "Shall we?" as he nodded in the direction of the bar.

Jamie nodded. Kissing his wife on the cheek one more time, he followed Sam over towards the bar. Alex watched the two of them go, shaking her head in mild amazement. They were an odd pairing. She could only assume that each was being polite to the other for her sake. She tried to control the mild anxiety she felt because she could not control the circumstances. Jamie wasn't supposed to have come and she had never expected to see Sam at a party like this. She held her breath as her past collided with her present. Then she turned to go and find her friend.

9

BAD NEWS BEAR
LATE-JUNE 2008

Alex lived exactly five blocks from her office. The walk took her fifteen minutes every morning when she was in a rush and about twenty-five at night, if she didn't stop along the way. Her whole life, it seemed, suddenly revolved around five square blocks in Midtown Manhattan. Everything she did was compressed into the area. Behind Jamie's back, she told her friends it was like living in an industrial wasteland. Everything was so corporate. She couldn't understand why so many people actually chose to live in the neighborhood where they worked. She felt like she never had any privacy, as if someone from work could discover her at any given moment. She called in sick to work one day and then a client spotted her in workout clothes headed to the gym while he hurriedly walked to a business meeting. Mortified, she had raced home after that thinking she might fall ill in earnest.

Privately, she fantasized about moving back to Soho, her favorite neighborhood. Overstepping her financial means, Alex had first lived in there when she moved to Manhattan after college. Wary of leaving behind all of the social comforts of college, Alex and her closest Harvard friend, Katya, agreed to bunk up in the city together. The city had felt electric down there, like anything might happen all of the time.

But Jamie had been persistent in his desire to live in Midtown. And when they had begun dating, Alex had set the precedent of being flexible with their overnight arrangements. For the majority of their early courtship, Alex had bent to accommodate Jamie's schedule more than she now cared to admit. But he had been so busy. And she had been so smitten. As a result, his apartment had morphed into their home base. And her apartment became a nauseatingly expensive, dust-collecting walk- in-closet. She resigned herself to living out of a small overnight bag she kept tucked in the corner of his bedroom and to retiring quietly to "their" room so as not to disturb Jamie's roommate in the small living room the three now all shared. So when it came time for Jamie and Alex to choose the part of town where they would formally move in together, Alex was left with little bargaining power. His priority was convenience and practicality. And Alex had acquiesced. If she let him "win" the apartment location war, then she was highly confident that she would succeed in her larger conquest, a marriage proposal. True to form, Jamie had proposed to Alex in the apartment itself the very day he signed the closing papers.

When spring finally rolled into summer, Alex gradually stretched out the length of her daily walks home. She had that summer itch. The heat was bearable even though the air hung, heavy and sticky. But the days were sunny and the streets were filled with people enjoying the city. Typically, Alex didn't step foot outside during a workday. After twelve straight hours under fluorescent lights, face to face with multiple computer monitors and surrounded by dozens of ringing phones, she couldn't help but to linger when walking home. She paused to look at the window displays at *Saks Fifth Avenue's* flagship store, salivating at the designer frocks. A long emerald green satin gown and minx fur cape were pinned to one provocatively arranged mannequin. Summer hadn't even begun and shops were already peddling for the fall and winter seasons. *As if time weren't already passing so quickly,* Alex thought to herself.

We must be still and yet still moving.

It was her favorite line from her favorite poem - a consequence of her father sneaking some T.S. Eliot in with the Dr. Seuss bedtime readings when she was a child.

We must be still and yet still moving.

The line ping-ponged across her mind as she stared at the fall frocks. Sometimes she felt still only. She would turn twenty-four in a few weeks and the impending angst was already mounting. Another year gone by with not enough accomplished yet. She loathed getting older. She feared getting older without accomplishing more. She ached with the desire to move faster, faster, faster, as fast as she could go.

Her mind wandered until she found herself back in front of her apartment building. Willy, her favorite doorman, greeted her with a nod and followed her inside through both sets of double doors and into the entry foyer. He jumped in front of her so that he could open the wrought-iron gate of the antiquated elevator. When she and Jamie had first found the apartment, Alex had found the elevator charming. More and more, the charm was wearing off and in its place she found frustration that she couldn't ever just ride the goddamned elevator alone.

"Jamie home yet?" she asked as he pulled the elevator to a stop on their floor.

"Yup, he's in there. Been home for a little while now I think. I haven't seen him go out unless he took the stairs down when I was on break."

Willy pulled back on the lever and pulled the iron-gate back open.

"You two have a nice night now. Let some of that summer air in."

Alex laughed. "Thanks Willy, I'll try. It's been a sauna in there. Some days I just stand in front of the air conditioning unit for the first ten minutes after I get home just to cool down."

She left the elevator and took the two quick steps to reach her apartment's door. With only four other units on the floor she almost never saw their neighbors, except for the octogenarian who sometimes coughed and wheezed so loudly that Willy would come up and bang on his door to make sure he wasn't having a stroke.

She stepped inside their apartment and dropped her purse on the floor just inside the door. The smell was a familiar mix of her perfume, Jamie's cologne, and the musk of all the leather from their Jennifer Convertibles living room furniture. It still had the same faint smell of paint though as the day they had first moved in. Otherwise, the apartment had changed so much since that first afternoon two years ago when Jamie had proposed. Then, the rooms were all completely bare. Jamie had scattered rose petals and lit tiny candles all across the floor. Alex remembered that there had also been a bottle of champagne and a soft beige blanket spread out on the floor.

That day, he had insisted that Alex rush right over from work. He had beckoned her with an urgent message about picking out paint colors for the new apartment. (They had settled on eggshell white). When Jamie had opened the front door for her he had tiny beads of sweat pinching his hairline and an awkward, nervous smile spread across his lips. He had taken her hands with both of his. This had momentarily struck her as quite strange. Giving her a quick, wet peck on the lips, he had then slowly led her from the small entry foyer into what would become the living room. His started in on a little speech, still holding both her hands in his.

"I love you so much and I think we have so many great things in front of us-"

Alex interrupted him. "I know babe, this apartment really is so great. I can't believe we are finally moving in together for real. It's so exciting!"

"No. I mean, yes. The apartment is perfect for us. Absolutely perfect. But I love you. And I can't wait to spend the rest of my life with you."

Jamie fumbled his hand around briefly in his pants pocket and withdrew a small blue velvet box. He bent quickly on one knee and choked a little bit on his words as tears welled in his eyes.

"That's why I...well, what I am asking is – Will you marry me, Alex? Will you marry me?" He gazed up at her with his nervous smile and his loving eyes. The hand that held the velvet box shook slightly.

Alex's mouth dropped. She stared at the dazzling engagement ring sitting atop the blue velvet. The large diamond, surrounded by smaller diamond chips, set in a cushion cut, was mesmerizingly beautiful. Alex had planned to anticipate this moment for so long but she had never actually been able to envision how it would unfold or what emotion she would have. Only weeks before it had seemed as though she and Jamie had been arguing endlessly, veering dangerously close to a breakup. But now, all that seemed to melt away. She had done it. She had arrived. She was going to get married. Alex looked at Jamie, embarrassed that he was on his knees, and pulled him back up and into her embrace.

"Yes! Holy Shit! Yes! Oh my god! I can't believe this is even happening right now. Yes! Yes! I will marry you."

Their lips met, as Jamie pulled her in for a long, deep kiss. Stepping back, he removed the ring from the box and slid it onto her finger. It was almost exactly a perfect fit. She stared down at it, still not believing that this stunning ring was actually on her finger. She had never before worn anything even remotely like it. *I should call my mom*, was her first thought.

She looked back up at Jamie, who was staring at her with adoring green eyes and a slightly goofy smile.

"You're going to be my wife."

He whispered in her ear as he pulled her gently onto the floor. They sunk into the blanket Jamie had prepared. He slid his hand up her thigh, inching her dress up along the way. Once it was half way up her midsection, she reached down for the ends and pulled it up herself and off over her head and then just flung it across the room as Jamie unbuttoned his shirt and slid off his suit pants. Then, they were fucking, the adrenaline of the proposal racing through them. There was a dull ache in her lower back as she slid off the blanket and her body pressed into the hard wooden floor. He slowed for a moment, staring into her eyes. She pulled him down against her, so their naked bodies pressed against one another. She wrapped her arms tightly around his back, catching another glimpse of the diamond now glittering on her ring finger as Jamie let out a groan of ecstasy...

◆ ◆ ◆

Now, Alex felt the heat when she stepped inside their apartment. She and Jamie had dutifully packed all seven hundred square feet to capacity. She tried to create the illusion of more space by placing floor to ceiling mirrors in as many rooms as the layout would allow. The first place a person's eye moved upon entering the apartment was to Alex and Jamie's Jewish marriage certificate. It hung in a large frame, elaborately designed and displayed as if it were art. Beyond that point, nearly every available space was filled with furniture that could display their wedding gifts. Dark wooden bookcases and glass tables displayed crystal bowls and superfluous dessert platters better than a department store might. Their kitchen cabinets held two sets of designer tableware, with service for twelve. The only time she had used them so far was when her mother and stepfather had come for Friday night dinner the month before.

Hearing Alex come in, Jamie called to her from the living room. She crossed over into the main room to find him sitting on the couch in mesh shorts and a t-shirt, feet up on the couch and watching TV. She checked her watch. It was just after seven. He looked like he'd been there for hours. He had been working such long hours for weeks at a time. Suddenly, he was always home.

"Hi muffin. How was work today?" he asked.

This was their routine now.

"Nothing special."

He didn't react.

She stripped off her top, which was clinging to her slightly sweaty body.

Jamie didn't take his eyes off the television.

"Market got crushed. I got a little beat up on one position but came out of it okay by the end of the day. They keep pounding on Lehman on CNBC. Just another bullshit story. It's like they just invent this shit out of thin air."

She parroted the remarks one of the guys used earlier.

"Like, it wasn't enough that the media pushed Bear Stearns over the edge? Now they're trying to sink their dirty little teeth into us too. We're practically neck and neck with Goldman Sachs in certain businesses – how can they even suggest the bank is in trouble!"

That got her husband's attention.

She looked up at him and seeing his face, realized she had let her emotions get the best of her and probably had hit a sensitive subject for Jamie.

"Sorry, you know what - I don't even feel like talking about Lehman. How was your day? Why are you home so early?"

She sat down on the couch next to him.

He moved closer to the middle of the couch where she was sitting.

"It sucked. They all suck. The new building sucks. The people suck. The work sucks. Nothing was really going on. I'm waiting to get staffed on more deals and I didn't feel like being there anymore on such a nice day so I just left."

"You just left? What do you mean?" She turned quizzically to face him.

He muted the television.

"What's the difference if I wait there or I wait here? They know where to find me. I don't need to be there to just put face-time in. I'm done with that shit. The whole place is just so different now. I don't even fucking care anymore. These new guys – they're so political. They treat me like I haven't also worked in this business for seven fucking years. The only deal I am working on right now is a pitch that I don't think will ever see the light of day. It's like they just want to torture me. I'm not going to stay there all night to hear back from one guy who is waiting to hear back from three other guys himself so they can give me some ridiculous changes to make to a stupid pitch book. They treat me like I'm no different than a darn intern."

He reached for her, needy, trying to pull her closer.

"You know what - I don't want to talk about work either right now."

He tried to snuggle up against her.

Alex eyes her husband cautiously, secretly. This wasn't like him at all. She was worried that he seemed so vitriolic about work. She was more worried that he was home. He seemed like he had no motivation. She had to help him. She needed him motivated.

"Let me get out of these work clothes. I'm so sticky. Why don't we go out for a drink somewhere? Sit outside."

"I'm not really in the mood."

"How about dinner then?"

"Can't we just order in?"

Alex could see that he was going to put up a fight.

"All we ever do is order in. Let's get out and enjoy the evening. Jamie, it is so goddamned hot in here. Don't you want to be outside?"

"Not really. I'm just not in the mood to go anywhere. Why don't we just order in some dinner and watch TV?"

She stood, hands on hips, and gave him a bug-eyed stare.

"I really should be home. I might have to do some work on this pitch book if comments come back in tonight."

"Jesus Jamie. You just said you didn't give a crap about the pitch book. You have been home for hours already. Let's just get out for a little. Why don't we at least just take a walk up to the park?"

He looked up at her standing over him, half-undressed, her suit pants still on, and he reluctantly caved.

"Fine. We'll go for a little. I'd really like to be home in time to watch *Grey's Anatomy* though."

Alex held back from rolling her eyes or making a smart-ass remark. The victory of getting Jamie out of the house on a work night had become a rare occurrence lately. It felt like it hadn't been that long ago that she used to long to have him home with her at normal hours. Now, it felt like he never left the house. He was there when she left for work. He was there when she got home too. He never wanted to go out to dinner. He never wanted to go out to drink. He never wanted to make plans with his friends. And he called or texted her constantly when she made any plans with her own friends.

He wouldn't do anything at all. It was driving Alex fucking insane but she felt helpless to help him. She felt so incensed that he wouldn't even try to help himself. She still believed they were going to be the dream team of corporate couples. But despite rounds of coaxing and counseling, her husband still seemed more enamored with *The Ellen DeGeneres Show* than with enhancing his career. The image of her once-confident, suave husband was starting to blur. She was determined to find him and bring him back.

Once outside the couple turned right towards Lexington Avenue, which was crowded with public buses, taxis, and general rush-hour traffic. The sidewalks were equally dense, with packs of commuters pushing past one another as they made their way in and out of the subway's entrance stairwell. Alex reached for Jamie's hand, intertwining her fingers with his as they headed uptown. They walked in silence for a couple of blocks. Alex looked around aimlessly. She stared into storefront windows distractedly and watched passersby, staring at some directly in the face to see if she could catch their attention and then stare some more until they looked away. She wondered about their lives – where they were going, whom they were going home to, what kind of work they did.

There were so many fucking people in this city, in this country, on this planet.

Alex thought about how many times she would have to multiply that number across history to calculate the number of people who had ever lived. Alex cringed at the thought. With so much competition it was tough to get a spot up in the trophy case, to make a difference, to be remembered.

The fear and the finality of death petrified Alex. It always had. She discovered death when she was five, while playing at her neighbor's house. She and the other girl, who was two years older, were sneaking around in forbidden rooms, playing with things they knew they were not allowed to touch.

The older girl had whispered gravely to her, "You know, this can make us die. Every morning from now on you should pinch your arm when you wake up to make sure that you are really awake and living and that you aren't really already dead and you are just having a dead person's dream that you're alive again. Because once you die you can't come back. Not ever. So when you pinch yourself, if it hurts, you know you're still alive. If it doesn't hurt, you're just in a dream you can never wake up from."

She stared at her neighbor in pure, all-consuming horror. She knew they were being sneaky. Alex's malleable young mind took hold of this frightening idea and never let it go. Each day after that Alex would pinch her own arm every morning. It became her ritual. Fear of death was her religion. For much of her childhood she was tortured by uncontrollable insomnia. When the busy activity and clatter of the day ended and she found herself alone in bed, all she could think about was the eventuality of dying. She would toss and turn uncomfortably, wondering whether or not that night would be the night. Maybe she would fall asleep that night and wouldn't be able to wake up from her dreams in the morning, like her neighbor had warned...

"Have you heard back from Harvard yet?" Jamie interrupted, pulling her back to reality.

She looked up at him. She was momentarily confused. Then she found her mental footing.

She shook her head no.

"Oh, no, not yet. I sent the Dean an email but she hasn't responded yet. I guess I can call her in the morning."

"I think you should. September is right around the corner and if you want to push back your start date for business school by another year then every day you wait probably lowers the chance of her saying yes to another extension for you."

"But, Jamie, I never said I one hundred percent wanted to wait another year. Remember? We talked about this? I was only going to explain the whole situation to her to see what she thinks. I just don't know what the right choice is right now."

"How could you not know? Do you really want to be away from me at least four, maybe five, nights a week?"

"No. Of course not. But I thought you were still willing to look for a job up in Boston? You hate your job. You're totally miserable."

She had been trying to avoid this conversation but they couldn't seem to talk about anything else since her family had been over for dinner.

"How many times do I have to tell you?! I can't interview unless I'm sure I want to leave because anyone I interview with will ask for references and even if I give them names of old Bear guys who got fired, I'm sure it will get back to JP Morgan. And once they find out I'm interviewing, they'll just fire me instead. And then I'm screwed. We'd both be screwed."

Hmm. He'd explained it a hundred times but she still didn't see how that logic made any sense at all. Her ambition hung in the air between them.

"Jamie," she softened her tone. "All you want is to get out of that place. You keep saying you couldn't be more miserable. Why wouldn't you want to come to Boston with me? When you say you can't do it - that you can't possibly look for a new job under the circumstances, do you really mean that?"

He glared at her. "I always say what I mean, Alex. I could lose all the stock they gave me from the acquisition. Nothing's vested. I just got it and I'd lose it all."

His circular logic was so frustrating. She tried to calm herself but anger overtook her.

"Who cares about the fucking stock! Think about it Jamie - if we live apart, we have to pay for two households on one income, not to mention all the traveling costs. If you find a new job at a place you love, in the long term you will end up making so much more money than you are waiting for on this stock. This place is holding you back from your own potential. And besides, your own happiness should be worth something to you. Who knows where that stock will even be trading by the time you can get your hands on it. The whole financial market has just been melting down all around us. They're just holding you hostage. They're holding us hostage. And to make matters worse, you're letting them."

He was silent for a minute.

"Can't you just hold off for one more year?"

He was trying to rationalize with her. She resisted.

"Jamie, I've already been pushing this off. Since before we were even married. Hell, since before we were even engaged. This is part of the plan. I feel like I'm getting behind."

"You feel like you're getting behind with me?"

He said it like his childhood dog died. Jamie stopped walking and looked at her with a wounded expression on his face. They had been trading quick comments like a verbal tennis match, with the ball shooting back and forth quickly between them. But Alex's last comment made Jamie freeze. She could tell her words had finally struck some real chord. But the look on his face made her retreat, instead of carrying on with a full-force assault.

"No. That's not what I meant. Obviously, that's not what I meant." She turned to face him. "Why would you even say that? How can I get behind with you? We're a team, remember?"

He exhaled.

"I'm sorry. You're right. I only said it because I love you so much. We just got married. Why would I ever want to be away from my wife for even one minute. I'd say anything to keep you here. Can you blame me?"

He grinned sheepishly at her.

She thawed a little.

"Well, when you put it that way...no I suppose not. But what am I supposed to do? Just keep pushing it off? The longer I put off going, the more disconnected I feel from that process. I just want to go and get on with it already. Otherwise I'm scared I'll never go."

"Would that be such a bad thing?"

"Jamie!"

"Relax. I just said it to get you going. Of course I want you to go. With a degree from Harvard Business School you'll be making the big bucks and I can retire early. But maybe you can just hold off one more year."

A stay-at-home dad?

She shuddered at the thought.

Dear Lord, that was not part of the plan.

She stopped walking so that she could face her husband.

Compromise is the key to a successful marriage, she coached herself.

"I'll give it some more thought, okay?"

She reached up to plant a soft kiss one his lips.

"Besides, I haven't really told too many of the guys on the desk yet. Delaying would give me another year to earn more street cred as a trader. Maybe the guys can even convince Lehman to hold my seat for me until I get back."

Jamie looked somewhat skeptical.

"What? You don't think they'd do that for me? Or at least try? They love me. I work my ass off for those guys."

"I'm not saying they won't. I'm not saying anything anymore!" he tried to joke. "But don't get ahead of yourself. I don't think they give a damn about you the second you walk out of the building every night. So I don't think they'll lose too much sleep over you when you leave for business school or for any other reason."

"Jesus, thanks for the vote of confidence. Way to make a girl feel special."

To herself she thought, *I'm a star and Lehman loves me for it. He just doesn't understand.*

"Alex! Come on! Cut me some slack. You can say anything you want to me but I can't even joke around with you?"

He was right. She was being overly sensitive. She had to shake off her mood. She was the one who begged him to go out after all, so that they could get out of their tiny apartment and escape their troubles for at last a night.

"I think we are both getting so worked up for no good reason. Let's just drop all of it. Come on, let's go. I want to try to enjoy this glorious summer day with my husband."

She grabbed his hand and tugged at it, giving him no choice but to follow as she dashed across the street before the light changed. They reached the other side with a flourish, running full speed for the last few steps as oncoming traffic sped up. She relished the rush, the speed, and the change of pace.

"Was that really necessary?" Jamie asked, leaning over and huffing to catch his breath. "I want nothing more than to enjoy the rest of the day with you too. But that city bus driver was definitely not slowing down. If I hadn't pulled you up onto the curb he completely would have hit you."

Determined to be playful, Alex shook her head at him in mock consternation. "Jamie Kramer, are you proposing that you saved my life just now? Because if that's the case, it would certainly seem like I owe you one." She emphasized the last word, swathing it in innuendo and staring intently at him as if she didn't even see the hundreds of passersby all around them.

Jamie finally caught her meaning. Relaxing his tensed shoulders, he seemed to allow his mood to shift too. He would play along. "Hmm, when you put it that way, yes, I believe you do owe me one, Mrs. Kramer."

"Well," she paused coquettishly for effect, "would you like to continue on our little walk to the park or do you want to go home and collect?"

"What if I want to "collect" as you say, in the park?"

She burst into laughter at that. "You would never!"

"Oh, wouldn't I?" Jamie was really playing along now. She knew her husband would never, ever have sex in Central Park. The leaves, the grass, the dirt, the possibility of strangers catching them - none of that would work for him. Alex knew it would never happen but just the thought of it was actually starting to turn her on in earnest.

She grabbed him and pulled him close, so that she was pressed up against the building's brick wall, and he was pressing up against her. She tugged at his shirt to pull him closer still, and kissed him hungrily, passionately; wholly different from the way she had kissed him only moments before.

Alex felt the warmth of his skin as they kissed. She looked at his face, eyelids closed, lips puckered. She had always kissed with her eyes open. Jamie had caught her once and horrified, begged her never to do it again. She had promised to try and break the habit for him but she was highly confident that she wouldn't. She loved the rush too much. She figured a crack cocaine addict had a better chance of breaking bad habits than she did.

Alex felt a vibration against her thigh.

"Jamie!" she exclaimed with a laugh, pushing him off of her slightly.

But then she heard the familiar ring of his cell phone following the vibration. Jay-Z's song, *Big Pimpin'*, blared from his pocket. Jamie reached for the phone and clicked it open without screening the call. Alex knew the only reason he'd do that was because he'd reserved that ringtone exclusively for his younger brother, Joshua.

"Hey Big Man! How's everything? I'm so glad to hear from you!"

He always spoke to Joshua like he was six years old. Joshua was in fact already a year older than Alex.

Jamie put one finger up to motion to Alex that he would only be a minute. She could hear Joshua's voice on the other end of the call. He spoke with a gruff and deep Midwestern drawl, tinted with some inner city slang. The first time she met Joshua, Alex had been highly amused by the expletives and the attitude that seemed to flow freely from his mouth. He couldn't have been any more different than his older brother. At the time that had endeared Jamie to her even more.

The first time they had met Joshua didn't hold back.

"You're the coolest bitch Jamie's ever dated. Shit, I'm just fuckin' happy that he's not bangin' that Indian hussy no more. Now if he doesn't treat you right, sweetheart, you just come and tell me. Big J's got your back. He might be my older brother. But I'm his bigger brother. I'll twist his shit up if he fucks this up with you, sweetheart. I just have a feelin' about you. You'll be a mighty nice addition to this here goddamned family. You meet our moms yet?"

Alex had just smiled sweetly. She had no clue how to respond.

"We can't wait to see you up here soon, Big Man. I'm so psyched you're coming to New York. You're still scheduled to come the third week of September, right?"

Forever homesick, Jamie couldn't wait to have his brother join them for the Jewish High Holiday season. Alex was quietly nervous to mix their families but she chided herself for thinking those thoughts. They were family now.

She saw Jamie's face drop slightly at whatever Joshua said in response. She wished for the hundredth time that Jamie could have just one normal conversation with his brother that didn't involve some sort of stress or disappointment.

"What do you mean you didn't buy your plane ticket yet? I thought we all made these plans months ago. We haven't seen you since the wedding. Now you are telling me you can't afford it? Jesus, Joshua. What happened to all of that hard-earned money from your new job that you told me you've been saving up?"

She could hear Joshua growing more animated on the other end of the phone.

"Eye surgery!"

Jamie bellowed. A few people glanced at him as they hurried by on the street. Alex steered them off onto a cross street, where the sidewalk widened and receded away from the busier street.

"You're saving up your money for elective eye surgery?"

He paused as Joshua shouted into the other end of the phone.

"Yeah, I know I told you that settings goals and saving up money for them is important. I just didn't think that you'd take my advice in this direction. And then, you want to ask me to pay for your plane ticket?"

He was incredulous. Alex could tell he was hurt.

Joshua was shouting so loudly now that even Alex could hear him clearly:

"Fine. If you don't want to see me then fuck that! I don't make the big fucking bucks that you do. I'm sorry if

I can't afford a fucking plane ticket. Forget this shit. I just won't come. I couldn't even afford a fucking hotel room even if I did show. How about y'all come visit me? How about that?"

"Joshua, take it easy."

Jamie responded in his soothing older brother voice. Alex noticed that he hid his own hurt feelings.

"I'm not trying to make you feel bad at all. I was just really looking forward to spending some quality time together. I'm just bummed out and surprised, that's all. What if we split the cost of your plane ticket? I'll book it and you can pay me back when you get here. And don't even sweat the hotel situation. You can just stay on our pullout couch."

Alex gave Jamie a sharp look, which caused him to stutter for a second.

"Well, uh, gimme a minute to check with Alex."

Before he could turn to ask her, Jamie couldn't help but chuckle into the phone at something Joshua must have said in response. He held one hand over the phone to muffle his voice and pushed his cell in Alex's direction.

"He wants to talk to you."

He could never stay mad at his baby brother for long. Alex begrudgingly took the phone from her husband, giving him a 'why the hell did you have to put me in this position' look. In return Jamie fixed his pleading eyes on her as if to silently say 'please, if you love me, do this favor for me.'

Silently, they agreed to disagree. And Alex acquiesced.

"Hi Joshua!" she chirped into the phone.

"Hey sweet thang," he replied with an exaggerated drawl. "How's my favorite sister doing?"

"I'm your only sister, Big J."

"Don't matter. Doesn't mean you gotta be my favorite."

Laughter escaped her lips. It was how they started every phone conversation. But the truth in his words made her laugh every time, despite herself.

"Good point."

"I know Jamie's practically begging me to come. But I ain't interested - even for him - if it's too much of an inquisition on you."

"It's not an imposition," she said without hesitation. "You know we'd be happy to have you."

Even as she allowed the words to flow from her mouth, she mentally played through what Joshua's visit would mean: the apartment smelling like cigarette smoke and cheap cologne, the living room being commandeered by his suitcase and clothing - invariably strewn inconsiderately all across the floor, the three of them sharing their one tiny bathroom. She'd have to get dressed in the closet, rather than the living room, where she usually checked her outfit in front of the big full-length mirror.

She realized that she had gotten lost in her own thoughts while Joshua was still talking to her. She zoned back in as he was saying his goodbyes.

"Okay, sounds good. Yup, we can't wait to see you too. Yes, I know you don't need to talk to Jamie again. Yup, we settled it. Talk soon. Bye."

She closed the phone and handed it back to her husband.

"Now, you owe me one. Big time."

He gave her an uncertain look, trying to decide if she was kidding around or not.

It was too late now to head to the park before it got dark. They retraced their steps in silence, following the same path back home. Alex felt restless. The phone call had killed the sexual tension between them. Now there was only tension. She wasn't ready to go back in to their apartment yet. She was dreading the thought of yet another night spent mindlessly on the couch, eating take-out in front of the television. She paused when they arrived at the entrance to their building.

"How about a drink?"

It was the first thing either of them had said to one another since Jamie's brother had hung up the phone.

"Alex —"

She already knew what his response would be by the tone of his voice. But she bit her tongue and let him finish.

"I'm just not in the mood. It's getting late. And it's a weekday. Do you really think it's a good idea?"

She felt like she was asking for permission to extend a curfew. But this time, she wasn't giving in.

"Yes, in fact I do think it's a good idea." She was resolute. "Jamie. I am not ready to go home yet."

She nodded her head to the right. He followed her gaze across Third Avenue.

"Let's just go for one drink at Smith & Wolly's."
"The Wall Street Bar?"

Jamie said it like it was a dirty word. He made it sound like she was asking to go to a strip club.

Alex didn't care where they went as long as they stayed out at least a little bit longer. She resisted the urge to point out that it was Jamie who had insisted they move to Midtown where *every* bar was a Wall Street bar.

"It's not just a Wall Street bar, Jamie. Plus, I know the bartender. We'll get served right away." She did her best to hide her exasperation. "C'mon, baby." She shifted tactics. "Who knows? Get me a little drunk and you might just get lucky after all - even though it's a school night."

With their unspoken argument over his brother still hanging in the air between them, Jamie gave in.

"Fine. But just one drink."

Alex knew that once she'd won the battle she's also win the war.

"Sure, baby," she was all sweetness now. "Whatever you say."

They held hands as they crossed Third Avenue. There was a small crowd of men in business suits standing under the front awning of Smith & Wollensky's, smoking cigarettes and cracking jokes. A polished doorman, complete with green suit and black top hat, held the front door open for Alex and Jamie. The restaurant was extremely busy. Groups of people crowded near the front, waiting for a table - or at the very least the opportunity to get the maître d's attention. Dozens of waiters dressed in signature white and green dinner jackets busily circled the room, filling wine glasses and inflating egos. The tables were crowded with business diners who eagerly chatted up one another, loudly enough for other tables to overhear all the dirty details. Alex breathed it all in deeply. The room was full of life. Sometimes she forgot that Wall Street was always just steps from her front door.

She held on firmly to Jamie's hand and led him to the left, over towards the front bar.

"Alex! How are ya sunshine? Nice to see ya again." His Irish accent was thick. "

"Manny! It's so nice to see you too!"

Alex stood on her tiptoes to reach across the bar to shake the resident bartender's hand. He took it, but instead of shaking it he raised it gallantly to his lips and kissed it with exaggeration. He made no effort to hide his appraisal of her casual outfit.

"I see this isn't a work dinner." He winked.

"So this must be the lucky man." He turned to Jamie. "Where have you been hiding our pretty little lady? We haven't seen her around here in weeks."

Jamie gave Alex a brief, quizzical look. Alex pretended not to notice. Of course she couldn't tell Jamie that she frequented the bar with colleagues. She assumed that if he knew she was a stone's-throw away from their apartment, he wouldn't ever understand why she had to stay out so late.

"What can I say? We're newlyweds," Jamie joked.

Manny laughed easily, slapping Jamie on the back.

"Where'd ya find this funny one?" he razed Alex. "He's alright." Turning to Jamie, "you're welcome here any time. It'll always be nice to see ya."

Jamie nodded appreciatively.

"Now, what can I get you kids to drink?"

Alex answered for them. "Just a glass of Pinot Grigio and a Knob Creek on the rocks. Thanks, Manny."

"Anytime, sunshine."

He winked and deftly poured them their drinks and slid them across the bar.

"Now don't be a stranger."

Alex took a sip of her drink and turned to face her husband, so that her back was perched up against the bar. He kissed her softly on the cheek.

"You sure seem to have an admirer." He paused. "He made it sound like you come here pretty often."

"Oh, he was just playing it up," Alex said breezily. "I get the impression he's like that with everyone. Part of the job description at a place like this."

She took another sip.

"I have been in here for one or two work dinners though," she added. "I guess I just stick out a little in this crowd," she tried to joke.

"Muffin, you think I don't know that?" Jamie asked sorely. "Don't forget, I met you at work. I know how these guys think."

She laughed, throwing her head back a little.

"Babe, please. Don't be crazy. First of all, you acted like I didn't even exist that summer I interned at Bear. We barely spoke three times. Second, I pursued you," she poked him in the stomach playfully. "And that was six months later. So don't forget that part. Third," she paused, becoming a little more serious, "please, please, please stop suggesting that all these men care about is the possibility of getting in my pants. I work my ass off. My looks have nothing to do with it. And fourth," she concluded, wiggling her fingers to show off her diamonds, "I am a married woman." She took a swig of the wine she'd been sipping the whole time, downing what was left in the glass.

"Just one more," she said to Jamie and the bartender, both promising and asking at the same time.

Jamie leaned in closer, kissing her softly on the lips, while discretely grinding his pelvis against her.

"I'll show you suggestive," he whispered in her ear. "Just one more drink."

God, it was good to get him out of the apartment, Alex thought to herself as she kissed him. It was good to distract him from his work troubles, find small ways for them to have a little fun.

A cacophony of deep laughter and guffaws interrupted her thoughts. She looked up, across the bar, at a group men dressed in expensive business suits. They were slapping each other on the back, some doubling over in laughter, while others stared in apparent awe. Everyone wore the same expression, except for one guy in the middle of the group. He was telling the story that had everyone else in fits of laughter. He was animated. He was captivating. No one else dared to speak. They were all mesmerized.

They looked like Wall Street guys. Alex straightened herself up, creating some space between herself and her husband. She smoothed her hair flat with one hand, shaking off the sexual flush from Jamie's suggestive touch. She mentally scolded herself for gallivanting like that. She was at a Wall Street bar. She didn't want to appear unprofessional if she ran into a colleague or client. She didn't want them to think of her as someone's wife. She only wanted them to see her as a trader. Alex checked the group of men; with a small measure of relief she concluded that she didn't recognize any of them. Still, she was drawn to the conversation, straining to listen in.

"...So our motto was: 'If it flies, floats, or fucks, just rent it!'"

Another round of uncontrolled laughter and backslapping ensued. One of the listeners shook his head in disbelief.

"You couldn't have taken a limo to the game, huh? You had to rent that chopper."

The listener shook his head again, confused, amazed, appalled, awed – all at once.

"Still sore I didn't give you the look?" the man in the middle replied with a laugh.

"No," the listener snorted. "I still can't believe all six of you assholes survived the crash. It's unheard of. It's a goddamned miracle."

The man in the middle chuckled, eyes shining. "It was a crazy fucking night. Crazy fucking story."

He paused.

"But I still fucking loved turning around at the game and seeing you sitting ten rows back behind me. What, the Goldman Sachs guys could only afford the cheap seats back then or you weren't a big enough client to deserve better?"

"I ran three billion dollars! Even back then that was a lot of fucking money, Hank." The second man replied self-importantly, puffing out his chest.

"It's not the money, my friend. It's the man."

The second man fell silent.

"Ah, hell, c'mon man I'm just fucking with you."

The man in the middle pulled the second guy into a friendly manbrace - half headlock, half hug.

"And if you start doing more business with me now, I'll tell the story differently so that you were sitting in front of me at the game!"

That brought another round of laughter from the rest of the group. Alex watched one of them beckon for Manny, who hurried to fetch the group another round of drinks. After the men had been served, Manny left his post at the bar to come around and exchange pleasantries with the group. Alex couldn't help but notice that he greeted them all the same:

"How are ya? Nice to see you again!"

"Do you know them?" Jamie asked, interested.

Alex shook her head. "No, never seen them before."

"Good," he breathed a sigh of relief.

"Why?"

"I don't know," he shrugged. "They just seem a little aggressive, that's all." He slipped his arm around her waist. "Ready to go home now?" He checked his watch. "It really is getting late, muffin."

They're all aggressive, Jamie, she thought to herself. Saying that would get her nowhere though.

"Sure, babe, I'm ready. Let's go home."

Jamie paid the bill and took his wife's hand, guiding her back through the crowd and towards the front door. Alex snuck one last glance at the group of Wall Street guys who were still loudly telling stories and throwing back drinks.

She followed Jamie home. Within two minutes, they were inside. Alex turned on the air- conditioner, washed up, stripped off her clothes, and crawled into bed. After he showered, Jamie crawled into bed next to her. He wrapped his arms around her and pulled her closely against his own body.

"I wish we could just stay here forever, muffin. I'd rather be in this bed with you than anywhere else in the world." He squeezed her tighter. "I love you. I'm too tired now tonight. You don't mind do you?"

It was as if his libido disappeared the second they walked back into their apartment, back into their real life.

"It's okay, babe. I love you too." She gave him a peck on the lips and rolled over. She stared at the wall even though she couldn't see it through the darkness of the room. Finally, she felt her eyes closing, thankful for the distraction that sleep would bring.

10

Alex tapped the microphone and waited. After a beat, the room quieted down. With a smile plastered to her face she spoke clearly.

"If Wall Street were an addiction, I'd be a crack-cocaine junkie."

She paused again, but this time it was for the self-emulation.

"Hi, my name is Alex Kramer and I am a junk bond trader."

She paused again to make sure she had everyone's attention. Deciding that all eyes were now focused squarely on her, accompanied by a few dropped-jaws, she continued by changing her tone slightly.

"Relax, you're not at an addiction meeting - well, at least not yet. But when we are done talking you'll see that I am head over heels crazy about this business. I love Wall Street. I can't get enough of it. If something tells you that you'd feel the same way about a business like this, then you've come to the right meeting after all."

A handful of girls laughed and the others cracked smiles. Alex knew she had disarmed them slightly, easing the tension in the room.

They were up on the executive floor of Lehman Brothers in one of the larger conference rooms that effectively doubled as a recruitment center. Instead of signs of Uncle Sam pointing down from the walls and convincing recruits that "We Want You!" the Lehman machine solicited younger employees like Alex to deliver rosy success stories of life inside a Big Bank. The room Alex looked out upon was filled with roughly one hundred female coeds, comprised mostly of sophomore and junior students at Ivy League Universities. The girls were there because they dreamed of working on Wall Street and wanted to show their dedication by putting in some face time with recruiters before the interview season began in earnest in another few short months.

Alex silently congratulated herself for being chosen as the keynote speaker for this recruiting event. The less Jamie tried at his job, the harder she worked at hers. The more he hated his Big Bank, the more she fell in love with hers. She needed her fix - a hit of excitement, a shot of adrenaline, even a little illicit dose of passion. Her marriage was limping along. So more and more, she started getting her kicks by throwing herself headfirst into her job. As a result she was quickly becoming the poster child for young traders. The fact that she was a woman and the Big Bank could use her to promote its diversity efforts made her the darling of Human Resources.

Alex looked down at the list of prompt questions she had received to help guide her presentation:

- Please discuss the product or service in which your group specializes.
- How did you get smart about this product specialty?
- Who are your clients and what services do you provide to them?
- What does it take to excel in a sales and trading role?
- What do you find most challenging about your job?
- How does a junior person add value?

Alex's opening introduction wasn't exactly on the HR cheat sheet.

"So, obviously you all are not here for an AA meeting. You're here to learn about Wall Street and what your life would be like working at a place like Lehman Brothers."

She saw some of the girls robotically nodding their approval.

"All kidding aside, it turns out that this business really is like an addiction. We're total junkies. People are consumed with their jobs and sometimes their jobs totally consume them. The thing I love about this kind of environment is that you end up working with people who are completely passionate about what they do. It's a culture of people who benchmark success and who always want to find themselves at the top of that heap. It's intense. People don't always agree. In fact, the amount of shouting and intensity that you imagine occurs on a trading floor – like the scenes you see from the movies – yup, that really happens."

She looked around the room at the all-to-eager faces.

Shit, this is too easy, she thought.

"I know you all go to phenomenal schools. I'm sure you all excel. I'm guessing you all know a thing or two already about competitive environments. Well, if you thrive in that type of environment then you'll do well on Wall Street and chances are you'll love doing it too. But, there are two sides to every coin. It is a wildly volatile climate. The highs are high. But the lows are, well – they are very, very low. You might go home one day up several million dollars only to come in the next and find that some unexpected news has blown up your trading strategy and cost you all of your profits. So one question you have to ask yourselves before you jump in is what your risk appetite really is."

Alex looked down at the notes she had long since stopped reading. She looked up and out at the sea of faces.

Fuck, they were eager.

"How much are you willing to lose in exchange for the opportunity to win huge?"

Alex paused here to try and make her last sentence really sink in with the girls. She looked around trying to read their faces, trying to remember the vision of herself in their shoes: when she was an undergrad she had firmly believed that she was invincible. All of that bra-burning women's lib shit didn't apply to her. She had believed that "Work-Life Balance" was a stupid term for weaker people. If you were strong, you could just will yourself to have it all, all of the time.

Alex thought about her life plan: *Wasn't she proving that she was on her way to having it all?*

Ivy League? Check. Hot Shot Wall Street job? Check. Prestigious business school in her sights? Check. Form-fitting husband? Check. Life plan? Check. Check. Check. She knew she had to remind herself that if she stayed the course, and continued to climb that Wall Street ladder, then she at least stood a chance of becoming someone really worth knowing. After all, the recently promoted CFO of Lehman was a woman. Anything was possible on Wall Street these days.

One of the girls' hands shot straight up. Alex motioned to the girl sitting in the third row. The girl had shoulder-length, stick straight, dark brown hair that was perfectly coiffed and secured by a demure headband.

Ugh. What fucking self-respecting woman shows up on Wall Street in a headband? It was like whispering: "look at me. I'm a delicate flower. If you shout too loudly I might wilt. So please be nice to me." Giving us all a bad name, Alex instinctively thought.

The girl cleared her throat and spoke with a confident and formal tone.

"Can you tell us why you decided to become a trader? Most of the people I've spoken to say that Sales is a more appropriate role for women. What is it like to be a woman on a trading floor?"

Alex paused. All she could think was that girls who wear headbands don't make it on trading floors. For the briefest moment she considered spouting off the downside to the job, all of the facts that would make this girl run for the hills: eating breakfast, lunch, and sometimes dinner in front of your computer, twelve inches away from every guy who inspected your meal choices and mocked you for them; watching the guys watch the secretaries as they walked down the trading rows and rated their asses on a scale from one to ten and then secretly wondering what they rated your ass; falling into a world where drinking to excess was the expected norm if you wanted to successfully socialize with clients and co-workers; biting your lower lip until the inside bled when you felt an uncontrollable quiver about to turn into a burst of tears when you inevitably fucked up some remedial task.

But none of that bothered Alex. She would never let it. And there were still plenty of women in the room who weren't wearing headbands. So instead, she answered:

"Look, trading's not for everyone. Many women are extraordinarily successful in sales. I think that trading is perceived as more of a "man's" role because it requires very quick decision-making, the ability to execute transactions, a high tolerance for risk, and the proclivity to gamble. Now, I know you and me - and I'm sure just about every other woman in this room believes that there's nothing a man can do that a woman can't. So why should trading be any different? For me, I always saw trading as the center of the action. And I wanted to be where the action was. It was never a decision between sales and trading. It was trading or nothing.

As far as being a female trader - I love it. People are so focused on making money that they don't care who or what you are. You matter if you can help them make money. You are irrelevant if you prove to be more of an impediment than an asset. Ironically, money is the great equalizer.

I think there is just one rule to live by as a woman on the trading floor:

Don't. Ever. Cry.

Don't ever fucking let one tear roll down your cheek while anyone else is looking. I don't care if you've had the worst possible day of your life. Everyone says "there is no crying in baseball." Well, there is no crying on Wall Street.

So if you want to play, that's the rule to live by. Otherwise, they'll never look at you the same way ever again."

Alex turned from speaking to the crowd more generally and returned her gaze to the headband-sporting coed.

"Did that help answer your question?"

The girl nodded her head up and down. Alex tried to gauge her reaction. Alex hoped she had sounded convincing. Most days she herself believed what she had just said about being a woman on the trading floor. But there were days when she questioned herself, when she questioned the way the guys treated her, when she wondered why she had even gotten the job in the first place.

Sure, she was just as qualified as the next person but she had her days where she had a lingering, sickening feeling that her looks and her sex had played a part in current role. Alex knew she had told the girls to "ask her anything" but she was pretty sure she'd be canned on the spot if she ever really spoke her mind on that subject.

Alex knew that she had to maintain control over her facial expressions so as not to betray even a hint of doubt to these young recruits. She turned her attention to another girl, who was sitting wide-eyed in the front row, patiently waiting to be noticed and called upon. She motioned to the girl who somewhat comically stood and introduced herself first.

"Hi, my name is Christina Lee from Harvard University; Economics Major, Class of 2009. Thank you for taking the time to talk to us today. Can you please tell us a little bit more about Lehman Brothers and its competitive advantage? My two older brothers work at Goldman Sachs. So I'm wondering if you can tell us more about why you love it here specifically and why any one of us would choose Lehman Brothers over another firm?"

The girl smiled broadly, handed the microphone back to the moderator, and took her seat.

Oh Christina, Alex thought to herself, *you are such a clever, manipulative little bitch. Well played. You will get so many job offers from so many Investment Banks you'll probably wet yourself in self-congratulatory glee. Phenomenal use of the Big-Bank reverser; Instead of asking questions about how to make yourself look better as a candidate, ask questions that turn the firms into candidates, competitors against one another. Make them want you. Bravo, Christina Lee. Bravo.*

Alex didn't hate the girl for asking. She absolutely fucking loved her. This girl was made for Wall Street.

Alex matched her bright smile.

"I'm so glad you asked that. Thank you, Christina. I think that a firm's culture is the underlying intangible that sets in apart from the others. You may look around as you go through this recruiting process and wonder what sets each bank apart. You may think, 'but aren't they all the same and I'm just happy if I land a job at any of them, I don't care much if it's Goldman Sachs, Morgan Stanley, Lehman Brothers, JP Morgan, or Bank of America.' But you should care. Because each firm is different. We all might do the same type of business but we conduct business in very different ways."

The women from Human Resources nodded their heads approvingly, like Kool-Aid Sipping Big Bank Bobble Heads.

Alex luckily caught herself before she added Bear Stearns to the mix. That would have been a disastrous fuck-up and completely undermined her advice since the firm didn't even exist anymore. Alex wondered if these girls even read the news or were following what was really happening on Wall Street. There was a different, disastrous headline out about Lehman Brothers every day. Alex tried to not pay too much attention to the details of all of the negative press her firm was getting, but you had to practically be living in a cave to not know that the firm's stock was down over eighty percent and had been trading below ten dollars a share for weeks already, after soaring close to one-hundred and fifty dollars per share.

But here she was, pimping the place out to these overachieving girls anyway. She knew she must still believe in the firm if she could proselytize about it with such ease.

"You want to find a firm where you will be valued, judged, and compensated for your work product and for nothing else. I look around at my time at Lehman to date and I can say to you that I think this is true. There are many women who hold senior titles throughout the firm. So to answer the last two questions in one fell swoop, I have never felt strange as a woman on a trading desk because the trading desk that I work on is at Lehman Brothers, and this is the kind of institution where I think you don't even have to give that sort of thing a second thought."

Well, the closing salvo was more than a little cheesy and aggressive, Alex thought, *but may as well end on a high note.*

"I have to get back down to the desk now, but thank you all for taking the time to come and learn a little more about Lehman Brothers. I'm sure I'll be seeing a few of you in the halls here in the near future. If anyone wants to email me with any questions or anything else about the process I'm more than happy to help out. I'll make sure I leave my contact info with one of the program coordinators. Thanks again guys. Good luck!"

Alex stepped away from the podium to applause, some enthusiastic while others were merely polite.

Can't win 'em all over. Whatever, the truth is you really do have to be one tough bitch to get anywhere in this business. At least half of these girls would end up in consulting jobs.

Alex headed out of the room, past all of the mahogany-paneled doors that led to executives' offices, and back towards the elevator bank down to the trading floor. As she walked past the executive offices she thought for the hundredth time how many years and how much hard work it would take her to try and reach these types of ranks within the financial world. If she was lucky, maybe she would have the opportunity to run a trading desk one day. But to get to the executive floor, to run an entire global institution, to oversee nearly twenty-five thousand employees - Jesus all that was something else. She knew that the media had been lighting up their executives in the papers and on financial talk shows. Dick Fuld, Lehman's CEO and Joe Gregory, its President, were vilified and ridiculed all day every day. But as far as Alex could tell inside the building, they were still worshipped. To Lehman employees, there was this idea that the building was under siege and all of them were banding together to defend its honor. By now, Alex was used to walking by the barricades and the news cameras as she entered and exited the building every day. She proudly and briskly walked by them, sometimes thinking, 'you schmucks don't actually do anything, you just report on what other people do. What talent is there in that?'

◆ ◆ ◆

When Alex walked back on to the fourth floor she could tell that something unusual was happening. People were really animated. Everyone was talking in excited whispers. Alex hurried down to her desk, walking as quickly as she could without breaking into a run. She sat down and looked around. The commotion seemed to be coming from the other end of one of the trading rows in an area just outside of the corner offices.

"What's going on?" she asked Josh, a mid-level trader who sat to her left.

"I don't fucking know," he said. "Who the fuck knows anymore. There's a rumor flying around that they just canned Joe Gregory and Erin Callan. I mean, she's a fucking idiot anyway. I don't why they made her CFO other than the obvious fact that she's fucking hot. But Joe's been at Lehman his whole career. With all the heat, all the press, looks like they're picking their sacrificial lambs. I don't know. It's just a rumor at this point. But I'm hearing Dick Fuld is on the trading floor right now. Maybe he's here to talk about it. It'd be fucking crazy if he's on the floor. In the eleven years I've worked at Lehman, I've never once seen him on any trading floor. See, there's that circle of people down there? It looks like they're surrounding someone. I don't know. Nobody fucking tells us anything anymore."

Alex was completely shocked. She stared at Josh like he had six heads. She didn't even know how to process everything he had just said, let alone believe it. They fired Erin Callan? Dick Fuld was on the trading floor? And why was Josh talking like he hated Dick Fuld so much?

She thought that Fuld was viewed as a demigod by all of the employees. Everyone had kept saying things were okay. But, it was becoming increasingly clear that things were not okay. What the fuck was going on? They'd been reassured for months that the firm was in great shape. They were told that all of the headlines were just reporters making noise because there was nothing better to talk about. They were trying to create a story where there wasn't one. Alex knew that some of the guys on the desk had been buying tons of Lehman stock in their personal accounts, thinking that they could double down and take advantage of the historically low price.

Alex shook her head. She had just told all of those college girls that Lehman was the greatest place on earth, basically that it was better than fucking Disneyland. She had mentally referenced the amazing fact that she worked at a financial institution that had a female CFO. And now that same woman was fired.

Alex now desperately wanted to know what in the hell was going on. So she did something she tried never to do while at work. She picked up the phone and dialed her husband. He answered on the second ring.

"Hi babe," she whispered as quietly as she could into the phone.

"Alex? Hi. What's the matter? Is everything okay?"

Alex had been firm with Jamie that they could not speak over the phone during the workday, but had to communicate only via email. The trading line was a public line that rang on everyone's desk. The guys whose wives called constantly were mercilessly ridiculed. Alex could only imagine the torture she would have to endure if her husband joined the ranks of spouses who made the Top Ten Calling List.

She knew he was surprised she had called and probably thought something was wrong. "Yeah, everything's okay. I mean, I'm fine. But I'm not really sure that everything's okay. But I have no fucking idea what is going on here. They're saying that they just fired our CFO and our President."

Alex thought she could hear those same exact words coming out of the financial news commentator yapping on the television screens above the trading desks. But there was so much pandemonium that she couldn't be sure.

"Holy shit, Jamie can you access CNBC? I think they're reporting that right now. I can't believe the news is reporting all of this before anyone's even said anything to us. This is crazy."

"Hold on. Calm down. Slow down. Relax. I'll check online to see what I can find."

Alex was amazed at how calm Jamie seemed, like he was on autopilot. Alex wanted to scream at the top of her lungs. She called him because she thought he would understand. She didn't know what was happening, but she remembered the sequence of events at Bear Stearns in those final days. She tried to convince herself that this was different. But there were eerie similarities.

Jamie was supposed to understand. He had gone through the exact same thing.

"I don't see anything on the newswires Alex. Just try to relax. You don't know what's going on yet. I'm sure it's all a bunch of bullshit."

Suddenly, everyone on the floor was standing, straining their necks to see towards the other end of the floor. She heard a voice come across over the hoot system. She couldn't see who it was but the voice was booming and authoritative. *This is like some fucked up version of 1984*, she thought to herself.

"Jamie, I gotta go," she cut him off. "Someone's making an announcement. I have to get off the phone and hear what's going on. I'll try to call you back." She clicked off without giving him time to respond.

"Is this thing on?"

The voice was commanding.

"I haven't used one of these in quite a few years."

By now, every trader, salesperson, research analyst, and assistant was standing. Dick Fuld was standing at the other end of the row, talking into the hoot, the internal microphone system that projected his voice across the entire floor. It looked to Alex like he was standing by the Investment Grade trading desk. Lehman's own corporate bonds were traded off of that desk and despite their high credit rating, activity had been very volatile and bonds had been trading at increasingly lower prices as investors wagered on whether or not the firm was in real trouble.

Ike Robinson was the Investment Grade financials trader who traded the firm's own bonds. Lately he had been making quite a spectacle of trading them, as if he were soldiering on an actual battlefield. Alex wondered if Dick Fuld was intentionally speaking from Ike's desk to make a symbolic point.

The entire floor was completely silent. It was as if someone had sucked all of the air out of it.

"I've decided that enough is enough. I know you all have been watching and listening to these absolutely ridiculous and outlandish news reports about our esteemed firm. This is an extraordinarily challenging time. But we, as a firm, have nothing to hide. We have nothing to be embarrassed about. In fact, we have only to be proud of ourselves, of our accomplishments, and of the great work that we do here at Lehman Brothers. The culture that we have built over many decades at this firm is one of dedication, of commitment, and of loyalty. At this time, I have asked a former employee, longtime friend, and lifelong advocate of those Lehman ideals to return to the executive ranks of Lehman Brothers and help me to steer this ship to calmer waters. I know that Bart McDade is a friend and a mentor to many of you and

I ask you to join me in welcoming him back to the firm as our new President and COO."

A round of loud cheers went up around the room, even while many were giving each other quizzical looks. There was no mention of former execs Joe Gregory or Erin Callan, but Fuld's meaning was clear. There would be no mention of them. Onward and upward. It was the Lehman way. Bart had come of age in the financial industry as a credit trader and so it was fitting – and Alex somehow guessed – no accident – that his re-ascendance was being carefully unveiled on the same trading floor that had made him famous in the business.

"So I ask that you all now remain steadfast in your dedication, your commitment, and your loyalty to this great firm. Use every amount of dedication that you have to pour your hearts into your work, produce better results than you ever have before, and help myself and Bart prove all of these naysayers wrong. I can assure each and every one of you that I will not stop and I will not rest until I correct every opinion of those who are inappropriately shorting our stock. You have my personal guarantee that we are going to get those sons of bitches!"

After hearing those words, the whole floor erupted once again into cacophonous cheers. People were really fired up. Some were high-fiving each other. Alex felt like she had unwittingly been recruited into this weird fucked up army to fight some outlandish battle. Dick Fuld was strutting around the floor like Napoleon. He was marching down the aisles, shaking hands and slapping backs.

Alex's head was spinning. It was as if everyone on the entire floor had collectively exhaled and suddenly the building was full of life again. The show continued for a few more minutes until Dick, Bart and their entourage had left the floor, presumably to go rally the troops in Equities, Commodities, Foreign Exchange, and other trading departments.

Ike Robinson switched on his iPod and held it next to the hoot system microphone. *A.C.D.C.'s I Wanna Rock* blasted through every speaker. Robinson moved the music aside for a second and shouted into the mike:

"Let's go motherfuckers! You heard The Man. Back to work! Long live Lehman Brothers!"

11

The pep talks might have helped build morale back up inside the building. But they did nothing to stop the groundswell growing outside. With each passing day, the headlines screamed louder and louder, warning of Lehman's imminent demise. First, the media prayed on the management shakeup:

> *"Shocker: Erin Callan to Leave Pity Post at Lehman."*

Then came the speculation of how the firm could right its course:

> *"Lehman to Sell Investment Management Division?"*
> *"Dick Fuld working feverishly on Asset Sales."*

Finally, when the detractors didn't get the instant gratification they demanded, the media started to go for the jugular kill:

"Say it. Just Say It. Can Lehman Survive This? I - I think – I Don't Know. I Just Don't Know."

July and August rushed by in a blur of negative headlines, lackluster business, and furious drinking. The dog days of summer were really nothing more than dog days. The final punctuation on the shit sandwich came on August 28th when the firm laid off 1,500 employees. Alex had never witnessed a mass firing before. It was sickening. After the first person had been let go, the other employees quickly realized what was happening. Most people were frozen, waiting by their phones to see if they too would receive a fateful call. Others tried to ignore the obvious tension by engaging in mindless banter and generic jokes. Alex watched as one person after another walked into a glass-encased conference room where several managers were seated around a table. Each person walked into the room with head held high. Each person emerged differently. Some still kept their heads high while others left with sunken shoulders and glassy eyes. By the time the fired people returned to their desks, they were no longer Lehman employees. There was a security guard, a human resources representative, and a cardboard box waiting at each desk. Alex saw her first direct boss, a middle-aged woman and veteran research analyst, get called in to the glass room to be shot. When Susan emerged, she stormed back to her desk, her eyes brimming with fire.

Spotting the additional personnel waiting by her desk, she looked like she might swing at of them.

"What the fuck do you want" she growled. "Here, take it. Fucking take it all."

She flung her employee pass and business cards at them.

"What else do you want? You want more? Here, how about eleven years of research? How about eleven years of dedication and hard work?"

She picked up a pile of research reports and hurled them into the isle. Papers flew everywhere. Row by row, the trading floor quieted down as more people turned to watch. "Eleven fucking years I gave this firm. Eleven years that cost me my marriage, custody of my daughter. I've worked my ass off for this firm. And this is what I get?!" She waved a green folder in the air. Alex guessed that it was some sort of severance letter or package. Susan's voice cracked.

"You can all go to hell. This firm can go to hell. It is going to hell. You just wait and see." Another analyst reached out to touch Susan's arm and try to calm her. Susan yanked her arm away.

"Don't touch me," she shouted.

"Don't. Touch. Me."

Susan repeated herself, this time in a voice so low, it sounded more like a whimper. She looked at the security guard.

"I can find my own way out, thank you. Don't worry - I'm not going to take anything with me. You have taken it all already."

That round of layoffs created a shift in attitude inside the building. Before people had really felt that they were more than simple employees. Some fancied themselves soldiers. Others thought they were part of a family. But when Mother Lehman turned her back on 1,500 of her "children" in the heat of battle, those who still remained were scarred by that memory. There was a real feeling that no one in the building was safe now. Alex noticed that the senior guys were more easily ruffled. Malcontent was now the default emotion for most.

By the second week of September the negative hype was literally squeezing the building into an unshakeable death grip. Every news channel had multiple vans parked outside the company's headquarters. News journalists and photographers stood poised by the entrances, with microphone or camera in hand, hoping to steal a quote or a photo of someone of consequence. Just north of Times Square, Lehman was starting to attract more than its fair share of tourists. An artist had set up a little studio for himself on the sidewalk directly outside the building. There, he sat and painted a colorful portrait of Dick Fuld. With each passing day the likeness took on a more grotesque visage, as if to convey the general public's disgust for a public figure that many believed was now more of a monster than a man. When the artist had finished he handed out several different colored markers to the crowd. Green was for employees. Red was for shareholders. Black was for members of competing firms. Blue was for New Yorkers. And yellow was for tourists. Some people just signed their names. Others left nasty messages. The board filled up quickly.

Alex passed by the sign one rare afternoon when she decided to leave the building during the workday to grab a cup of coffee at the Starbucks across the street. She saw that the space was nearly filled and wondered to herself it she should sign it too. *Jesus, Fuld looks like a monster*, she thought. It resembled some fucked up, modern day capitalist-hating interpretation of the portrait in *The Picture of Dorian Grey*. She wondered who the artist was going to give the painting to and whether he was going to try to deliver his masterpiece to Fuld himself. Anything seemed possible. Nothing seemed too audacious when it came to Wall Street.

◆ ◆ ◆

September 11th was never a normal day in New York City. It hadn't been normal in seven years. The entire trading floor, along with the rest of Manhattan and maybe the rest of America, stood in silence two separate times that morning just after nine o'clock, in recognition of those who had died in the 9/11 terrorist attacks. Alex noticed that some people looked lost, deep in thought or memory while others stared off in to space, like they were trying to do anything other than remember the events of that unspeakable day. Lehman's headquarters had been in the World Trade Center back then so the carnage hit very close to home for many.

And then, just as quickly as it had arrived, the moment passed in a New York minute. It was back to business as usual on Wall Street. As the rest of that day unfolded, it became increasingly clear that the "business" to be tended to that day would be the destruction of what was left of Lehman. The firm had prematurely reported its quarterly results the day before and the market had no patience left for Lehman's perceived shenanigans. The stock dropped forty percent the day of the announcement and showed no signs of letting up. After months of public debate and speculation, there was suddenly a general consensus that day: Lehman Brothers could no longer exist as a stand-alone entity.

Financial analysts, reporters, employees, shareholders, bondholders, and competitors were suddenly, seemingly inexplicably, all on the same page. This understanding had the perverse effect of emboldening many of Lehman's employees. Inside the building, talk of a corporate takeover was seriously gaining momentum.

Traders, true to form, started making markets and taking odds on who would buy the firm. The most popular rumor to circulate was that Bank of America would purchase Lehman Brothers over the weekend. And at that time, anyone even remotely involved in finance was in the business of believing rumor as if it were reality. This led employees to puff up their chests even more and to repeat the same theories to one another until everyone believed it all. The hope that people religiously clung to was rooted in their fundamental beliefs: one, the United States government would not let Lehman Brothers file for bankruptcy because the firm was "too big to fail"; two, with the recent sell-off the firm's stock was now so cheap that competitors were surely falling all over themselves to buy the company at such a steal of a price; and three – this was Lehman Brothers goddamnit. An institution wouldn't just disappear after fully functioning for almost one hundred and fifty years.

So in some very perverted way, people just carried on. Alex was amazed that most of the salesmen were still keeping their client engagements, planning to entertain as if nothing at all was amiss. Thursdays were typically the premier entertaining night and every salesman made every effort to book his best client. By all appearances, that Thursday would not be any different. Alex listened while DiVeccio called to confirm his plans with one of the multi-billion dollar hedge funds he covered. The only difference in the schedule was that Alex had been invited to attend. She had been invited to a handful of client dinners but never to one of Bobby's. He had also invited three senior traders – Greg, Joe, and Josh - so they would be five in total from

Lehman with another four guys joining the group from the client's side.

Nanni's was a dated Italian eatery on East 46th Street. There were only about twenty-five tables in the restaurant. The space was small and crowded with the tables set only inches apart from one another. The décor was simple with several oil paintings adorning the walls, scuffed wooden floors, low-ceilings, and dim lighting. Alex noticed a photograph dated from 1968 of an old man with a broad smile – she guessed the owner – sitting inside. From the look of the space little if anything had been done to update the restaurant in the forty years since it first opened. The waiters were all old men with grey hair and thick mustaches. They stood slightly stooped over and spoke with animated, Italian accents.

Bobby was greeted warmly and royally and Alex could tell that this "authentic" Italian spot was a fine-tuned part of his sales pitch. She was quietly amused that he suddenly seemed to develop a thick Italian accent and took to speaking with animated hand gesticulations. Several tables were pushed together in the far corner of the room to accommodate the group.

The waiter didn't bother passing around menus. He and Bobby conferred briefly with one another and agreed that everyone would enjoy a sampling of all Nanni's had to offer: seafood platters to start, pasta samplers after that, and then steaks and chicken all around. Alex inwardly groaned, mentally calculated the unavoidable caloric intake and promised herself she would make it to the gym at five the next morning before work. Then she ordered a glass of white wine. Bobby pointed out that he had already ordered several bottles of red for the table. Alex assured him that she wouldn't discriminate. Everyone laughed.

The conversation shifted easily to the market. The clients asked about the mood insider Lehman. Alex's more seasoned colleagues asked about the current perception of Lehman Brothers amongst the client community. Everyone answered with cautious optimism. Alex wondered if anyone was really telling the truth. She hadn't been directly invited to join the conversation though, so she simply nodded her head in agreement at one group or the other every few minutes. She sipped her glass of wine, trying to make that first round last as long as possible. She hoped to stay as sober as possible while the others drank leisurely so that she could remain alert to the financial discussions that were still a bit over her head.

The men's glasses were quickly being drained and refilled time and again all around her, as they talked louder, laughed harder, and ate more. With little to contribute to the early conversation, Alex had no choice but to drain her wine glass too. Their waiter was highly attuned to every movement at his VIP table. The very instant she had put her glass down, the old Italian reappeared at her side, smiled broadly so that his mustache expanded across his cheeks, and poured her a generous refill.

The second glass went down smoothly and quickly. Her muscles began to release and she allowed her mind to relax a bit. Without paying much attention she began to converse easily with the client sitting to her left. They talked shop and Alex found that after a few drinks she too could deftly steer the conversation to topics and companies on which she was respectably knowledgeable. If she got caught she found that she could simply ask enough questions to keep the client speaking at length, pleased to display his vast Wall Street acumen and seemingly more than happy to hear himself talk. The client asked Alex how she had come to join Lehman and become a trader. She gave a brief summary, careful to exclude the part about "falling down the rabbit hole." He marveled that she had gone to Harvard, drawing the attention of the others at the table. Her senior traders then sung her praises and even Bobby unexpectedly paid her a compliment. She took a chance and joked to the group about his obsessive-compulsive personal space issues and lightheartedly bemoaned her plight in having to sit next to him each day. The group laughed harder still and Bobby motioned to his waiter for another bottle of wine.

It felt more like a celebration than a client dinner. Alex reminded herself that she must have one of the greatest jobs in the world.

They all carried on in this way for several hours. When the check finally arrived Bobby slid his American Express corporate card into the waiter's hands without even checking the sum.

"Who gives a shit – this dinner's on Bank of America!" he declared.

Everyone roared with laughter. Now deliriously drunk, all agreed that Bank of America would buy Lehman within the next few days and all of the market madness would be behind them.

Someone suggested that they continue on to a nearby bar and the group labored loudly toward the door and out onto the street. When Alex fumbled with her jacket Greg appeared instantly to help her. He let his hand linger on her shoulder for an extra moment. Her face flushed as the wine, the chilly fall air, and a wave of confusion hit her all at once. She checked her cell phone and saw a text message from Jamie asking when she'd be home. She typed a quick reply - *out with important clients. Don't wait up. xo* - and quickly slid the phone back into her bag. She re-centered her concentration on putting one foot squarely in front of the other, suddenly aware that she was extraordinarily drunk and couldn't imagine anything more embarrassing that tripping on her four inch stilettos and falling flat on her face. They passed by an unattractive middle-aged man with a splotchy face who was accompanied by two women. He had his arm around each on either side of him. Alex stared closely as the groups passed one another and in a moment of drunken clarity she divined that he was a distantly famous character-actor actor. Alex swore he looked just like the guy who played the impish, hated, redheaded principal from the cult-classic *Ferris Buehler's Day Off*.

"Rooney!"

She was too drunk to control herself.

"Rooney! Is that you, Rooney?"

At first he didn't turn around, pretending not to hear her. But she persisted.

"Roo-ney."

She crooned, emphasizing both syllables this time.

"I know it's you! I'm a huge fan!"

Finally he turned around, swinging both of his women with him in a drunken, clumsy pirouette.

"I get that all the time, sweetheart," he slurred. "All I ever hear is Rooney! Rooney! Goddamned mother-fucking movie. I can't get away from that crap. Rooney! Rooney!" he kept chanting. "Well, Rooney's right here baby. You want some of this? Come and get it. Come and get your autograph," he motioned lewdly.

Alex burst in to laughter. She was horrified but too drunk to care. Now that she had the chance to stare at him for an extended period, she wasn't even sure if it really was the actor after all. Before Alex could take the opportunity to escalate the situation even further Greg steered her away from trouble and into their next destination.

Once inside the group immediately made their way over to the bar. The bartender looked up as they approached, sensing his evening was about to get more profitable. Up until they had arrived the place had been fairly quiet. Smaller parties of two or four lounged at cocktail tables, speaking in discreet, nearly inaudible voices. A handful of old men in equally old, but nevertheless expensive suits sat at the bar, taking long, slow swigs of whiskey on the rocks. None appeared to know the other and not one of them seemed to make any attempt to change that status quo. The room was dimly lit. The wooden floors were mostly covered in expensive looking rugs. Traces of cigar smoke hung in the air.

"What the hell was that little outburst? Maybe if you started speaking up like that on the desk you'd be trading more. I never heard a broad yell so loudly before." Bobby laughed heartily.

"Very funny Bobby," Alex replied sweetly. "That was just the alcohol talking. Maybe I should just start drinking on the desk then."

"You wouldn't be the first honey, so don't flatter yourself," he said without hesitation.

Greg winked at her, running his hand through his hair and repositioned himself closer to her.

Bobby turned to the bartender and slid his corporate credit card across the bar.

"Can we get a couple of drinks? We're dyin' of thirst over here. Let's get a round of Patron shots to moisten these parched throats."

The bartender nodded obligingly and deftly poured nine shots. Holding their shot glasses in hands raised high, the group toasted: "To old friends! To new friends! To good business! To better times! To Lehman Brothers!"

Alex chimed in: "To Bank of America!"

Everyone looked at her. Bobby raised a single eyebrow.

"What?" she asked rhetorically. "They'll be paying for these drinks on Monday when your corporate card gets transferred to them in a merger."

Everyone laughed.

"To Bank of America!" they echoed with feeling.

The group banged their shot glasses on the bar top, threw their heads back and drank. "Bartender, we'll have another!" Bobby insisted.

They all had another, and another, and another after that. Mixed drinks were ordered too. The booze just flowed and flowed. Everybody talked. Hardly anyone made any sense. Nobody listened. The last conscious decision Alex made was to take a seat in a barstool because she no longer trusted herself to stand. Hours flew by like minutes as everyone stopped caring about the time. The last thing Alex remembered clearly was holding a shot of vodka in one hand, a glass of white wine in another, and lecturing the men around her about controlling "mind over matter" before she downed one drink after another.

"It's just mind over matter, boys. Mind over matter."

12

MISSING THE BELL THE NEXT MORNING

The shrill and persistent beeping brought her to the fore of consciousness. She heard a voice repeating her name. The voice was coming closer and closer but she still couldn't identify him. When he physically shook her Alex finally awoke from her dreamless sleep. She opened her eyes and immediately regretted it. Her husband was staring down at her, shaking his head. She knew he was still talking, probably lecturing her, but she couldn't decipher any specific words. Her whole head throbbed, like a hammer was being smashed into it every few seconds. The combination of the light streaming through the window shades and the beeping that wouldn't seem to stop was unbearable. Closing her eyes immediately, she rolled over and grumbled something incoherent to no one in particular. She had no idea what day it was but assumed it must be the weekend if she was still sleeping.

"What time is it baby? Why is the alarm going off on a Saturday?"

She squeezed a pillow over her head, hoping the pressure would stop her head from throbbing so badly.

"It's 8:45 and it's not Saturday morning, it's Friday."

His tone was sharp. His words were clipped.

"And you still reek of alcohol. I could get drunk just lying next to you. What the fuck happened to you last night? I was worried sick about you. You stopped answering my text messages. I must have called you fifty times. I don't even know what time you got home."

Alex couldn't think. Jamie never swore at her. Why was he swearing at her? And couldn't he just turn off the damned alarm. She was sure her head was going to explode.

"My phone must have died," she grumbled. "I'm sorry. I lost track of time. Would you mind turning off the alarm?" She added meekly. "I feel like my head's going to explode."

"I'm sure it does."

He reached across her and turned off the alarm.

"I don't get how you could be so irresponsible. What, did your colleagues give you the day off from work or something when you were out partying it up with them all night?" The sarcasm dripped uncharacteristically from his voice.

Alex didn't respond. But she was suddenly alert.
Fuckkkkkk!

She mentally screamed at herself. She just registered the very first thing Jamie had said to her. It was Friday and she was supposed to be at work. She had never, ever before missed the bell. She felt sick to her stomach. She couldn't think straight. She couldn't see straight. She threw the covers off of herself and jumped up. Bad decision, she realized immediately. The sudden movement must have stirred all the alcohol still coursing through her system. Now she could add overwhelmingly nauseous to splitting headache on her list of hangover ailments. She raced around their tiny apartment in a manic daze. She was panicked to the point of hysteria about what the reaction would be when she showed up. She was showered, brushed, combed, washed, dressed, and altogether arranged to the best of her ability in about twelve minutes. The entire time Jamie had sat and silently stared at her. She walked over to him, stood next to his bedside, and waited to see if he would speak first. The seconds that passed felt like hours and Alex knew he was holding her there on purpose because she was so desperate to get to work. Finally, he spoke.

"You rush around like a mad woman to race to work for them but you sure do take your sweet ass time getting home to me."

She knew she'd just been verbally slapped in the face. Only she was still too numb and delirious from the alcohol to feel the sting. She knew that that statement was the opening to a much larger conversation but she didn't know what to say. And she certainly didn't think she had the time at that exact moment. She took his hand and squeezed it. Her stomach churned. She fought the urge to gag. Instead, she swallowed hard.

"I'm sorry. I don't even remember half of last night. I should have come home when my phone died so that you wouldn't be worried. I wasn't thinking. We were all just blowing off a little steam with all the pressure at work, and the takeover rumors. I would think you could understand that."

She paused to look into his eyes for a response of recognition. There was none. She gave his hand another squeeze.

"I love you. I swear I'll make it up to you. I know you're angry with me. But know that I love you. I'm sorry we can't talk about this more now, but if I don't get to work right away I don't even know what is going to happen to me. Can we just talk about this later?"

She didn't wait for a response.

"I love you," she said again.

"I love you too," she heard him say begrudgingly as she grabbed her purse and a jacket and raced out the door, trying not to let it slam behind her. She took the stairs down, deciding that there was no way on earth she could handle benign elevator pleasantries with a doorman. She reached the landing of the lobby in a huff and paused for a moment to catch her breath. Running down five flights of stairs in stilettos still completely drunk off her ass was not her finest hour. She slowed as she passed the doorman, smoothing her hair and trying to look casual, even though Willy knew it was out of character for her to be leaving the apartment at this late hour. She cursed New York City doormen under her breath for their never-ending ability to invade her life without actually knowing anything about it. Once out the front door, she broke into an awkward run-walk as she made her way across town. This was not a sustainable pace. She would be late and sweating like a dirty animal by the time she got to work. She hailed a taxi and settled into the backseat with a sigh of relief. She momentarily thought about asking the driver to just drive aimlessly around the city while she slept in the backseat for an hour. The nausea was returning and she was already late anyway. Against her own will, she directed the cab to Lehman headquarters instead.

As she leaned back against the sticky leather seats, relieved just to be sitting peacefully, she tried to focus on Jamie's accusations. She squeezed her eyes tightly shut, using all her might to try and remember what had happened the night before. There were so many black holes. She remembered the restaurant, the wine, the food, the stories, and the bar they went to afterward. She cringed when the "Rooney" episode flashed across her mind. She could not bring herself to believe she had taunted a grown man in the street like that. *Stupid, stupid, stupid*, she reprimanded herself.

She tried to remember more. She could recall all the drinking they did at the second bar - all the shots the group had done. But after that, nothing was clear.

"Just fucking remember," she scolded herself out loud.

She saw the cab driver peer back at her in the rear-view mirror.

"Sorry," she muttered. "I wasn't talking to you."

"Whatever lady," he responded with his eyes, and went back to focusing on the gridlock in front of him.

She remembered stumbling on the street and someone propping her up, grasping her arm with another hand around her waist. The image flashed through her mind. It disappeared as quickly as it had arrived. She tried to catch it but the memory was gone. She had no fucking idea what had happened. Her mind was literally blank. She didn't even know when she got home or how for that matter. She counted her blessings that she woke up in her own bed next to her husband. She cringed at the mere thought of any alternatives.

You would never, Alex.

She tried to reassure herself. Then she thought of Jamie and the look he had given her that morning. He had scolded her like a child. She wanted so desperately to yell back at him but she didn't know how to defend herself because she couldn't even remember what had happened. She had only blacked out from drinking once before in her life - at Daniella's twenty-first birthday party. She remembered waking up the next morning with two of her friends hovered over her, a mixture of concern and relief washing over their faces when she finally showed signs of life. It had been years since then and Alex still couldn't recall what had happened that night. She groaned. She was dreading walking on to that trading floor with every fiber of her being. The cab stopped in front of Lehman. The driver stopped the meter and put his hand out automatically to collect his fair. Alex silently pleaded with him to keep driving. He gave her another long stare in the mirror. His look said it all: *you think you're the only stupid chick in this city with a hangover and a problem? Get over yourself and get outta my cab, lady.*

Alex paid the fare and forced herself to get out of taxi, walk into the building, swipe her card through the turnstile, get into the elevator, press the button for the fourth floor, swipe her card again, pull open the daunting double doors and walk onto the trading floor.

It was 9:30 already and the floor was bustling with activity. Alex kept her head down and tried to make her way over to her desk as quickly and unassumingly as possible. She had no such luck. As she passed research and approached sales and trading she could see that people started to notice her. Being late to work was one of the cardinal sins of trading floor etiquette. And Alex was a serious offender. A few traders stood and started to applaud her. Others followed. By the time she reached her desk, a full two rows of traders and salesmen were standing and clapping. *Oh my god*, she thought. *I am going to literally drop dead right this very second.* Alex could not think of anything more embarrassing that had ever happened to her in her entire life. Inwardly, she thought for the first time, *I have the worst job in the world.*

Alex could not remember experiencing a worse feeling. Fucking up that equity trade now seemed like a pleasant walk in the park compared to this complete and utter public humiliation.

There were hoots, hollers, and whistles mixed in with the cacophony of clapping. Someone somewhere on the floor kept pressing a button that mimicked the sound of a bell ringing, to signify that Alex had missed the opening trading bell. Some people were smirking while a handful of others were flat out laughing at her. She hurried over to her desk, trying to remove herself from most peoples' direct line of vision. For the first and only time that day Alex was momentarily relieved that she was so completely intoxicated because the sensation served to dull the sting of indignation and embarrassment. She gave a little generic wave to no one in particular and smiled meekly, trying to join the joke herself and mask her mortification. She then slumped into her seat and tried not to make direct eye contact with anyone. After what seemed like an eternity to her - but could not have been more than ten seconds in reality - the mob quieted down and returned to work.

Alex stared at her computer monitors. She tried to log in first to the system and then to the Bloomberg network but her hands were unsteady and sweaty. She had to re-enter her password three separate times before successfully keying in the correct combination. She stared at her screens for a few more minutes, trying to appear busy even though it was abundantly obvious to anyone who cared that she was not working on anything specific. Finally, she hazarded a sideways glance at Bobby. He was waiting for it.

"What in the fuck happened to you last night?"

He demanded to know. His voice was hard but Alex thought she detected mild concern in his eyes.

"You wanna roll with the big boys? You wanna drink with the big boys? You gotta show up for the goddamned trading bell like the big boys do. All that respect you've been building up with everyone around here - remember - you can lose it all in an instant with these monkeys. Don't let yourself get sloppy. You understand what I'm saying to you?" He stared intently at her, letting the emphasis of his last question hang in the air between them.

Alex nodded her head yes but secretly she meant no. "How bad was I?"

Her voice was so low it was nearly a whisper.

"Did I make a total ass out of myself in front of your clients?"

"Hardly," Bobby snorted. "You were the goddamned life of the party. They loved you - kept asking where we'd been hiding you all this time. I'm sure they'll throw a few trades our way today because of it. But," he continued pointedly, "It seems that I left well before you did. I tried to convince you to get into your own taxi when I was leaving but you wouldn't hear of it. You kept blabbing on and on - kept saying you only lived three blocks away so you didn't need to take a cab home. In fact, you kept telling everyone that you didn't have a curfew for a change so drinks were on you. I think you did a shot every time you made that little proclamation."

He chuckled.

"Then, when you were good and sauced, you started asking everyone to whisper and not to make too much noise. You kept saying that if we were too loud your husband was going to be able to hear us all having so much fun and he would come and break up the party. I left right about then."

He stopped talking and looked at her ashen face.

"Look, kid, I'm just telling you so you hear it as friendly fire. If you're gonna get totally sauced, you've got to make the bell in the morning. Do a trade. Change the topic."

Alex stared at him. She required every fiber of her self-control to remain composed, and she hoped, somewhat stone-faced. She bit her bottom lip so hard that she could taste the small drops of blood. After a few long seconds, she felt composed enough to speak.

"I can't believe I said that. I really can't believe I did that. I don't remember-"

She stammered.

"Bobby, I don't remember a goddamned thing after we got to Sparks. I remember doing a few rounds of shots, but saying all those absurd things..."

She studied his face, trying to decide if he had told her everything.

"Is that...everything? I mean, the clapping, and the standing ovation - it's a little extreme, no?"

"Look, kid, that's all I saw. This old man here ran out of steam well before you did last night. Ask those guys for the rest."

He jerked his head over in the direction of the traders who had been there.

"When I left, you were with them. But stop beating yourself up about it. You gotta let it roll off your back - or at least make everyone think it's rolling off your back. It's just part of the gig. Either way, today is your lucky day."

Alex stared at him, perplexed. She could not think of any aspect of her current situation that left her feeling "lucky." She felt shitty, drunk, humiliated, nauseous and depressed. And that was before she considered the bundle of joy she would have waiting for her at home that night with a pissed off husband inside an already small apartment. And his younger brother was due to arrive any day.

Ugh, she inwardly groaned. *Fuck.*

Bobby helped her to the answer.

"It's your lucky fucking day little lady because you decided to get shit-faced in the middle of our corporate meltdown. Nobody's gonna give a fuck about you in ten minutes. All anybody's focused on today is Lehman Brothers, Lehman Brothers, Lehman Brothers - our stock, our bonds, and any news that affects all of our futures."

"Thanks Bobby," Alex managed a tiny smile. "The 'nobody gives a fuck about you because we might go bankrupt' speech is always such a pick me up."

"Look, I don't give a fuck how wasted you are."

He was suddenly furious, nostrils flaring.

"I don't want to hear the word 'bankruptcy' out of your mouth. We all know Bank of America is going to buy us on the cheap. Now fucking get to work will you? I can't be seen talking to the drunk junior any longer. People are gonna think I've gone soft or something."

"Your secret's safe with me, Bobby."

❖ ❖ ❖

Bobby ended up being right. For the rest of the day, everyone quickly forgot about Alex and worried only for themselves and their futures. Mostly, people tried to ignore the news correspondents and focus on their clients. However, as the day progressed, it seemed as

THEY ALL FALL DOWN

though the phones were ringing less and less frequently. Friday was typically a painstakingly slow market day but the complete lack of incoming calls struck some people as odd. Some salespeople spoke quietly to one another of what they had noticed, but no one wanted to bring it to the attention of a manager because no one believed their own clients had halted doing business with the firm. It seemed as though the entire market was collectively holding its breath and waiting. By the middle of the day the only discernible business activity was coming from Robinson's desk, where the increasingly irate trader continued to trade the firm's own bonds with clients and competitors. He had ACDC's classic *Hell's Bell's* blasting through a speaker at his desk as he took phone call after phone call and sent out message after message. By two o'clock, his were the only Bloomberg messages anyone was paying any attention to. They were a mixture of actual trading updates and an expression of his (everyone's) frustration with the news media and the firm's persistent detractors:

1:15 PM: THIS IS ABOUT AS CLEAR AS I CAN BE: EVERYONE ON CNBC IS AN IDIOT

1:27 PM: HERE'S ANOTHER THING I WANT TO BE CLEAR ABOUT. WE ARE NOT AXED TO GIVE AWAY FREE MONEY IN OUR OWN BONDS TODAY. IF YOU HAVE CLIENTS LOOKING TO PICK SOMEONE OFF, TELL THEM TO LOOK SOMEWHERE ELSE.

203

1:52 PM: JUST GOT LIFTED ON OUR 2012 AND 2013 PAPER. LEAVES ME AXED AS A BUYER. STILL SWINGING. WILL KEEP SWINGING ALL DAMN DAY.

2:07 PM: I THINK WE SHOULD ALLOW CNBC TO FAIL. THAT WILL TRULY REMOVE SYSTEMIC RISK.

2:15 PM: BUYING ANOTHER BLOCK OF LEHMAN BONDS. WHO ELSE WANTS A PIECE OF THIS?

3:05 PM: WINDING IT DOWN. WE WILL BE BACK IN THE RING IN ONE FORM OR ANOTHER ON MONDAY. AND WE'RE LIKELY TO BE FAIRLY RILED UP. PROUD AS HELL OF EVERYONE IN THIS BUILDING. TO OUR FRIENDS: THANK YOU.

4:55 PM: IT HAS BEEN ONE OF THE GREAT HONORS OF MY LIFE TO BE IN THE TRENCHES WITH EVERY SINGLE ONE OF YOU FREAKS. LONG LIVE 'THE BRUDDAHS.'

13

Alex was standing in the bedroom, in between the foot of her bed and the small writing desk that she and Jamie had squeezed into the room. She was trying to clean and organize the apartment, on her best behavior as she tried to curry favor with her husband. He had barely spoken to her on Friday and was still bitter on Saturday. Sunday was almost over and the cloud of Thursday night still hung in the air over them. She was trying to simultaneously remember the details and just forget about the whole night altogether. She was pursuing both avenues with equal dedication. With no success in either direction, she just continued to walk on eggshells, waiting for the weekend to finally end.

She was mindlessly sorting through a pile of papers and junk mail when the blackberry she had tucked into the back pocket of her jeans buzzed, signaling an incoming message. Her heart skipped a beat when she saw the sender's name and the subject title. She immediately clicked on the message to open and read it.

Dick Fuld had sent an email to all of the firm's employees Sunday afternoon, September 14th, 2008. He was breaking up with 25,000 thousand people digitally; he didn't even have the decency or the balls to do it in person. The message was short. After all, there really wasn't much left to say. The firm had run out of options. Management had been unable to facilitate a sale. Lehman was finished. Bankruptcy was the only option left. Employees would be apprised of more details if and when those details became available.

Alex couldn't feel her hand even though she could see it shaking slightly, still holding the device. This was not the outcome she had been expecting. Where was the email declaring they'd be sold and saved? The panic hit her like a wave, crashing down over her head, suffocating. She yelled for Jamie, who was in the living room watching baseball, still making every effort to ignore her. No response. She swallowed her pride and walked the few short feet into the other room. She needed her husband now. She had no idea what the bankruptcy filing would mean for her yet. She had no idea how it would impact the day-to-day practicalities of her life. But this was certainly not part of her plan. She couldn't very well climb a corporate ladder without a goddamned corporation. And all of the men in her life had just talked her into delaying graduate school for another year. She thought for a moment about the academic calendar and how she could have been ten days in to a business school semester, coddled snugly in the make-believe perfect world of Harvard academia. She shook her head in disbelief. Would that one decision change the course of her future?

She wordlessly handed the device to Jamie so he could read the news for himself. He grabbed the television remote and muted the voices of the sports announcers calling the baseball game. She sank down onto the couch next to him and watched expectantly, judging his reaction by his facial expressions. He stared at the small device for a long time. He didn't say anything. He whistled softly under his breath and shook his head. Finally he looked up at her. They stared at each other in total silence.

"Did they say anything about the employees yet? Did you get any other emails?"

Alex just shook her head no. She felt a lump growing in her throat and wasn't in the mood for crying.

He took her hand and squeezed it. "It's going to be okay. Okay?"

She was still staring at him wordlessly. She tried to nod her head slightly.

"We'll figure this out. We have some money saved up if we need it, and I'll be getting my bonus from Bear, er, I mean JP Morgan in a few months. You just have to solve for one year of work before going back to school.

Who knows - maybe this is the best thing for us - for you. You've always said that you don't want to do this forever. So you have a year to do something totally different - get away from Wall Street for a while."

Alex nodded her head in agreement. She was trying to find the right words. She was so relieved at her husband's support even though she couldn't help but be a bit annoyed at his comments about leaving Wall Street. She chalked it up to his still being sour about the other night. She knew that if she challenged him things would escalate into a full-blown fight. She didn't have the strength for that now. Her mind flashed back to the first night of their honeymoon, when Bear Stearns was on the ropes. Six months later, almost to the day, she had that hopeless feeling of déjà vu.

"I can't believe this is happening to us. Again. It's happening all over again Jamie," she finally said, mournfully.

He laughed without bitterness. "We sure do know how to pick 'em," he tried to joke.

She groaned. "I wish I could laugh. This is so fucking surreal. I have no idea what to do. It feels like someone I know just died. Is that a totally fucked up thing to say?"

"No...Yes...Hell, I don't know. Why did we think these professions were a good idea again?"

He pulled her in towards him until she was nestled against his chest. He wrapped his arms around her, enveloping her in a long, hard hug. She rested her head against his body, allowing herself to be hugged.

"I'm sorry."

"I know."

"It won't happen again."

"I know."

"I promise, Jamie."

"Thank you, Alex. I really needed to hear you say that. Do you understand why I was so upset?"

She sat up so she could see him. She shook her head yes, like a little girl. She hated to be reprimanded but she knew she deserved it.

"Alex, I just love you so much. You need to understand that you are my responsibility. Do you have any idea how much I worry about you when I don't hear from you? I mean, anything could have happened..."

His voice trailed off.

"But Jamie, nothing happened."

She emphasized the word, trying to convince them both. He gave her a hard look.

"I know.   But why risk it? Do you think they really respect you more for getting so drunk?"

"But everyone was drunk," she muttered.

He did have a point. She worked too hard to earn their respect to throw it all away. She leaned back over to cuddle up against him, laying her body down on top of his.

"I really am sorry, Jamie. I won't let it happen ever again. I swear."

Jamie kissed the top of her head. They sat in silence for several minutes. Alex squeezed him tightly. She felt a tidal wave of love for him then. She hated that he had been angry with her. Alex sighed, relieved that he had forgiven her. Fuck up. Fight. Forgive. She listened to the thumping beat of his heart and felt the rhythmic rise and fall of his chest. *Yes*, she thought to herself, *this is marriage*.

As she lay there she thought about Jamie's question. *Why had they chosen these professions?* She certainly hadn't come out of the womb wanted to be a bond trader. Maybe this was a perfect opportunity for them to get out before it was too late. Get out and do what they really wanted to do. She had no fucking idea what exactly that was at this point but if both of their companies were going to go belly up then it must be some sort of sign.

"Jamie," she started slowly. "This could be the year I've always talked about."

Alex felt her way around to find the right words without looking up at her husband.

"Forget experience in another industry. I'm going to do that anyway after graduate school. Maybe you should quit your job. We can travel the world. Just think, Jamie - we could see it all. Bring nothing but one backpack each. We could get those plane tickets I read about - the ones that let you take unlimited flights for one year to destinations all over the world. We could country hop. Explore. Live. Imagine what an adventure we'd have."

She sat straight up, full of enthusiasm for her developing plan.

"We could just forget everything for a year. Come back a few months early so I could get ready for school and you could find a job. We'd be complete nomads for a year. We'd be free. Just the two of us. Wouldn't that be the most romantic thing in the world?"

Jamie paused.

"Well, it certainly wouldn't be the most practical."

She felt compelled to build her case before he could kill it.

"It would be the experience of a lifetime, Jamie. This is probably our only chance. Once we have kids we'd never be able to do anything like this."

"Okay," he said slowly. "But we just talked about trying for a baby. You didn't change your mind did you?"

Hmm. She had forgotten about that with all of the insanity at work and Jamie being so angry with her. It didn't seem like the most opportune time to have a baby. But the baby was tied to the business school part of the plan. That wouldn't happen for another eleven months. They had plenty of time.

"That's not until next year? We only agreed to practice a lot, remember?"

She gave him a playful nudge but he wasn't biting yet.

"What about our mortgage?"

"We can sublet the apartment."

"In this real estate market?"

"Sure, why not? It's a beautiful apartment. You remember how we fell in love with it right away. I'm sure we could cover our costs."

"And our car?"

"Leave it at my mom's house."

"What about the payments?"

"You just finished telling me we have money in the bank. Or we can just sell it, either way."

"Sell it?? We just bought it!"

"Who cares? Cars only depreciate in value."

He gave her a look that said 'don't lecture an investment banker about depreciation'. But he didn't pursue that angle any further.

"And then, you just want me to - quit. Just quit my job, just like that?"

Here they were again. Back to his fucking job.

"Yup. Just like that. Just do it. Let's just do it. Fuck it."

"Fuck it? By "it" do you mean the seven years of hard work and relationships that I've spent building up? Just throw it all away...to travel?"

"Well, first of all, I hardly think you'd be throwing it all away. If anything, you'd be enhancing your credentials by broadening your worldview. You can position it to people that you are taking a sabbatical. I have heard that people do it all the time."

"A sabbatical? You really think people would buy that? Please, Alex."

"If you can sell it, then yes, I do think people will buy it. This job is more about marketing and politics than finance, anyway."

"Oh, and you are suddenly the expert on Wall Street? You've barely been in the business a year."

She felt like he'd slapped her.

"Maybe not," she shot back. "But I'm an expert in not continuing to do things that would make me totally miserable. And you are beyond miserable. You haven't come home with anything good to say about work in months now. You hate everything about that place. Why not make a change? Do something drastic? Maybe it's just what we need."

He sighed.

"I don't know, Alex. Slow down, will you? It's not that I wouldn't want to do something like that. You know how much I love you. Having you all to myself for a year would be a dream come true. But we have so much responsibility right now. Not to mention you've only been unofficially unemployed for approximately thirty-five minutes. You have no idea what is actually going to happen. Let's just wait and see, okay? We don't need to make any rash decisions. Let's get all the facts first, see what they do with all of the Lehman employees, and then we'll develop a strategy. Sound like a plan, Mrs. Kramer?"

She still hadn't adjusted to being called "Mrs. Anyone". It always sounded so strange to her. She had anguished over the decision to give up her maiden name. But Jamie had been unrelenting. He had made her feel that she wouldn't be a good wife if she didn't assume his name as her own. She felt she had to do everything she could to be a good wife. So she had to give up her name. In exchange, she had talked him into the practicality of maintaining their separate pre-marital bank accounts in addition to the joint account they had opened together for show.

"Yes, Mr. Kramer," she reluctantly agreed. "I suppose I can wait at least that long."

She stared at the muted television screen. She hated to be wrong and to be chided for it, but her husband had a fair point. After all, he was the levelheaded one. She was the crazy one. *That's why we are supposed to be such a good match*, she reminded herself.

"Why don't I take you out to dinner tonight? Take your mind off of this whole mess."

Alex looked at him in shock. For the past couple of months he had been loath to spend money on a night out to dinner, especially a Sunday night. With Wall Street in disarray and their jobs hanging in the balance, Jamie felt obligated to watch every penny and to spare most expenses. If she dare shopped for clothing off her own paycheck, she hid the bags at the bottom of her side of their single closet.

"Really?" she asked tepidly.

He nodded. "Yeah. We deserve it. What was that expression you used again? Oh yes - fuck it!"

She smiled slyly at him and giggled. He sounded adorable when he cursed. It wasn't natural to him at all.

"That would be amazing, baby. I would love nothing more than to go to dinner with you tonight. Dare I call it a date? Where should we go?"

"I darn well think you should, ma'am."

You can take the boy out of Kentucky, but you can't take Kentucky out of the boy, she thought to herself, but refrained from saying aloud.

"I'm gonna go shower and get ready," she said instead, giving her husband a peck on the lips and standing up from the couch.

"But it's only five o'clock?"

"I know. I want to hurry and get ready before you change your mind."

"You are so ridiculous. I am taking my wife to dinner tonight. And that's a fact."

"Mm-hmm. I know babe. I won't be long," she called over her shoulder retreating into the bathroom and closing the door behind her.

She turned on the shower, let the room steam up, slipped off her clothes and stepped into the scalding hot water. The heavy drops felt so good as they rained down on her body. She sighed and closed her eyes. A scene from Bangkok flashed through her mind again: *their honeymoon suite at The Peninsula.* She remembered stepping out of the shower there, so exhausted but still so excited to be on this grand adventure she had planned with her new husband. Then, walking out into the bedroom and seeing Jamie's crestfallen face, defeated as he had received the news about his firm going under. That moment had changed their whole trip. She reflected. It had really changed Jamie. Maybe it had even changed their whole relationship. Images of the past six months snapped through her head. Panic. Fear. Frustration. Disappointment. Hope. And again. Panic. Fear. Frustration. Disappointment. Hope. Disappointment again. They had asked their realtor to come in again to evaluate whether or not they should consider selling their apartment even though they'd owned it less than a year. Weekend adventures meant trips to her mother's house on Saturdays followed by a rendezvous at the nearby Costco on Sundays. They ate out on rare occasion. She tried to cook a few times, which had made for some laughs. They had visited his family in Kentucky. She had stretched their budget for a trip out to the vineyards in Napa Valley. On most weeknights they sat on the living room couch and watched TV. She started to lose touch with several of her still-single friends. They spent more time with couples, mostly Jamie's other married friends. They barely ever fucked anymore, but made love quietly two nights a week. They were living a married life, cautiously, quietly, anonymously, and slightly on edge. Jamie's newfound dissatisfaction and disillusion with work weighed on them. Or at least it weighed on her. She wondered what would happen now. *Fucking goddamnit*, she silently cursed. *How was this happening to Lehman of all places? How was this happening to her?*

Jamie opened the bathroom door, jolting her out of her thoughts.

"I've been calling your name for five minutes. You okay in here? I was getting worried."

"I'm in the shower, silly. You sound like my mom. I can't hear you in here with the water running."

"Your phone is buzzing and ringing off the hook. It's beeping with new emails every thirty seconds."

He paused.

"And it looks like you have a handful of text messages too."

Alex turned the shower off. "Who were the texts from?"

"I don't know. I didn't check."

He's lying, she thought. *Why is he lying?* She held her hand out for a towel. He passed it to her without a word. She dried herself quickly and then wrapped the towel around herself. She whipped the shower curtain to the left, pushing it aside so she could see Jamie. He was standing casually in the doorway, arms crossed.

"Baby, why are you being such a weirdo?"

"I think I'm being perfectly normal," he said very casually.

She ignored the extra emphasis in his words.

"Good. Well, I appreciate your concern for my ability to successfully take a shower without hurting myself," she said mockingly. "Now, where are we going to dinner?" she asked as she stepped past him to go get dressed.

"I'll let you choose. Anywhere you want."

"Hmmm, let me think." She bought some time while eying the room for her blackberry. She found it lying face down on the bed, which was not where she remembered leaving it a few minutes before. There was a flood of new messages in her inbox. She scrolled down to the first one. Clarke had sent a message that all of the traders should come in to work immediately. The email thread that followed was a combination of responses to Clarke and reactions to the email from Fuld.

A text from Greg popped up on her screen. "Where are you? We are all here."

She clicked on the message to respond and saw that there were four other messages from him in the past ten minutes.

"Are you okay?"

"Just tried calling"

"Heading to the office ...U coming?"

"We'll get through this."

Alex felt sick. Jamie had probably seen these texts. That explained his bizarre behavior in the bathroom. She had nothing to hide, she reasoned to herself. They were just colleagues. But she knew her husband would find incrimination in those messages. Or at least he would drive himself mad trying to find something that wasn't there. Greg probably just felt guilty for convincing her to stay at Lehman instead of going back to school. He and Clarke had locked her in a corner office a few weeks before and sweet-talked her into staying, presenting Lehman as the bastion of all opportunity. They told her she'd be a fool to pass up a once in a lifetime opportunity for more unnecessary schooling. She thought about explaining all this to Jamie but she wasn't sure that would help her either. He had been convinced that their talk on the street a few months ago was the real reason why she had pushed her plans back. He thought she stayed just for them and their young marriage. Making matters worse, she actually had to go into the office immediately. Everyone was there. She had to find out what was going on. Maybe there was news about their jobs or some update about what would happen to them. Or maybe people were rushing in to clear their belongings, download their files. She couldn't be sure if the building would even be open tomorrow morning. Things were happening at that exact moment. She had to be there.

"So did you decide where you want to go yet? I'm sure you have a long list in that crazy mind of yours."

He came over and stood above her as she sat on the bed, her towel still wrapped around her.

She looked up at him and smiled, lips closed, eyes pleading.

"It looks like I actually have to go in to the office."

She placed her hand softly on his thigh. She looked at the hurt in his eyes.

"Please don't be angry. I have to go."

"Of course you do. I understand."

There was no understanding in his voice.

"Jamie don't you remember? When we were in Bangkok and Bear went up in flames. Don't you remember the panic, the way you wanted to come home, to go into the office, to get all of the details from the guys who were there?"

"But I didn't go Alex."

"Of course you didn't - we were on our honeymoon! In Thailand! It wasn't like you could just hop in a taxi and be there in five minutes."

"Yeah, that's true. But we stayed the full two weeks. I made sure we did every last little thing as planned. Do you have any idea how hard that was for me? Did you ever think of how panicked I was? Trying to make you happy on such an expensive trip and not even knowing if I was going to have a job when we got back? Every single day we were there a part of me wanted to get right on the next flight back to New York."

She didn't say anything for a minute.

"Why didn't you ever tell me that before?" she finally asked.

"I don't know. I didn't want you to feel bad or be upset. I wanted you to just be happy and not have to worry. That's what husbands do you know?" Then he added, "I just wanted our honeymoon to be everything you ever imagined it would be."

"It was the most amazing trip of my life," she said knowing it was a lie. "I'm sorry you felt that way. I didn't know."

She waited but he didn't respond.

"Will you really be upset if I go in to the office for a bit? I don't have the close friends there that you had at Bear. I - we - can't afford to miss what's going on there. Jamie, I have to be there to find out for myself what is happening. I promise I won't take more than an hour or two. I just need to be there for myself. I'll call you when I know more. We'll still go to dinner together afterwards, if that's okay?"

"I'll try and keep my dance card open."

He grinned, despite himself.

"Go. But call me. I'll be waiting."

◆ ◆ ◆

The scene unfolding on the desk was not at all what Alex had expected to see. She was shocked to see people in shorts, t-shirts, polo shirts and flip-flops. Alex was mildly embarrassed that she had come in regular work attire, modified down slightly to 'Sunday, we just filed for bankruptcy chic,' (which meant no blazer and lower heels). Some people were sitting at their desks going through documents but most were milling around the trading desk, congregated in small groups, discussing the email from Fuld. People were searching for information, grappling for answers. But no one seemed panicked. It was strange to see her colleagues at work but not working. It was even stranger that no one appeared to be freaking out or having a complete meltdown. The mood was eerily light, a sort of state of suspended animation, where most people hadn't really processed the change in their lives yet.

Alex walked over to her desk. Josh was in his seat next to hers, staring intently at some typed piece of paper he was holding.

"So this is totally fucked up."

He shook his head in disgusted agreement.

"Couldn't be worse. Could not be worse fucking timing. Fuld's gonna need some serious fucking security now. He's got twenty-five thousand people looking to put a bullet in his brain. Melanie's pregnant you know?"

Alex was taken aback. She hadn't known. She knew little about any of the wives or children or the lives in general of the people she worked with.

"Yeah, our second. She's due around Christmas. Fucking unbelievable. We'll probably end up having another girl too at the rate I'm going. That'll be just my fucking luck. I promised her she could quit her job when we had our second. Here, read this," he said abruptly, flinging the paper he had been staring at into her hands.

"What is it?" She was bewildered.

"Isn't it fucking obvious, Harvard. It's my resume."

She could not hide the shock from her face.

"We're all gonna need them now. Just read it and tell me if you think it needs any work, will you? And don't fucking show it to another soul or let anyone know what you're reading."

She was about to tell him how ridiculous he was being but the look on his face stopped her. Beneath the anger and the resentment he was petrified. The anger dug in to the creases in his face. The fear shone straight through his eyes. She picked up the paper.

"Sure, let me take a look at it. At Harvard we were practically professional resume writers. Though I'm sure you are more than qualified," she felt she had to add.

Someone somewhere on the trading floor connected an iPod up to some speakers. Music blared across the room. A crowd was forming in one corner area by some of the filing cabinets. Alex strained to see what was going on. Someone moved and she caught a glimpse of stacks of pizza boxes and what looked like cases of beer. Alex looked around the room in astonishment. For some it looked like a party. For others, a wake. Alex felt again like she was in some alternate reality. Time felt like it was passing very slowly and very quickly all at once. She was sitting there reading a resume of a guy who was at least ten years her senior while traders and salesmen ate pizza and slugged beer as music blared. *What the fuck was everyone doing? This could not get more fucked up*, she thought. It was like watching some people dance on a warm grave to alleviate the tension and the grief while other mourners wept uncontrollably just beside them.

"Alex, grab a beer. What are you so busy working on over there? Didn't you hear, we're bankrupt!"

She looked up just in time to catch a beer can that her boss had hurled at her.

"Canned beer at Lehman Brothers? Shit times are really tough."

Clarke walked over and patted her paternalistically on the shoulder.

"It's all gonna work out, kid. We just gotta wait to see what the Big Man has to say now. We fought the good fight. There's nothing we can do about any of it today, other than just drink to Lehman, that bitch."

He clinked her unopened beer can against his nearly empty one.

"Was good working with you, Harvard. See - wouldn't have mattered either way now if you'd lost me six million bucks on that stock. At least we had some laughs along the way. Now let's go, open that sucker and drink up."

She slyly shifted some papers on her desk, covering Josh's resume. Then she lifted the tab and cracked open the can. "To Lehman," she said meekly, taking the smallest sip possible.

"To Lehman!" he roared back, chugging whatever was left in his can, before heading back over to the cases to grab yet another.

"Here, sign this."

She turned to face the other junior trader.

"What it is?"

"Contact list," he said matter-of-factly, with a simple shrug of the shoulders.

He handed her the sheet and methodically pointed at each column - "Name; phone number; contact email. Make sure to list you personal email, not your work one."

She rolled her eyes at him and took the paper.

"Thank you, Captain Obvious."

Privately, she felt like a little girl on the last day of summer camp. The thought of simply never seeing so many of these people ever again suddenly hit her hard. They were the source of eighty percent of her human interaction. What was she supposed to do without them? What was she going to do every day? She felt the wave of panic setting in again.

"I need to get a job," she said aloud without meaning to.

"No shit, we all do," Greg said coming up behind them. "Contact list, huh?"

He folded his arms across his chest. He was wearing khaki shorts, a t-shirt, and flip-flops. She had never seen him dressed in anything other than work clothes before.

"So, I'm guessing trading isn't exactly shaping up like you guys thought?" he asked rhetorically, but with his boyish smile. "Well, me neither," he said before they had a chance to answer. "But just hang in there. I think we'll get more color on what's happening in the next few days, hopefully sooner."

He looked at Alex.

"And you both have been invaluable to our efforts. Clarke and I are going to shop the desk to other firms as a group, and I'll do everything I can to make sure you two are included."

"Thanks Greg," Zach said affably. "But I just don't know if I even want to do this anymore. My dad's been trying to get me to come and work for his business. With all of this happening, I'm starting to think that that might be the right direction for me. It just feels like Wall Street is falling apart."

"Look, don't make any decisions on the wire," Greg said. "It's clearly been a crazy day for all of us. Why don't you go grab us a couple of beers if there are still any left and you and I can sit down and talk about it, okay?"

Zach nodded readily and went searching for more booze.

Greg turned more privately towards Alex and lowered his voice.

"Are you okay? How are you doing? I meant what I said about trying to get you guys jobs with us at the next firm."

"Thanks, I'm okay I guess. Just taking it all in. This is pretty insane."

"Yeah, I thought you might be taking it kind of hard. That's why I sent you those text messages. Did you get them?"

"My husband did."

"Ouch, sorry about that," Greg mindlessly ran his hand through his hair. "Was he pissed?"

"He's still worked up about Thursday night. It's driving me nuts. I was a schmuck for getting so wasted but I don't even remember what happened. Total black out after a certain point. He's so mad at me and I don't even know if I had a good time or not!"

Greg stared at her intently, searching.

"You don't remember Thursday night?"

"Well, I remember Nanni's and Sparks. But total black hole after that. Next thing I knew I was late for work Friday with a splitting headache, a bruised ego, and a standing ovation from you guys. Thank you for that, by the way."

"If you wanna run with the big boys…"

"I know, I know. Please not another lecture. Bobby already gave me one Friday morning. He was very serious about it too."

"He was? Why do you think he was so serious?"

Greg looked serious himself now.

"Don't know. I was still drunk when he was lecturing me I think. It's all sort of a blur. Were you there when I was a disaster? I'm so embarrassed. Did I do anything extraordinarily stupid?"

"You don't remember anything?" Greg asked again.

"Christ. No. Just tell me, what was it? How bad was it?"

He stood silently, seeming to weigh his response. After another long, pregnant pause he finally said, "Don't beat yourself up. You really weren't that bad. I dropped you off in a cab on my way uptown to make sure you got home safely."

"*You did?*"

Alex was shocked. She strained her memory for an image of a taxi ride. Nothing. She must have been completely intoxicated if she needed a taxi and an escort to go just a few short blocks. She readily accepted his explanation, though, determined to close the gap on that night. Still, she thought she might just leave that detail out if her husband continued to press her for information. She hoped they could both just forget the whole episode entirely.

Zach returned with his hands full and Alex and Greg quickly fell silent.

"I figured I should grab a bunch while there was still supply," Zach explained.

"Always thinking my man."

Greg patted him on the back.

"Join us?"

He handed Alex a beer. She was still holding her barely-touched first beer.

"Sure. What the hell. What else are we gonna do right now, anyway?"

She felt her shoulders start to relax as she willed the tension out of her body. Fuck it. *May as well just enjoy myself and keep hanging on for the ride*, she thought to herself.

Just as she was reaching out to take hold of her second beer she felt her phone buzzing. She took it out of her purse and looked down at it as Jamie's name popped up on the screen.

"Hello? Where are you? Everything okay? STATUS?"

She hadn't realized that three hours had passed already. Where had the time gone? Shit. He was going to be so pissed. She fired off a quick series of guilty, overly-emotive texts.

"Yes, sorry baby!!!!!"

"things just so crazy over here!!"

"Probably just another hour or two. Sorry!!!"

"Waiting to see if any meetings with happen No new news yet:("

"I love you!!"

"Where should I meet you for dinner?"

She didn't wait for an answer before slipping the phone back into her bag. She looked up to find Greg smirking at her.

"Husband?" was all he said.

"Yup," she nodded with a knowing grin.

"Mine too," he said sympathetically.

"The wife won't stop calling. Guess I was also in the doghouse after Thursday night. Knocked over a lamp when I stumbled in and woke the kids up. Then I went to bed and left her to get them back down since I couldn't go without at least a little shut eye."

"What the fuck are we gonna do?" she asked, surprised at the mirth in her own voice.

He held up one finger motioning for her to watch and wait. Greg snapped the tab on his beer can and taking a deep breath, he shot-gunned it, downing all twelve ounces in one go. After the last swallow he looked back at her with devilish eyes.

"We're going to finish all these beers, get good and drunk on Lehman one last time. And then we're each going to go home and take them to dinner."

14

On Monday morning, Lehman Brothers had a hung-over look and a stale smell to it. The rest of the world was waking up to the news of the largest corporate bankruptcy filing in history, but inside the building, the employees already knew and now the paralysis of this new, daunting reality was setting in. Many of the men were haggard, unshaven, once again dressed in casual clothing. Others, unsure of what to do, came dressed for business as usual, in full suits and with vacant stares. It was obvious that people had drank too much, gone home later than promised, and been confronted by angry spouses who demanded answers and confused children who asked too many unanswerable questions. Nobody knew anything yet but they all still filed into work like loyal corporate soldiers waiting for instruction. That morning people greeted one another like they might at a funeral - unsure of what to say, compelled to say something, incomplete after the conversation ended, and just deflated from the overall effort of maintaining appearances.

Instead of their normal morning meeting, the traders were summoned to Ted's office for a private huddle. Ted waited until everyone had crammed into the small room and the last guy in shut the door. Arms crossed against his chest, he was dressed for business as usual, in a crisp white collared shirt and dark navy suit pants. Without clearing his throat or showing any sign of hesitation, he spoke.

"Look guys, I know you all have a ton of questions. Unfortunately I still don't have a lot of answers for you yet. I know the firm was in negotiations all weekend long, trying to find a solution, trying to sell the business, and we were close. We were damn close to getting it done. But at the last minute, I'm told Bank of America got cold feet. I don't know exactly what happened. It's mystifying really. I know the Fed's guys were heavily involved. There's talk that Goldman Sachs started to meddle. It's unclear really. We'll get more information I'm sure as the day goes on. You know that as soon as I know more, you'll all know it too. But look, we've still got a job to do and executing today is probably more important than any other day since any of us have been at the firm. We need to get our portfolio of positions off of the books immediately. It's not entirely clear yet, but we might need the proceeds to pay our salaries and our bonuses."

Several of the guys made eye contact with one another, with looks filled with skepticism and confusion. But no one said a word.

Ted continued: "Look guys, none of us expected to be here. None of thought this could ever actually happen to such a great firm. But here we are. And we have to fucking deal with it right here, right now. If you are standing in this room then I already know you've got balls of steel and if you don't and you've somehow been sneaking along all this time without anyone noticing then hurry up and fucking grow a pair since we're all gonna need them. I want the books liquidated as quickly and as calmly as possible. Leverage your client relationships. Guys are going to know they're getting serious bargains from us today. So let's handle the task at hand because our livelihood could very well depend on it. We'll go from there. Like I said, when I know more, you'll know more." He paused, running one hand over his bald head to wipe away invisible beads of perspiration. "We all have nothing to be ashamed of. We work at one of the greatest firms on earth and we did our jobs damn well. Best in class. We just got fucked. Caught with our pants down - wrong place, wrong time. That doesn't mean we did anything wrong. We just got fucked. Go do what we're here to do today and don't let anyone tell you any different. Everyone clear?"

"Are we still getting paid this week or are our paychecks just going to stop?"

The question on everyone's mind came from Josh.

"Because I need some fucking answers before you can just tell us to march out there and be the best we can fucking be for this fucking firm," he continued, his voices rising. "This place is bankrupt for fuck's sake! Do I have a paycheck? How about healthcare? Are we getting severance packages? Our stock's obviously a fucking donut. I've got a kid, a pregnant wife, fucking bills and commitments up the ass, and this job is all I've ever done. It's all I fucking know how to do. Don't tell me to grow a pair of fucking balls Ted when I don't know if you even have a heart anymore."

He exhaled, his face now flushed in a deep crimson color. Nobody moved. Alex's eyes were wide.

"Josh, calm down," Ted replied coolly. "We're all in the same place. We've all worked together for a long time here. We've all got the same commitments, obligations, fucking fears and concerns. You think I wanted to come in here this morning and give a 'rally the troops speech'? C'mon, you fucking know me better than that. I'm just trying to keep things organized and keep everyone as calm as possible until we figure this out."

He looked around the room, taking stock.

"Guys I know we're all feeling it. Josh was just the only one to fucking stick his neck out there and say it out loud. I wish I had more answers already but I don't. I'm not trying to feed you a bunch of bullshit. I'm just telling you what I know and what I was told to do. So let's just all try to do the best we can today, okay?"

All people could really seem to muster in response were a few grunts, mumbles and nods. Everyone looked exhausted. They were drained and the day hadn't even begun yet. As they filed out of the office many of the other employees on the floor turned to stare at them. Alex guessed that they were trying to read their faces, their body language for some sort of hint or clue that would reveal their collective fate. Traders always had information first. That's how a trading desk worked. That's how they controlled the flow.

Alex thought back to the atmosphere on the floor Friday afternoon. It had only been three days ago but already she felt like it had been in another lifetime, perhaps even on a different planet. Almost overnight the bravado had transformed into disbelief, the defiance into a state of sullen disdain. But even through this haze, people started to rally and the trading floor burst to life again. Alex wondered what was driving everyone to action - belief in the company, disbelief in their new reality, self-interest, or common interest? Or were they all just propelled forward by pure muscle-memory? Trading and selling was all they knew how to do. Rather than thinking, feeling, processing, or attempting to comprehend what would happen next, they just tuned out all of the madness and they did the only thing they could do without thinking. They traded.

For an instant, it felt like just another day on the trading floor at Lehman Brothers. Dozens of phones rang in unison. The whole floor was abuzz with activity and conversation. Salespeople and traders were standing, engaged in animated negotiations.

"I sell." "I sell." "I sell."

"You're done." "You're done." "You're done."

This exchange continued for nearly three hours as the group sold off the desks positions to eager - though suspecting and confused - clients. They worked until there was almost nothing left to sell.

The activity stopped more or less as abruptly as it had started. When it stopped, the distraction was gone too. People looked around at one another and at the trading floor like they were surveying the scene of a crime, sizing up their co-conspirators to determine if there were any rats among them. Secretly they knew that all of the effort they had just expended didn't matter at all. They had merely been playing with monopoly money. Now they had to wait. They had to wait for instructions. They had to wait for information. The paralysis was torture. Here was a group of people highly addicted to the instant gratification of action, transaction, and access to information. With trading activity all but halted, the ever-present voices of the financial media commentators blared from the television screens.

"So what exactly are all of the employees - er, former employees - of Lehman Brothers doing right now?"

A man's nasally voice filtered through the speakers. There was a slight delay from one television to the next, causing his words to echo slightly across the vast floor.

"We'd like to think this could have been avoided, but let's not kid ourselves. Lehman has been a train wreck for months. And I don't know if the buck necessarily stops with senior management. I mean, we - the public - are really going to have to examine this story in detail. What responsibility should each of the employees of Lehman Brothers feel? This bankruptcy filing could really bring down a lot of other major players in the financial system. How many people at Lehman really have blood on their hands? We have a right to invest-"

Robinson stood up angrily, grabbed a remote controller to turn the volume off. In his fury, he simply hurled the device at the television instead. It cracked. Several people jumped. Alex inhaled sharply. An annoying hissing sound now streamed from that one television while all the others still let the news reporter drone on.

"Fuck this shit!" Robinson yelled at the broken television. "They want to see what's really going on up here. I know they're right downstairs, right outside, pussyfooting around with their microphones, like they're worth a damn. Fucking bring 'em up here! I'll show them what's really going on inside Lehman Brothers!"

One of the other traders got a grip on Robinson's shoulder and managed to steer him back down to his seat. They spoke in hushed voices, though Ike still gesticulated wildly. After several minutes of persuasive coaxing he finally seemed to relax a bit, though more than a few eyes around the floor remained focused on his desk.

Then it was eerily quiet again. People checked emails, gathered more information off of their computers, and made some phone calls - though there were fewer and fewer incoming calls as the day progressed. There was a growing sense that they were all a little bit trapped in the building, both mentally and physically.

An email arrived from Corporate. Finally. Management had been officially silent since the bankruptcy announcement email from Dick Fuld. Desperate for information, everyone hungrily devoured the contents of this new message. The email was several pages long but Alex stopped reading after the first paragraph:

YOU ARE NOW PERMITTED TO TRADE IN THE FIRM'S SECURITIES

The sentence was underscored in bold and further emphasized in all caps. The words jumped off the page, mocking its readers. Alex thought that any good will people might still have for their Mother Lehman faded into the abyss with that one sentence.

Technically, Corporate had to write it. For several days before a company reports its earnings anyone affiliated with that company is strictly prohibited from trading its stock. This blackout period saves people from the temptation of trading on what may or may not be insider information. It removes even a hint of impropriety. It is standard procedure for every public company. But for Lehman's employees, this rule meant that they had no choice but to sink along with the ship. As the stock had traded from a few dollars a share down to twenty cents all they could do was watch with restrained horror. So it was standard for management to remind employees after earnings that the blackout period was over and the trading restrictions were all lifted. But in that moment anything normal seemed completely absurd. Management looked heartless and ruthless. How could they write that without any qualifiers as if it were just another passing day? How could they present this statement so benignly? Alex only owned a minuscule amount of stock. But in that moment she hated Lehman Brothers with every fiber of her being. Judging by the growls of discontent all around her, her more seasoned colleagues were filled with unabashed rage. The desk was starting to overheat from anger.

After the email most people walked out for the day. Those few who remained sat in a stupor of dejection and melancholy. They were hollow, disenchanted men. One by one they also left early. The room emptied out. There wasn't a discernible reason to stay and see the day out. Alex sat at her desk, unsure of what to do. Only yesterday, she had felt liberated by the infinite possibilities of being forced into unemployment. She had been enrapt with the romantic vision of roaming the world with her husband

- young, free, loved and in love. Now, she felt foolish, trapped, and more than a bit frightened. In a word, she was afraid.

◆ ◆ ◆

Lehman's employees carried on in that state of suspended animation for the next two days. Then, without warning the announcement came that would change everything: Barclays, the British Investment Bank, was going to buy Lehman Brothers.

The reaction to the news cycled through people in waves of emotion: hope followed by elation followed by confusion followed by fear. Hope, elation, confusion, then fear all played on repeat. People were hopeful that the news might actually be true, elated that their careers were not now in an uncontrollable downward spiral, confused by what a Barclays takeover would actually mean for them, and of course, fearful that their jobs could be lost in an inevitable "synergistic" combination. Barclays didn't have an Equities division, but it had its own Fixed Income Trading juggernaut. It had hundreds of its own employees trading the same bonds, calling the same institutional clients, and analyzing the same companies. Attrition was going to be an inevitable, ugly side effect.

Clarke was the first to break the news to them. The Distressed and High Yield traders gathered around him. He sat casually on his desk, looking more relaxed that

Alex had ever seen him. He looked like the weight of the world had been lifted off his shoulders. His lips were upturned into a slight, smug grin as he delighted in holding information that all the others coveted so deeply.

"It's a done deal. They've been working on it non-stop since the weekend. They tried to buy us before we were forced to go under but the regulators couldn't get comfortable enough with the deal in time. So now those lucky British bastards are getting us at a fraction of the price they should be paying. But there's a deal done and that's the important part. From the conversations I've had so far I think it'll take them about thirty days to work out the details. So until then, we can breathe a little easier. But tonight, we celebrate! I'm taking everybody out for cigars!"

Alex found that she was exhausted from trying to process the roller coaster of events. Clarke seemed so nonchalant about it all. She thought it must be a facade. Only moments earlier they were all wallowing in various stages of self-pity. Now they were suddenly rescued and he just wanted them to all run off and celebrate? There were still so many questions left to answer: would they be paid in the interim? Would they have to relocate to Barclays' offices? Would any of their stock be saved? Would there be another round of layoffs to cut out excess corporate fat?

Alex ventured a question. "Who works in Distressed at Barclays? Do they have a big trading desk?"

Clarke gave her a dubious look. Then his smug grin returned.

"Just a bunch of nobodies, really. They really have only one guy there who is worth his weight. Hank Martin. Real piece of work. He runs the desk there. But it'll be our show when we get there. I'll never work for that asshole. Trust me. He'll be working for me."

Alex noticed that a few of the other guys exchanged looks with each other. *Who was Hank Martin?* She wondered to herself.

She had never heard of him but it certainly seemed that everyone else knew exactly who he was. She wondered which of the guys it would be safest to question.

Before anyone could say anything more they were all distracted by a commotion at the other end of the floor. The last time the place had stirred to life like that was earlier that summer when Dick Fuld had been down on the trading floor. Alex realized that that now felt life a lifetime ago.

"Hi, I'm Bob Diamond, CEO of Barclays Capital, for those of you who didn't already know."

His voice projected with authority over the hoot system and rang out across the entire floor. Those who hadn't been standing already rose immediately out of their seats, standing quietly and respectfully, as if the Queen of England herself were in their presence.

"It was really important for me to come here and to break the news to you personally."

Someone had the balls to jokingly yell out "you're fired!" There were a few scattered laughs. But mostly a nervous silence continued to hold the room captive.

Bob Diamond continued with his monologue, undeterred and unfazed.

"Later today, I will announce to the world that Barclays has completed a transaction to purchase the true value of this great organization - you, the employees. Our two institutions will merge and together we will create a force to be reckoned with all across the globe. If the integrity of your leadership is any measure of the integrity of your firm as a whole, then I have no doubt that this merger will be a success. I have worked closely with your President, Bart McDade, over the past four days. In fact, I have probably spent every waking hour with him and I can tell you what I think most of you already know - he is a great man, and a great leader. I want you to know that he has been fighting for each and every one of you every step of the way."

A cheer of approval swept over the entire floor. People clapped, shouted or whistled their approval. The building was restored with a little bit of self-respect, to finally hear an outsider refer to some of Lehman's management in a positive way. Throughout Diamond's speech, he never mentioned Dick Fuld once. It was as if he had been expunged from the narrative. Diamond waited for the cheers to subside before concluding:

"This is a great culture and a great firm. Together with Barclays, we are all going to make one plus one equal three. I can't tell you how excited I am about the prospects of our two great firms, merged as one."

Another roar of applause went up across the room. Alex felt tiny goose bumps tingling on her arms. Bob Diamond ceremoniously shook a few hands and then marched off of the floor with Bart McDade in tow.

While they were still within earshot, Robinson hit play on his iPod and turned it on to the hoot system. The musical introduction to *God Save The Queen* echoed across the room.

Alex laughed as she shook her head. The highs were high and the lows were fucking low. *Well, this next chapter certainly wasn't going to be boring,* she thought to herself.

15

The first thing Alex noticed was the ceiling. The ceiling was so stiflingly low. The second thing she noticed was the lighting. Even though the bulbs that lined the ceiling were florescent, they emitted a pale yellowish hue that gave the place a sickly and sterile feel. The third thing she noticed was the artwork. It looked like it had been acquired at a garage sale from someone looking to rid himself of the artistic residue of 1987. She was sure it was expensive but it made the place feel dated and cheap.

So this is Barclays, Alex thought to herself. *Ugh, gross.*

A month had passed since the Lehman bankruptcy and the subsequent Barclays acquisition. In that time, the Lehman employees partied their faces off while the Barclays employees were reportedly cowering under their desks. The guys at Lehman treated the month like a paid vacation, coming and going from the office as they pleased, if they came to work at all. Across town, the Barclays office in the MetLife Building was turning in to a ghost town too, albeit for different reasons. To make room for the new Lehman soldiers, Diamond had ordered the firing of many of his own employees.

Alex had heard that over seventy percent of their trading and sales teams had been fired. Reportedly, this guy Hank Martin and the seven he saved were the only ones left.

Since the merger had been announced she had heard a few stories about this so-called famous trader. She had always looked up to the senior guys on her desk who had trained her but they all spoke about this other trader with a strange mixture of awe, adulation, and a hint of what she thought was jealously. She had never heard of him before and now she seemed to hear nothing but his name.

It seemed that he was the most storied Distressed Bond trader on Wall Street. After seventeen years in the business, he had worked at many of the Big Banks, including Lehman Brothers, UBS, and now Barclays. He'd traded every major corporate bankruptcy everyone in the business could recall – WorldCom, Enron, Dow Corning, Kmart, and now, ironically, Lehman Brothers. Everybody knew him. Everybody said the same thing. *Greatest junk bond trader I've ever seen. Craziest motherfucker I've ever met! Did you hear about the time he - ?*

From what Alex could gather, Hank was apparently also renowned for his prowess off the desk. He partied just like he traded – with the appearance of reckless abandon while quietly maintaining complete control. Nearly everyone had a treasured story about a night out with Hank that they would tell and tell and then retell again. The stories were filled with escapades in New York, Las Vegas, Atlantic City, Miami, and Brazil, complete with movie stars, professional athletes, strip clubs, and midgets. Nothing was out of bounds for him.

Like many of the stories that emanated from his trading desk, the weight bets were legendary almost immediately after they had happened. Alex was strangely fascinated by these ridiculous weight-betting stories. They reminded her of one of the first "lessons" she had been taught: Traders bet. Because that's just what they do.

It turns out that traders can make markets on a person's weight more easily than on a risky security. Unlike the analysis required to value corporate securities, weight bets never required anyone to pause and to question annoying mathematical factors like "yield," "recovery," or "basis." Weight bets are a more carnal form of betting - all traders need to know is that there is a data point open to interpretation – and therefore they can place their wager. Instinct overtakes analysis. Bettors mentally predetermine the weights of those on the scales. Bookies determine the line or the point spread, which is used to even the odds between two teams. It doesn't matter what these random people actually weigh so much as how their weights stack up in relationship to one another. Because traders can bet on this outcome. And Traders bet. That's just what they do.

Trading volumes were light one afternoon earlier that summer, even before the Lehman bankruptcy. Hank had already amassed a tidy sum in trading profits for his firm and the desk was coasting into year-end. But traders bet. That's what they do. If Hank wasn't going to make markets on bonds, he was determined to find something else to trade.

The story going around was that it all started with one salesman who was built like a brick house. He weighed at least two hundred and sixty-five pounds but swore on his mother that he didn't weigh more than two hundred and ten. His name was Jimmy Jones. Everyone called him J.J.

Hank used to say, "My man, I will pay you $500 bucks just to get on a scale. There's no fucking chance that you weigh anything under two-fifty. You are so fat, JJ, I'm gonna have to start calling you Triple J."

It didn't take long to send an intern out to the nearest drug store to buy the first scale he could find and race back to the desk, breathless to please. Jimmy was on the scale in no time, clocking in at more than fifty pounds over his personal estimate, much to the desk's overwhelming glee. That meant $500 in Hank's pocket. It wasn't the money he cared about though; it was the prospect of a new game, something else to bet on.

Hank was feeling hot. Now the gloves came off. The weight bets began in earnest. Guys started taking odds like they were calling up their bookies. Hank stacked a bond salesman versus a bank debt salesman next with the bond salesman laying - or giving - ten pounds. Typically, a match-up was shouted across the desk to hoots, hollers and more than a few snickers.

"Who wants in?"

"I'll take a little one on that," a junior Distressed trader piped in.

"Excuse me son, you'll have to speak up," one senior trader from another desk said in a hoarse voice, mimicking a bookie who mocked novice gamblers for placing puny bets.

"Pussy!" The bank debt salesman shouted, leaning back in his swivel chair, feet up on the desk.

Laughter and a few jeers followed. (A little one was only $100 in gambling terms).

"Alright, I'll take the other side but let's make it a nickel," the head of High Yield Sales challenged to the junior trader. (A nickel meant $500). "I didn't come to work today to play against the fucking junior varsity."

The junior trader hesitated. That kind of wager pushed the limits of his bank account. Not to mention his wife was six months pregnant with their first child and was watching their small nest egg like a hawk. He typically didn't allocate funds for off-the-cuff desk shenanigans.

Here, Hank interjected, agreeing to take the other side of the bet at a nickel. He loved to bet more than anyone on the desk, but this wager wasn't about the money. With a salesman challenging one of his traders like that, now they were also gambling with the desk hierarchy. Hank protected his team of traders with ferocity. It didn't matter that the junior trader was a knucklehead – with a thick city accent, a gap between his two front teeth, and an Internet porn obsession that would have made anyone who caught him blush. He was one of Hank's. And he was protected.

One after the other, the bank debt salesman and the bond salesman ceremoniously loaded themselves onto the scale. The intern shouted out the results, much louder than was necessary, overjoyed to be able to contribute to the desk's activity. The bond salesman was fourteen pounds heavier. Hank had won. The Head of High Yield Sales threw five $100 bills in Hank's direction, disgusted. Everyone clapped.

"I can't lose!"

Hank gloated, drawing out the word "can't" with an extra beat. If he had been wearing suspenders - which he never did, though he revived the popularity of the three piece suit with uncanny ease - then he would have snapped the suspenders between his thumb and forefingers, allowing the bands to pound his chest in mannish satisfaction.

There was a momentum in the room. It was a force people couldn't stop. No one was working. Everyone was weight-betting or watching. All the guys wanted in. And with egos raging, everyone wanted a shot at the title, which meant beating Hank.

Things escalated. The wagers increased. The match-ups were more difficult to call. It was like the slow climb up a roller coaster ride; the car's gears clicked in against the metal of the track one at a time just before the car reached the top. But it hovered at the top for only a moment. Then, it went screaming downward to a combination of gleeful shouts, terrified cries, and at least one person hurling his lunch up by the time the ride stopped.

The ride stopped when Hank stacked a woman in High Yield Sales against a small Indian guy who worked on the Corporate Syndicate desk. And the saleswoman was giving six pounds. It wasn't meant as an insult to her. It's not like she was fat or anything. Well, she was no lingerie model either. She was a little on the chunky side. But that wasn't the point. It was just another bet. But the Saleswoman didn't really see it that way. Making matters worse, the best analyst on the desk was all over this match-up.

Ronny was a skilled research analyst. He was also one of Hank's guys. So he was protected. And he knew it. So he was also a total dick. Ronny was recently married and already soon-to-be-divorced. As a result, he took frequent daytime trips to the bar downstairs.

The irony on Wall Street was that the very characteristics that made Ronny such a phenomenal credit analyst also contributed to his ability to be a monster dick; he honed in on strengths and weaknesses, cut straight to the core point and he rendered his opinion quickly, instinctively and loudly. So Ronny was pretty vocal on his view that hell would freeze over sooner than the guy from Syndicate could possibly outweigh the woman from High Yield Sales. And, being the astute research analyst that he was, Ronny saw fit to "publish" his views on this bet in a Bloomberg message that he promptly blasted out to the entire desk. Now, there was a paper trail of the desk's illicit activities.

Everyone read Ronny's research and therefore the bets placed here were much larger than usual. Despite the large sums and intense scrutiny placed on this particular wager, it never materialized. Indignant, the High Yield Saleswoman flat out refused to weigh in. Once the commotion dissipated, guys reluctantly turned back to their computer screens to scroll through Bloomberg messages, track markets, and get back to the business of calling clients. When the attention finally shifted away from her, the Saleswoman sulked off to the bathroom to cry her eyes out. At least she had the common decency to leave the desk before crying. Women cannot just cry on the trading desk. No one ever forgets a woman who cries on a trading desk. No one ever respects her afterward.

Like any good Wall Street rumor, the story spread and spiraled like wildfire. The head of the department was briefed. The Human Resources department was called. Security was alerted. All signs pointed to someone getting shot. After all, every story needed a sacrificial lamb, the figurehead to take the fall.

Human Resources tried to fire Ronny.

But they couldn't get it done on Hank's watch. He got wind of it all and jumped in front of Ronny like he was taking a bullet for a brother. Determined, Human Resources sent a woman down to settle the score with Hank directly. That woman weighed about two hundred and seventy-five pounds. Well, that was a pretty fucking funny thing to do. The traders were all beside themselves – sending a fat chick down to yell at them for betting on a woman's weight – what would they think of next?

Hank began by patiently explaining to this innocuously heavy employee that no one on the desk was claiming, implying, or in any way suggesting that the High Yield Saleswoman was fat. Once he had killed her with kindness, he deftly turned the conversation into a deposition, accusing the department of failing to supervise. If they were going to try and fire Ronny, wouldn't they have to also try and fire him, since he was Ronny's direct manager? And if they fired Hank, what about the head of the department, who managed him? (The department head just might have snuck in on a little of the action too, Hank winked.) Sacrifice one and she would have to slaughter them all. Then he asked if she realized how much money he had already made for the firm that year. He knew that she knew. Everyone knew. And Hank knew that everyone cared. He had them by the balls. All he had to do was just threaten to squeeze and they'd back down.

So the weight bets were officially over. But Hank had still won. Oh, and no one from the Distressed Desk did a trade with the saleswoman's accounts ever again.

◆ ◆ ◆

The guys all told and retold the story to each other with such satisfaction and admiration. The story had stuck out in her mind and she wondered what he would be like in person. Would he be approachable enough to ask him about it directly? Maybe not on the first day, she cautioned her over- eager self. Looking around the empty floor, she tried to imagine the scene that had allegedly unfolded there.

She was having a hard time believing that such a lively story had unfolded on this lifeless trading floor. The room lacked a pulse. It barely seemed to have a heartbeat. Alex thought back to the mood on the floor at Lehman during the last round of layoffs just before the bankruptcy. Quadruple the number of people had been laid off here in the post-merger purge. And it wasn't because the bank was performing poorly. *It was to make room for us*, Alex realized. *Ugh, what a shit show.*

She scanned the cavernous room, trying to identify her new seat. She found the row where several of the Distressed traders were already seated and made her way over. Greg caught her eye and motioned to the seat next to him, a broad, boyish grin plastered on his face. When she reached their desks he indicated for her to sit and leaning closer, whispered in a voice only audible enough for her to hear:

"I moved you next to me so I could keep my eye on you; make sure you stay out of trouble with all of these new Barclays guys around."

Alex flushed and looked at him quizzically. *What the fuck is that supposed to mean?* She wondered silently.

"Good," she said aloud. "Because I plan on proving that I can trade my ass off and run with the big boys here." She exuded over-confidence.

Greg raised an eyebrow in amusement at her unusually fiery outburst. "I look forward to seeing that. Let's get to work then."

Alex bristled slightly at his suggestive tone. She decided to mentally brush aside their strange conversation, chalking it up to their new surroundings. Instead, she set about rearranging her desk area in the few small ways that would distinguish it as her own. She switched the mouse from the right to the left-hand side of her keyboard, stacked her notebooks and trade history books next to her computer monitors, and removed the framed wedding picture of herself and Jamie from her purse and placed it just behind the notebooks, trying to angle it so that it was less obvious to others than to her. She switched the computer and all the monitors on. The familiar hum of the systems loading sent a rush of nervous adrenaline through her body. They hadn't really been allowed to do much of anything over the last month; trading had all but halted while management untangled the dirty details of the bankruptcy and merger. She missed the electric rush she felt from the noise, the madness and the organized chaos of the floor. She longed for the instant gratification she experienced from trading. She felt her body tingle slightly in giddy but nervous anticipation that she would finally get her fix.

◆ ◆ ◆

Hank didn't come to work the first day that all of the Lehman employees started. He kept everyone waiting, allowing the anticipation to build around him. When Alex arrived on the second day, he was already in his seat, silently watching everyone who walked in. Alex made a mental note to arrive even earlier the next day, something she hadn't thought about since her earliest days on the trading floor. She paused for a moment to take in the image of this guy who was part man, part myth and part legend.

His hat seemed out of place. It was impossible not to notice it. He was still wearing it despite otherwise looking like he had comfortably settled into his seat some time ago. It was a tweed Irish lid that reminded her of something a 1920's gangster might have worn. Beneath the lid, Alex could see the hint of a military-style buzzed haircut. He was dressed in a purple cashmere sweater, grey slacks, and expensive-looking alligator skin loafers. He sat tapping both feet against the floor, as if he were at the starting line of a race, waiting for the gun to go off and the competition to begin. He had a hard copy of the *New York Post* newspaper open in front of him and he was making something of a spectacle of reading it, licking his forefinger and flipping the pages in an exaggerated manner. He stopped reading periodically to look up at each new person who walked through the door and size them up without betraying so much as a hint as to what he was really thinking. Her eyes caught his momentarily and she quickly looked away - down, up, anywhere but back at him. She hurried silently over to her chair, a few seats down, opposite Hank Martin. She felt him staring at her as she moved, though she dared not look up at him again.

Lindsey summoned all of the traders for their morning meeting, trying to create a post-merger semblance of normalcy. Everyone filed off the desk and into a conference room to figure out how to best get back to business. Hank stayed in his seat. He gave no indication that he planned on joining the meeting. Apparently, he would wait for them all to come to him. To Alex's surprise, they did. The meeting didn't last long since most of the traders had not had any material client interaction in nearly a month. The guys all wanted to get back out there, feel the pulse of the market, get back in on the action. As they all shuffled out of the conference room Alex noticed that the trading floor was much livelier than before. Hank was standing by his seat, holding a phone to his ear with his hand over the receiver so the client presumably couldn't hear him. Several sales people were standing, also jabbering into phones or talking animatedly to each other.

"How many you got? I'm open on twenty-five to fifty million," he shouted in the direction of one salesman - Alex couldn't tell which one.

"Fifty million!" Two voices shouted back at the same time.

Hank looked from one salesman to the other. They in turn both looked at each other with competitive death stares, intent on being the one who got his client's order executed.

"You're done. I buy." Hank said loudly, with authority.

One salesman looked at him in total confusion. "Which one of us?" he asked.

"Both. I'll take 'em all. One hundred million."

Hank waved his hand as if to gesture the bonds in towards him. Then he whispered something into the phone before turning back to the sales desk.

"Well, don't just fucking stand there. You clowns look like you haven't traded bonds in a while. Little rusty from the Lehman vacation? How does that leave you? Do either of you have more to sell?"

Another hundred and fifty million bonds traded all in a flurry in the next few minutes. Hank lowered his voice back to a normal decibel level and removed his hand from covering the receiver so he could converse freely with the client on the other end. When several of the other traders were back within earshot as they approached their own desks, Alex heard him say,

"Yeah, of course. You got it. Anything for you. So we're done on two hundred and fifty million Lehman bonds. I'm selling them to you at $15."

He was talking to the client but the whole time he never took his eyes off of the Lehman traders, staring them down as if in a duel, even though he had already clearly fired the first shot.

Alex was dumbstruck. She had never seen so many bonds traded so quickly and so deftly. She also kept stealing glances at all of the other traders to see how they were reacting. These were the same bonds that had been trading at eighty cents on the dollar on that day right before Lehman had filed for bankruptcy. Alex couldn't believe that she had lost track of the market so completely over the last month. But even more to the point, she couldn't believe that Lehman's bonds were trading at only fifteen cents on the dollar! With the bonds trading at such depressed prices, it must have only served as a reminder to the senior traders that their stock was worthless, with the equity value completed eviscerated.

But to Alex's amazement the guys all seemed to shrug it off. They too seemed to be more focused on the show-stopping display of trading. In succession, they approached Hank to say hello with a handshake, a slap on the back or a little story to remind him of their mutual connections. Hank stood patiently, shaking hands and making small talk, holding court.

"Hey man, showing off already?"

Clarke asked affably with a wink and a friendly but firmer than necessary slap on the back.

"Just getting warmed up."

Hank replied with a thin smile, deliberately crossing his arms across his chest.

"We missed you in the meeting in there."

"I'm not a meeting kind of guy."

"I hear you, brother."

Clarke slapped Hank on the back again.

"Let's get to it then."

He cracked his knuckles, took his seat next to Hank and loosened his tie.

Hank seemed to hold back a snort of amusement.

"I'll take a lap then and give you some time to catch up. I'm up five million bucks from that trade."

Hank sauntered over to the rows where the salesmen sat. He commended the men who had just executed all of the large Lehman trades with him only moments before. He joked with them and laughed a deep, deliberate belly laugh that rang out across the trading floor. Only moments before he had been consumed with intensity, fire and deep concentration. His eyes had blazed directly at the salesmen, his presence commanding the attention of the entire room. But now, as if executing a scene change, his temperament appeared completely altered. Those same salesmen and all those around him were now laughing heartily, mesmerized and hanging on his every word. Alex wondered in amazement how he could turn the intensity on and off like the flick of a switch. She had never seen any of the other traders execute such extreme mental control over the sales force.

As she pondered the scenes she had just witnessed she fell lost in thought, momentarily losing track of her surroundings. When she looked up and back over to the sales row Hank was no longer there.

"Not planning on introducing yourself?"

Alex turned, startled, to find Hank Martin standing right behind her.

He waited.

Alex silently prayed that she wasn't actually gaping at him.

"I'm Hank," he finally said, extending his hand. His voice was gruff, his handshake was firm.

"Um, Alexandra. I'm Alex Kramer," she finally managed.

Alex had a much clearer view of him now. He looked vaguely familiar. *Have we met?* She silently wondered. She didn't have the balls to ask.

"What do you do? Trading assistant?"

Alex bristled at the question, taking offense and consequently regaining her composure immediately.

"No. I'm a trader. No assistant. Just a trader," she said firmly.

Where have I met him? He looks so goddamned familiar. She racked her brain but couldn't place it.

Hank's lips twitched as he tried to avoid smiling.

"A trader?"

He repeated her words, a hint of intrigue in his voice. "Interesting."

His eyes wandered across her desk, her twelve inches of personal space and then back over to her. He took his time surveying the scene. His eyes betrayed nothing. She suddenly felt so awkward. He reached out to shake her hand again.

"Good to meet you, Alex Kramer, bond trader. Make sure you pay close attention if you want to become a real trader and not just one of these guys." He pointed his thumb over his back at the Lehman guys.

She stood this time to shake his hand once again. Speechless, she simply nodded her head in affirmation.

"Good." He stared at her intently. "Lesson number one" he started, leaning in closer to her and lowering his voice. Then he whispered in her ear:

"Leave your wedding picture at home. It's a sign of weakness you can't afford to betray here. Any chinks in the armor get used against you. And that," he tilted his head towards the framed photograph, "is a gaping fucking hole."

16

She felt the nervous, electric energy from the crowd rubbing off on her. There was anticipation in the air. She felt the tiny goose bumps tingling across her entire body. Dawn was breaking over Washington, D.C.

Thousands of runners strode purposefully towards the starting line. The powerful outline of the Pentagon was painted against the sky. United States Marines were positioned throughout the area, giving instructions and providing directions.

Jamie took Alex's hand confidently in his own and guided her through the masses.

"Don't worry, muffin. You're going to do great. Just remember everything I taught you. Breathe. Focus. Stretch. Stay loose. Pace yourself."

He was full of instructions for her.

"Remember, the expression 'it's a marathon, not a sprint' is used for a reason."

He chuckled knowingly.

"I'll be waiting for you at the finish line."

He leaned in to give her a light kiss on the lips and then he jogged off to find his spot further ahead, closer to the starting line.

Then Alex was alone. She was surrounded by thousands of strangers. But she was alone. What a strange sport. She and Jamie had flown in to the capital to race in the Marine Corps Marathon. Well, to be exact, Jamie was racing; she was just running. A few months before, Jamie had tepidly asked her if she would be interested in running a marathon with him. She had mixed feelings about it but when she saw the expectant, hopeful look on his face she had said yes immediately. It seemed that running was the only activity that brought her husband any joy lately. It was the only thing that seemed to boost his confidence and raise his spirits. It was the one time of the day when he wasn't in a dismal, semi-catatonic funk. Alex desperately wanted to see that side of him again - the confident, youthful exuberance that she had always found so attractive. She saw glimmers of it when he ran or trained for a race. She wanted so desperately to reach inside of him and pry that capability back out of him, externalize what she was sure was still there somewhere. When Bear fell, he stumbled. But she still believed he could get back up. He had to. He had to do it for them. She believed he would do it for her.

So she had agreed to run with him. She had never been a runner before. But, she reasoned with herself, completing a marathon would be such an accomplishment. She could check that box. And she assumed that it would help them spend time together, doing something that Jamie really enjoyed and poured his heart into. To Alex, that was marriage. Compromise. Doing things she didn't otherwise want to do solely because it made her husband happy.

It was something special they were going to do together. But here she was alone. Well, it's important to Jamie that he registers a good, fast, strong time, she reminded herself. *But why?* There was that little voice. It questioned him now from time to time. It's not like he was running to win the fucking race. She had trained because it was important to him. Why wouldn't he just run this one race a little slower than usual so that he could run it with her? He had run so many; did this one really matter? What did he have to prove? It makes him feel good about himself, Alex reminded herself for the hundredth time. He could use the ego boost these days. She thought about the comments that Hank Martin had made to her at work. He had overheard her talking to Clarke and Greg about her upcoming race. They had been complimenting her, extolling her for what an accomplishment it would be. Joining the conversation, Hank had offered up his opinion:

"Marathons are bullshit," he scoffed. "What are you really running for? What are you running towards? Where is it going to get you? I'll tell you where: nowhere. Marathons are just puff pieces. Bullshit races that mean nothing. They just fluff the egos of people who don't have anything else going on. It's for people who think they want to compete but don't think they'd ever actually win."

She had been so taken aback. Her face turned bright red. What could she say? She scrambled to think. Finally, "well, have you ever run one?"

He paused, leaning back in his chair. He studied her long and hard. For a minute, he was completely silent. A slow smile spread across his lips. He finally responded.

"Yes. I ran one. A very long time ago."

He was ignoring Clarke and Greg entirely. He just stared straight at her.

"Good luck, kid. Let me know how it goes. We'll compare notes."

The shotgun sounded and they were off. Alex felt a rush of adrenaline carrying her. She fell into an automatic rhythm, benchmarking her pace against the strangers all around her. She ran through the picturesque suburbs of Arlington, Virginia just outside Washington, gaping at the sprawling homes she passed, wondering about the lives of the strangers behind their doors. After a few miles, the runners crossed a bridge over the Potomac. The early morning sunlight glinted off of the late fall foliage, making the leaves on the trees look like they were polished in exquisite shades of bronze and copper. Alex lost herself in the beauty of her surroundings. She just breathed in this world around her.

Inhale. Exhale. Inhale. Exhale.

She felt the crisp air as she sucked it in through her nose and pushed it back out of her lungs, through her mouth.

Inhale. Exhale. Inhale. Exhale.

She concentrated on her breathing, just like Jamie had taught her. She mindlessly grabbed a cup of water from an anonymous, outstretched arm at a water station, gulping it down without pausing.

Inhale. Exhale. Inhale. Exhale.

She fell into a rhythm, head down, watching her feet pound against the pavement, running to the beat of the music that blared through her headphones.

Inhale. Exhale. Inhale. Exhale.

She looked up and looked around. Surprised, she saw the mile marker demarcating Mile 13. *Halfway there already*, she thought. Wow. She had completely lost track of time. She picked up the pace, a little extra bounce in her step. Alex couldn't remember the last time she had lost track of time like that. She never operated on autopilot. She always made a conscientious effort to control all her actions. She never just let herself go. It was too risky. She was always thinking. She was always running.

What are you really running for? What are you running towards?

His words echoed through her head again. Why couldn't she shake those questions? They had pierced some part of her. She couldn't tell where.

She was in the heart of the capital now, pushing her way past the famed Washington Monument. The crowd of supporters was dense, with family, friends, and spectators packed four or five deep, cheering the runners on, encouraging them to press ahead. Alex felt another rush of adrenaline, motivated by these strangers to press on, to keep running.

What are you really running for? What are you running towards?

She thought about the last time she had been in Washington; sophomore summer of college she had lived in the city while working for a Senator. Back then she had still believed that politicians could change the world and that Washington could shape the course of history. She imagined a gilded city, filled with men and women driven by noble causes who stopped for nothing until they changed the world. She followed the senior statesmen around the Senate buildings on Capitol Hill, awestruck, hoping to get a glimpse at the true men behind the proverbial political curtain.

Much to her chagrin, Alex got her glimpse. Washington was slow, petty, bureaucratic, and archaic in its practices. It's guardians we're not puritanical, saintly noblemen. They were just men. They were just like everyone else. Alex remembered her disappointment, her disillusionment. She experienced a pang of sadness. The magical city of her idealistic childhood imagination fell from grace as she grew up and saw the realities of adulthood. She had made up her mind that summer: she would never work in Washington. Instead, she would go to Wall Street. At least there, people gave no pretense of creating Camelot.

What are you really running for? What are you running towards?

"Alex!! Alex!! Alex! Look over here!!"

The sound of someone calling her name pulled Alex out of her own head. She looked out at the crowd, confused. She only saw a sea of strange faces.

"Alex!!!" Waving hands and arms. Suddenly two familiar faces came into view up ahead. Jamie's dad was waving at her, smiling and cheering enthusiastically. His girlfriend stood beside him, calling out Alex's and jumping up and down with equal enthusiasm.

"Woot Woot! Go Alex, go! You can do it!"

Alex smiled and waved as she approached. *What is marathon etiquette?* She wondered to herself. *Was she supposed to stop?* She didn't want to lose her momentum. She wanted to keep running. As she approached they got more excited. No, she wouldn't stop. She waved to them to acknowledge that she had seen them. When she was a few feet away, she waved her arms in a little victorious fist pump, like a boxer at the end of a winning match.

"Alex!! Great job!! We're so proud of you!!"

Jamie's dad put his hands out, presumably to hug her. She didn't want to stop running. Instead, she reached one hand out and awkwardly gave the older Kramer a high-five. She shouted her thanks, too, focused on her marathon breathing to say more, and then she continued running.

Continuing her pace, she turned to look back at them. Their faces had a small, crestfallen look to them. She turned away, looking ahead once again. She wondered where Jamie was on the course. She figured he might even be done already. She hoped he had seen his dad too. She expected that that would have made him happy.

Jamie had had another epic brawl with his mother about the marathon. She had tried to insist that she would come to see him run this race. She argued that his father had been to all the others and it was her turn this time. She had stomped her feet and pouted like an adolescent, even crying a little. By now, Alex had become accustomed to her mother-in-law's temper tantrums. Alex just tried her best to tune them out and to pretend that they weren't a part of her new reality, of her new family.

What are you really running for? What are you running towards?

She looked up and saw the mile marker for Mile 25. Wow. Almost done. Alex couldn't believe it. She was actually proud of herself. She had another solid box to check. She looked around and saw that many runners had slowed to a walking pace. Several looked exhausted, panting, hands on hips. A handful had stopped all together to take a little break, overcome. They were all so close. Alex wouldn't slow down. She wouldn't walk. She wouldn't stop. She had to finish strong. She had to finish running.

What are you really running for? What are you running towards?

Alex could hear the cheers get louder. She turned the corner of the street she was on and a huge mass of spectators, family, friends, and fans came into view. The roar of the crowd was deafening. She pushed on. She could see the finish line now. She couldn't even feel her feet or her legs. They just carried her body over the finish line. Finally, it was over. She slowed her pace and came to a full stop. Suddenly, she was overcome with a wave of mixed emotions. Inexplicably, she wanted to cry. She shook her head from side to side, as if to shake the thought, and began walking slowly - to where? She didn't know. Now that she had stopped she realized how much her legs, her, feet, her arms, her whole body was fucking killing her. She heard someone call her name. Looking around, she spotted Jamie standing next to her dad. They were both smiling at her and waving, Jamie wrapped in a post-marathon foil to keep him warm. Somehow she found the energy to run over to them. She reached the pair and grabbed her dad to hug him. Again, she felt like crying for no reason.

Her father looked at her expectantly.

"Well, how was it, dear?"

She released her dad from her embrace and stood back, looking up at him.

"Dad, that was the stupidest fucking thing I have ever done in my life."

He looked at her, eyes widening, a belly laugh escaping from within him.

Jamie reached around to grab his wife.

"I'm so proud of you, muffin! Great job! See, we did it!"

He was so enthusiastic.

"I think we should keep doing these together. I'm going to sign us up for the Miami one next month, what do you say?"

What are you really running for? What are you running towards?

She smiled lightly at her husband, exhausted.

"Sure, baby, let's do it."

17

"Alex. Are you busy right now?"

She turned to look at him and shook her head no.

"Good. Take a walk with me."

His questions never sounded like questions. She stood nervously and followed Hank off the trading floor, out towards the elevator bank.

"Where are we going?"

She was so curious. She clasped her hands together in front of her, like a schoolgirl. She didn't want to fidget.

He was nonchalant.

"Just for a walk. Maybe we'll grab a coffee. Do you drink coffee?"

She nodded yes. Why couldn't she answer even the stupidest of questions around him? She chided herself. *There's no reason to be so tongue-tied, Alex. Stop being such a moron.*

"So how you been? Alex Kramer, Bond Trader. You learning a trick or two on this desk?"

Tricks? She hadn't learned any tricks. Had she? She couldn't be sure.

Just answer the fucking questions, Alex. Real traders can't get nervous over fucking basic questions. They have to bet, to act and to react. They don't turn red-faced and get their panties all tied up in a bunch. You are a trader, she coached herself.

She nodded her head yes. Swallowing, she forced the words out:

"I like it. I mean - I love trading. And the place -" she shrugged her shoulders. "You know, Barclays is okay I guess. It's not the best environment, but I am happy I am getting to trade a little more. And I'm learning a lot."

Before she could stop herself she added, "especially from you."

All Hank ever wanted to do was to win. He was tenacious. He was electric. He was unrelenting. He made it all seem effortless – like the world just came to him.

He paused to look at her. *How come he always looked at her like that? She wondered not for the first time.*

"Barclays is a fucking mess, Alex. Too much politics. Not enough trading. Those clowns don't really get it. They're missing the bigger picture."

He looked at her again, like *that*.

"Something tells me you get it."

Then he was silent again.

Alex didn't know what to say. She was flattered, shocked, embarrassed, excited. It was early February and the employees of the two firms had worked together for a few months now. But they didn't *really* work together. Hank and his guys stuck to themselves. There seemed to be no love lost between the two groups. Alex felt torn. She thought that she owed an allegiance to the Lehman traders, the ones who had raised her. But there was something about Hank and his group. They carried themselves differently. She could tell they had some sort of secret sauce. She just couldn't put her finger on it. But she knew she wanted badly to taste it. They were tight knit. They were really friends, not merely colleagues.

"I'm going to give you some of the bonds in my book to trade.

He looked at her and waited for her to react. When she didn't respond, he continued:

"If you think you can handle that."

Alex was stunned into total silence.

"Don't look so surprised. I've been watching you on the desk. I see what you are capable of. Those clowns aren't giving you a fair shot. You think you are a trader. But they treat you like a fucking assistant."

His voice had a bitter edge.

"You deserve a fair shot. A couple things might change around here soon. I wanted you to take these bonds before they do."

He paused to look at her again.

"Either of your parents ever work on Wall Street?" he asked.

She shook her head no, again wordlessly.

"Good. First generation. That'll keep you hungry. Stay hungry, Harvard. Life doesn't come to you on a silver fucking platter. You've got to bring your own food and then go find your own fucking fork."

"I don't know what to say, Hank. Thank you?"

Alex felt like a schmuck but she didn't know what else to say.

"Don't thank me yet. You've gotta do something with it first."

Alex looked at him, more than a little confused.

"Do you want me to take the positions too?" she asked, worried. When Clarke had given her a few small names to trade when they were back at Lehman, he had also saddled her - unbeknownst to her- with shitty exposure that caused her to lose half a million bucks almost out of the gate.

Hank looked at her pointedly. He made no effort to hide the offense he took to the question.

"Who the fuck do you think I am?" he nearly growled. "I'm not one of them, Alex. I'm not like them at all." He stared at her fixedly.

"Oh, no, Hank, that's not what I meant at all! I'm sorry,"

The last thing she ever wanted to do was offend Hank Martin in any way. The man, the myth, the legend.

"Thank you. I really mean it more than you know. Thank you!" she said again. "Do you have any, um, advice?"

"Yes," without skipping a beat.

"Traders bet," he said simply. "That's just what we do." He let his words sink in. "You can't be afraid to bet. Just look around, all the time. The other players at the table, the dealer, they're just as important as the cards in your hand."

She was silent for a long time. She turned his words over in her mind. Many of the legendary stories about Hank Martin revolved around his rumored excessive gambling habits. Hearing this, Alex started to wonder if there was more to know about Hank than met the eye.

He watched her think. "Let's get back upstairs. They're going to wonder what we are doing gone for so long. I don't give a fuck but you still have to be mindful of them. At least for right now."

Alex wondered what he meant by that. She nodded her agreement though. This time she was purposely silent, digesting everything he had said.

"I'm taking my guys out to meet some clients tonight. I'd like for you to come."

Alex forced a confident response. "I'd love to. Thanks for thinking of me."

This time it was Hank who nodded his head wordlessly, smiling. "Eight o'clock at Smith & Wollensky's. Do you know where it is?"

"Of course. I actually live right across the street," she slipped.

Alex regretted her response from the moment the words escaped her lips. She had violated rule number one, disclosing too much personal information. She had been on her guard about that ever since Hank had given her that introductory lecture. But he was so goddamned disarming. She barely spoke around him for fear of what she might say. She wondered how he even thought highly enough of her to give her these bonds in the first place.

"Well that's good to know."

Alex couldn't tell if he was mocking her or not. *Ugh, why did she even care if he knew where she lived?*

"I'm at the bar there almost every night. We're practically neighbors then." He smirked. "Stop by for a drink anytime."

Alex didn't know how to respond. By now they were already back at the elevator bank leading up to the trading floor. They stepped into the vestibule and Hank hit the button for their stop. With no one else in site, Alex couldn't avoid making eye contact.

"Well, um, thanks for the coffee." She clutched the steaming hot Starbucks paper cup with two hands.

Hank raised an eyebrow at her in amusement. Alex caught herself.

"Oh, and of course thank you so much for the trading book. It's an extraordinary opportunity. I promise I won't let you down."

Hank simply nodded. The elevator doors opened and he held the door for her to pass through first. As she exited he put his hand on her shoulder, squeezing it slightly.

"Knock 'em dead, kid."

She felt a shiver run down her spine.

◆ ◆ ◆

Smith & Wollensky's hadn't changed at all since the last Alex had been there with Jamie. The steakhouse was packed with patrons. The bartenders operated efficiently in their posts, serving up drink after drink to boisterous clients. Waiters hustled around the room, serving course after succulent course.

The place hadn't changed but the experience was completely different when traveling with Hank.

Each person from the maître di to the busboy fell all over himself to accommodate him. Hank rewarded each one with a handshake, where he slyly slipped them all hundred-dollar bills.

It took their group longer than necessary to make their way over to the bar because so many people stopped Hank to say hello. From where she stood Alex could see Manny behind the bar. She waved to try and catch his attention. Finally, he looked up. When he recognized the group, he immediately excused himself from the customers he was serving and rushed over to the group.

"Hi Man—"Alex began, proud that he had recognized her.

Ignoring Alex, Manny made a beeline for Hank. He threw his arms around the trader, pushing a few others aside. Alex quickly clammed up, her face brightening from embarrassment. She quickly surveyed the others to see if they had noticed her slip. No one seemed to be giving her presence a second thought.

"Hank! How ya doing buddy? It's nice to see ya again!"

Hank gave Manny an avuncular pat on the back. "I was just in here last night, Manny."

"Ah, heck, I know that. But you know this place isn't the same without you."

"In my experience, no place is." Hank grinned. He shook Manny's hand, slipping him a hundred dollar bill.

"Who you got with you tonight? What can I get you guys to drink? The usual?"

"Yeah – usual crowd, usual drink." Hank gestured to the group. "Can't teach old dogs new tricks, Manny."

Manny noticed Alex then. "And who's this lucky lady? Your girlfriend?"

Alex blushed fiercely. "Hi Manny," she said quietly.

"Oh my gosh!" Manny slapped himself on the forehead like a cartoon character. "Alex is that you honey? Jeez. I didn't even recognize you. I'm sorry honey. It's nice to see you again! You're looking more beautiful than ever."

"Yes, it's like staring at the sun."

She turned to look at Hank, her eyes widening. She was scared to even imagine how red her face must be.

"I'm not his girlfriend, Manny. Hank and I just work together, that's all."

"Oh, of course honey. I shoulda known. I just didn't recognize you at first. How is that man of yours doing? I haven't seen you two in here in a while."

"Yeah, neither have I."

Alex looked at Hank, confused.

"What do you mean?"

"Well, I'm assuming that was your husband you were making out with over at the bar here last summer wasn't it?"

Alex racked her brain. What the hell was he talking about? Last summer? She'd only met Hank in October.

"The girl looks like she needs a drink, Manny. Why don't you go grab us a couple?" Manny took the hint. "You got it, boss. Coming right up."

Hank turned to Alex, so his back was to the rest of the group.

"I saw you that night. I was here with clients. You were standing right over there."

He pointed to a spot across the bar, where Alex and Jamie had in fact been carrying on.

"It dawned on me when I saw that ridiculous wedding picture you keep on your desk. It's hard to forget a face like yours – especially when you're with such a scrawny looking punk. He must be great in the sack. At least, I hope so for your sake."

Alex's head was spinning. Hank kept going.

"I still don't know why you keep that fucking picture on your desk. Didn't I tell you? It's a sign of weakness. One of you must be insecure. Let me guess – he asked you to put the picture up at work? He's not respecting you, Alex. He's just pissing on his territory."

Alex blushed. Her cheeks burned.

"I love my husband, Hank."

The statement came out sounding defensive.

Hank brandished a devilish smile.

"I do!" Alex insisted.

Hank shrugged nonchalantly.

"I never said you didn't. You're the one who seems to feel the need to justify yourself."

Alex stuttered. "I don't know how we even started talking about this."

Manny returned with their drinks and Alex took a large gulp of her white wine.

"I think it started when I said looking at you was like staring at the sun."

He stared straight at her, unfettered.

Manny gave Hank a friendly nudge. "Couldn't agree with you more. I say that every time she comes in here."

Hank smiled. "I know. I got it from you. I overheard you saying it the first time I saw Alex in here. Never woulda thought it would always be sunny at Barclays." He winked at Alex.

"Can you guys excuse me for one sec? I'm just going to use the restroom."

Carrying her wine glass, Alex squeezed her way past the two men and walked quickly towards the bathrooms. Once inside the small women's washroom, she placed her purse and her wine glass on the sink counter and exhaled deeply. She checked her reflection in the mirror. Shit. Her complexion was completely flushed. Turning on the faucet, she splashed some cold water on her face.

Pull your shit together, Alex. You're the one who wanted to roll with the big boys.

She took a deep breath and patted her face dry with a hand towel. Retrieving the necessary materials from her purse, she carefully reapplied her makeup until she had almost successfully masked her redness. She pursed her lips and smiled at herself in the mirror.

Game time, again. She could handle him. She could handle any of them.

She downed the remainder of her wine and quickly checked her phone. She was relieved to see that there were no messages waiting for her there. She shoved the phone back into her purse and quickly slipped back out of the bathroom, feeling fortified enough to rejoin her group.

"Oh! Excuse me. I'm sorry."

A man's voice.

Alex spun around to face whoever had just bumped into her in the narrow hallway.

A boyish grin.

"Alex! What are you doing here?"

He ran his hand through his hair.

"Client dinner."

She shrugged, as if she attended them all the time now. Then she added, "It's great to see you too."

Greg reached over to give her an affectionate hug.

"Me too." He pointed to the restaurant behind him. "Have a whole crew in there. I've been entertaining non-stop since I started at the new shop."

Alex hesitated before asking, "How is it over there?"

Greg had shocked her when he'd quit the month before. He left to go run a trading desk at a competing Big Bank.

"They're all the same at this point, Alex." He smiled wistfully. "I hope you're still planning on going back to business school. See what else the world has to offer other than this crazy shit show."

Alex nodded. Privately, she was surprised to hear Greg talking like that. It hadn't been that long ago since he and Clark had convinced her to stay, to trade, to live the dream. Of course, that was before Lehman had gone under.

"Hey," Greg interrupted her thoughts with a grin. "It's fancy meeting you here anyway. Scene of the crime and all." He winked.

Alex furrowed her brows, questioning.

"Alex, you seriously still don't remember?"

Alex felt her chest constricting. "What are you talking about?"

"That Thursday night before we went under. The night you chased some poor guy down the street trying to confirm whether or not he was some C-list actor."

The color drained from Alex's face. "Oh god. I was hoping no one would ever bring that up ever again." She tried to joke lightly.

"You and I came here that night."

Alex searched the recesses of her mind. She had no memory of ever coming here with Greg. "We did?" She asked quietly. "What happened? I don't remember."

She was sick to her stomach.

"You wouldn't let me drop you off in front of your apartment across the street. So you insisted that we come here instead. Said you wanted one last drink." He chuckled. "Man, you drank us all under the table that night."

Alex stared at him wordlessly. She wasn't going to say another word until he finished the story.

"So, anyway - you and I came here. I got us a table in the back where it was quiet. It was so late though that the place was pretty empty anyway. You started spilling your guts to me. Told me that you were miserable. You started telling me all about your marriage. You said things had been pretty rough. You went into detail."

"Oh my god." Alex shook her head in disbelief. She felt her stomach tighten. Greg had to be fucking with her.

"You're kidding, right?"

He ran his hands through his hair again.

He smiled his boyish smile.

He was always so cool and collected.

"Yeah, I'm just fucking with you. We did make out though."

Alex thought she was going to throw up. She stared at him wordlessly, panicked.

"That's a joke, too, right?"

She could barely get the words out.

"C'mon, Alex. Does it really matter?" He winked.

She tried to sip from her wine glass, forgetting there was nothing left.

"Listen," now he was her mentor again. "This kind of thing happens all the time. Trust me. And nothing really even *happened.*"

He put his hand on her shoulder and she practically jumped.

"Why didn't you tell me before?"

"You should have seen the look on your face the next day at the office. I could tell you were already beating yourself up pretty bad. I didn't see the point."

She squeezed her eyes shut. Blinking:

"Do I even want to know the details?"

Alex was mortified.

This kind of thing happens all the time. Trust me.

His words were ringing in her head.

She had spent all of these months sitting next to Greg. He had acted like nothing had ever happened. She had been totally clueless. She thought about the wedding picture she kept on her desk. *Fuck, Hank was right, wasn't he? Why the hell did she keep that thing there?*

"Actually, don't even tell me. I'd rather not even know at this point. As long as that was all that happened, *if* it even happened?"

She couldn't tell what was true and what was a lie. She wasn't even sure how to tell the difference or if it even mattered. She got nauseous again thinking about the other traders. *Were they all smirking at her all of the time now? What did they think happened? What had Greg told them? It didn't even matter if it was true. It was Wall Street. Rumors could take you down too.*

"As long as what was all that happened?"

Alex turned to see Hank standing right beside her. He moved in protectively, positioning himself in between her and Greg.

"Thought you might have fallen in back here. I came to check on you." He looked at Greg. "But I see you've been otherwise detained."

Alex looked back and forth between the two men and down at her empty glass.

"I think I'll go get a refill. Thanks for coming to find me. I ran into Greg. We were just catching up."

You don't need to explain yourself, Alex. She coached herself.

Alex looked back towards Greg.

"It was nice running in to you. Thanks for the – the update."

"It was good seeing you too, Alex. Don't be a stranger."

Greg winked, laughed, and ran his hand through his hair. Alex thought she might vomit.

Greg extended a hand to Hank. "Good to see you too man. Things good?"

"Never better," Hank grinned. "See you in The Street. Good luck keeping up, trading against me now."

18

Two weeks later Hank quit too. Alex had been on vacation. It was the first one she had taken in a year. She and Jamie went away for a long weekend to celebrate their one-year anniversary. She hadn't found out about Hank until she got home and returned to work. She had been excited to get back to work, excited to see him, excited to get back to the action.

Her vacation had been a silent disaster. Jamie had surprised her with a trip to the Dominican Republic, dutifully booking a vacation to a place she had never traveled to before. Her heart warmed at his gesture but her mind wandered the whole time.

It's no big deal. It happens all the time. Trust me.

She couldn't get Greg's words out of her mind. She still didn't know whether or not to believe him. She had made up her mind that he was just kidding. There is no way she ever would have done that, she kept reasoning with herself. But the fact that she couldn't be certain was eating her alive. She felt like a little girl again, waking up each morning and pinching her arm. Even if she'd only confessed her marital woes, it was still as if she had broken the seal. Now all sorts of things seemed to creep in, to invade her mind. She thought about the framed wedding photo on her desk. She thought about Hank.

It's no big deal. It happens all the time. Trust me.

She thought she would be relieved to get away with her husband for a few days. So much was happening between them, around them and to them. But on the first day it hit her that when it was just the two of them she was bored beyond belief.

They went to breakfast. They walked on the beach. They ate lunch. They each read their books. She asked if he wanted to play tennis. He say no. She made a face and then made a lesson for herself with the tennis pro. They ate dinner in silence until she said that she wanted a cocktail that wasn't included in their prix fix meal. Then, they argued. That night he watched movies in Spanish with English subtitles. She rolled over and went to bed.

It's no big deal. It happens all the time. Trust me.

On the second day, he went for an early run. She brought her book to the beach and stared blankly at the pages. During lunch they called a truce. And after lunch they went for a bike ride. The pavement on all of the streets was cracked. There was barely any vegetation. The single-story, two-room houses looked half-built and half-deserted all at once. She decided that she hated the Dominican Republic.

It's no big deal. It happens all the time. Trust me.

On the third day he made love to her in the morning and she let him. Afterwards, she talked about work and he listened. She asked him about work and he said he didn't want to talk about it. He asked if she was finally ready to talk about what had happened and she said no. So they went to breakfast.

Secretly, Alex didn't think that he had even taken her because of their anniversary. It just happened to be good, solid coincidental timing. He had brought her to the island as an apology, as a distraction, as the path of least resistance. *If he was sorry should she be too?*

A few weeks before Alex had snuck home from work uncharacteristically early. She had wanted to guarantee that she would be home alone in their apartment. She needed to do this without him there. And lately he was *always* there.

Alex had left work a little early, as discretely as possible and stopped by a pharmacy on her way home. Once inside, she slinked around the store, peeking up and down the aisles. She wasn't even sure where to find the home pregnancy test section. She grabbed a few other unnecessary items along the way and tossed them into a shopping basket, a thinly veiled attempt to mask the real purpose of her trip. Finally, after locating the necessary products she joined the line at the checkout counter. *Why are you nervous? What the hell are you embarrassed about? You are a married woman, Alex. If you're pregnant no one will judge you.* When it was finally her turn, she made sure to flash her ring at the sales clerk multiple times, in an effort to silently justify her purchases.

She walked back very slowly to her apartment building. She had never been this late before. She had agonizingly counted the extra days and then, finally, on the tenth day, she had gone to the drug store. What would she do if she were pregnant? Just the thought of it made Alex break out into a cold sweat. Sure, she and Jamie talked about having kids. But they hadn't talked about it in a while. It was just this **thing** that she expected would happen at some mythical future point where every piece of her life plan fit perfectly together. Could they even afford kids now? What would happen when she went off to school by herself? Would Jamie reconsider a move to Boston under the circumstances? But then he would have no job! How would they support themselves and their child without any income? No, Jamie wouldn't leave work. Not even for this. He was too stuck. But what about her job? How ridiculous would she look as a pregnant trader? Goddamnit, how would anyone take her seriously? The thought of a pregnant lady waddling around the floor, trying to shout at salesmen to execute trades was not the vision of authority Alex envisioned for herself. She didn't feel ready.

Once home she hurried into the bathroom, locking the door behind her just in case. She spilled the bag of pregnancy tests out on to the floor in front of her. She had bought multiple just in case. She had never taken one before and she didn't know what the hell she was supposed to do. She took one and then waited, holding her breathe expectantly. After what felt like an eternity, she looked down at the results. She stared at the little device for several seconds. Shaking her head, she ripped off the packaging from another and took a second test. Almost like a maniac, she repeated the process four times, using up everything she'd bought. Each time the results were the same. From outside the bathroom, she suddenly heard the front door to the apartment slam. Fuck. She checked her watch. It was only four-thirty. She silently cursed her husband. She heard him pause. He must have seen her purse on the floor in the front hallway.

"Alex?" Jamie's voice called out, with a hint of alarm in it. "Alex are you home?"

"I'm just in the bathroom." She shouted.

Shit. She searched the bathroom hopelessly, trying to figure out where to hide the evidence. She was desperate. There was no place to put it. The sink, the cabinets, the garbage were all in a little separate powder room on the other side of the door. She heard Jamie getting closer. He knocked.

"Alex? Are you okay? What's going on? Why are you home?"

She was stuck. Finally, she turned the doorknob and the door creaked open. Jamie was standing on the other sides, with his hands on his hips and a concerned look on his face.

"What on god's earth are you doing in here?"

Wordlessly, she held up the four tests. He looked at her quizzically. Then, recognizing what she was holding, his eyes widened. He put his hand on the sink counter to steady himself.

"Are you - ?"

She stared at him for what felt like a long time. Finally, she shook her head no. She handed him the tests so he could see for himself. He took them and looked back at her, bewildered. Then she started to cry. Quiet tears trickled down her face. She didn't even know why she was crying. Sadness? Relief? A mixture of the two?

"Alex, why are you acting so strange? What the heck is going on?"

"I thought I might have been pregnant," she answered simply, wiping her tears away.

"But, why wouldn't you tell me? How long have you been wondering? I'm your husband, Alex." He sounded offended.

"I don't know," she mumbled. "It just felt personal. Like I had to know myself at first."

The events of the past few months rushed through her mind. So many things had happened and had changed them just by happening. She was full of an uncertainty and a hollow distance that she couldn't dislodge now, like she'd been shot and it hadn't killed her but she still couldn't get the bullet out. She and Jamie had slept together only a handful of times in the past month. But it had hardly felt intimate. How could she possibly make a baby from that?

"That's strange," he said, sounding strange himself. He looked at her more closely. "Is there something you're not telling me?"

She felt affronted by his tone.

"What the hell are you talking about Jamie?"

Why was his tone accusatory? Shouldn't he be giving her a hug or something? Telling her that it was okay, that it wasn't the right time for this to happen anyway.

"I just think it's odd that you wouldn't have told me sooner. Like when it was happening, not after the fact. I'm your husband. So why wouldn't you share this with me. Unless you were trying to hide something?" He gave her a hard look.

"Jamie, what the fuck are you talking about?" she exploded. "Have you lost your mind?"

She stormed past him and into the bedroom. *This is insane*, she thought to herself. Thank god she wasn't pregnant. Her husband was acting like a loony tune.

He followed her into the bedroom. He looked at her helplessly, wildly. "I'm sorry," he stuttered. "I don't know what came over me. I guess my mind has just been jumping places lately. You have been going out so much for "work" and I see the way you talk about these other guys. Do you talk about me with that same awe? I wonder."

He sounded so insecure. Alex was so fucking mad at him right at the second. "I go out for *work* because it's my fucking job, Jamie." She had raised her voice and was yelling at him. "How dare you. Maybe if you actually went to work yourself and focused on your own shit you wouldn't be so concerned with me and mine." She pointed to her watch for added emphasis. "It's fucking four-thirty. What are you doing home anyway?"

"Don't turn this around on me! You know how miserable I am there. I just came home to take a little break from all those assholes. You know my office is only three blocks away. I was going to walk back over in a little bit," he lied, defensively.

She couldn't hide her disgust. "Thank god I'm not pregnant," she practically spat. "We are obviously in no position to have children right now."

His eyes flew to find hers. She stared at him icily. She felt drained. "Just get out and go back to work, will you? I want to lie down. I'm tired. And I really just don't even want to talk to you right now."

"Alex -" he began. He tried to approach her but she motioned for him to stay away. "I'm sorry. I don't know what came over me."

"Neither do I Jamie. But obviously something did. Please just leave," she said again. "I really just want to be alone right now."

He stared at her silently for a few minutes, sizing up the situation. With resignation, he realized he wouldn't win. He knew that when she got like this her will was unbending. He turned and closed the door softly behind him, leaving her alone.

Alex lay down on the bed, silent tears streaming down her face. She stared mindlessly at the blank ceiling, pinching at her arm over and over and over again.

◆ ◆ ◆

Hank had quit without warning. He quit without apology. He quit without looking back. Or so it seemed to her. The ensuing weeks passed slowly, lethargically. It was impossible not to notice the change in the atmosphere on the trading desk. It was missing its spark. It had been unplugged.

Alex plodded through each day, bored and mildly resentful. Now she was bored at home and at work. It felt like a very long time had passed since she had graduated from college, silently pledging to take the world by storm. Now it just seemed dull and cloudy all the time. So she tried to just will the time to pass more quickly until she could leave and go back to school again, and reset the clock.

The phone on the desk rang. She answered in her usual way: "Trading, Barclays Capital."

"Alex!" The jovial voice exclaimed. "Alex. How you doin, buddy? It's Tommy!"

Tommy Good Times! Alex hadn't heard from him in so long. He was one of the more fun and hilarious Street brokers Alex knew. Whenever he called, she knew something good was in the works.

"Alex. I wanted to call to invite you to a party. It's a charity event up at my bar. You have to come," he paused for effect. "This one's going to be too great to miss, mama. Everyone on The Street is going to be there. It's coming up in about a week - March 15th. Promise me you'll come?"

A night out? A fun Wall Street party? An excuse to break away? Alex didn't need to hear anymore. He had her at hello.

"You know I'll be there, Tommy. Thank you for the invite," she said warmly. "You know I wouldn't miss your parties for the world."

19

THE YELLOW BRICK ROAD
MARCH 16TH, 2009

"*A*sshole, get your fucking hands off of my wife!" *Alex felt like the wind had been knocked out of her. The groper stopped in his tracks. Jamie stared blindly.*

The four of them froze, perfectly still.

A measure of silence engulfed them, despite the drunken din all around. Someone somewhere hit the mute button as the four stood there, unmoving. Alex was shell-shocked. She shifted her gaze back and forth, Hank then Jamie, Jamie then Hank.

The angry, white-haired groper ultimately broke the silence, which could have been hours not seconds from Alex's drunken, awe-struck position.

"What did you say little man?" He pointed his finger in Hank's face, and moved closer as if to demonstrate his six-inch height advantage. "Watch yourself." He squeezed Alex's backside once more, still eyeing Hank menacingly.

The rest was a blur. Hank rocketed towards the groper. He curled his right fist and smashed it into the groper's face, sending him crashing back into the wall.

"You don't talk to a lady like that." Hank growled. He jumped on top of the groper and pounded.

Alex jumped back. One of the bartenders caught the glass he was flipping, mid-bar trick. He shouted at them with a heavy Irish accent. Someone else yelled to get the police. Women scattered. Tongues wagged in disbelief. Several burly waiters closed in around the fight. The crowd was in a panic. Nick and Ronny finally reached Hank and tore him off the groper. Hank had a rip in his dress shirt and blood trickling down his face, in between his left eye and the bridge of his nose. Salty and Jason appeared next. The four of them closed in around Hank, creating a human wall. The unit moved deftly towards the door of the bar. Hank looked over at Alex. Then his friends pushed him out the door.

Next, she was outside. Alex's head was spinning. It was cold. The guys were already plowing their way down the street, heading east toward Third Avenue. Jamie physically tugged at Alex's arm, pulling her southward, toward home. She resisted.

"We should at least go for one more drink," she reasoned. Jamie paled. "Did you see what just went on?"

"Yeah," she countered. "That's why we should go have one drink with them. He just punched a guy in the face for me."

There it was.

She said it.

No defense countered.

They stared at each other for a long, hard minute.

They started down the street after the others, breaking into a brisk walk to catch up to the group. Jamie held her hand in his. They caught up about half way down the block.

"Holy shit," she said, to all of them and to none of them.

"I'm so fucking mad right now," Hank said.

"Are you ok?" she touched his arm.

"You never should have pulled me off Ronny. I wasn't done with that asshole."

"Hank," Nick broke in, "the cops would have been all over that place. They're probably filling out a report as we speak."

Jason kept his hands buried in his pockets, shoulders hunched. Ronny and Salty walked side by side up ahead, Salty measuring about a shoulder taller.

Somehow, Alex felt they'd played out this scene before. Jamie walked silently, nose tucked into his zipped up jacket, and still holding her hand. "Are you bleeding?" she asked Hank.

"No," he replied, not noticing the blood on his face.

"Yeah, Hank, I think you are," she confirmed as he turned his head to face her.

"Shit. That fucking asshole. Are you okay? He didn't hurt you when he grabbed you, did he?"

Ronny jerked left up a few stairs and into a small bar Alex had never noticed before. The rest of them followed behind. Inside it smelled of stale cigarette smoke. The bar was otherwise empty. Music blared from somewhere in the dark room. Ronny pulled up at one of the empty stools and ordered everyone a round of shots. Alex hid her yawn. She realized she was drunk and tired.

She downed her tequila shot, shaking her head side to side.

Hank got up, walked past the bar, and disappeared through a door on the left. Alex followed. She pushed open the door behind him. His back was to her. It took her drunken blue eyes an extra second to adjust. They were in the men's restroom. His back turned away because he was at the urinal. Shit.

"Uh, I just wanted to say thanks. Um, you know, for before."

Hank flipped his gaze over his right shoulder, keeping the rest of his body fixed. His face was still streaked with a little blood. He wore the widest shit-eating grin.

"Trust me ..."

She couldn't hear what he was saying. She strained to listen but the music was too loud. He just kept grinning at her.

"What?" She shouted? "I can't hear you! What did you say?"

◆ ◆ ◆

"Alex!" Someone called to her. "Alex! Wake up!"

She opened her eyes.

Her husband was calling her name. He looked down at her, concerned.

"You were having a nightmare babe. You were shouting in your sleep. Are you okay?"

She sighed, still sleepy.

"I had such a weird dream." She shook her head. She tried to clear the fog of sleep. Her head ached slightly and she felt the start of a mild hangover migraine as well. They had been drinking, she remembered. She looked over at her husband.

"I didn't dream it, did I?"

He shook his head no, chagrinned.

Alex felt dizzy. She rolled back over and let her head sink into the pillow.

"Alex, I - " Jamie started.

She held her hand up to stop him. She didn't want to hear it. She just wanted to go back to sleep for a few more minutes. She wanted to hear the end of what Hank had to say.

20

Jamie's mom never touched a sip of alcohol. But she chain smoked cigarettes and guzzled diet sodas like any proper addict might. When she visited them in New York City, she usually carried a twelve ounce bottle of Diet Coke in her purse, which she would sometimes refill from the larger bottles and other times from the soda fountains at restaurants. She coupled that with the nervous habit of lighting a series of cigarettes at fundamentally inopportune moments — like her first dinner at Alex's mom's house. But when she was in the comfort of her own home, Jamie's mom would sit on the steps just inside the garage of his childhood home and smoke and drink nonstop. Dressed in an oversized men's sweatshirt and bell-bottom jeans, she could sit there for hours, smoking and staring aimlessly out into the backyard. Sometimes she'd let the cigarette hang loose from her lips so she could pick nervously at her fingernails, which she oft did until they were raw and bleeding. The smell of her combined vices was sticky-sweet and clung to her like the smell of perspiration hangs on clothing. She kept an old, oversized coffee can that had the label peeled off at the foot of the steps so she could just drop the butts right in, only emptying the can when it was nearly spilling over.

Every time Alex and Jamie had been down to Kentucky to visit they had always gone into the house through the garage off the driveway. They had always passed through the sticky sweet stench. Alex never once remembered using the front door. The door they used off of the garage led directly into the kitchen. There was a neatly stacked pile of local daily and weekly newspapers and promotional magazines in the center of the kitchen table. One lone copy of the weekend edition of The New York Times was carefully arranged in its own separate pile. Jamie had gotten his mother a one-year subscription for Mother's Day and she worshipped that paper. The other newspapers, though, she tore to shreds. She would clip coupons on promotions for every store within a fifty-mile radius, sometimes traveling the distance to shop because she had a too-good-to-be-missed deal that couldn't go to waste. She was committed to clipping, spending, and saving with maniacal fervor. Sometimes, Jamie told Alex with embarrassment and anger, his mom would return and re-purchase items she had bought only days earlier because another coupon had arrived. At first, Alex had just chalked up Jamie's comments to standard parental-related exaggeration. Down in Kentucky though, Alex saw firsthand the fruits of this manic labor. When they visited, she and Jamie would sleep in his childhood bedroom, which had a walk-in closet that connected through to his younger brother's old room. With the boys long-gone, the closet was now packed tightly with a petite woman's clothing. Nearly every hanger had an article of clothing that still had the sales tags on it. There were piles and racks of jeans, dress pants, blouses, sweaters, sweatshirts, and t-shirts – all looked unworn.

"Um, Jamie, what's up with this closet? Whose clothing is this?" Alex had asked the first time.

"That's my mom's second closet. Well, actually, it's her third. Since we don't live here anymore and my dad moved out, she also has the hallway one filled too."

"But – what's up with all the new clothing? There's more shit in here than in a department store."

"Oh. That," Jamie had said, "is evidence of my mother's situation. She just buys this stuff to return it. My dad tried to make her see a psychiatrist for it. She stopped doing it for a while. But she never really admitted that it's, like, a problem. It drives…I mean it used to drive my dad absolutely crazy."

Jamie's brother was raw and redneck. He stood about six feet, five inches tall and had a belly the size of a bear. The two were always a funny picture together, like a pair of mismatched fraternal twins. Jamie always liked to say that his little brother's bark was worse than his bite and he was really just a big teddy bear. He proudly called him "big man" but usually coddled him like a little boy.

Joshua was living in a special facility for recovering gamblers and alcoholics when Jamie and Alex started dating. He was back in his hometown six months later when Alex visited Kentucky for the first time. She went to her first Alcoholics Anonymous meeting in the basement of a Kentucky church. They'd driven there in his brother's old Toyota, where she had silently held her breath the whole way for fear that her stomach wouldn't hold against the sickeningly sweet combination of cigarettes and cheap cologne; the cologne having been sprayed to mask the cigarette stench that hovered in the tiny car. Joshua hadn't told them where they were all going when he had picked Jamie and Alex up from the airport. He only said that he had a surprise for them. When they had pulled up to the church Jamie immediately realized what his little brother intended and balked at the plan. Alex stood quietly off to the side, unsure of what to do or how to act. Within thirty minutes of meeting her boyfriend's only brother, Alex was sitting in a semi circle of plastic chairs in a linoleum-tiled, dimly lit room of a Kentucky church basement listening to him pour his heart out about his addiction, his temptation, his struggle with recovery. He talked about being a disappointment and an embarrassment to his family. He talked about never being half as good or remotely as talented as his older brother, whom he idolized. Then with the same fervor he began to speak about the rush, the adrenaline and the toxic high that sucked him back in time and time again. Alex stared quietly at the floor. She heard a choked sob of agony in an otherwise dead silent room. Looking up, she saw her boyfriend clutching his brother's hand tightly, as uncontrollable, noisy tears streamed down his face.

Their family dinners often took place at casual, chain restaurants popularly known in the Midwest. Alex had never heard of a Cracker Barrel before, nor was she entirely sure she wanted to. The first few times were disarmingly new and amusing to her but after a few years there was nothing even remotely sexy about gravy-soaked biscuits at a $19.95 all-you-can-eat buffet.

◆ ◆ ◆

This was without a shadow of a doubt the most excited she had ever been to go to Jamie's hometown. It was the first weekend in May. She, Jamie, Daniella and her boyfriend had all flown in to attend the Kentucky Derby. It was the one weekend a year where Alex beamed with pride that her husband was from the state; where Joshua walked everywhere with swagger because he was a very close friend of one of the country's top jockeys and got them in to all of the celebrity parties; when Kentucky was decidedly the coolest place to be in the entire country. The girls had packed their most Derby-appropriate dresses and offensively large and hysterically ridiculous hats. For their part, the guys went all out with matching light blue seersucker suits, pink bowties and suspenders, and light brown loafers. They were ready and more than a little eager to smoke cigars, bet the races, and drink mint juleps from morning till night. For once, Alex was excited to play the part, to be a Kentucky Woman.

She also hoped the trip would serve as a distraction and to help lighten the mood between them. She had been having a really tough time with Jamie over the past month and a half. Ever since the incident with Hank and all of the other guys from work at P.J. Clarke's, husband and wife had been more fraught with tension than ever before. He went out even less. She started going out even more. He became more dictatorial about her whereabouts. In turn, she became more secretive about her plans, more defiant against her husband's growing demands to have her home and all to himself all of the time.

At first, Alex hadn't thought much of the fight at P.J. Clarke's. In her mind it had just been another crazy night out with the guys, punctuated by the presence of her husband and the crazy drunk guy who tried to grope her. She still couldn't believe that Hank had beaten the shit out of the guy. He really was as crazy and intense as the stories about him suggested. She wondered if that night would become just another weapon in his arsenal, added to the library of war stories about him that made him larger than life. She couldn't imagine herself actually becoming a character in one of his fabled tales. They all seemed so extraordinary, larger than life and she was just an ordinary girl, trying to find her way in order to do extraordinary things with her life. But she hadn't really done anything yet.

But she couldn't stop thinking about him. Hank seemed so different from anyone she had ever met before; he seemed to care so much and care so little all at once. The contradiction was confounding and intriguing. After a while, she had started to wonder why he had gotten into that fight in the first place. Sure, they had all been drunk. But he had seemed highly alert. Why had he done it? Did he do it for her? Did he do it for himself? Was he trying to prove a point in front of his new trading partners? Or was he trying to remind the guys who worked for him, who followed him loyally from one Big Bank to another that he was always on the winning side of a good fight? Was he trying to show up her husband? Alex couldn't imagine why he would want to do that. She couldn't imagine why he would care. The two men were so different. In fact, Alex couldn't think of two people were more divergent, polar opposite figures. Then she started thinking that Hank had nothing to prove to Jamie because he was already so much more masculine, so much more of a man. She let her thoughts run down this path before she could fully process the direction of her mind. By the time she caught herself it was too late. It had already run too far and she couldn't catch it. She started to obsessively think back on that one fateful night. And the more she thought about it, the angrier she became at her husband. Why the fuck hadn't he been the one to protect her from the angry groper? What if the man really had been dangerous? Was Jamie just going to stand there and watch? How could he have just stood there and done nothing at all - not to defend her honor or his own? What kind of a man was he?

That's when it happened. It was a sudden, irreversible feeling. She tried to shake it. She dared not voice it to another living soul. She tried to bury it, to will it away. It hurt to think about. But it was all she thought about. Her mind was overheated. And she slowly started to look at him differently. She no longer respected her husband as a man. He had tripped and was slowly falling from the pedestal she had so delicately placed him on, falling from grace. Her shifting perception was taking hold of their reality, altering its course. It was as if someone had opened the gas tank and the fuel was secretly leaking out the side, even though the car continued to barrel forward.

Alex didn't know what to do. She couldn't stop it and she tried everything she could think of to hide it. But the loss of respect was slowly being replaced with a building resentment. She resented him. She resented herself. She resented this life that they had, this life that she had chosen. She felt that she had folded too soon. And now for the rest of her life she was going to be joined to this man who was so hopelessly paralyzed. The feeling of despair grew inside of her, secretly, a little lump that grew a little bigger each day. It was starting to fill her to the point where she couldn't breathe. The foreboding sense of claustrophobia was setting down upon her, smothering her from the inside out. She wanted to crawl out of her body, out of her apartment, out of her life.

That's when she started to think the unthinkable. That's when she permitted herself to start thinking about crawling out of her marriage too. *Divorce*. The thought started to privately haunt her. She tried to grab hold of it with both hands, to strangle it out of her mind and out of reach. She couldn't get divorced. That would be so humiliating. It would be such a failure. Goddamnit, it wasn't part of her plan. She had to prove she could have it all. All her life she had been told she could do anything she put her mind to. So she resolved to re-entrench herself and put her mind towards saving her marriage.

Jamie's dad picked the group up from the airport. Alex had requested that they stay at his townhouse apartment, instead of Jamie's childhood home. She had never brought any of her friends to Kentucky before. While Daniella was one of her closest friends and they had known each other since they were fourteen, she wanted to take extra precautions to ensure that their weekend would be perfect. She was worried it would all be too much pressure to share a house with Jamie's mom for the weekend. So his dad had graciously offered to stay with his girlfriend so that they could have free reign over his two-bedroom.

They settled into the house quickly and Alex urged the group to get ready to go out for the evening right away. Joshua had gotten them all invited to an exclusive celebrity-sponsored charity fundraiser at a club downtown. It was pegged as the hottest spot in town that night. Alex didn't want to miss a minute. She wiggled into the sexiest dress she had packed. It was a sleeveless mini red and white striped dress that only reached the middle of her thighs. She completed the look with a pair of four inch white stilettos and pearl earrings. After a second thought, she removed the white headband that was holding her newly bobbed blonde hair in place. *Just naughty, no need for nice tonight*, she smiled at her reflection approvingly in the bathroom mirror. Jamie came into the bathroom to finish getting ready himself and whistled softly when he saw his wife. He came up behind her and wrapped his arms around her waist, nuzzling her neck softly with his nose. She felt small goose bumps tingling across her body as he kissed her lightly behind one ear.

"You look gorgeous," he whispered in her ear. "Sometimes I still can't believe you are really my wife. I would be happy to just stay home and keep you all to myself tonight." He squeezed her tighter and she felt his erection building, pressing in to her backside.

She placed her arms over his and squeezed a little tighter, smiling as broadly as she could at the reflection of the two of them in the mirror. It was nice to see an easy, relaxed smile on her husband's face. He seemed calmer, more sure of himself in his hometown.

"You always want to have me all to yourself. We are going out tonight to paint this town red," she said firmly but sweetly. "You're supposed to show me this other side of Kentucky you always talk about."

"After this weekend you will love Kentucky so much you'll never want to leave. Who knows, maybe you'll warm to the idea of moving here." He paused for a moment, thoughtful, as an idea seemed to pop into his head. "We could buy a huge house for less than we spend on our apartment in the city. We'd get jobs here in a heartbeat. It would solve so many of our problems. Life would be so much easier. You see how amazing the quality of life is here? I could golf with my dad after work or on Fridays. I could coach our kids' Little League teams one day, just like my dad did for us. You wouldn't have to work on Wall Street anymore. Maybe that's something to really think about?" He looked expectantly at her reflection in the mirror, in search of a reply.

MOVE TO KENTUCKY! She silently screamed. There were alarm bells ringing in her head. Oh dear lord. What in the fuck did he think she was going to do it Kentucky? She just wanted to have a fun weekend in his home town where he could show off a little to their friends and feel good about himself; where she could get dressed up and feel pretty and girly and good about herself; where they could try to find that carefree spark to reignite the passion in their relationship. But she sure as shit didn't want to move to Kentucky. Alex did her best to mask her repulsion. Jamie's suggestions were outlandish. *Remain calm*, Alex silently coached herself. *Remain calm, and slowly step away from your husband.*

"Baby, you know moving to Kentucky isn't part of our plan," she said soothingly, calmly, robotically.

She turned to face him and cupped his face with both her hands. Because she was in her heels already she could reach him without raising her tiptoes.

"Let's just try to have fun together this weekend. I think we both know we could use it."

She looked deep into his eyes and planted a soft kiss on his lips before he had time to respond. Stepping back, she examined him at arm's length.

"Now, let me see what you've picked out to wear tonight. I don't want to be fending off all these old Kentucky flames of yours all night long."

She had never really been worried about other women hitting on him when they went out together. But, she recalled with a mild hint of jealousy, his college sweetheart was a very attractive, bubbly blonde who was much skinnier than Alex and had decent size implants that gave her a knockout, hourglass shape. They'd stayed together for years and had always been expected to marry, from what Alex gathered, until Jamie broke it off when he first moved to New York.

Alex approved of the ensemble he had picked out for himself: dark army green dress shirt, denim jeans, and smart looking brown leather loafers. She reached for his shirt and untucked the bottom from inside his pants, fixing it instead so that it hung loosely. His habit of tucking his dress shirts in drove her mad as it had the distinct effect of making her husband look too skinny and a bit like a nerd.

"There," she said, smoothing the edges of the shirt. "Now you look handsome. Let's go."

They walked downstairs to find Joshua sitting on the couch smack in between Daniella and her boyfriend. He had his arm casually slung over Daniella's shoulder. The three of them looking ridiculous stuffed into that small couch with Joshua's big frame. Alex heard Joshua recounting some outlandish story, his Kentucky drawl more pronounced than usual. She tried to suppress a little smile, Amused that he was making such a blatant effort to hit on her friend, with equally- blatant disregard to her boyfriend, who sat there looking hopelessly annoyed.

Daniella's boyfriend needn't worry; Joshua didn't stand a chance with her perfectly manicured friend. She came from a Good Jewish Family in New York and she was damn sure going to marry a Good Jewish Boy from New York. They were respectable members of their community, a picture perfect family. Her father was a self-made businessman. Her mother was a former schoolteacher who became an active volunteer for community projects after her children were born. Her father gave the best advice - he always had a thoughtful solution for every problem. Her mother cooked the most delicious dinners and stayed up late gossiping with her girls. Daniella and her sister were both beautiful, with perfect figures and impeccable wardrobes to match. Their younger brother deftly mastered every sport and was the apple of every pre-teen girl's eye. They skied in the winters, boated in the summers, and spent holidays at a quaint family vacation bungalow in upstate New York that was nostalgically reminiscent of summer camp. Ever since they had been friends, Alex had spent just as much time with Daniella's family as she had with her own. The girls were polar opposites but fast friends and fiercely loyal to one another. Alex had watched her friend easily date handsome guys from good families. Her single status earlier that year had not lasted long after they had attended that charity event.

"Alright guys, let's go already," Alex interrupted. "Joshua, am I going to have to keep an eye on you this weekend?" She asked playfully.

"Sweetness, I am fully suspecting both of your pretty little blue eyes on me this here entire weekend. Anythang else would be 'n insult."

"We wouldn't be here without you this weekend, Big Man'" she complimented him. "Now let's get this party started." He stood and she linked her arms through his, as they walked towards to the door.

"Hey not so fast!" Daniella chimed in, faking a pout, her voice filled with light laughter. "There'd better room for one more." She bounced towards them, linking her arm through Joshua's other one. She giggled and slyly winked at her friend. Alex envied her friend's carefree demeanor but it was infectious tonight. They were a ridiculous sight, with Joshua towering a foot and a half over them, one girl dressed on each arm. He spun them around to face the other guys, an action that for a split second jogged a distant memory in Alex's mind. She pushed it aside.

Joshua was all fired up. "Shit, y'all. Some guys really just do have all the luck," he smirked at his brother. "I gots my dates for the night. We'd better go find you suckers some ladies."

◆ ◆ ◆

The rest of the night had been a blur of fun. They had skipped all the lines, been granted ready access to all the VIP sections, rubbed elbows with many of the celebrities in town, and hit all the hottest parties. They'd stayed out until almost four am. Jamie had even gotten uncharacteristically drunk. And he played along when Alex and Daniella made a scene at the last bar, climbing up onto the tops of the couches in the lounge to dance and swigging shots of vodka from magnum bottles of Grey Goose. The girls had posed for photographs with some of the professional football players at the party and Jamie didn't even make a scene when one had asked for his wife's phone number. The couple was still slightly euphoric when they finally turned in and made a concerted effort to consummate their night of revelry. But ultimately Jamie had been too drunk to get it up and Alex had been too smashed to get him off, so after some fumbling and fondling they finally collapsed in each others' arms, entwined in a state of drunken, safe, oblivious marital bliss.

The next morning Alex woke with a mild hangover and a major sense of relief that they hadn't done it in his father's bedroom. Now that she was almost sober the thought of fucking in her father-in-law's bed made her a little bit nauseous. She glanced across the bed at her sleeping husband, whose unconscious facial expression was a slightly goofy, though blissfully unaware smile. She moved closer to nuzzle up against him. Sensing her presence, he pulled her closer; his eyes were still screwed shut, stealing a few more minutes of sleep. She lay cuddled against his chest, facing him with their faces a few inches apart. She listened to his peaceful, rhythmic breathing and smiled to herself. Last night had been fun, really fun. She couldn't remember the last time she and Jamie had carried on like that together. She hadn't seen him that drunk since they celebrated the night of their engagement at the Russian vodka bar on the Lower East

Side where they had also gone on their first date. He had danced, mingled, and even did a few shots with her towards the end of the night. When a DJ had played one of his favorite songs, he had crooned along, belting out the lyrics with feeling. He seemed to revel in introducing people to his wife, and she thought he even beamed a little with pride when a few guys had innocently hit on her. His smile had come easily, his laughter had been genuine, and his charm was subtly disarming in his mildly midwestern, unique way. He had perfectly resembled the man she had fallen for. There was no trace of the New York malcontent he had become.

They could still make it, Alex thought, her heart warming against his sleeping touch. She just had to try harder and she had to do better. She could be a better wife to him. They still had their spark, she reasoned. And last night proved they could still rise above the madness that had seemed to engulf their lives. They had lost track of the intimacy and the levity of their relationship replacing it instead with a more stayed, careful marriage. The fall of Bear had knocked them against the ropes. They were still teetering, trying to catch their footing when Lehman collapsed, nearly knocking the couple to the ground. She hadn't been doing them any favors with all of her nights out. Then there was the persistent emotional drain she felt from his family, the way they seemed to invade Alex and Jamie's life with their constant, petty bickering. She thought all of their problems might have been solved with a baby. But that false alarm only made her more insecure about the strength of their union. Did they really need a baby to keep it all together? She shuddered at the thought. She had never failed at anything in her entire life. And she had never quit either. Marriage sure as shit wasn't going to be the place where she made a habit of either. But were they even the same people anymore? She wondered not for the first time. How had she gotten here? When she and Jamie were at home together she had the growing, sickening feeling of boredom. They were so goddamned normal. Her life was so normal, so predictable. She got up every morning to go to the gym just so she could escape the confines of her small apartment. Then she went to work, cringing each day before she walked through the glass doors to a place that she increasingly resented. Then she came home to an expectant husband who wanted nothing more than her undivided attention and adoration. Where was the fire, the passion? She wasn't even twenty-five. Did she really have to come to Kentucky to light a fire?

That made her think of Hank again. The fight at the bar that night had really turned into a trojan horse. *Fuck*! She couldn't escape it. Not even here. An image of Hank briefly flitted through her mind; an image of his face, a tight smirk across his lips and intensity in his dark eyes. Where was the fire in Jamie's eyes?

Stop it, she scolded herself. She pushed the image out of her head before she could play with it anymore. *What the hell is wrong with you? You are a married woman. You have no business thinking about another man while lying in bed with your husband.* She scrunched her eyes shut, trying to physically squeeze the image into oblivion. When she opened her eyes, Jamie's green ones were open, awake, staring straight at her.

"Morning muffin," he said with a lazy yawn. "Why were you squeezing your eyes shut like that? You looked like you were making a wish or something."

She breathed deeply. "Something like that." Then she forced a smile. "I had fun with you last night. There must be something in the air down here. Kentucky really does agree with you."

Suddenly he was wide awake. "So you would consider moving?" his voice was full of hope.

Jesus, god. Not this conversation again. Didn't he remember anything at all about their life plan? He had talked her out of a prenuptial agreement, logically, because they hadn't had any assets when they married; for a split second she wished she'd had one with a single clause: no Kentucky living. It was too early for a fight. And she didn't want to ruin the afterglow of their fun evening out.

"No baby. I just want to bottle the air. I intend to keep the man out of Kentucky. I just want to take his good humor with us when we go home - to New York - which is our home," she couldn't help adding with a little extra emphasis. "C'mon, we've got to get going anyway. We promised to squeeze in brunch with your mom before we head to the racetrack."

"I know. It really is an inconvenience," Jamie scowled, his voice souring a note. "I'm sorry to pull you in so many directions. It's just she was so offended when I had to tell her that we weren't going to stay at the house this weekend. And then she really nearly lost it when I told her that we were going to the Derby with my dad."

Alex wished that she could cringe too, but she kept the reflex to herself. Somehow, it was okay for Jamie to bemoan his mom's nutty and needy tendencies but the second Alex brought any of them up, Jamie transformed into a protective bloodhound. *Better leave well enough alone,* Alex thought. *You aren't going to change the woman and you only need to see her a handful of times a year.* Plus, the softer side of her conscious reckoned, if anyone understood the intense pressure of feeling dragged in different directions by both parents, literally pulled apart at the emotional seams, it was Alex. She had felt it nearly her entire life. Jamie was new to the world of divorced parents and she thought it was her responsibility to guide him. So she never batted an eye when they double-booked all of their plans when down in Kentucky. And she never let on that any of the overcompensation drove her bananas. After all, she couldn't fault Jamie for trying to do the same thing she often did herself: please everyone.

◆ ◆ ◆

Lunch at Cracker Barrel was just like any other weekend outing for the most part. The buffet was still disgustingly decadent. The crowd was still overwhelmingly overweight. The place was still frightfully packed. Only this weekend, everyone at their table was dressed to the nines for the Derby. Everyone except Jamie's mom, who made a point to wear her personal uniform of baggy jeans and a men's college basketball sweatshirt. She even furnished her own bottle of Diet Coke when they sat down at the table.

Daniella leaned over to consult her friend. "Babes, why are we eating in a shopping center parking lot," she whispered in Alex's ear.

"A table at the Ritz wasn't available," Alex responded dryly and also in a whisper.

Daniella flushed. "Sorry, babe, I didn't mean it that way. They're really sweet and all. I just meant," she stuttered. "I just meant I thought we'd be going straight to the race track. I figured we'd take it all in since this is all of our first time down here. And Jamie made it all sound so cool and fun," she concluded on an accommodating note.

Alex sighed. "I know and I'm sorry babe. I don't think we'll be here long. Jamie just felt so bad between not staying at his mom's and then basically having to tell her she wasn't invited to the Derby with all of us. He doesn't really know how to juggle his parents separately down here yet. He feels so guilty when he is having a good time with his dad and his mom is home alone. But then when he spends time with his mom she just nags and nags at him until he nearly explodes. I feel so badly that he is caught in the middle. You know I know how it is... It's still pretty new to him and he's not used to it. He felt bad for her and I guess I just felt bad for him. What's a wife to do," she shrugged, mildly defeated.

Daniella nodded sympathetically. She couldn't really relate but she did feel for her friend. "Let's go get some food?" she offered, not fully knowing what else to say.

"Yeah, sure. Buffet?" Alex asked jokingly.

The two girls burst into laughter at that.

"I thought you'd never ask," Daniella giggled.

"I thought I'd never have to," Alex said trying to subdue herself.

"All you can eat or pay as you go?" Daniella could barely get the words out between her growing hysterical gasps.

"Can you believe this is my life?" Alex quietly laughed, wiping a few stray tears from the creases of her eyes. "Me? Of all people in the world. Married to a Kentucky man. Sitting in a Cracker Barrel. In a parking lot. Eating a buffet-style lunch. While dressed in cocktail attire and a massive hat for the Kentucky Derby."

Daniella hugged her friend. Suddenly she was very serious. "You always did march to your own drum beat, babe." Before Alex had time to think or to respond, Daniella grabbed her hand and pulled her towards the buffet. "Come," she uncharacteristically commanded. "If we can't beat em, we join em!"

They returned moments later with small side salads and an assortment of fruit, cheese and crackers. Sitting to her right, Joshua had also returned from the buffet. Only he was taking full advantage, with four plates overfilled with food laid out in front of him. He was tearing into the first plate with unabashed and reckless abandon. In between forkfuls he came up for air and grinned at Alex, a shit-eating grin that revealed some of the food he was still chewing.

"Shit," he said with a long drawl, "these sons of bitches sho' are losing money on me. Suckers." He laughed heartily.

Alex caught Jamie's eye and gave him a cold stare that said *I thought you talked to your brother about acting up in front of her friends.* Jamie shrugged helplessly, busy trying to assuage with mother, who in turn was busy listing her latest litany of complaints.

To Joshua Alex said, "J, maybe you should tone it down a little. You look so great in your Derby suit - you wouldn't want to carelessly get food over it."

She knew a compliment was the quickest way to his heart.

"You're right, sugar," he purred with a mischievous wink. He readjusted himself in his seat to pull out the napkin he'd been sitting on. When he lifted his leg, he let out a noisy, obnoxious fart, like a farm animal. Unperturbed, Joshua broke into fits of laughter. Alex paled in embarrassment. Daniella cringed noticeably.

"Joshua!" Jamie said sharply from across the table.

"Sorry," he tried, still laughing uncontrollably. "Guess your little lady just makes my nerves light up." Laughing and talking at the same time, with food still filled in his mouth, he began to choke. His massive body heaved and all of the key lime pie he had just shoveled into his mouth he now let pour out and back onto the plate.

"Joshua!" Jamie shouted, not holding back this time. "We talked about this. What the hell is wrong with you? You are embarrassing all of us."

Some people at other tables had stopped eating to stare.

Alex wanted to crawl under the table and die. It was pretty tough to become embarrassed at a place like Cracker Barrel, but somehow they had managed it.

Joshua wiped the pie off of his face and threw his napkin down on the table in exaggerated anger. "Fuck you Jamie. I was just havin' a little fun. I'm always embarrassing you, ain't I? Except when you need somethin' from me like arrangin' this whole Derby weekend. Does that embarrass you too? You come down here with your city wife and your fancy city friends and all of a sudden Big J's an embarrassment? Well, screw you, brother."

"Joshua!" This time it was their mother who interceded. "Cut it, right now."

"Screw this. I'll be waitin' in the car, since it seems I ain't nothin' more than a chauffeur for the weekend." He stood up, knocking his chair back to the ground, and stormed out.

Jamie was about to get up and chase after him when his mom started. Her lower lip quivered as she looked around the table.

"I'm so sorry y'all. He has been acting up lately," she made excuses for her youngest son as if he were still a child. "It hasn't been easy on him down here with his father and I splitting. He's caught in the middle and it's making him anxious." She looked at Jamie pointedly, her voice catching. "He's mad at your father for walking out and he's taking his anger out on all the wrong people."

This time it was Jamie's turn to become defensive. "Mom, stop dragging dad through the mud. This has nothing to do with him. Joshua is a grown man and you need to stop treating him like a little boy."

"You're never here anymore Jamie!" Tears were now streaming down his mother's face. "It's been so hard, honey. I'm all alone now," she wailed. "Your father's life hasn't changed at all. Sure, maybe he moved out of the house and all. But he lives around the fucking corner. With his new fucking girlfriend. And all of our friends have turned on me like I don't even exist anymore. He still goes to the club with them, out to dinner with them, biking with them, to shows with them. And I'm like a fucking pariah. Now it's just like his new girlfriend just took my place. Twenty-nine years of marriage together and now he is just carryin' on like this right around the corner from me! Shit, Jamie. Your father can't be the only one who gets to be happy. I need to get fucked. I deserve to get fucked too," she sobbed, throwing herself into her son's arms.

Jamie hugged his mother back, trying to sooth her. He peered over her hunched shoulders at his wife, giving Alex a helpless look. Alex returned his gaze, but her eyes were steely, burning in anger and embarrassment. He had sworn to her that his mother wouldn't make a scene around their friends. Jamie's mom had broken down to them with this same exact story countless times over the past two years. Couldn't she just keep herself under control for one weekend, for one hour? Alex was mortified that Daniella and her boyfriend had just witnessed this outburst. She couldn't help but hold Jamie responsible for his family.

"I'll be waiting outside, too," she seethed through tightly pursed lips. "I'm not sure if this was 'all you can eat' or 'all you can stomach.'" She stood and left, motioning for her friends to follow. She felt a stab of guilt as she saw her husband recoil but she was too angry to do anything other than keep walking out the door.

◆ ◆ ◆

The group had been sullen and mostly silent on the way to the track. Jamie had sat in front with his brother, stealing glances in the rearview mirror at his wife, who sat in the back between her friends. Daniella and her boyfriend tried to lighten the mood with innocent questions about the details of horseracing, the history of the derby and this year's favorites. By the time they pulled up to the entrance everyone was talking, though not necessarily all to one another.

Churchill Downs was just as picturesque as she had imagined. They entered through a horseshoe -shaped pavilion, with the tall white building that bore the track's name standing proudly in the background. Alex had read that 150,000 people came out for the event and judging by the teaming crowds, she believed the estimates. Most of the people were very dressed up for the event. Everywhere she turned, Alex saw women bumping in to one another because their views were obstructed by large, decorative hats. Alex had rummaged through her mother's closet in preparation for the day, finally choosing an extra large white wicker and lace hat with a huge lace flower appliqué affixed to the top. She wore it tilted in exaggeration to one side, a style she that she determined was evocative of Southern style and Midwestern charm. She had chosen the hat to compliment the strapless, A-line, calf-length black and white polka dotted dress, the only piece in her wardrobe with a Derby sensibility to it.

"Come here, you two," Daniella called to them excitedly. "Let me take a picture of you in front of the entrance. "You two look adorable together."

Alex gave her friend a rueful but appreciative look. She knew she was only trying to help. Alex had been too ashamed to discuss her budding fears and anxieties even with her closest friend, but Daniella was no mental slouch. She knew everything was not entirely okay with her friend. After all, she had been there that night of the bar fight. Even though she had left early, Alex had filled her in on all of the details.

Alex posed next to her husband, her lips pursed in a tight, forced smile. Jamie wrapped his arm around her waist and pulled her closer. She held her purse with both hands in front of her, her shoulders arched back and her body stiff.

"Don't be mad," he whispered in her ear.

"Ready? Smile!" Daniella chirped from a few feet away.

They both held poses for the camera.

"How can you say that?" Alex whispered back, without turning her head. "I'm sorry Jamie but your family is fucking humiliating," she seethed. "It's the same shit every time."

"Let me get one more!" Daniella called over. "I want to make sure I get the perfect angle." They smiled again for the camera. This time both with tightly pursed half-grins. "They're your family too now, Alex."

"Don't remind me." She turned to face him, pretending to straighten his already straight bowtie. "Let's just make the best of this day and try to get through it. We promised Daniella and Eric a superb weekend. We can talk about the ridiculous stunts your family pulled in therapy next week."

"Shhh. Alex! What's wrong with you? We both agreed that we wouldn't tell anyone we're seeing a therapist. Don't say that so loudly or they might hear you."

"Please, Jamie. Do you honestly think we look like a happy, picture-perfect couple right now? Daniella is my best friend. She's not a moron."

Alex took Jamie's hand and turned back to their friends. "So, how'd we do?" she asked brightly. "Will we make it into *People Magazine's* Derby pictures?"

Daniella laughed. "Not yet. But maybe if we add a few mint juleps and some winning race tickets to those pictures."

"Let's go then," Jamie exclaimed with extra enthusiasm. "It's time for me to show you New Yorkers what Kentucky's all about."

They made their way inside to the crowded track, lubricated themselves with several specialty cocktails and went to place their bets. Alex knew little to nothing about horse racing but she thought it was fun to choose horses with clever names and of course, she had grown to love betting in general. She chose to wager her money on 'Hold Me Back' and 'Flying Private,' while Jamie chose 'Musket Man' to win, and Daniella and her boyfriend pooled their money to place their collective lot with 'Mr. Hot Stuff' and 'Join in the Dance.' Alex listened as Jamie expertly explained the nuances of horserace betting to their friends. Daniella's boyfriend was impressed and asked how much he usually wagered on races. Alex rolled her eyes to herself as Jamie admitted he never anted up with more than a fifty bucks a race. He wasn't a gambling man.

After a few beverages, Alex and Jamie had cooled off a bit. Despite a splitting migraine, Alex had to admit that she was having a pretty good time. It was an experience like no other for her. Things were happening all around them. There was a feeling of chaos and exuberance to the crowd that she just let herself get swept away in. Jamie also eased into a more affable humor, helped along by Daniella's boyfriend who was easy-going and a good-natured sport. He bought a couple of cheap cigars and the two guys jokingly puffed away, thumbing their suspenders and parading around with wide grins as Daniella happily snapped dozens of photos.

After a few of the races they wandered over to the back paddock area where the jockeys and owners walked the horses for display before each race went off. Alex thought a rude passerby kept knocking into her shoulder but then she realized someone was purposely tapping her.

"Alex! How you doing mama? Sheesh don't you look fancy. Someone sure cleans up nice." Tommy Good Times checked her out admiringly before enveloping her in a sweaty bear hug.

"Tommy!" she shrieked with genuine excitement, returning the hug despite the sweat. "What are you guys doing here?"

He pointed to a group of about dozen guys standing an arms-length away. "Down with a whole bunch of the guys. Bachelor party," he said smoothly, winking. "It's an annual trip for us. Soon some of us are going to have to start getting divorced just so we can get remarried and throw more parties. We are starting to run out of real bachelors." He winked at her again.

"Oh, somehow I'm not too worried about you guys. I'll think you'll manage just fine. It's so great to see you!" She squeezed his arm.

"You too, kiddo. What a great surprise. I forgot the old man is from Kentucky. Let's all go do a few shots." He acknowledged Jamie then. "Hey bud! Great to see you! Great town you've got here." He made a grand sweeping motion with his arm, as if to suggest that the entire city was inside the track.

"Tommy," Jamie nodded his head curtly in recognition. "Nice to see you too. It's been a while."

"Yeah, that's right bud. Great to see you again!" He slung his arm sloppily over Jamie's shoulder. "Gosh, when was the last time I saw you two lovebirds? I barely get to see Alex at all these days." He gave Alex a sly wink over his shoulder. "Where have you been hiding your gorgeous wife? You've got to let her get out with the boys more. It's part of the job you know? Gosh, when was the last time I saw you?" He slapped his forehead with his free hand. "That's right! It was at my last charity event. I was hammered that night, bud. Sorry I didn't get to catch up with you more then. I heard I missed quite the late night show."

Alex watched Jamie tense uncomfortably, still locked in Tommy's sweaty man-brace. Tommy grabbed for Alex and enveloped her in a similar hug on his other side. "Don't worry, mama. I would have slugged the guy, too. Crazy fucking story. Nobody puts baby in the corner." He laughed heartily, releasing them both.

So Tommy knew too! She wondered who else knew. Everyone must know. The realization hit her. Tommy had even used that line from *Dirty Dancing* that Hank had let slip that night. That meant he was retelling the story.

"C'mon, let's go grab some drinks. I'm parched." Tommy motioned for them all to follow him back over to his group.

"No, thank you though," Jamie said with a cool but even tone, one Alex had never heard him use before.

"We really should be getting back to our seats. The final race is going to start soon."

"Aww heck, c'mon bud. Let's just all grab one. It's not every day I get to see your beautiful wife. These horses have been racing all day. Seen one, seen 'em all, right?!"

Jamie grasped Alex's hand tightly, with ownership. He smiled tightly. "Yes, she is beautiful. But unfortunately we can't. I'm sure you'll see her back in New York." He turned to his wife. "Let's go, muffin," he said with a light voice and hard eyes. "We have a large group waiting for us."

Alex cringed at his usage of that awful pet name in front of her Wall Street colleagues. There was no large group waiting for them - only Daniella and her boyfriend, whom they'd temporarily lost in the crowd.

"Sure," she said, mild resignation in her voice. "Tommy, rain-check back in New York?"

"You know it, mama." He winked. "Don't you worry. We'll get the whole band back together."

21

I heard you ran into Tommy.

Alex froze as she read the message that flashed across her cell phone. She hadn't spoken to him in two months. She hadn't contacted him. He hadn't reached out to her. A little voice in her head sometimes pestered her. *Call him.* But then another, more rationale voice would counter. *Yeah? And say what?* She looked around the floor to see if anyone else had noticed. There was an unspoken understanding that no one would speak of him anymore. Senior management wanted to erase any trace of his powerful presence. Even now, she felt she was breaking the rules merely by reading his text message. She forced herself not to smile though she was mentally grinning from ear to ear.

Yes, at Derby. She typed then paused to think. Should she say more? No, she decided. Just wait. She hit send. The seconds ticked by. She realized she was subconsciously holding her breath. *Exhale, you moron,* she scolded herself. *Don't get so worked up over one little message.*

What are you doing tonight?

Alex sat back in her chair, shocked. She started to type back that she had plans when another message came through.

I've got something big planned. I want you to be a part of it.

She stopped typing immediately and stared at the screen. Something big? Most everything Hank did was "something big." If he was classifying it as such it must be a really big deal. She deleted her original message. Instead, she wrote:

Wow. I'm honored. Can you fill me in on any dets?

His response came quickly, in several messages.

No.

You need to show up in person.

Ten p.m.

Pietro's.

Damn. She was curious.

I would love to. But I can't. They're having a going away party for me tonight. It's my last day here.

He was silent for several minutes. *Crap. Had she blown her only chance? What did he have planned? Stupid, stupid, stupid,* she cursed herself.

You quit?

She sighed in relief.

Sort of. I'm going back to business school. Leaving on good terms.

His response seemed mirthful.

So it seems. I didn't get a party when I left.

She felt him laughing at her. Laughing at them. What could she say? Then, he messaged her again.

You're wasting your time with school. Ten p.m. Leave the party early. You don't need to celebrate your past. Not when you can celebrate the future. Ten p.m.

Pietro's. See you then, Harvard.

◆ ◆ ◆

For the rest of the day she thought about the mystery meeting at Pietro's. She kept telling herself she wasn't going to go. She felt she shouldn't go. But deep down she knew she would. There was a magnetic pull there. She had to know what he was planning. *It's just a meeting*, she rationalized. *You can always just say no. C'mon, Alex, who says no to Hank Martin?* There was the other voice again.

"Ready for tonight?" Bobby's question startled her. The color drained from her face.

"What are you talking about?" she asked cagily. Were they reading her text messages? Holy shit. She hadn't actually done anything, but she felt caught nonetheless.

"For your party. Tonight. The one we are throwing in your honor. Remember, Harvard? Jesus, how'd they let you in anyway? I thought you had to be sharp to go to that school. Let alone to go twice," he joked with gruff affection.

She grinned at him. "Hahaha. Sorry, I am so spaced out today. I guess my mind is just on leaving. It's strange to think about it. It will be so weird to not see you guys every day. Trading has been my life for the past few years. You know, Bobby, in all seriousness I really appreciate you looking out for me. I know it's not really your style to be caught consorting with the junior traders."

"Hey, you're no junior trader anymore, kid. We're all really proud of you. Just don't ever fucking tell anyone I said that, capish?"

She shook her head in amusement. He would never change.

"And listen, it's not too late to change your mind. This whole Harvard bullshit, it's impressive and all, but you don't need it. You're a natural at this."

The wheels in her head were turning. "Thanks, that really means a lot," she said genuinely. "But I made this decision a while ago. Part of the life plan," she confided. "I have a question, though - do you think everyone would mind if we started drinks a little earlier tonight? Something important came up last minute with my husband." She felt bad lying to Bobby but the words just tumbled out before she could stop herself.

"Really?" he was surprised. "I thought you got the pass for the night, kid? How he landed you..." Bobby thought twice and trailed off before finishing his thought. "I'm sure it won't be a problem getting this crowd to start boozing on the early side. You just cut out when you have to. Don't take this the wrong way, but after a couple of hours they won't even notice if you're there or not. You know how it is these days - any excuse..."

She nodded knowingly.

Bobby sauntered off to go inform some of the others about the time change. An earlier tee-time for drinking was always good news. Alex turned back to her computer and took a deep breath. She stared silently at the wedding photo next to her computer screen, thinking long and hard about her next move. *He'll never let you go. It's the only way*, she told herself. Taking another deep breath, she picked up the phone and dialed her husband's work number.

"Jamie Kramer speaking."

"Hi Jamie," she said lightly.

"Well, hello to you!" he was surprised to hear from her. "To what do I owe this honor?"

She tried to make out if there was any sarcasm in his tone. She didn't think so.

"So the party for me got moved back a couple of hours. There's some important meeting here that they don't want to push off. So, we'll probably all be out later than I initially told you."

There was an extended silence on the other end. "Sure, Alex," he said carefully. "I want you to have a good time tonight." Another pause. "Why don't I stop by? Where is it again?"

Fuck. She hadn't anticipated this. After the disastrous night at P.J. Clarke's, Jamie hadn't dared ask to attend another one of her work-related events. Now what? *This is absurd that you think you have to lie to your own husband,* she thought to herself.

"No," she said firmly. "I'm going myself. It's work-related and I don't think it's appropriate for you to come with me. Jamie, we discussed this last week with Dr. Jane. You need to show me that you trust me more."

God, she felt like an awful human being - awful and in the right all at the same time. Was that even possible? She felt vindicated in her belief that she shouldn't have to feel badly about going out to work events or even going to the dinner at Pietro's for that matter. Yet she still felt compelled to lie to her own husband about the real reason she was going to be out later than anticipated. She realized they really were in a terrible place. She didn't know how to get out of it.

Wearily, she turned her mind back to their phone conversation. The line on the other end was silent now but she wasn't even sure if he had responded while she had be locked away in her own thoughts.

"Jamie?" There was no response. "Jamie? Are you still there?" Again, nothing. "Jesus Christ, did he really hang up on me?" She muttered into the mute phone. "Whatever, it's probably easier this way anyway." Just then, she heard the line click dead. *Shit.* He had still been on the phone. He was going to be so pissed off at her when she got home. How had she tangled things up so badly? Her desire to stay out even later now, just despite him, was building fervently inside of her. She checked her watch. Was it time for that first drink yet?

◆ ◆ ◆

She didn't stay long at her own event after all. Bobby had been right. All anyone really cared about at the end of the day was an excuse to get out for a few drinks on the company tab and delay the inevitable host of issues waiting for them at their respective homes. People stopped by to wish her well. Several insisted on "buying" her rounds of shots, some of which she managed to deftly decline or avoid. They asked questions about what she planned on studying, what she would do upon graduation. A few half-heartedly proposed that she come back to Barclays when she was done, though they all knew that wasn't even a remote possibility. People had been heading for the exits as quickly as they could. As it was, Hank, Greg, Clarke and a host of others had all already quit. Alex had little connection to most of the guys she worked for now, which had made it much easier for her to walk away this early. Even though she was thrilled to be leaving Barclays, she still felt a slight melancholy at the thought of leaving the business. *It's just fear of the unknown,* she told herself reassuringly. After a few hours and more than a few drinks Alex decided it was safe to sneak away. She walked quickly to the corner so no one would spot her outside through the bar's windows. She paused to compose herself and gather her thoughts. Three blocks north and she'd be home. Three blocks east and she'd be at Pietro's. She turned her choices over in her head. *Life doesn't happen twice*, she thought to herself. She had to know. Her feet carried her, automatic, to the famed Italian eatery.

◆ ◆ ◆

When she walked into the restaurant she felt like she had just stepped into another time. She knew it not from memory but from her imagination. She had just stepped back into a time when Wall Street had titans, when business had been booming, when life was fucking fun. The place was packed with wealthy and important looking business diners. She spotted them right away. They had the entire back area reserved. It was raised up a few feet like a small balcony, so they were on display for all the other patrons. Hank was seated in the center of a large oval table with his back to the wall so he had an open view of the entire room. He was surrounded by a few of his guys from Barclays and many others Alex didn't recognize. The table was riddled with red and white wine bottles, mixed drinks and opulent platters of Italian food. The group was loud, rancorous, and exuberant.

Alex felt drawn to them with a certain measure of subconscious magnetism. They looked happy. They sounded crazy. They seemed untouchable. They were carefree but cognizant. They were going to try and take over their small part of the world. And everyone at that table believed that they would.

Alex ascended the few stairs in the back. She looked around tepidly, unsure of where to sit, what to say or whom to approach. She paused at the top of the landing, taking it all in. She was right there. She could reach out and touch them. God, this was so different from the "party" she had just left. The world she had been living in was hollow compared to this. Hank's words echoed in her head: "you don't need to celebrate your past. Not when you can celebrate your future." She took a deep breath, as if she were breathing in all of the life and experience the group was emanating.

"Harvard!!!!!!"

The voice bellowed from across the room, somehow full of both levity and authority. She turned to face Hank. All eyes turned to face her.

She watched him turn to the guy sitting to his right and heard him say loudly, "What did I tell you, Michael? It's like staring at the sun. I've never met anyone like her."

To the room, he announced: "Here she is: part of the future of Wall Street, boys. Alex is coming with us. And we are going to change the course of history."

She blushed but no one noticed. He raised his glass in salute. "Fuck the Big Banks!" he exclaimed. Then he looked directly at her. "Come." He pointed at the open seat across from him. "Sit." He commanded. She couldn't refuse.

"Welcome to the other side." He spread his arms wide, gesturing to demonstrate that he effectively controlled the group; he owned them. "Glad you came." He stared straight at her. "I knew you'd make the right decision."

"I haven't decided anything yet," she replied softly, completely unsure of herself.

"Yes you have," he said knowingly. "Yes. You have."

She checked her watch. He read her thoughts.

"Time doesn't matter anymore. Relax."

She flushed. This was insane. How did she get here? Why was she here? She tried to take a deep, unnoticeable breath. But he wouldn't take his eyes off of her. So instead she just held her breath, watching, waiting, thinking.

"Don't think so hard." He read her mind again.

Fuck. How did he continuously do that?

All around her the revelry continued. Wine, liquor, shots - the alcohol flowed freely. People high-fived, swapped storied, laughed with true contentment, spoke with real excitement. There was a buzz in the air. Finally, she found her words.

"Hank. What is all this?" She leaned in closer. "Who are all these people?"

A waiter whizzed by and with a flourish refilled all the glasses.

"This," Hank gestured around the table, "is the dream team I've been building for the past few months. These are the craziest mother fuckers you'll ever met in your life." He pointed to a few people around the table, introducing them in turn. Alex recognized several of the names. These guys were legendary in the business. Like Hank, they had reputations that long preceded them and they would leave legacies that would long outlive them. Hank told her a few select stories about a handful of the guys and her jaw literally dropped in awe and admiration.

"But where?" She asked simply.

"I'm taking them all to a boutique shop. You've never heard of it. My money says most people haven't. But that's all going to change in a few months. I'm not in it any more to be king of the dipshits. I'm taking on Goldman, Morgan, Chase, Barclays - all the Big Banks. We are going to build the most respected and most feared firm on Wall Street. It's different now. Wall Street has changed forever. All the banks are gonna go down in flames. I've seen every cycle there is. And this one is different. I can tell. I can feel it in my bones. It's like a trade. Boutiques are the future. You know I sell sizzle. It's what I do. And this," he pointed again around the overcrowded room, "is sizzle."

"Sizzle?" she asked, confused.

He laughed a deep, deliberate laugh. He shook his head, presumably at her relative innocence. He pointed to a steak that was plated on the table.

"Take notes," he winked. "I might let you use this one day, Harvard."

He cut a piece of the steak and bit into it, chewing it thoughtfully. "Why do you pay more for steak?" he asked rhetorically and then paused for effect. "It's not taste. It's not the quality. It's the sizzle. You get it?"

She nodded yes. But she really had no fucking idea what he was talking about. "So you're the sizzle?" She was so confused.

He laughed heartily, like he was really genuinely enjoying himself. "No, Harvard. I'm the steak. But I sell the sizzle." He looked straight at her, holding her gaze. "And nobody sells the sizzle better than Hank Martin." He grinned in a way she had never seen before.

One of the other women at the table must have overheard him because she turned around to join their conversation. "The sizzle speech?" She asked knowingly.

Alex nodded wordlessly.

"He's not fucking around. He is better than anyone else out there." She shook her head. "Hank sells the fucking sizzle. We all know it. Shit. Look at me. I was his fucking assistant. And he gave me a shot. Taught me everything I know. I wouldn't be here today without him." She smiled affectionately at Hank and they clinked wine glasses.

"Alex, meet Lauren. She's the best fucking female trader on the street. Probably the best I've ever trained. Well, maybe second best. Once you come up the curve she might have competition." He winked at Lauren.

Lauren looked like she was in her mid-thirties. She had shoulder length black hair. A series of light freckles dotted her face. She had a huge rack, which she unabashedly displayed with a very low cut shirt. She carried herself with authority. Alex could tell right away that her opinion mattered.

She laughed and gave him a playful nudge. "Fuck you, Hank. I am the best there is. Other than you of course." She turned to Alex. "He changed my whole life. I was his assistant," she repeated herself. "But he gave me a shot. Believed in me. He taught me. He showed me. Not just trading, but life. I thought I fucking had it all figured out before. But I had no fucking idea."

Hank smiled at Lauren like a proud father might. "I'll never forget when I made my first million," she said. "It was the craziest fucking high."

Alex stared at her in awe. She hoped she wasn't gaping.

"Don't gape. You'll get there too. Once you come and work with us. When do you start?" Lauren asked her.

Alex shook her head, confused. "I'm not starting," she stuttered. "I'm, um, I'm going to business school in the fall."

Lauren couldn't hide her surprise. She gave Hank a quizzical sideways glance. To Alex, she said "That is the worst fucking idea I've ever heard in my life. Why on earth would you do that?"

"I'd like to know the answer to that too." Hank looked very serious.

"This is the first I've heard of what you guys are building." Alex said simply. "We haven't spoken since the night at P.J. Clarkes."

"You're the girl from the P.J. Clarkes fight?" Lauren asked, eyes widening a little. She broke into a fit of loud laughter. "Oh honey, you're coming with us. Trust me. You might not know it yet, but you're coming."

"Yes," Hank agreed. "You have to choose. The life you planned or the one you didn't."

"But I've planned this for so long," Alex said in a whisper, almost to herself.

Hank shrugged. "You can change them." He looked at her pointedly. "You can do anything you want to. You can choose."

Alex thought about her plans. Her precious life plans. She thought about all the boxes she had checked. All the boxes she still expected herself to check. Where had that gotten her so far? The power couple she had imagined herself and Jamie to become was far from materializing. And she wasn't sure it ever would anymore. Jamie didn't want to move to Boston with her. She had dutifully told him she would support any decision he made. So they had decided they would split their time between the two cities and commute to see each other as frequently as possible. She would get a tiny apartment, maybe even live in the dorms. They had budgeted out everything. It would be tight for those two years with two homes, one income, and student loans. But it would be worth it because she'd become so much more credible and marketable on the other side. But once they had decided they would live apart, Jamie had become even more possessive. He started grilling her on the men who would be up at Harvard just liked he grilled her about the men she worked with. They couldn't have a conversation any more without him bringing it up, his questions filled with his insecurities. She had started to look at school as an escape. Maybe if they just had some time apart things between them could get better, she reasoned. Or, maybe they wouldn't improve but at least she'd have more freedom. Hell, she would be in a totally different city. Maybe she'd take a lover, she thought on some days. He already accused her of it every day anyway.

She looked back at Hank. "I know I can choose," she said finally, carefully. "But I'd be choosing so much more than just the job."

He smiled knowingly.

"I know. I'll give you two weeks to decide."

22

"Over my fucking dead body." He shouted. She had never seen him this angry. But she had never been this angry with him either.

They were standing at opposite ends of their narrow galley kitchen. The homemade dinner Jamie had prepared sat untouched, behind them on the small dining room table. A set of lit candles flickered silently, casting a soft light on the room. Melancholy Jazz music played softly from the stereo system.

"It's not up to you, Jamie!" she exploded. "You are being unbearable."

"It's not up to me? You think it's not up to me?" He thundered. "You are my wife! Goddamnit Alex, when did you become so selfish? It's all about you. What you want. All the time."

"All you do is hold me back." Her voice was rising to match his. "This could be an unbelievable opportunity. No, actually it is an unbelievable opportunity."

"That's all you care about now. It's all about work. All about your career." He crossed the few steps to reach her. He grabbed her shoulders and shook her, squeezing her arms tightly. "When did you become such a monster? You are a monster now, not my wife."

He bellowed. His nose was nearly touching hers.

"Where is my wife? Where is the woman I thought I married? Is she even in there anymore?"

He acted like he was trying to see through her eyeballs right inside her brain.

Alex struggled to break free of his grasp.

"Let me go!"

He had never grabbed her like that before. She choked back sobs, sinking down on the marble-tiled floor. She wept, folding her face into her hands as he stood over her.

"I don't even know who you are anymore," he said again, this time in a quieter, somber tone.

They stayed that way for several minutes - he standing in angry silence and she sitting with tears of resentment streaming down her face. Her thoughts were a jumbled blur. She had kept her meeting with Hank a secret for nearly two weeks. But she had to make a decision and that had meant she had to finally tell her husband. She knew she should have consulted Jamie, included him in the process. But she felt his vision was clouded when it came to Hank. He would never want her to work with all those guys again. He wouldn't see the bigger picture. She had negotiated an unbelievable deal with them. She also hadn't included Jamie because of the deal she had been able to negotiate. She would have a title and a paycheck that were superior to his. She thought he should be happy for her, for them, but these days she never knew how he was going to react. *He should be fucking thrilled*, she seethed. She was even going to try and put off school for another year. She'd be in New York with him. Wasn't that all he really wanted anyway? And how dare he call her a monster because she worked hard. She felt her anger building. Finally, she looked up at him.

"Maybe I am a monster. But I'm the same girl I've always been. So you must have married a monster. I guess you just saw what you wanted to see."

"Alex, why are you doing this?" he sounded helpless. "I love you."

"It's not enough Jamie. You don't love me. You smother me."

She stood up.

"I can't fucking breathe. Don't you get it?"

She threw her hands up in exasperation.

"This is why I didn't tell you!"

"What do you mean? How long have you kept this from me?" He was back to shouting again. "I can't believe this is happening!"

"Well, that makes two of us!"

"I just wanted to have a nice quiet dinner with my wife tonight." He spread his hands out pointing behind her. "How many husbands do you know who cook for their wives? I came home early from work, took the time to buy all of your favorite foods, and to cook them for you! When is the last time you did that for me? Forget the last time you did it, actually. When is the last time you even thought about doing something like that for me? Wives cook for their husbands you know?"

"I'm not a fucking housewife, Jamie," she swore. "If you wanted some pretty little arm candy who was going to be home at four, barefoot with an apron on, here to bake you fucking cookies then you should have married that bimbo from back home.

"See. You can't even thank me for cooking you dinner. I never thought in my life I would be married to someone so selfish."

She recoiled.

"I didn't want to eat at home tonight," she said coldly. "I told you we were invited to that dinner party my old colleague is hosting and that it would be fun for us to go. But god forbid you should want to be social."

"Why do you even want to hang out with them on a weekend? You are OBSESSED with the people you work with. You were supposed to be leaving work, leaving Wall Street, leaving this insidious, addictive lifestyle, but here you go again, just letting them all suck you back in. It's been two weeks since you quit. Why do you still want to see them? What kind of power do they have over you that you constantly feel like you have to choose them over me? Over your own husband."

"Why can't I have both?" she shouted. "Why is it okay for you to have it all but it's not okay for me? First you give me grief over school. Then you go for the jugular on work. Then school. Then work again. You never fucking let up! You tell me when to come home, when I can go out, what time I should go to sleep, who I can hang out with and who I can't. You try to control what I wear and when I eat. You follow me around this fucking kitchen with Windex, spraying the counters immediately after I eat like you are disinfecting it from my fucking touch. You have rules like 'no outside clothes inside the bed.' What kind of crazy person does shit like that?"

She grabbed at her own hair, tugging it, a subconscious demonstration of her anxiety.

"You.

Are.

Driving.

Me.

Insane!"

"What do you want from me, Alex? What do you want me to do? Nothing I ever seem to do or say is good enough for you anymore."

His voice quivered with anger and exhaustion.

"Do you want to divorce me?"

Her eyes flew to meet his. She couldn't believe he had actually said it out loud. That word. Her body felt cold all over. Her head was throbbing from the tension. She felt bile rising up from her stomach into her throat. He must have been thinking about it too.

"Because if that's what you want then just do it already. Let me move on with my life. I'll be a thirty-year-old divorcee. Is that what you want?"

A low moan of agony escaped her lips. She stared at him wordless, helpless. He had said it out loud. He could never un-say it. Just like she could never un-think it, no matter how hard she had willed herself to do just that.

"Say something. Damnit, Alex. Just say something. Talk to me." His eyes looked so very sad.

She stared at him with a mixture of emotion coursing through her. At that moment, she pitied him, resented him, maybe even hated him a little bit. His face was long and his shoulders sagged. Had he always been so skinny? His hairline looked like it had receded noticeably too.

"I'm going to go to the party," she said simply.

She picked up her purse off of the counter and slipped her shoes back onto her feet. She moved to slide by him in the narrow kitchen and he positioned himself to try and block her path.

"Have you lost your mind completely?"

He stared at her like she was a rabid dog.

"First I'm a monster. Now I'm insane? Sounds like you married your mother, Jamie."

He slapped her across the face. Once. Hard. Quickly.

She gasped, her hand flying to her face, where his had been in anger. She wondered if the look in her own eyes mirrored the sheer terror she saw now in his. She had pushed him to his own limits. She had practically goaded him into doing it. But he had done it. And now he looked terrified. She had to get out of that goddamned apartment. She couldn't breathe.

"Don't touch me," she hissed. "I don't want to be anywhere near you right now." She stormed to the door. "Don't wait up. Don't call me. Don't fucking ask what time I'll be home. You're not the fucking boss of me."

She slammed the door behind her, creating a small gust of wind that blew one of the candles out.

She forced herself to call the elevator and wait for the doorman to bring it up. She would not race down the stairs in a fit of tears. Maybe she would not even cry at all. She stared vacantly at the closed door and counted the full thirty seconds it took him to reach her floor. She smiled mechanically at him and was relieved to see it was the nighttime attendant who didn't speak a lick of English. They rode back down in silence. She appraised her disheveled-looking appearance in the mirror.

Alex stood outside the front door of her apartment building. For a second, she thought about turning around and going back upstairs. But the thought was fleeting. She couldn't be there. She had to think. She knew she wasn't really going to go to the dinner party. She looked like a fucking mess. The rims of her eyes were bloodshot red. The area under her nose was raw and crusty. Her hair was far from brushed, though she combed through it with her fingers in a futile attempt to control the tangles. She wondered again where she should go. Turning left, she picked a direction at random and just began walking. She wanted to get away just in case Jamie came after her. *Would he come after her?* He should, goddamnit. Maybe he didn't even want to be in this marriage if he wouldn't even chase after her. She walked listlessly down Third Avenue. She had nowhere to go. She thought about taking a taxi out to New Jersey to her mother's house. But she wasn't sure if she could talk to her about all this yet. She didn't know what she would possibly say. Where would she start? Alex felt so humiliated. She felt so ashamed. She cried even harder, unabashedly wiping her nose with her sleeve. What would her mother say? Would she be angry with her? Disappointed? She couldn't face her family, not yet. She stared at the people walking past her on the street, a few couples dressed smartly for an evening out on the town. Some stared at her with sympathy, others with pity. Most ignored her altogether. She cried harder. How had she gotten here? She wondered yet again. This isn't the life that she planned.

She wandered the streets aimlessly. Somehow she ended up at Smith & Wolly's. Trying desperately to wipe away the evidence of the torrent of tears from her face, she slipped inside. Her neighborhood bar. The Wall Street bar as Jamie had called it. She was so close to home. But she had never felt further away. The Friday night bartender eyed her wearily and Alex silently thanked the drinking gods that it was Manny's night off.

With nowhere else to go, Alex polished off two bottles of white wine herself and stared listlessly at the small television screen. When she felt the bartender might cut her off, she paid the bill and made her way back home, finally slipping back into the apartment after two a.m.

The door to their bedroom had been closed. She had wrapped a throw blanket tightly around herself and curled up on the couch, tucked into a fetal position. She didn't even bother undressing or washing the makeup off of her tear-stained face. After a few minutes she had heard the bedroom door creak open. She screwed her eyes shut and pretended to be asleep. She heard his footsteps as he padded into the room. She could feel him standing over her but she refused to let herself open her eyes. He stood there like that for a little while. Then without ever saying a word he turned and went back into their bedroom and shut the door behind him. With the door closed again, she opened her eyes and choked back a sob. Fresh tears sprang to her eyes and she could taste their saltiness as they littered her cheeks, then her lips, and finally rolled over her chin and down her neck. Everything hurt.

23

She checked her watch and realized she had to pick up the pace. *Crap, this is the last thing I need,* Alex thought. She had agreed to meet Jamie on the corner of 40th and Third Avenue so that they could walk to the therapist's office together. Alex couldn't figure out why he insisted on pretending they put on this united front when they were clearly in a state of marital free fall. She wished she were going anywhere else on the planet at that moment.

Alex saw Jamie before he saw her. He was standing on the corner busily typing away on his blackberry. As usual, every item of clothing was neatly tucked, freshly pressed and perfectly in place. She frowned at the site of him. How was it possible that she didn't even feel attracted to her own husband anymore? She looked down at her wedding ring, spinning it around on her finger. She had put it back on before leaving Daniella's apartment. She was afraid of what Jamie might do if he knew she hadn't been wearing it. Her finger felt naked without it. But she had forced herself to try, to see how she would feel when she took it off.

"Hi," he said, shyly grinning at his wife.

He bent to try and kiss her but she turned her head so that he could only have her cheek. He looked so wounded. Still, she felt nothing. *Maybe you really are a monster,* she told herself.

"Can I at least hold your hand, Alex? I'd really like to."

"Okay." She had to keep trying.

He took her hand and they walked south together. There was a heavy silence between them.

"It's beautiful out," she said.

"Yeah. It is. I went for a fifteen mile run in the park this morning. I've been getting up earlier again," he said eagerly, hoping to please her.

"Good. That's really good, Jamie," she said without really caring.

He squeezed her hand. "I'm glad we are going to see Dr. Jane again. I think today will really help us."

She looked skeptical. "We'll see," was all she said.

They walked into the building. It bothered Alex that the shrink's office was located in a residential building. Jamie had found her through their insurance though so it was practically free. When she had complained he had defensively asked if she wanted to make the effort to find a different doctor. She really didn't want to so she just went along half-heartedly with his plan. It was the path of least resistance.

Dr. Jane buzzed them into her office. The doctor's little French poodle barked crazily and jumped up onto Alex's legs.

"Oh, I'm sorry honey!" Dr. Jane exclaimed. "Is Nietzsche bothering you? She loves all the sweet ones," she winked. "My apartment is being renovated so I've had to bring her with me to work lately."

Of course your stupid dog is bothering me, Alex thought. Only a shrink would have a poodle named Nietzsche. What kind of real doctor keeps a dog in the office, anyway?

But aloud she only said sweetly, "No, no it's okay. She isn't bothering me at all."

She bent down to pet the poodle, as if to demonstrate that she was telling the truth. Alex couldn't help but care what the therapist thought of her. She wanted the doctor to like her, to take her side, to tell her that she wasn't crazy for thinking about getting a divorce. Alex knew Jamie was here to try and help fix them. Alex already knew in her heart that they were broken beyond repair. She was here hoping for medical validation, something to help her sleep at night. She thought that the dog might be a test and she wanted to make sure that she passed.

Jamie gave her a sideways glance. He knew she hated dogs. Dr. Jane watched them.

"Come sit down, you two."

The office was outfitted with a small couch, two uncomfortable looking armchairs, a little coffee table and the doctor's desk. One wall held a floor to ceiling bookshelf that was adorned with medical books and a handful of personal photos. Dr. Jane took her seat at her desk. Alex eyed the seating options.

Another test. Would they sit together or apart?

Alex made the first move, sitting down on the far end of the sofa, making room for Jamie to take the opposite side. He sat down on the couch too, but saddled up right beside her so that their thighs were touching. She took a deep breath and made every effort not to squirm uncomfortably in front of Dr. Jane. She sat with her hands clasped firmly together, resting in her lap.

"So, any updates for me?"

Jamie answered the doctor. "Alex hasn't been staying at our home as of a week ago," he said quietly.

Dr. Jane couldn't hide her surprise. She turned to Alex, questioning. "You moved out?"

Alex squirmed. She felt her face redden. "I haven't moved out exactly. I just needed some space. I need some room." She motioned to show how closely Jamie had sat down next to her, as if to demonstrate that he was smothering her.

"Did you move your things out as well?" Dr. Jane sounded concerned.

"Oh, no. Nothing like that." Alex didn't like the doctor's tone. "I'm staying with my best friend," she offered.

"I thought I was your best friend," Jamie said quietly.

"Jamie you know what I mean!" Alex's voice detonated before she could control herself. "I'm staying with my close girl friend, Daniella," she explained to Dr. Jane regaining her composure. "It's only been a few days."

"How do you feel about all of this, Jamie?" Dr. Jane turned to her husband. "Do you want to say anything to Alex about this?"

"I'm obviously devastated." His voice caught. He paused.

Alex furrowed her brows. Of course Jamie was going to play the victim. That was his go-to move. She would have been angrier if she weren't busy being disgusted.

"I don't know how we are supposed to fix things between us if we never spend any time together. Just meeting like this here, in your office, it can't become the only time we talk." He sounded helpless. "I want to make it work." He said more firmly. "I still love my wife."

"Don't tell me," Dr. Jane said. "Tell Alex, Jamie."

Jamie turned to face Alex. "I love you. I love you, muffin."

Alex turned to Dr. Jane. "I hate when he calls me 'muffin'. It's beyond ridiculous. It drives me insane. I don't remember how it started. I only wish he'd stop."

Dr. Jane continued to facilitate the conversation. "Alex," she said gently. "Is that the only feeling you experience? Is that the only thing you focused in on?"

Shit. Another test. Focus, Alex!

She concentrated. She knew the answer. "I love him, too." Then she corrected herself before Dr. Jane could speak.

"I love you, too Jamie," she said to her husband. "But I hate when you call me muffin. You sound ridiculous. And it's not very manly," she added. She felt liberated, finally saying that out loud. She sighed, mentally exhausted.

"Good! That was good, positive communication, Alex." Dr. Jane complimented her. Alex beamed. "Jamie, can you commit to Alex that you will work on this for her. Can you acknowledge the way that she feels?"

Jamie sat still, thoughtful. "But I thought you loved that name?" he asked, the pain bleeding through his voice.

Her shoulders sagged. She took his hand in hers. He looked at her with surprised, cautious delight in eyes. She hadn't initiated physical contact between them in so long.

"I hate it," she whispered. "I always have."

Jamie withdrew his hands. He looked at her like she was a stranger. His words from their fight in the kitchen rang through her head, haunting her: *You are a monster.* She couldn't get the words out of her mind.

"So, did you both prepare your lists?" Dr. Jane cleared her throat, startling Alex.

Jamie exhaled. He patted the breast pocket of his shirt comfortingly. "Yup," he said, suddenly confident again. "I've got mine right here."

She squeezed her eyes shut momentarily.

Fuck! Fuck fuck fuck fuck fuck.

She had totally forgotten about the lists Dr. Jane had asked them to make.

Fuckkkkkkkkkk.

She looked around helplessly, searching the walls of the office, hoping the answers to this test would somehow materialize. Finally, in defeat, she lowered her head in shame.

"I forgot."

She felt Jamie staring at her, hating her. He slid away from her ever so slightly, moving to the other end of the couch.

"That's okay, Alex," Dr. Jane said reassuringly, her voice dripping with empathy.

Don't pity me! Alex silently shouted. *I fucking hate pity.* Suddenly, Alex had the overwhelming desire to run.

Dr. Jane stopped her. "Alex, why don't you go outside and spend fifteen minutes writing your list. Remember, you are supposed to record what you want in a partner, in a husband. Write down what you value the most."

Alex nodded silently. She hated being unprepared. She felt like Jamie had the upper hand now. Dr. Jane handed her a blank notepad and a pen and she stepped out into the hallway to think. She was distracted by the sound of the muffled voices behind the closed door and tried to guess at what Jamie and the therapist were discussing. She tapped the pen thoughtfully against the side of her head, hoping to knock the right words out. *What do I want in a husband?* She thought about Dr. Janet's instructions. I should have done this before we got married, she laughed bitterly to herself. She thought back to the list her mother and stepfather had given her in college that detailed the characteristics of a suitable husband. They had actually given her a goddamned list! She had only been twenty at the time but they were hot on her case to find a boyfriend who was husband material. She recalled some of the characteristics:

1. *At least six feet tall, but not taller than six foot four.*
2. *Jewish (preferably orthodox).*
3. *From a good family with strong values.*
4. *Wants children.*
5. *Makes a good living but isn't too wealthy (around one million annual salary).*
6. *Athletic and likes sports (some sports like golf better than others).*

Alex remembered laughing the list off with her roommates, printing a copy of the email to show them.

But deep down she had internalized the pressure she felt from her family.

She began to write her list for Dr. Jane:

1. *Passionate about career*
2. *Committed to traveling the world*
3. *An adventure-seeker*
4. *Madly in love with me*
5. *Intellectually curious*
6. *Ambition to achieve power and wealth*
7. *Respects me, a lot.*

She stopped there. ***Were seven enough?*** She thought it was a good start. Plus, they were on the clock with Dr. Jane. She looked down at her list one last time. Did these actually resemble her husband? She tapped the pen to her head again and sighed. She knew in her heart that the answer was no. This was an exercise in futility. She knocked on the door and went back into the room.

"That was quick," Dr. Jane said.

"It was easier than I thought," Alex replied. "I think I know what's important to me."

Jamie smiled hopefully at her. She tried hard to avoid making eye contact with him.

"So, who wants to go first?" Dr. Jane looked at them expectantly.

Another test. Alex thought hard. Jamie had told the therapist that Alex was very domineering. She would prove him wrong. She waited, letting Jamie offer to share his list first. He unfolded the paper and cleared his throat. He looked up at his wife and then back down at his notes. He read them aloud like he was ticking off items on a grocery list:

"These are the qualities I value in a wife, a partner:

1. *Someone who is kind*
2. *Someone who is supportive*
3. *Someone who wants children (preferably two boys)*
4. *Someone with strong family values*
5. *Someone who compromises*
6. *Someone who wants to eat dinner together as a family every night*
7. *Someone who doesn't run when life gets hard*
8. *Someone I can share my passion for running with*
9. *Someone who is grounded*
10. *Someone to grow old with."*

Jamie looked up to indicate that he was done. Alex gulped. This fucking therapy session certainly didn't feel very therapeutic. She cringed when she thought about how different their two lists were. She didn't even want to read hers aloud anymore. This was hopeless and stupid. She searched the walls for Dr. Jane's medical degrees, proof that she was a licensed physician. "Alex," Dr. Jane said gently. "How did hearing that make you feel?"

Alex was sick of talking about her feelings. All she and Jamie ever fucking did anymore was talk about their feelings. They were clobbering their marriage over its proverbial head with a baseball bat, verbally clubbing it to death. She felt like certain of the qualities on Jamie's list were meant as a direct, passive-aggressive attack on her. Obviously she wasn't several of those things. She could never be what he wanted her to be. She hated him for making her hate herself.

"I feel like that was the validation I needed," Alex said.

They waited for her to elaborate. She was silent.

"Can you elaborate?" Dr. Jane asked. Both she and Jamie looked hopeful, like they were staring at a hospitalized patient who might be waking from her coma.

"No," Alex said simply. "I don't think I am ready to yet."

"Okay." The doctor didn't press her. Instead, she checked her watch. "Well, unfortunately we are already over our slotted time. I have another patient who is probably waiting out in the hallway. Alex, why don't you hold on to your list for next time? And we'll start off with you going through it. I also think it would be helpful to increase the number of times a week you two come to see me."

Jamie looked like he was going to burst from desperation. "Doctor, I don't think it's um, healthy, for me to have read my list and to have to wait to hear Alex's.

I know we're over our time, but it's not..." He paused, searching for words. "It's not fair."

Dr. Jane was sympathetic but firm. "I understand Jamie," she said as if she were speaking to a child. "If Alex feels comfortable, maybe she can share it with you privately. That would also be a good way for you both to spend some more time together out of my office." She looked at Alex. Alex nodded, acquiescing to the doctor's suggestion. She just wanted to get the hell out of that office. The couple confirmed a time for their next meeting, stood, shook Dr. Jane's hand, and left the building.

They hadn't spoken since leaving the office. "Do you want to have lunch?" Jamie asked hopefully.

Alex shook her head no. "I need to do some prep work in advance of starting that new job," she lied.

Jamie opened his mouth to protest but Alex stopped him. She reached up and kissed him softly on the lips. He couldn't hide his shock. It was the first time there had been any sexual contact between them in weeks. He grabbed her around the waist, pulling her as close to him as he could. His kiss deepened with his embrace, feverishly and urgently tonguing every crevice inside her mouth. After a minute she gently pressed her hands against his chest, pushing him off of her, breaking the embrace. His eyes watered, a sea of confusion, hope, fear, love, longing.

"Here," she said. "Read this later." She handed him her list, which she had folded.

He took the paper and smiled at her. "Okay," he whispered.

She took a deep breath and braced herself. "And Jamie," she paused again.

Am I really about to do this? She questioned herself.

"I think it would be best if you went home to Kentucky this weekend. Spend some time with your family. I think I am going to do the same."

He looked at her like a little boy whose dog had just died.

They stood there on that street corner, paralyzed, staring at each other, with the entire city running all around them. For that instant the world only held the two of them.

"Jamie, I'm going to go now." Her voice was no more than a whisper.

He nodded, helpless. "Thanks for this." He held up her list, still folded. "I'll wait till I get home. I don't want to do it while I'm at work. I'll call you after I read it."

She nodded. *No, you won't,* she thought. Alex turned and walked away. She could feel him watching her go. She forced herself not to turn around. Once she turned the corner, she reached into her purse to retrieve her cell phone. She dialed her mother's work number.

"Hello?"

"Mama," Alex said tearfully. "Can I come up to your office?"

"Alex? Honey, what's the matter? What's wrong? Are you okay? You never call me during the work day. Did something happen to you?" Her mother's voice dripped with concern for her baby girl.

Alex did her best to hold back the flood of tears. She was so sick of crying. "Physically I'm fine. Sorry. I didn't mean to scare you. But mama, it's Jamie and me. I need to talk to you. To really talk to you. Would it be okay if I came to see you?"

Her mother was calm, authoritative. "Meet me at your stepfather's office. I am on my way there now. We have a meeting with his business partner. He is a trained psychologist and a business coach. I never told you kids this but he helps us a lot. We meet him once a month to talk through business, family, life. He is very smart and a good sounding board. We'll talk it through together, honey. We are here for you no matter what. Let me call your stepfather right now to tell him you're coming."

Alex was skeptical. She just wanted her mother. She didn't want a life coach. She didn't want to talk to another professional stranger about how she had royally fucked up her life. She just wanted her mom. She wanted to lay her head in her lap and cry with total abandon. She wanted to let her mom soothingly stroke her hair, singing soft lullabies like she used to when Alex would get sick as a little girl. Alex felt so sick now.

Everything hurt. Her head. Her bones. Her heart. It hurt so much that the pain was starting to actually have a numbing effect on her mind.

"Okay, mama," Alex resigned herself. It was better than nothing. "I'll meet you guys there. Please don't say anything to anyone else in the office. Please." Her older stepbrother worked for his dad. She would just die if he found out why she was there. She was always the perfect child. She imagined his glee at the thought that perfect little Alex had fucked it all up. She burned with shame just thinking about it.

"Honey, I love you." Her mom's voice brought her back into the present. "It's all going to be okay. Whatever it is. I'm glad you called. You need to talk to me. We'll help you figure it out."

◆ ◆ ◆

"So you're basically saying your husband is a pussy?"

Despite the situation, Alex had to choke back laughter. Apparently, Glen, the family life coach, didn't mince words.

"A what?" her mother asked, bewildered. Alex was sure her mom had never heard the word *pussy* before in her entire life.

"A pussy. Glen is saying Jamie is a pussy." Alex's stepfather repeated. "At least in Alex's view. That's how she sees him."

It was all Alex could do to control herself. *At least you can maintain a sense of humor*, she told herself encouragingly. She had just finished retelling them about the fight at P.J. Clarke's as well as all of the other dirty little details about her marriage to Jamie. She calmly recounted everything that had been hidden behind their closed door, careful to maintain as stoic a disposition as she could manage. She wouldn't betray her real emotions. She refused to look weak to them.

"You're obviously a very strong woman," Glen said.

Alex hung her head in appreciation, feigning a humble appearance. "Thank you," she said quietly.

"Do you think it can be fixed? Do you think you can ever look at him the same way again? Can you get the respect back?" Glen peppered her with questions.

"No," she said simply. "My mind is made up. It's over. I can't keep living like this."

"But honey, it's all so sudden." Her mom looked so sad and shell-shocked. Alex's stepfather patted her mother's leg comfortingly. Alex felt a nauseating wave of guilt wash over her whole body. She swallowed her tears. She would not cry in front of them.

"I'm sorry, mama. I'm sorry. I know, the wedding and everything-- But it only seems sudden to you. It's something I've been living with for months. It's like a cloud has been hovering over us ever since Bear collapsed. I just hate my life," she said sullenly. "I have to get out."

"Honey, we don't care about the wedding! Don't even think about that. We just want you to be happy. That's all we care about. Do you understand?" Her mother looked at her daughter intently.

Alex took a deep breath. God, this sucked. She thought about the inevitably long road ahead. "Thanks mama. So what do I do now?"

"Are you sure this is what you want to do?" Glen asked again. "Do you want to give it a little more time? That would be my recommendation."

Alex vehemently shook her head no. She had given it enough time. What did they want her to do? Wait for ten years to pass and two kids to come for her to come to the exact same conclusion? She was a betting woman. And she knew in her gut that the odds weren't in her favor here.

"Okay," Glen continued. "Well, let's be practical for a minute here. Are your things still in the apartment?"

Alex shook her head yes. She hadn't told them that she'd been living at Daniella's. Her mother would have been devastated to think that her daughter had gone there instead of coming home.

But somehow, Glen seemed to know. He could read Alex like a book. She knew it. And he knew that she knew it. He gave her a look that said *Tell me. I won't tell them. But tell me and I'll help you.*

"So you need to get your things out of the apartment," Glen continued in a matter-of-fact tone. "And you need to do it before you tell your husband officially that you want to end the marriage. I'm assuming you don't want to stay in the apartment, correct? And you said it is solely in his name anyway?

"That's right," Alex said evenly. "On both accounts."

"Okay, so how are we going to do this?"

Alex felt so deceitful, like they were plotting a murder. And so calmly. "You really think I need to move my things out first?"

Her mom interjected. "Honey, once you do this, everything will change. Everything will be different. Do you understand? He will become a different person. People do crazy things in these situations."

Alex couldn't believe her. Jamie was so tepid. And he loved her. He would never hurt her. She was the one hurting him.

"Your mother is obviously right," Glen added. "You need to think about yourself. You need to protect yourself. When the gloves come off, they're off. You can't put them back on. You can only put your own fists up and protect yourself. Let's hope it doesn't get ugly, but we need to prepare for it."

Alex nodded skeptically. She still didn't think Jamie would ever do any of the things they were suggesting. "Okay," she said slowly. "Well, I told him to go to Kentucky this weekend to see his family. So he won't be home."

"You did?" Glen actually sounded genuinely surprised.

"Yeah, it just seemed like the right thing to do." Alex was so lost she didn't know what was really right anymore.

Glen eyed her. He looked like he wanted to say more, but he held back. "Okay," he said simply. "Can you do it this weekend?"

Alex nodded yes.

"Her little brother can help her," Alex's mom offered quickly.

"No!" Alex was adamant. "I can do it myself. I'll hire a car service or something." She paused. "I got myself into this mess. I can get myself out too." Here was the guilt again, creeping back into the forefront of her psyche. God, they were going to be so embarrassed because of her.

"Alex, stop this foolishness right now." Her mother was using her authoritative voice, all business now. "We are your family and we are going to help you! You can't do this alone."

"Fine. Eli can help me." Alex was so tired. She just wanted to undo her whole life. If her mother was going to be so insistent that her little brother helps, then she couldn't really argue with her. All Alex ever did was argue these days it seemed.

Glen patted her knee awkwardly. "It's all gonna work out in the end, kiddo."

❖ ❖ ❖

Alex sat on the living room floor of her apartment, taking it all in. She looked around gravely, feeling the full weight of her actions. All of her bags were packed. Now she had to decide which of their communal items she should take. She was fearful now that Jamie really never would let her back in. It wasn't going to be her apartment anymore. If she wanted it, she had to take it now. The instinct made her feel like a thief. She was raiding her own home. *It's not going to be your home anymore*, she coached herself, trying to stay calm. She realized this could be the very last time she was there. This could be the very last time this was home.

She pulled their wedding album out from the bottom shelf of the coffee table. She started thumbing through the pages. God, they looked so happy. She was radiant, just glowing. Everyone had always said what a beautiful bride she had been. Images of the day flew across the pages. She had so many dreams for her life on that day. She had had so many expectations. She had been filled with hope, exuberant for life. It had been a perfect day. Now, tears were streaming uncontrollably down her face. She curled up on the floor, lying protectively over the album. She rocked herself back and forth, as she left herself cry, scream, mourn. She howled without relief, her whole body convulsing. She mourned the life that they'd had, the life that she'd wanted, the life that she'd dreamt. She wept over all their fights, all of the yelling, the screaming and the misunderstanding. They were dead. And she was mourning the loss.

She forced herself to sit up. She wiped the snot and the tears from her face with her sleeve. She didn't care about her shirt. She didn't care about her life. She didn't care about her husband. She didn't care about anything. She took a deep breath, steadying herself. The sharp pain was followed by an all-consuming sense of hollowness. It was like someone had removed her organs, her bones, her emotions, her mind. She was just a shell of a person, functioning on autopilot. She decided to take the wedding album with her.

Next, she turned to the computer. Most of their life had been on his laptop. She took out a memory card and started to methodically download all of the files. She didn't know what she would need. She didn't know what she would want. So she just copied it all. Next, she went to the filing cabinet. Carefully, she removed all of Jamie's diligently filed paperwork. She took out the documents for their mortgage, their car, their insurance, and finally, their marriage. Careful not to jumble the order of the papers she hid them in her bag and calmly went downstairs. She rode the elevator unassumingly, like it was any other day. Willy eyed her warily. She knew that he knew she hadn't been living in the apartment for weeks. But still, she pretended.

Once outside, she practically ran to the Kinkos store down the street. There, she copied all of the pertinent documents, replaced them in their original folders and hurried back to the apartment. She was sweating profusely.

She felt like a spy, an assassin, a thief.

She got back to her apartment and sat back down on the floor of the living room. She didn't want to lie down on the bed for fear she wouldn't get up. The sound of the doorbell startled her. She looked around like a mad woman, trying to think of where she could hide the evidence of her escape. Calming herself, she realized it was her little brother, who was there to dutifully help her do the dirty work.

She unlocked the door and let him in.

"Hey sis. How are you?" Eli hugged her, innocent concern in his eyes. Even though he was nearly three years younger, he towered over her at six foot, two. His sandy brown hair, green eyes, and distinct nose always made him look a little like the famous actor whose name she could never remember. Alex noted that he looked a little more fit, his muscles more pronounced in his black and white striped shirt, which hung artistically from his otherwise lanky body. He was dressed in starving- actor, hipster chic attire - his usual uniform. He had just graduated from college and was pursuing his dream of becoming a professional actor, much to their mother's dismay. Alex had always tried to be a source of sound advice for Eli. Now, here he was, helping his big sister untangle the mess she had made of her life. Again, she was ashamed.

"You know, just another day in paradise." Sarcasm dripped from her voice.

"Hey, it's all gonna be okay." He gave her shoulder a little squeeze.

"Promise me you will never get married, Eli." She felt a fresh wave of tears coming. *Were there any left inside her?* She felt the wave of nausea a person feels when a stomach virus wretches her insides and there is nothing but bile left to vomit.

"C'mon. It's gonna be okay." He smiled his boyish smile at her. "You are the strongest person I know," he said with reverence. "You are gonna be just fine. Nice new 'do by the way." He tried to change the subject.

Eli was the first person to mention her drastically different appearance. In addition to dropping ten pounds, she had chopped her hair super short and dyed it platinum blonde. It was nearly white. *God, I'm such a cliché*, Alex thought to herself. *Change your hair. Change your life.* To Eli, she forced a smile and said, "You know what dad always told me, 'when all else fails, just look hot.'"

"The fact that our father gives that advice will never cease to amaze me," Eli grinned. They both thought of their father, with his mad scientist, Albert Einstein hair, his washed out old jeans, and the same flannel shirt he had been wearing for twenty years.

"He does give good advice," Alex smiled.

"Yes, he does." Eli was suddenly serious. "Have you called him?"

Alex mirrored his shift in mood. "Not yet." Her voice caught just thinking about it. "I can't. Not yet. God, I don't even know what I'd say. Eli, I'm so embarrassed. I feel like such a failure". She looked down, thinking of the speech her father had given at her wedding. How could she face him? How could she tell him? Should she try to pay him back for all the money he had spent? Maybe she'd work all summer just to do that, instead of putting the money towards her graduate degree.

Eli saved her from herself. "Sis, stop beating yourself up. It's okay. Shit happens."

She wondered how her baby brother had suddenly become the smart, wise one?

"Okay, let's do this. You ready?" He asked.

"Yes." Alex took a deep breath. She had the plan all mapped out in her mind. "So here is what we are going to do: I will call the elevator up, distracting the doorman. When you hear him, you run a few of the bags downstairs." She looked around the apartment, realizing the last few years of her life could be fit into only a handful of bags. "It should only take us a few trips."

He looked at her like she had completely lost her mind. "Stop. Alex, are you kidding me? You want to sneak everything out? Don't you think it's a little late for that? A little unnecessary? I mean, they are going to know you are moving out."

Alex just wasn't ready to face the world yet. She had to do it on her own time. She didn't want to have to look Willy in the eye. She didn't want to face him when she was betraying Jamie like this, effectively sneaking out in the middle of the night. She thought of her husband back in Kentucky and her heart tugged a little bit. She shook her head hoping to expunge the thoughts from her consciousness. *Just go. You can't look back now.*

"Please Eli, just help me do it my way," she pleaded. "I just don't want them to know. Not yet. Not before I can tell Jamie myself."

He nodded, agreeing. "Let's do this."

They proceeded to execute her plan to perfection. If she hadn't been on auto-pilot she would have stopped to laugh at how ridiculous the two of them looked, running up and down the stairs, ringing the elevator every few minutes, inventing multiple reasons to call the doorman on repeat. They repeated their ridiculous exercise five times. It took thirty minutes. On the last trip, she looked around one last time, left the key inside and let the door slam behind her.

◆ ◆ ◆

Hi Alex. Honey, since you don't seem to be answering my phone calls I have resigned to email☺ You should be proud that I am getting to be a very fast typer on my new blackberry ☺ ☺

In all seriousness, I tried calling you a few times already. I guess you're not picking up your phone, which I understand. But, after you read this please try to call me back. It's important to not go into seclusion even though I know that's all you want to do right now. I am just feeling very sad today...you have all of these hopes and aspirations as a parent when your children get married. I want only the best for you and your siblings. I know that you will survive and that you are strong like me. I also know that there will be some lonely moments... it is a balancing act of feeling good about yourself and where you are in your life and trying to live with another person at the same time. It is not always easy and there are compromises. It sounds like you tried to tell Jamie that you needed space and a place for yourself and he did not always understand it and that you needed it within the marriage. He wanted a more traditional type of relationship – where he might have breakfast, lunch, and dinner prepared for him every day. He wanted what he sees your grandparents have together. While they have an amazing marriage, grandma pretty much gave up everything to get married – number one in her class, a future as a doctor...she never really fully did for herself and we all became her life and still are her life...if that is not who you are then you are making the right decision. You need to be true to yourself and if you both could not do it within the marriage then divorce is the right answer. A fundamental element to any relationship is mutual respect...from mutual respect there is the trust and the love...My advice having gone through this is that you need to take care of yourself..lots of exercise.. fun, active things..and looking good! It makes others want to be with you and will make you like being with you too, even when you are feeling blue. Kisses and hugs. Call me back. Or at least please respond to this email. I need to know you are okay. Please. And you can always come back and live at home with us. You know I think you should. I love you, honey.

Love,

Mommy

Alex exhaled, clicking out of the message on her phone. She was sitting on the bed in Daniella's apartment, reading this gut-wrenching message from her mom. After moving her things out and dropping them off at her mother's she had quickly returned to the city. She felt claustrophobic, manic even. She didn't know where to go or what to do. She only felt that she needed the option to do whatever she wanted. She needed to feel free. She couldn't go back home. Other than the obvious fact that it would be so utterly humiliating to move back in with her folks, she didn't want to feel imprisoned by them either. She had gotten married in the first place so that she could prove she was her own person. She married so she could be free from their rules. If she had her own household then she did not need to justify not obeying their house rules anymore. She couldn't fight so hard to free herself from Jamie's world just to fall back into theirs. She had to live her own life. She had to find her own way. Still, she couldn't fight the tears. *God, when will I fucking stop crying*, she moaned to herself. It was too much. She lay her head down just as her phone buzzed again, signaling another message. Her mom just didn't stop. Alex resigned herself to cut her mom some slack. She was only trying to help. She had already helped so much. It was emotional for all of them, Alex reasoned. She looked down at the device to read the message. She froze when she realized the message was from Jamie, not her mother. There was no subject title. Fuck. She wondered if he had somehow found out she had moved her things out. *How could he know already?* It had only been one day. He wasn't due back from Kentucky until late the next night. Tepidly, she clicked on the message, her heart all but stopped.

AK,

I think it may be best for us to not speak until Monday morning at the session with Dr. Jane, so I figured I'd write you instead.

First, as you already know, I love you very much. I care deeply about you and our marriage and that's why I'm so driven to make things work between us. I realize all of our conversations recently have been about us and our difficulties, because frankly, I can't think about anything else. I also don't think these conversations are helpful or informative; they are only driving a wedge further between us.

Second, I want you to know that over the last several months, I've done and said things that are very much out of my character and are things of which I'm not very proud. When I look back at my actions and comments, I realize and regret how they must have made you feel and react. For some reason, I've developed an insecurity regarding my trust for you, and there is absolutely no basis behind this at all. Additionally, the issue you have regarding me smothering you is a direct result of my need to hear reassurance that all is okay with us. This is a characteristic that I've developed over the last several months that I want to work on and change not only for the better for our marriage, but also for myself.

Again, and I've said this a million times previously, I'm not happy with the position I'm in right now, but know that I'm doing everything in my power to change and improve this.

Have been apart from you for 2 of the past 3 weekends, I've had time to reflect and think about my actions, priorities and statements. I understand that just "loving you more" or showing you more affection isn't enough. It will take effort and change on not only my part, but yours as well.

The key thing that I want to have resolved at Monday's session, and which I'm hoping Dr. Jane can obviously help with, is to get clarity from you with regards to whether you want to make this marriage work. I realize that right now it's broken, but I know that if you put the drive and determination which you put into your school studies and work, we can fix this. I hope that you have enough faith in us and care enough about me and our marriage to want to make this work.

Things have definitely spiraled out of control over the last few months to the point where I think we have lost a sense of why we married each other. I hope that

Dr. Jane can not only bring clarity to you as to whether you want to pursue this, but also to guide us and help us make things the way they were when we were dating, engaged and early on in our marriage; all times that were the happiest and most fun in my life.

I want only the best for me, you and our marriage. I want to look back at this difficult time as simply a speed bump in the road of a long, loving marriage where we are both successful, happy and build a wonderful family.

Since your iPhone tends to 'act up' a bit, if you wouldn't mind responding and letting me know that you got this, I would appreciate it. I hope you are doing okay and are getting the space that you need.

Love, JK

Alex put her phone down. She collapsed back onto the bed. She grabbed one of the pillows and pulled it down over her own head, trying to drown out reality. First her mom's email. Then Jamie's. It was too much to handle. The pressure was so intense. She felt like the worst person in the world. Jamie must have known she was going to move her things out while he was gone. She could tell his dad had probably coached him in writing that email, finally saying everything she had wanted so badly to hear. It didn't even sound genuine to her. She couldn't tell if it was her perception or his reality but it didn't even matter anymore. She had pulled the pin out of the grenade already. Now she just had to let it explode and see what happened next.

She picked up her phone and dialed Jamie's number before she chickened out. She had to tell him what she'd done. He needed to be prepared for Monday. He needed to know in his heart that she was going to end it.

24

On 6/26/09, at 1:15 PM, Jamie Kramer wrote:
Are you available to speak on Monday sometime to finalize our discussion from yesterday and discuss recommendations we've each gotten for divorce mediators?

> **From: Alex Kaufmann [mailto:Alexkaufmann@gmail.com]**
> **Sent: Friday, June 26, 2009 2:11 PM**
> **To: Jamie Kramer**
> **Subject: Re:**
>
> Yes. That works for me. What time?

From: Jamie Kramer
To: Alex Kaufmann<Alexkaufmann@gmail.com>
Sent: Friday, June 26, 2009 2:38 PM Subject: RE: Re:

Noon?

On 6/26/09, at 9:32 PM, Jamie Kramer wrote:
Does noon work for you? PLEASE RESPOND.

From: Alex Kaufmann <Alexkaufmann@gmail.com>
To: Jamie Kramer
Sent: Sunday, June 28, 2009 2:48 PM
Subject: Re: Re:

Can we actually talk this evening if that works for you?

On 6/28/09, at 3:44 PM Jamie Kramer wrote:
Fine.

From: Alex Kaufmann <Alexkaufmann@gmail. com>
To: Jamie Kramer
Sent: Sunday, June 28, 2009 5:13 PM
Subject: Re: Re:

9.30?

On 6/28/09, at 7:15 PM, Jamie Kramer wrote:
Let's do 10.

On Mon, 6/29/09, at 10:52 AM, Alex Kaufmann <Alexkaufmann@gmail.com> wrote:
Hi,
Per our conversation last night, please send me the list of your terms as you would like them. I don't think I received them. I am planning on meeting with the mediator you recommended to assess whether or not I feel comfortable using her. That's my plan. I'll touch base with you tomorrow. Tentatively, she said she is available to meet with us on Thursday from 2-4pm.
-A

On Mon, Jun 29, 2009 at 8:19 PM, Jamie Kramer wrote:

Hi,

You haven't received them because I haven't sent them yet. I'll send them tomorrow. I can't meet on Thursday afternoon. If you don't feel comfortable meeting with her, let me know.

-J

On Tues, Jun 30, 2009 at 11:19 PM, Jamie Kramer wrote:

Hi, here is what we have agreed to, as I understand it:

Alex gives/returns:

1. Engagement ring (in original blue box)
2. Diamond wedding band (in original blue box)
3. Cartier watch
4. Pete Rose picture
5. Bag of DVDs and miscellaneous books
6. Month of your June medical insurance which I paid for
7. Half of the payment for your new laptop, since you used wedding gift money to purchase it
8. Half of the parking bill for June – you began paying for that over the last several months (in cash) and used my car numerous times

9. Bose specialty headphones from my dad – you took the wrong pair - and Stereo and speakers (currently stored in a box at your mother's house)
10. Half of the cost of the mediator –including meeting session(s),
11. Cost to file divorce papers and any related court costs

Jamie gives/returns:

1. Jewish divorce (Ghet)
2. Platinum wedding band
3. Rolex watch (in box, with warranty)
4. Set of china/dishware and silverware
5. Silver wedding gifts left in the apartment (please be specific, I have no idea what you're referring to)
6. Alex's half/share of $15,000 in wedding gift money less deductions for all of the above items

On Wed, 7/1/09, at 6.30 AM Alex Kaufmann wrote:

Let's discuss the specific pieces of silver at the mediator session today. I'm at work. I cannot talk now. I'll see you at noon.

On Wed, Jul 1, 2009 at 8:55 AM, Jamie Kramer wrote:

One other thing I want to discuss is our wedding album from the photographer. I'm not sure as to why you think you had the right to just take it while I was gone last weekend. We can discuss how to handle this at the mediator.

On Wed, Jul 1, 2009 at 4:05 PM, Jamie Kramer wrote:

Glad that everything ran smoothly with the mediator. Let me know what days and times you're available to do the "exchange." Just so we're on the same page, can you edit my last email of items and re-send to me after our discussion today?

Have a great day!

From: Alex Kaufmann [mailto:AlexKaufmann@ gmail.com}
Sent: Thursday, July 02, 2009 7:18 AM
To: Jamie Kramer
Subject: Re:

Yes, I agree that the meeting went well -A

From: Alex Kaufmann [mailto:AlexKaufmann@ gmail.com}
Sent: Wednesday, July 08, 2009 11:00 AM
To: Jamie Kramer
Subject: Mediation

Hi, Do you have any update? I spoke with the mediator and she said you have not been in touch yet.

On Wednesday, July 08, 2009 at 11:10 AM, Jamie Kramer wrote:
DO NOT email my work email regarding this. I spoke with the mediator earlier. We will both need to reply to an email.

Fri, Jul 10, 2009 at 1:41 PM, Jamie Kramer wrote:
Just wanted to wish you a Happy Birthday. Have a good weekend,
JK

From: Alex Kaufmann <AlexKaufmann@ gmail.com>
To: Jamie Kramer
Sent: Mon Jul 13 13:16:51 2009
Subject: Mediator

Hi - did you email the mediator back last week. She just sent an email saying you did not.

On Mon, Jul 13, 2009 at 1:41 PM, Jamie Kramer wrote:

That's correct. I have not emailed her yet. I want to finalize and have us both sign off and agree on the list I sent to you last week.

On Mon, Jul 13, 2009 at 1:54 PM, Alex Kaufmann <AlexKaufmann@gmail.com> wrote:

Oh, it was not clear to me that you are waiting for that. I agree to your list. Will send you that email now.

From: Alex Kaufmann <AlexKaufmann@ gmail.com>
To: Jamie Kramer
Sent: Mon Jul 13 13:56:50 2009
Subject: Re: Mediator

I just sent official email. I have no changes. Are you going to respond in kind?

On Mon, Jul 13, 2009 at 2:16 PM, Jamie Kramer wrote:

Respond in kind? Who am I emailing with, a corporate financing attorney? I just need to add one more thing to the list - the nightstand that is also out at your mom's house. Other than that, I should be good to go. If you want to revise the list for that and then respond again, I'll be sure to respond 'in kind' and send the mediator an email tonight. Don't worry, Alex, it will all be over soon enough.

I'm assuming you're not wearing the watch anymore (or maybe you've bought yourself, or someone else has bought you, a new one already), but if you did wear it today, can we meet so you can drop it off with me today, preferably this afternoon before 5pm? I've made an appointment at the Cartier place to have it serviced and have the links replaced that you seem to have damaged.

From: Alex Kaufmann <AlexKaufmann@ gmail.com>
To: Jamie Kramer
Sent: Mon Jul 13 14:26:30 2009
Subject: Re: Mediator

Jamie, there's no need to make those kind of remarks to me. I am not wearing the watch. I would be happy to drop it off later. Can you leave me the Rolex with everything please? You can leave it with the doorman if you'd like and I can swing by. I will revise and resend.

On Mon, Jul 13, 2009 at 3:10 PM, Jamie Kramer wrote:

If you're not wearing it, then I won't be able to get it before the store closes anyways. Don't worry about it - we'll just exchange everything this week sometime.

From: Alex Kaufmann <AlexKaufmann@ gmail.com>
To: Jamie Kramer
Sent: Mon Jul 13 15:32:02 2009
Subject: Re: Mediator

You asked me not to wear it, SO I AM NOT. Send me a couple of dates that work for you to exchange stuff and we'll make a plan. Thank you.

On Thu, Jul 16, 2009 at 1:13 PM, Jamie Kramer wrote:

I'd like to get the rings back either today or tomorrow, since I delivered already on the return of the watch. Can we arrange a time for you to meet me with them? Thank you.

I reviewed the list you sent back and am "responding in kind".

I, Jamie Kramer, agree to the below list and agree to deliver the items in a timely fashion.

From: Alex Kaufmann [mailto:AlexKaufmann@ gmail.com]
Sent: Thursday, July 16, 2009 1:37 PM
To: Jamie Kramer
Subject: Re:

As far as the rings go, we will do that in conjunction with the signing of the Ghet, as we agreed.

On Thu, Jul 16, 2009 at 1:50 PM, Jamie Kramer wrote:

We didn't agree on that - we agreed that I would get them in advance of the signing. What difference does it make when you give them to me, if I'm going to get them anyways?

Also, you're welcome for sending back the watch - that's clearly a showing of me not holding things back and delivering without being prompted.

From: Alex Kaufmann [mailto:AlexKaufmann@ gmail.com]
Sent: Thursday, July 16, 2009 2:15 PM
To: Jamie Kramer
Subject: Re: Re:

I think we should just do everything all at once. One day next week. What works for you? I will make myself available.

On Thu, Jul 16, 2009 at 2:20 PM, Jamie Kramer wrote:

Again, I don't understand why it's so difficult for you to deliver the rings tomorrow?

You're clearly not wearing them, so I'd really prefer you not continue to play games and try and "control" the situation.

I've given you no reason to not trust me through this whole process thus far and have delivered on more than what I've been asked.

From: Alex Kaufmann [mailto:AlexKaufmann@ gmail.com]
Sent: Thursday, July 16, 2009 2:29 PM
To: Jamie Kramer
Subject: Re: Re:

I have done the same Jamie. I am not trying to control the situation. When we spoke at the mediator's office we said we would do everything all at once, so let's just do that. In any event, the rings are in New Jersey and I cannot get them. Let's just set a day for next week and exchange all items and do Ghet all at once. Want to do Monday? You and I don't even need to be there at same time.

On Thu, Jul 16, 2009 at 3:20 PM, Jamie Kramer wrote:

Have you spoken to your mom yet? Just want to make sure they received the watch.
If you're able to get everything and bring it in the city over the weekend - let's meet on Sunday night for you to deliver everything to me.

On Fri, Jul 17, 2009 at 7:06 AM, Jamie Kramer wrote:

Hello????

By this point, I'm very used to trying to contact you and not hearing back for hours, but I'm trying to confirm that (1) your mom got the watch which she needed to get back and (2) Sunday night works for you to exchange the items

From: Alex Kaufmann <AlexKaufmann@ gmail.com>
To: Jamie Kramer
Sent: Fri Jul 17 07:34:18 2009
Subject: Re:

Yes, my mom got the watch, thank you. No, I do not think Sunday works for me. I think one night after work is best.

On Fri, Jul 17, 2009 at 9:03 AM, Jamie Kramer wrote:
Again, I'm having trouble understanding why we can't exchange the majority of the items on Sunday night - won't take more than 5 minutes for you to grab your precious dishes and your other things and drop off my few items - and I don't think you'll have any client dinners on that night.
Every day, weekend and week that goes by makes me more and more speculative of your guarantees and promises.

**From: Alex Kaufmann [mailto:AlexKaufmann@
gmail.com]
Sent: Friday, July 17, 2009 9:23 AM
To: Jamie Kramer
Subject: Re:**

Look, Jamie, I'm not going to mudsling with you
over email all day. All of your stuff is in New Jersey.
I do not have a car and I do not know if I am going
to be out there this weekend. If you want to take
the car out there and get everything and leave
a key for me or whomever you prefer to get the
dishes/mirror from the apartment, I am happy to
do that. Otherwise, I just have to schedule to get
everything together and we will definitely do it
all - stuff/rings/check/Ghet exchange this week.
I am not trying to hold anything up in any way,
trust me. I am sorry you feel that way.

**On Fri, Jul 17, 2009 at 1:53 PM, Jamie Kramer
wrote:**
To reiterate, I'll be home on Sunday night around
8 or so. Bring everything over then and I'll give
you your stuff.

    If you're not able to pick the mirror up then,
I can leave it down in storage on the day that
you can pick it up and you can grab it at your
convenience.

Also, speaking of storage, I need you to return the storage key, which you took from my apartment. Thanks.

From: Alex Kaufmann [mailto:AlexKaufmann@ gmail.com] Sent: Friday, July 17, 2009 2:26 PM To: Jamie Kramer Subject: Re: Re:

Jamie, I CANNOT do Sunday. I just said that to you earlier. Can we please just pick one night next week? I also put a call in to schedule the Ghet. They will call me back on Monday to schedule a time for next week. It is $500. I will incur the cost. You said around noon any day except Monday/ Friday works for you?

I will look for the key. I have to find it. If I lost it I'll buy you a new lock.

On Fri, Jul 17, 2009 at 2:44 PM, Jamie Kramer wrote:

Alex,

Just to clarify - I told you that I couldn't do it on Sunday, you were the one who said "If you want to do it Sunday, that's an option." I can now do it Sunday night around 8pm.

If you now say that you can't, let's do Monday night then.

Bring over your own box to put the dishes in - I'll have them waiting for you in my own container, although they won't be wrapped at all and I'd like to have the container back. I'll have everything stacked in the lobby for you.

Let me know if you'll be picking up the mirror then as well, so I can have that ready to go.

I can't do Tuesday now either for the Ghet, so it will have to be arranged for either Wednesday or Thursday.

Did you see my note regarding the key to storage? Please bring that with you as well.

From: Alex Kaufmann [mailto:AlexKaufmann@ gmail.com]
Sent: Friday, July 17, 2009 2:55 PM
To: Jamie Kramer
Subject: Re: Re:

I would like to do the Ghet on the same day we exchange all items. Please let me know what works for you. I will make myself available any day next week. I wrote back to you about key. See my last email.

On Fri, Jul 17, 2009 at 3:44 PM, Jamie Kramer wrote:

Here's the thing - and we've already discussed this ad nauseam - I am absolutely not signing the Ghet until I get all of the items I have requested.

You agreed to the fact that I would be receiving everything beforehand, not "afterward."

Are you even reading my emails? This entire email chain has only further solidified to me how speculative I am of your promises to deliver - you have no idea how soon I want to give you your stuff back, and get my items back from you.

For someone who wants this to be over as soon as possible, you sure are making it difficult to finalize everything.

From: Alex Kaufmann <AlexKaufmann@ gmail.com>
To: Jamie Kramer
Sent: Sun Jul 19 20:38:27 2009
Subject: stuff

Hi Jamie, I am going to go to New Jersey tomorrow evening to pick up all your stuff. I will also go get your Pete Rose picture and bring it back. Can you tell me what clothing you think you have at my mother's? I did not see anything last time I was there. The only thing I might not have is the key to storage. If I can't find it, I'll buy you a new lock. I will bring you everything except the engagement ring. I promise you I am not trying to be difficult but my mom wants me to return it when you sign the religious divorce docs. I will bring it to our appointment this week and give it to you outside beforehand. I know you want it before - that's fine with me.

Can you please have all of my stuff ready? Dishes, wine cup, check, coats, roller blades, and plane ticket info. I can pick it all up tomorrow. Can I come by tomorrow evening? Probably between 8-10pm to exchange. Only thing I ask is that you put the mirror in storage - I will not be able to pick that up for several weeks.

Thanks - please let me know if this works.

On Sun, Jul 19, 2009 at 9:33 PM, Jamie Kramer wrote:

I don't remember what clothing I had out there - you were the one who said that you had some of my clothing out there in an email last week. Tomorrow night works - please bring boxes to put the dishes / silverware / cup / other items in. I'll have everything down in storage for you - let me know 30 minutes or so before you get here so I can put it downstairs and have it waiting for you. I can't leave the mirror in storage - it'll stay in the apartment until you can pick it up - don't worry, it's just sitting here.

As for the engagement ring exchange - I'm unclear as to why your mom is involved in this at all. You're 25 years old and you should be making your own decisions - we agreed I would have the ring beforehand, and to be completely honest with you, I'd like to have it well in advance of the signing of the Ghet so I can look at it - I hope you can appreciate this as this is an extremely "material" item. If we exchange everything tomorrow under your terms in your email, that would mean that I have given up everything "material" up to this point and have gotten nothing material back in exchange. IF my dad or mom was involved in this process like yours are, they surely wouldn't agree with those terms.

Just bring everything of mine tomorrow night and I'll give you everything. I'm tired of having to deal with this. It's amazing and shocking to me that in a matter of several weeks you and your mom have gone from having me as a part of your family to thinking that I'm going to take the engagement ring and never show up to sign your fucking religious divorce papers. WHO DO YOU THINK I AM?

From: Alex Kaufmann [mailto:AlexKaufmann@ gmail.com]
Sent: Monday, July 20, 2009 10:35 AM
To: Jamie Kramer
Subject: Re: stuff

We'll exchange all the "stuff" this evening. I will give you the ring before either of us signs the Ghet. You will have it in your physical possession. Go back and check all the emails. THAT IS WHAT I HAVE SAID ALL ALONG. The engagement ring is in the vault and I can't get it tonight anyway. At the latest, we'll have everything exchanged by Wednesday, including signing of Ghet and ring. I'm not gonna do this back and forth over email all day, so just let me know.

On Mon, Jul 20, 2009 at 10:48 AM, Jamie Kramer wrote:

That's fine. You'll get everything except for the check tonight then. I'll give that to you at the same time as you give me the ring before the signing of the Ghet.

Using excuses like "the ring is in a vault" is really pathetic and I can see right through it. If you wanted (or if your mom ALLOWED you) to give it to me tonight, you certainly could.

Again, I can't tell you how amazed, insulted, hurt and offended I am that your mom (and I'm assuming you) would honestly think that I would take the engagement ring tonight and then just not ever show up to sign the Ghet. Don't forget that no one wants to "release you" from me more than I do.

I'm the same person I was 3 years ago, as I was 3 months ago, as I was 3 weeks ago - a trustworthy and honest individual who is a man of his word.

What time do you think you'll be over tonight? I'm not going to wait around 2 hours for you.

From: Alex Kaufmann [mailto:AlexKaufmann@ gmail.com]
Sent: Monday, July 20, 2009 10:56 AM
To: Jamie Kramer
Subject: Re: stuff

Ignoring all of the usual mudslinging that accompanies your emails because I am immune to them at this point - I will be over between 8:30 and 9:30 tonight, depending on traffic. Are you going to just leave everything for me downstairs? I will have one of the doormen bring all of your things up to you. Who is going to be working tonight?

I am waiting on a final call back from the religious court and will confirm with you when I know the final appointment time. We can do ring/check before. That's fine.

On Mon, Jul 20, 2009 at 11:20 AM, Jamie Kramer wrote:

Mudslinging? You think you're taking the higher, mature road through this? Okay, believe what you want.

I'll leave everything downstairs in the storage area. Please bring boxes to place those items in, as I want to keep the plastic bin some of the stuff will be in.

Take the Ketubah as well – I took it off the wall and I'll leave that downstairs - your grandfather said we may need to bring that to the Ghet signing.

Also, I got that bank check you sent me from the residual in our joint account - it was for $271, not $285.

From: Alex Kaufmann [mailto:AlexKaufmann@ gmail.com] Sent: Monday, July 20, 2009 11:35 AM To: Jamie Kramer Subject: Re: stuff

Feel free to adjust my check by $14. I confirmed the appointment for 2pm on Thursday for the Ghet.

On Mon, Jul 20, 2009 at 11:41 AM, Jamie Kramer wrote:

Can't do it then. My only available times are around noon on either Wednesday or Thursday of this week.

Maybe give the guys a few more dollars than $500 so we can get a good time slot.

From: Alex Kaufmann [mailto:AlexKaufmann@ gmail.com]
Sent: Monday, July 20, 2009 11:57 AM
To: Jamie Kramer
Subject: Re: stuff

The only time slots available this week are either 2pm or 4pm on Thursday.

On Mon, Jul 20, 2009 at 12:04 PM, Jamie Kramer wrote:
How long will it take and where is it?
Can't your grandfather make a few calls – use his connections?

From: Alex Kaufmann [mailto:AlexKaufmann@ gmail.com]
Sent: Monday, July 20, 2009 12:08 PM
To: Jamie Kramer
Subject: Re: stuff

It will take about 20-30 minutes and it is on 7th Avenue and 28th street. My grandparents have been nothing but amazing to you, even now – so don't be a fucking asshole.

On Mon, Jul 20, 2009 at 12:09 PM, Jamie Kramer wrote:

4pm definitely doesn't work. 2pm may work. I'll know more on Wednesday. Reserve that slot and we'll cancel as needed.

From: Alex Kaufmann <AlexKaufmann@ gmail.com>
To: Jamie Kramer
Sent: Mon Jul 20 12:14:25 2009
Subject: Re: stuff

It's reserved.

On Mon, Jul 20, 2009 at 12:34 PM, Jamie Kramer wrote:

Just so I'm clear, you're bringing over the wedding band tonight, which has been stored in a separate box and not in the "vault"?

From: Alex Kaufmann <AlexKaufmann@ gmail.com>
To: Jamie Kramer
Sent: Mon Jul 20 12:39:24 2009
Subject: Re: stuff

Correct.

On Mon, Jul 20, 2009 at 7:23 PM, Jamie Kramer wrote:
Btw, is "vault" code word for your mom's pocket?

On Tue, Jul 21, 2009 at 6:47 AM, Jamie Kramer wrote:
Also, when you get the engagement ring out of the "vault" this morning, can you pls put it in the blue velvet box I originally gave it to you in. I just don't want to have to "wear" it back to the office.

On Tue, Jul 21, 2009 at 8:55 AM, Jamie Kramer wrote:
Also, I moved the bed frame into the basement. The super said I can't keep it there past this weekend. If you want to pick it up to keep it or sell it or whatever, you'll have to do it by then. Otherwise I'm going to donate it.

From: Alex Kaufmann [mailto:AlexKaufmann@ gmail.com]
Sent: Tuesday, July 21, 2009 9:23 AM
To: Jamie Kramer
Subject: Re:

Donate it.

From: Alex Kaufmann [mailto:AlexKaufmann@ gmail.com]
Sent: Tuesday, July 21, 2009 10:28 AM
To: Jamie Kramer
Subject: Re: Re:

Oh, and regarding your absurd phone call to me yesterday, I can promise you that I am not trying to be difficult at all. I went to my mom's, aunt and uncle's yesterday and rented a car service to pick everything up. I drove around like a fucking mad woman picking up all of your shit – which took me six hours – only to be interrupted with calls from you demanding the ring immediately and accusing me of swapping out of the diamond for cubic zirconium. I'm clearly not asking for recognition - that's not where we're at - I'm just saying that I am clearly not trying to be difficult. Please don't misinterpret the tone of this email. I do not want to escalate to the tone we were at yesterday.

On Tue, Jul 21, 2009 at 10:35 AM, Jamie Kramer wrote:

Understood. No worries. Thank you for making those trips yesterday - made the process very easy. If we can't get an appointment today, I should be able to make Thursday work.

From: Alex Kaufmann [mailto:AlexKaufmann@ gmail.com]
Sent: Tuesday, July 21, 2009 10:42 AM To: Jamie Kramer
Subject: Re: Re:

Okay, sounds good. I will keep you posted as I hear.

On Tue, Jul 21, 2009 at 10:42 AM, Jamie Kramer wrote:
Would you mind bringing the ring in a box? I just don't want to "wear" it back to the office.

On Tue, Jul 21, 2009 at 10:53 AM, Alex Kaufmann   <AlexKaufmann@gmail.com> wrote:
I will bring it in a ring box.

From: Alex Kaufmann [mailto:AlexKaufmann@ gmail.com]
Sent: Tuesday, July 21, 2009 11:04 AM
To: Jamie Kramer
Subject: Re: Re:

I just got a call back. We can do 12:15 today. Does that still work for you?

From: Jamie Kramer
To: 'Alex Kaufmann' <AlexKaufmann@gmail.com>
Sent: Tue Jul 21, 2009 11:42 AM
Subject: Re: Re

Yes. I'll be there.

25

She walked out onto the busy city street. She looked up at the clear, bright blue sky. It was so incongruous to the way she felt. She looked around at all the strangers rushing by, coming and going, like any of it mattered.

They just don't get it, she silently scoffed. *It's all one big charade. Nothing matters.*

She felt like she was falling. She clasped her hands tightly, squeezing her ring-less fingers together. Her father's wedding speech crossed her mind. Maybe she still was the little girl in her father's dream after all, falling through the clouds and laughing. But no. She was not laughing. His closing line rang in her ears: *I realized at some point, I will have to just let go.*

Maybe it had meant she had to let it all go, not him.

Alex couldn't believe what she had just experienced. She officially felt like she wasn't on planet earth anymore. She stared back up at the nondescript building she had just exited. Inside, there was another world. She didn't feel like she was leaving a midtown Manhattan office building. She felt like she was escaping from a medieval tribunal court.

After several unnecessary delays, it was over. She had agonizingly waited, caught between her mother who wanted her Jewish divorce and her soon-to-be ex husband who wanted his shit back. She just wanted her freedom. Everything else seemed negligible. Despite her rigorous religious upbringing, she had never learned about the process of getting a Jewish divorce. Apparently, that had been left off of the curriculum. So she had just assumed it was the same as the civil process: agree to disagree, sign a few documents and move on. No one ever told her any different. She had never thought to ask. So she had raced downtown during lunch, hoping she could make it to the court and back within an hour. She was consumed with her new trading job and she didn't want to miss a minute.

More than one jaw dropped when Alex walked into the *Bhet Din*, the "courthouse." She was wearing a bold blue and fuchsia knit dress that stopped midway down her thigh. Her platinum blonde bob was slicked back. Her black Jimmy Choo stilettos were sky-high. She looked hot.

She definitely didn't look Jewish. The modestly clothed receptionist asked if she could help her, assuming Alex was lost.

Alex carelessly threw her Amex down on the desk. "They told me I could charge my divorce on a credit card," she said, too nonchalantly. Alex resisted the urge to joke that she wanted the extra points. *Who charges a divorce on a credit card? It was so fucked up.*

She had to wait thirty minutes. Then they escorted her into an archaic-looking makeshift courtroom. There were three intensely religious looking old men sitting at an ancient, battered wooden table at the front of the room. They wore long black coats, religious black hats, and no- nonsense looks. Each one had a beard longer than the other. Alex felt like they were judging her, chastising her, staring straight through her into her empty soul.

"Approach," one said, with a thick eastern European accent.

Alex wordlessly walked forward.

The second man handed her a plastic binder. "Page seven," he said without looking at her.

Alex flipped the pages, her hands trembling slightly. The first one spoke again.

"We talk. You repeat. It's all outlined in the pages. Understand?"

Alex nodded yes.

"Do you speak Hebrew?" he asked in the native language, testing her.

"Yes," she responded, also in Hebrew. He didn't hide his surprise.

Don't judge a book by its cover, she couldn't help thinking.

He read a few lines and she responded, reciting her part when instructed. It was like paint by number. No thought was required. *Man, this is fucked up*, she kept thinking.

"Okay, now please open you palms. Cup them together, and hold them face up in front of you." Alex did as the rabbi instructed.

"Good." He took her marriage contract, the beautifully ornate work of art her grandparents had so thoughtfully gifted them, and folded it several times, until it was nothing more than a small square. He placed it into her open hands.

"Now close your hands."

Again, she did as she was told.

"Now raise your hands over your head."

Shit this was embarrassing. She thought of the growing sweat stains underneath her armpits. She lifted her arms over her head, gaining mild satisfaction from the fact that her already-short dress was now hiked up several inches higher, no doubt making the good rabbis squirm.

"Now walk backwards to the door. Stay facing us." The rabbi didn't flinch.

Shut the fuck up, Alex silently cursed. But still, she did as she was told.

"Good. Now approach the bench again."

Alex thought the humiliation would never end.

"Now put your hands over your head."

Alex stared at him, dumbfounded. *And what, do the fucking hokey pokey?* She exerted every effort not to blurt that out. Instead, she just did it.

"Good. Now hand me the document." Alex wordlessly passed it to the old man.

"I will now void your marriage, understand?"

"Finally," she muttered under her breath.

"What?" The rabbi looked at her quizzically. He was running the show. This wasn't in the script.

"Nothing," she apologized. "Thank you," she added like a fool.

The rabbi unfolded the parchment, laying the huge document out across the table. Then he took a black permanent marker out of his pocket and before Alex knew what was happening, he wrote 'VOID' in huge block letters, defiling the page, the oath, promise.

Alex gasped in horror.

The old man didn't acknowledge her reaction. He refolded the paper and handed it back to her. She felt like someone had just taken a shit on her life.

"So that's it?" she managed to ask,

"You can pay at the front," he responded.

Alex turned and stormed out, making no effort to hide indignant displeasure. *It's all a bunch of bullshit*, she thought to herself, fuming. She didn't know why she was so angry. But she was uncontrollably furious. She felt duped. Bear. Lehman. Jamie. Religion. Marriage. Life. She felt like it was all for show. Nothing could last forever. Everything she had ever thought she was supposed to work for. Everything she had ever been taught to believe in. None of it was real. She knew she was walking down the street, but she couldn't really feel the pavement beneath her feet. She was floating.

She hopped a cab and headed back to work. She dialed her mom's number. When Alex heard her voice she said, "It's done."

She felt like she was calling to report a successful hit. "Thank God," her mother breathed a sigh of relief.

"That's one way to put it," Alex replied sardonically. She didn't say more. She didn't care anymore. She was perfectly hollow now.

"I've got to go, mom," Alex said firmly. "I need to get back to work."

"Okay," her mom said slowly. "Well, why don't you come over for dinner tonight? I'll pick you up. I'd really love to see you."

"Sorry, can't. I have a client dinner," Alex lied. She just wanted to be by herself.

As the cab approached her office, Alex redirected the driver to the next block instead. She got out outside of the Irish pub that somehow managed to always be both open and empty. Sneaking inside *Conolly's*, she ordered two shots of vodka and then a glass of wine. She downed all three quickly and promptly ordered a vodka soda. The bartender eyed her warily.

"Rough day already, honey?"

The bartender wiped some errant liquid off the counter and placed the fourth drink in front of his lone patron. Alex rested her elbows on the bar, letting her head sink into the palms of her hands. She held the straw of her drink between her lips like a little kid sipping a milkshake at a diner.

She took her time polishing the last drink off. Muscle memory alone carried her out of the bar and back towards her new office. She was about to walk inside the building, when a well-oiled thought occurred to her. She pulled her cell phone out of her purse and searched through her contact list for the number of the Dean of Admissions at Harvard Business School. She pressed the call button and took a deep breath to prevent herself from slurring her words. She spoke a few random words into the phone, to no one, to make sure she didn't sound as drunk as she felt. When the receptionist answered, she asked for the Dean. She was put straight through. *How about that*, Alex thought proudly to herself. But her smile faded when she remembered: nothing really mattered. It was all just a game. And even when you won, you still lost.

"Alex, so nice to hear from you." The Dean's voice was crisp, professional. "To what do I owe the pleasure?

We are looking forward to seeing you up here in a few weeks. It's certainly been a long time coming. "

Alex hesitated. *Was she really going to pull the ripcord on everything all at once?*

Traders bet, she coached herself. *Because that's just what they do,* she heard the addict in her talking.

"Hi Dean. I am so sorry to call you like this. But the thing is-" Alex paused to compose herself, feeling her voice cracking. "Well the thing is I just don't think I am going to be able to come after all." Alex explained the incredible opportunity she had been given at a boutique-trading firm. She detailed how well she had been doing. She explained again that it was a once in a lifetime opportunity. It was a gamble too good to miss.

"Alex," the Dean said sharply. "I think you are making a huge mistake. *This* is a once in a lifetime opportunity. The HBS experience changes lives, charts courses. What does your husband think about your decision?"

The Dean had known Alex for a long time. She had chronicled her courtship, her engagement, her marriage, the fall of Bear and then the collapse of Lehman - all demarcated by Alex pushing off her matriculation, pushing off her own future for another year.

Alex swallowed hard. "Um, about that." She paused for a long time, leaning against the side of the building to steady herself. "Dean, we're not together anymore. We got divorced."

That was the first time Alex had said those words out loud.

It doesn't matter. Nothing matters. Remember, in the end, nothing really matters, she coached herself.

The Dean was silent. Alex could feel her weighing her words.

"I'm so sorry to hear that, Alexandra," the Dean's voice dripped with sympathy. "I'll tell you what - why don't you sleep on it. This is a big decision. Sleep on it. Then call me tomorrow. I'm still willing to let you defer another year. It's never been done before but I feel there are extenuating circumstances. Just sleep on it," she had motherly concern in her voice. "Call me tomorrow and we'll talk gain. Just think it over. This decision will change the course of your life."

"I'll think it over," Alex promised, knowing she was lying. Her mind was made up. Nothing really mattered anyway.

She clicked off the call and walked into her office building. It was sleek, modern, and bright. It was the antithesis of a Big Bank. She walked purposefully back onto the trading floor. She exuded confidence and reeked of alcohol. She didn't care about anything. For the first time in her life, she just bet.

She saw Hank looking at her out of the corner of her eye. He was the only one there who knew where she had been. Everyone else thought she had a doctor's appointment. Alex settled back into her seat. She tuned out her life and zoned into her job. The trading floor was alive. Phones rang constantly. Salesmen humped orders. Traders directed traffic. The people were sharp. The business was agile. Shit got done.

Alex continued to operate on autopilot. After she was back in her seat for a little while, Franco called to her from across the trading floor. He was one of the most senior salesmen. And he was an extraordinary salesman. He was also a crazy motherfucker. He had seen it all and done even more himself. He was one of the guys Hank had introduced her to that night at Pietro's. Before Bear and Lehman, a professional like him would never have worked at a Boutique Bank. But everything was different after the fall. Realities were shifting.

"Alex, I've got a big one for you," he called from across the room, dollar signs lighting up his eyes.

"How big are you?" Alex shouted back, louder than necessary.

They were putting on a show. A few of the other traders and salespeople looked up, intrigued. The possibility of big trades always aroused mass interest, got the room hard.

"I'm big. I'm huge. I'm as big as you want me to be."

Alex laughed. Franco's double meaning wasn't lost on her. But it was part of the game. It was part of the show. And she had grown to love the stage. It was the only place she felt alive.

Franco called her to privately explain the details of the bond order he had just taken from his client. If they played it right, they could put up one of the largest trades in the market. And Alex knew exactly which client to call on the other side of the trade. It was like she could see the ball coming in slow motion, just like Hank had explained it to her. It would happen when she let go. It would happen when she stopped thinking and started living. It would come naturally when she understood what it really meant to bet. She hung up the phone, a shit-eating grin spread across her inebriated face. She had gotten the answer she needed.

"Franco," she called to him loudly. He looked up, expectant, his eyes lit up. "You're done. I buy."

Franco let out a victorious shout. He called his client to confirm the trade. Alex couldn't hide her delight. Hank called her over to his desk, in the center of the trading floor, to inquire about the trade. She quietly filled him in on the details. He looked at her proudly. He raised his hand, high-fiving his young protégé. He was grinning from ear to ear. He looked at her with knowing eyes, victorious. He leaned back in his chair, satisfied.

"I'll tell you one fucking thing -" Hank paused.

Alex waited.

"Harvard's not doing this!"

Alex let herself smile.

No, she thought, *Harvard certainly wasn't doing this.*

ABOUT THE AUTHOR

A. K. Mason is a graduate of Harvard College, who turned down Harvard Business School on three different occasions in favor of working on Wall Street. As a bond trader from 2007 to 2013, she experienced the financial crisis first-hand, and was on the trading desk as Lehman Brothers underwent bankruptcy.

In 2013, Mason earned her MBA from New York University's Stern School of Business and left Wall Street to build a fitness technology and media business. She currently resides in Washington, DC with her family.

Made in United States
Orlando, FL
31 July 2024

49767661R00246